Unperfect

Susie Tate

Contents

For my husband, who now admits that unperfect is a real word and that his wife is always right.
I love you to the moon and back x

Unperfect

Verb

(transitive) To mar or destroy the perfection of.

Chapter 1

No offence, kid

MIA

I gritted my teeth as the pain shot through my ribs like a knife. Holding my breath I waited for the pain to slowly subside, all the time trying desperately to stay awake. But the office space, even though it was open plan, was warm. Warmer than any environment I'd been in for the last week. So, despite the pain, my eyelids started to feel heavy. Digging my nails into my hands, I sat straighter in the chair – the last thing I needed was to fall asleep now. I just had to hope that the adrenaline from my interview nerves (and the double shot espresso I'd bought with my last fiver this morning) was enough to keep me going.

Eyes open, I chanted to myself. *Stay awake, stay awake, stay awake. Pain is just a chemical process. You don't have to focus on it. You can choose to ignore it. Stay awake ...*

But it was so warm and the chair I was in was so comfortable, even with the pain in my ribs and shoulder. *Just for a moment*, I thought. *I'll close my eyes just for a few seconds.*

"Ms Lantum?" I felt somebody shaking my shoulder gently,

1

but couldn't seem to work my way up to consciousness. Who was Ms Lantum?

"Ms Lantum?" Another gentle shake. "*Mia?*"

My eyes flew open and I flinched in my chair sending fresh stabs of pain through my ribcage. Cripes. *I* was Ms Lantum. That was the name I'd given these people. I had to get it together. I had to get this job. The 27p in my pocket, and the bread and peanut butter in my backpack were all I had left. Ignoring the pain from my ribs and shoulder and straightening in my chair, I forced a smile for the woman hovering over me. My heart sank when I realised that it was Verity Markham, a partner at this firm and one of the most intimidating people I'd ever met.

When I'd popped in last week to check if my application had come through, one side of my face had still been slightly swollen and my arm was in a sling. The receptionist (a beautiful blonde who I swear was wearing a surfing rash vest with her ripped jeans) had taken in my injuries and, before I could say anything, started recommending a variety of herbal remedies and explaining how a plant-based diet combined with some sort of crystal healing could accelerate my recovery. When I thanked her but said I was there to ask about the job advertised her face fell and she apologised. Apparently they no longer needed anyone. I had been all set to leave, but that was when Verity Markham strode over to us, her sky-high heels clicking across the floor of the office. Everyone in the office broke off what they were doing to watch her: perfectly tailored shift dress, expertly styled hair and a laser-focused look in her eyes, which directed straight at me.

"Interview next Wednesday, two o'clock sharp," she'd told me in her posh, cut-glass accent.

"Oh, that's great! V, you should–" the receptionist started.

"Set it up, Yaz," Ms Markham clipped, turning back to me and barking, "Don't be late."

It was all business and efficiency, but I hadn't missed the way she'd scanned me top to toe, or the cogs that had been whirring behind those sharp eyes. All I could do at the time was nod. And now here I was at the interview – fast asleep.

"Ms Markham, I'm so so sorry," I said, my face flushing as I stood and extended my hand, I managed to ignore the wrenching pain in my shoulder as she shook it.

"It's fine, honestly and please, don't give me any of that Markham bullshit," the other woman said, her accent so outrageously posh that from anyone else it would have been ridiculous, but from her it seemed so natural and carried such authority that it was anything but. "My parents are complete fuckers – I don't much care for the reminder. Call me Verity."

"Er ... okay," I said, a bit taken aback by her rampant swearing and direct manner, but also kind of loving it. I'd never been confident enough to swear like that, and Nate would never have tolerated it anyway – it wouldn't have fitted with his vision of perfection. I decided to take it up as soon as I could muster the ladyballs required.

Verity's sharp gaze settled on my face for a moment. "Are you ... ?" she trailed off and her forehead puckered in a small frown of concern. "Are you feeling better?"

I forced a smile. "Yes, yes of course. Totally back to normal. Last time I attempt stairs in heels though." My small, fake laugh sounded forced, even to my own ears. Verity gave me a polite smile but I didn't miss how her eyes narrowed on me just a fraction. Her scrutiny made me feel edgy. I dug my nails into the palm of my free hand to keep from fidgeting.

"Okay," she said, dropping my hand and stepping back. "If you'll follow me, you can look at our system. Have you worked with design programmes before?"

"Yes, of course." At least this wasn't a lie unlike minor details like my actual name. I bit my lip as I followed Verity across the office space, trying to ignore how each step jarred my ribs and blinking against the bright light. A whole wall of the office was glass and there were skylights all over the place. Some people were working at computers while others were drawing at huge easels. One of the non-glass walls was lined with long racks from which a load of bikes were suspended, like a cycling work of art. There were large green plants dotted between the tables and hanging from the ceiling, and a large table in the centre of the office was covered with models of buildings – all made of white materials with clean lines and a unique, modern beauty. I wasn't an artistic person, but even I could tell they were exceptional.

"Yo, V!" I heard shouted behind us, and turned to see the receptionist I remembered from last week jogging across the office. "Soz about that. Fell down on the old reception gig again. Mark needed an urgent spot of reiki."

Most people in the office were dressed casually. Architecture was a creative industry and I wasn't surprised by the lack of suits. But this girl was, yet again, taking casual to a new level. She no longer had the rash vest on, but was now sporting a sloppy jumper which fell off one shoulder revealing what looked to be a bikini top tied behind the back of her neck, along with jeans and flip flops. Her wavy blonde hair fell around her tanned, make-up free face. It looked as though she'd been swimming in the sea not long ago and had let her hair air dry, without making contact with a brush once.

"The 'reception gig' is in actual fact *your job*, Yaz," Verity replied, not breaking her stride across the floor. "Mark did not need urgent Reiki. Nobody has *ever* needed urgent Reiki, because Reiki is a bunch of bullshit. What Mark wants is to get into your knickers. Why on earth the man would think that you rubbing his feet will naturally progress to polishing his knob I have no idea."

We arrived in Verity's office where Verity attempted to shut the door on Yaz, but Yaz pushed past her.

"Reiki is *not* bullshit and Mark does *not* want me to polish his knob," Yaz said, giving Verity a grumpy look before her expression softened. "You're terribly cross today and your balance of oestrogen to progesterone is off. I think someone needs a good shot of oxytocin ... aka a hug." Arms open, she took a step towards Verity who retreated rapidly behind her desk with an alarmed expression on her face. Yaz sighed and rolled her eyes, then directed her attention at me.

"Well, I wanted to come and say hi," she told me. "Sorry I left you to dragon lady. You never know when another complimentary therapy emergency might crop up. I had to give Dan a back massage in the copy room yesterday after his egg and bacon bap got taken by a seagull on his way back from Greggs."

I blinked. There was a lot to unpack there, and I thought Verity may be right – Mark and this Dan most definitely wanted Yaz to polish their knobs. She was the most naturally beautiful girl I had ever seen in my life.

Verity cut in. "Yaz, I will remind you that I am, at the present time, your employer, and you cannot call me *dragon lady*, tell me I have a *stick up my arse*, or comment on my hormone levels."

"Whatevs, V." Yaz turned back to me. "So, you here for the interview? Whatcha do? Bricks-and-mortar-loving-design-monkey? Money-fiddler?"

"She's here for the tech support role," Verity said. "Now if you can–"

"Hurrah for tech support!" Yaz shouted, punching the air. Punched the air ... for *IT*? Was she on drugs? "I'll need your number so we add you into the WhatsApp. Monday is vegan curry night at The Raj just across the road and we can ..."

"Yaz," Verity cut her off, her tone indicating that her patience may be waning. "I'm just *interviewing* Mia. We don't even know if she'll take the job yet. Slow down."

Yaz frowned. "Why wouldn't you take the job?" she asked, looking genuinely bewildered. Little did Verity know that I would take *any* job at this point. I'd gone beyond desperate a couple of nights ago. "Well," she said, her smile back again, "have a pre-interview hug."

"I–" Before I could say anything, Yaz had launched herself at me and I was engulfed in a tight hug. My arm and ribs protested and I felt the blood drain from my face but I managed to keep myself from emitting a low moan of pain.

"Yaz," Verity clipped, having gone beyond annoyed now, that laser focus back on my pale face again. "Get. Out."

"Okay, okay, it's back to boss-lady-mode. Yeesh," Yaz said as she pulled back, much to my relief. Her smile dropped when she took in my ashen face. "Hey," she said, her tone now softer, "you okay there, love? Your aura's gone all wonky."

"Yaz," Verity snapped.

"I'm fine," I managed to get out, giving Yaz a small, probably unconvincing smile.

"Hmm," Yaz said, tilting her head to the side as she studied me. "Do you–?"

"*Now*, Yaz," Verity snapped and Yaz put her hands up in surrender, backing out of the office door.

"Don't worry, Yaz isn't a regular feature of the office," Verity told me once we were alone. "She helps out when we're short, or when she feels like the atmosphere in the office needs 'readjusting'. You'll get used to her. Right, shall we start?"

After a few questions about my background (all the information was technically true, it was only the names of my old employer and, in fact, *my* name that were altered) Verity asked me to sit at her computer. The desktop was crowded with files and completely disorganised.

"What ... er ... what would you ...?"

"We need an overhaul of the system and advice on how to upgrade. The way we store all the old projects, our referencing system, our payroll, leave rota, it all needs to be ... oh!"

I had started tapping away at the keyboard as Verity was speaking and brought up the document filing system. I reorganised it, formulated a new system for accessing the files, downloaded a programme to sort the leave rota and made a start on the payroll. It took two minutes and fifteen seconds. Verity blinked at the transformed screen and then at me.

"Ah ... I–I thought that would take a bit longer if I'm honest." She laughed. "That was supposed to be your first week of work. The desktop looks unrecognisable."

I bit my lip and waited, aware that I may well have typed my way out of a job. Sorting this entire system *was* less than an hour's work, tops. I looked down at my hands and took a deep breath, despite what it cost me pain-wise. Verity cleared her throat.

"Right, jolly good," she said, her bright, no-nonsense tone back as she recovered from her surprise. "Let's go through to the conference room and have an actual bloody interview shall we? I'm sure we can tweak the job description a bit so that you have *some* work to do."

∽

Mia

"V, what the fu– " the huge man who'd burst into the conference room started to say, then glanced at me and cleared his throat. "Sorry," he muttered, then turned back to Verity.

Max Hardcastle – eco architect of the moment. He'd made waves recently after appearing on *Dream Homes,* the most popular architectural design programme in the UK, with an affordable eco house and telling Dermot McWilliam, the show's famous host, that designing affordable, environmentally friendly homes 'wasn't rocket science' and that most of the other projects featured on the programme were for 'reight poncy bastads who want to spend a grand on a shite tap'.

Dermot actually seemed to take to Max, as did the country as a whole – well at least the female half (maybe even some of the men if they were that way inclined). It didn't hurt that Max had the whole Sean Bean gorgeous-but-rough-around-the-edges Yorkshireman vibe going on. That clip of him talking about 'poncy bastads' and 'shite taps' had gone viral. Apparently, by unwittingly making architecture sexy Max had caused a huge increase in school leavers applying to study it at university. It was called The Max Effect.

But, despite his huge popularity, Verity had taken over most of the other interviews during the rest of the programme, telling Dermot that Max 'wasn't a people person'. I'd loved that episode of *Dream Homes* even though it always put Nate in a bad mood. He *hated* Max. Didn't have any time for "all that eco-design idiocy".

"What the chuffing hell is going on?" Max bellowed, his deep Yorkshire accented voice a stark contrast to Verity's. "I thought we discussed this in the last meeting?"

"Max," Verity said in a warning tone. "I'm in the middle of an interview. Can we talk later?"

Max threw his hands up in the air and I stifled a flinch. I wasn't good with large, aggressive men, or sudden movements. Irrational fear crawled its way up into my throat and I choked it back down with some effort.

"It's the bloody *interview* I want to talk about!" he said, scowling at Verity as he towered over the table. Up until then I had thought things were going pretty well. The name on my CV may have been false, but the CV itself was not: I could easily back up all my claims. I had my real documents with me in my backpack (along with *all* my other belongings – but nobody needed to know that). If Verity asked for them I would give them to her, but so far that hadn't been an issue. Verity had suggested that I could take on other duties as well as IT support (it had become clear that there was not enough work for just this). Although I was not keen to be facing the public in any capacity, I would do it if it meant I had an income. At this stage I wasn't ashamed to say I would do just about anything.

"We don't need any IT support. *I* can do the IT support. It's a waste of bleeding money."

"Max," Verity said and I marvelled at her bravery. Her tone was more like that which you would use on a recalcitrant teen than a fully grown, pissed off, very adult man. "You are too busy to do that. We jolly well need you on the creative side exclusively and you know it. We–"

"Ugh!" he spat out, his head tipping back to look at the ceiling and his hands going into his thick, dark hair. I stared at him. Everything about him was so intimidating. He wasn't just tall, he had muscle bulk to him; you could see it, even under the scruffy jeans and ill-fitting jumper he was wearing.

Nate had been fit and had worked at it, but he didn't have half the physical bulk of Max. And I knew from personal experience just *how* strong Nate had been. In comparison, Max could squash me like a bug. I suppressed a shudder and shrank further back into my chair. Becoming invisible was a technique I had perfected over the years. "There's not enough work and we can't afford to hire another – "

"Lorraine's leaving at the end of the month and Yaz is barely here as it is. We can afford it."

I kept my eyes down and squeezed my hands together in my lap. I needed this job.

Max huffed and started pacing up and down the conference room. He reminded me of a caged tiger: huge, magnificent, and scary as hell.

"I don't want anyone messing with my system," he told Verity. "I've got it set up just the way I ruddy like it and–"

"There *is* no system, you stubborn arse," Verity snapped at him. "It's total chaos ... just like your mind."

I blinked and froze in my seat. For Verity to snap at a man *this* intimidating and *this* angry and call him an arse ... it blew my mind. Verity was a freaking Amazon.

Max huffed and threw himself into the nearest chair, crossing his arms over his chest. Despite his size he actually looked like a moody ten-year-old boy in that moment.

"I know where everything is," he muttered and Verity rolled her eyes.

"We need you actually being an *architect*. You know, that thing you spent ten plus years training for? I'd rather you concentrated on that." He huffed again and, much to my terror, focused his gaze on me, his blue/green eyes flashing with annoyance.

"No offence, kid," he said, and I felt my spine stiffen despite how scared of him I was. I knew I looked a lot younger than my twenty-eight years, but calling me a kid? Granted, I had become even skinnier over the last month, and the fact that my hair was dyed almost black instead of my natural sandy blonde (not to mention the dark eyeliner I'd taken to wearing) did give me a bit of an emo, angsty edge. But I didn't look *that* young. I pulled on the sleeves of my high-necked grey jumper, which I'd paired with my black skinny jeans, and tucked my scuffed ballet flats under the chair. The outfit was actually all designer. It had cost a fortune originally. But now the cashmere of the jumper was bobbled and my shoes were scuffed. Unfortunately, I had a sum total of two outfits at my disposal at the moment. And the leggings, hoodie and trainers in my backpack (also designer, but also well worn) wouldn't have looked much better.

Max narrowed his eyes at me and continued, "But are you trying to pull a fast one? You must know as well as I do that there's not enough work for a full-time employee to do this bollocks."

Oh God. He wasn't going to employ me. I summoned up all my courage and took a deep breath in which became stuttered due to the pain.

"I–I can do whatever you need," I whispered, and then cleared my throat, willing my voice to be stronger. "And you can cut the hourly rate if that works better. I don't–"

"Have you guys discussed pay yet?" Max asked, his eyebrows going up and his gaze flicking from me to Verity.

"No," Verity said. Max's eyes narrowed on me again.

"If you haven't discussed pay yet then how do you know you'd take less?"

I bit my lip. If I told them I'd take *anything* then I'd look desperate and a little weird. And I was damn sure they wouldn't be employing me if they knew that the backpack at my feet contained all my worldly belongings. Or that I'd slept in a homeless shelter last night and a bus stop the night before. The address I'd put on my employment forms was fake, picked randomly from a map of the area.

"Er, I ..." I looked down at my hands again and clasped them together when I realised they were shaking. "What about your Building Information Modelling? Do you need help with that?" Building Information Modelling, or BIM, is an intelligent, 3D model-based programme that gives architecture, engineering, and construction people the tools to plan, design, construct, and manage buildings and infrastructure much more easily. It had revolutionized the industry and companies that didn't fully embrace it were in danger of being left behind.

Verity tipped her head to the side, her eyes sparking with interest. "We outsource our BIM, but if I'm honest not everyone has taken to it." She gave Max a strong bit of side-eye. "We could do with more support. Is that something you could help with?"

"I bloody hate BIM," Max mumbled and my heart sank. It was rare nowadays, but there were architects out there still reluctant to modernise. The only thing left to do was put aside my pride. To be honest I was surprised there was any of it left.

"I really *need* this job," I said quietly at my hands. "I don't have to do just IT ... I can do anything else; I *will* do anything else. Please, *please* give me a chance."

Chapter 2

Teen emo freak

MAX

I was in a bad mood. Not that this was out of the ordinary. By all accounts I was a moody guy. *Grumpy northern arsehole –* that was Heath's favourite way to describe me. But this situation was starting to annoy me. The image of those wide, dark, chocolate-coloured eyes accompanied by that whispered *please* had been going round and round in my head since I'd interrupted that bloody interview in the conference room.

It was the edge of desperation behind her whispered words that had got to me, and I'd relented on the job.

She was good.

I had to give her that.

She was so ruddy good that she'd sucked in not only Verity, but me as well. Some might think I was a daft bugger, but I did *not* get suckered, and I did not like to be made to look like a mug. But there was something about her that was so ... fragile. In that moment in the conference room she'd reminded me of the hedgehog I'd found as a child behind the hayloft. It had been injured and couldn't really walk. I'd carried it home, its prickles piercing my hands until blood was running down my arms. Mam had rolled her eyes at yet another stray: the hedgehog was one of a long line of strays I'd rescued on the farm – the most recent being a fox that had been caught in a trap set by me da. Being a sensitive, animal-loving child was not ideal when you lived on a farm and your father would rather drown a litter of kittens than find them new homes. True story. But when it came to the hedgehog, Mam relented after seeing the pain I'd gone through to get the thing home. She helped me contact the RSPCA to see what to feed it and how we should keep it, and had set up a box for it in the airing cupboard. The hedgehog may have become stronger over time, but it did not appreciate my efforts as its rescuer, nor did it think I was anything but a threat. I'd kept it for two weeks and when I let it go it shot off into the undergrowth without a second look.

So, whilst it might be a tad bizarre to compare a grown woman to a hedgehog, that didn't change the fact that Mia's eyes, so full of fear and hopelessness, did remind me of that animal. She looked hounded. On that basis I'd shrugged and told Verity *fine* and to *just set it up*. But the more I thought about it, the more I started to feel something was off about this girl. Something I couldn't put my finger on.

Every time her full name was mentioned she looked down and to the left. Why would she lie about her name? And that backpack she had with her ... it was tattered and dirty. Not just a bit scuffed, but covered in real dirt. Why would she bring that to an interview with her? After I'd noticed the bag I also noticed that she never lost contact with it. Even in the conference room it was tucked behind her legs, and as she left the building she had been clutching it so tightly that her knuckles were white.

Not. Normal.

And her hair colour. It was so stark. It didn't match her skin tone at all. The whole emo look screamed teenager. But I'd read her CV and her date of birth told me a different story. She didn't look a day over sixteen. Was she lying about her age to get the job? There was no denying that Mia was good at IT. That much she did not lie about. But she was absolutely taking us for a ride if she had convinced Verity there was enough tech support work for her to do here. It was a waste of bloody money and I hated it when we wasted money on pointless shite – that was something I did have in common with me da. Yes I was a tight-arse, but there was no use pissing money away whilst you were trying to keep a business afloat.

Although I had to admit that despite Mia only being here for three days, the new system she'd established *did* seem to be making my life easier – not that I'd ever admit that to Verity. But now that she'd rearranged the whole system, run all the searches we needed running and analysed all the data that needed sorting, there was precious little *IT support work* for her to get on with. So, this morning I'd found her sitting behind the reception desk, looking like she was going to vomit and flinching every time the phone rang. Yaz had buggered off to the sea as soon as the wind picked up. Typical of my bloody sister.

And ... Mia hadn't made me any tea.

Yaz might be useless in general, but she made a decent brew and she always saved me the chocolate digestives. The absence of my morning tea and biscuits had put me in the mother of all bad moods – and it was all this skinny, little, lying teenager's fault. My phone rang and I made a grab for it, needing the distraction.

"What?" I grunted, holding the phone to my ear with one hand as I checked the latest design with the other.

"Nice greeting, you grumpy git," Heath said in his normal happy tone. Bastard was in a perpetual good mood, which always managed to piss me off more. "Do you want to have lunch today or not? You were going to show me the plans again. I *am* a client you know." Heath had bought a small bungalow overlooking the sea that we were converting into a massive house with an entire wall of glass looking out over the clifftop. It was costing him an insane amount, but it was safe to say he wasn't short a bob or two.

I rolled my eyes. "Only if you're paying. And only if we can go to the Badger and Ferret and not some swank place that serves me hal-fucking-loumi."

Heath laughed. "Well, you're on rare form today.'

I sighed. "Look I'm swamped here and t'top it off your sister's hired some fucking teen emo freak and stuck her on reception. I've already had a complaint from a client, and she's too much of a lazy article to even make me a brew. You know how I get without me tea."

Something caught my eye in my peripheral vision and I swivelled on my chair to see teen emo freak blinking at me from the doorway.

Ah shite.

"Verity wouldn't have hired someone dodgy. My sister has many flaws but she's a scarily accurate judge of character. Ever thought of making your own tea? And maybe even … I don't know … make one for the new member of staff who's probably nervous, you massively entitled bastard." During Heath's mini rant, Mia scuttled into the room, giving me as wide a berth as possible, and deposited a cup of tea on the very edge of my desk before turning and running out of the door. No woman had ever actually run away from me before. I knew I was rough around the edges, but I'd never scared them into a sprinting retreat.

"Arse," I muttered. Her wounded expression now lodging

into my brain along with those chocolate-brown eyes and that desperate *please* for the interview.

"So articulate as always," Heath said.

"Listen, I'm up t'eyeballs today. Let's make it one o'clock tomorrow, okay? You can come here and meet me seeing as your lazy arse in't at work where it belongs," I said.

"My lazy arse has just been on seven straight night shifts you bloody pr–"

I ended the call before Heath could finish, then stared at the plan on my desk for a moment before closing my eyes and rubbing the centre of my chest, which for some reason was feeling too tight. I refused to believe it was because I might have hurt teen emo's feelings. I shook my head to try to clear it and settled down to the design.

～

MIA

I stared at myself in the mirror of the bathroom. A small, dark-haired, deathly pale girl with dark circles under her eyes stared back at me.

Teen emo freak.

That was what I looked like. Max Hardcastle might be a complete bastard, but at least he was an honest one. I felt my lips start to tremble as I gripped the sides of the sink, willing the moisture I could feel building behind my eyes back. I hadn't cried since That Night, and I wasn't going to start now just because some arrogant twat thought I was nothing. Something to be sneered at. A freak.

"Get it together," I whispered to myself in the mirror. "You've had worse insults chucked at you for *years*. You can handle this. Horrible men are not a new phenomenon. He can't hurt you. You're in control of your life now."

I sighed and let my head fall forward, closing my eyes. It didn't *feel* like I was in control if I was honest. I'd been lucky last night that the shelter had still been taking in people when I made it there. The three-mile walk from the office seemed to take forever. What would I do tonight if there wasn't space? Verity had asked me to stay until after everyone had left so that I could lock up. She said I'd be paid until seven, and whilst I needed the extra money, I really didn't want to stay any later than five and jeopardise a space at the shelter. But Verity had been so kind that I didn't feel like I could turn her down.

I swallowed past the lump in my throat and then threw my head back, giving my body a quick shake and telling myself to woman up. Once I was sure no more tears were threatening I pushed open the door and started along the corridor. Feeling stressed about the amount of time I'd spent hiding in the toilet, I glanced down at my watch and picked up my pace until I walked smack into what felt like a solid brick wall. Pain flared up my side. I stumbled back and, just as I thought I was going to go down on my arse, a pair of huge hands shot out and engulfed my upper arms, keeping me on my feet. I froze and looked up and *up* until my eyes met his blue/green gaze.

Max towered over me and didn't look any less annoyed than he had been earlier. A muscle was ticking in his jaw and it caused a spike of adrenaline to shoot through my body. To my absolute horror I made an involuntary small noise of fear. A sound I had made many *many* times before. One I swore I would never make again. I was furious that it had escaped my lips. It was weak and pathetic. *I* was weak. But that feeling of being trapped in someone else's grasp had invaded me again, triggering such a violent reaction that I wrenched free of his hands and took a few rapid steps back, searching wildly for a way past him in the narrow corridor which his big body was currently filling.

~

MAX

I blinked as I watched Mia stumble away from me. The girl had torn out of my hands like I was a serial killer. For fuck's sake I'd stopped her from breaking her arse on the floorboards after she'd careened into me like a bat out of hell. Why was she looking at me like I was the devil incarnate? And that terrible noise she'd made. It'd gone right through me. What did she have to be scared of?

"Hey, you okay?" I asked. If I could have gentled my voice I would have but it was tricky to make my low, gruff tones any softer.

"Fine," she whispered. I had to strain to hear it, even in the silence of the corridor. She took another step back and I felt myself frowning. The way she was backing away from me felt … wrong. It made my chest feel tight again. "Excuse me," she whispered again, looking more and more like a trapped animal as she tried to peer around me.

"You should look where you're going," I told her, immediately regretting my words and wishing that I could pull them back. A perceived reprimand from me was not going to help this situation but, once again, I had let my quick temper get the better of me. I was pissed off that I was feeling like a monster when *she'd* been the one to run into *me*.

"S-s-sorry," she stuttered and I felt like an utter bastard. Her hands were shaking at her sides, but when she noticed me glancing down at them she balled them into small fists.

I sighed but it came out as more of a huff. Mia flinched then backed up another step. Being smart enough to realise that I wasn't going to get anywhere with her in this confined space, I stepped to the side, trying to give her as much room as possible. As soon as she saw the opening Mia sprinted past me. Shoving my hands into my pockets, I scowled after her rapidly retreating back. I hadn't handled that well. I shook my head to clear it. The last thing I needed at the moment was to be worrying over some child-woman. Not when I had to concentrate on winning the biggest contract of my career. I'd wait until she had calmed down and then I'd apologise. And, in the meantime, I would try not to allow that small sound of terror she'd made ruin my concentration for the day, or make my chest feel any tighter.

Chapter 3

Do you two know each other?

MAX

"Hey, big man," Heath smiled at me as he strolled into the open plan office. "Got you your fave sickly pseudo-coffee. No whipped cream I'm afraid but I convinced them to give you extra chocolate sprinkles." A ripple of laughter went through the office floor – only quieting when I scowled across at the cheeky buggers.

Everyone found it hilarious that big, gruff, northern Max liked mochas instead of 'real coffee'. Apparently men like me should be main-lining black Americanos all day to maintain their alpha personas.

"You're hilarious," I said dryly as I snatched the mocha.

I rolled my eyes as Yaz giggled from her yoga position in the middle of the office floor.

"Good for you, bro," she called out. Apparently two of my junior architects needed some *urgent centering,* and so were now with Yaz copying her downward dog. There were a number of things that wound me up about this situation. Firstly, there was no reason for Yaz to even *be* in the office today. Secondly, the blokes she was *centering* had no interest whatsoever in yoga – they were far more preoccupied with my sister's arse, which was currently up in the air for all to see. Thirdly, she had laid yoga mats out in the middle of the office space, obstructing any movement in my supposedly free-flow environment. As Yaz transferred from downward dog to an upward one – my employees' gazes went from her arse to her ample chest at lightning speed and I rolled my eyes. "It just shows how comfortable you are in your masculinity," she continued. "Don't fall into the trap of societal norms. Embrace your feminine side as well. Fight the patriarchy."

I was so bleeding tired of my goddamn sister hanging out in the office.

"Yazmin," Heath addressed her. "Hard at work as always."

"Bugger off, Heath," Yaz said, her smile dying as she stared up at him.

"Sorry, sorry," Heath said, holding his hands up and backing away. "Do go back to your little floorshow. Keeping the troops happy and all that."

Yaz's face reddened as she scowled at Heath and I pulled him away before there could be any further bloodshed. Heath seemed to turn on the charm for everyone but my sister. They'd been at each other's throats for years. Yaz was definitely the exception to his rule. Then again, my sister seemed to be the exception to every rule.

The walk to my office was slowed by Heath waving at and charming the rest of my staff – the great, personable show-off. Everyone loved Heath. He had the same outrageously posh but charming vibe as his sister, and the same immaculate, cutting-edge dress sense, that gave them both the air of having just stepped out of *GQ* magazine. Even I could admit that the bugger was good looking. I mean, don't get me wrong, I did alright with the lasses (or at least I had done, before everything went to shite), but Heath's perfectly styled (the vain article) hair, clean-shaven face and open expression was more appealing than my scruffy clothes, messy hair, stubble and perpetual scowl. Heath was pleasantly muscular where I was just plain huge, always had been – one of the consequences of all the childhood physical labour I'd endured growing up.

We were unlikely friends, but for some reason the git had taken a shine to me from the start. After Mam left Da when I was ten, and remarried a doctor, my life had changed dramatically. I'd gone from living on a bleak, northern farm with a cold, abusive father to a life of relative luxury down south with a kind gentle stepfather and then a new sister a year later. When it had then emerged that I was academically gifted, instead of dismissing me as a smartarse (something Da would definitely have done), my stepfather had arranged for all sorts of testing and put me forward for entrance exams to a whole range of posh schools. I'd managed to get a scholarship to one of the top boarding schools in the country, however, it turned out that being a chopsy northern chancer didn't go down too well in one of those posh establishments. If it hadn't been for Heath and Verity – who were twins in the same year as me and had buddied up with me for some reason from the first week – I would have had a pretty miserable time of it. See, Verity and Heath were from up north like me, but they weren't proper Yorkshire – they were the type of northerners that lived in an actual castle (yes, *castle*) and spoke the Queen's English. Heath and Verity's parents had been appalled by me. I think that was the main reason Heath liked me so much – he always did relish winding those buggers up.

So, I had been adopted into their fold as an 'honorary triplet', and, seeing as within a term they practically ruled that school, everyone else had to follow suit. For some reason they both thought my scowls and grumpiness were delightful. Heath used to joke that being my friend was like culturing bacteria – all you needed to do was provide the right medium for me to flourish. Meaning that I had to be around buggers I liked in order to have a laugh. My tolerance for dickheads was, and still is, very low.

"I'm doing this as a favour to you, so you might want to tone down the pain in the arse routine," I grumbled as I led Heath through to my office. Most of the floor was open plan, maximising the light coming in from the skylights and floor-to-ceiling windows. My office only had glass for walls. Verity had one very similar to mine, but she tended to keep her door open, encouraging anyone to walk in at any time.

My door was invariably shut.

"Oh, I'm frightfully sorry," Heath said through a chuckle. "I thought I was paying you, quite a lot actually, to build me a house."

"A carbon neutral, state-of-the-art, architect-designed, *single* house, knobhead. Something we don't do anymore, 'cept for the likes of you."

Heath's grin only grew wider. "Oh of *course*. You're too much of a big deal now to build itty bitty houses for little people like me."

"Exactly." Since the business had expanded we'd only taken on big projects: designing eco-hotels, wings of museums, eco-office buildings, carbon neutral villages. "And yes I *am* a big deal. My time is precious. So if you could ... Heath?"

We had both moved to sit in my office with me at my desk and Heath on the other side. But something had caught Heath's eye beyond the glass wall. His grin fell and he pushed up onto his feet abruptly.

"Who is that?" he asked. I followed the direction of Heath's gaze and saw Mia sitting at a monitor to our left, typing at the computer, her fingers flying over the keyboard at a furious pace and a small frown of concentration marring her forehead.

"Oh, that's the emo lass I was complaining about the other day. The one V hired."

Heath took a step towards the glass as he shoved his hands into his pockets. His mouth was set in a grim line and a muscle was ticking in his jaw. I moved from behind my desk to come and stand beside him.

"How long has she been working here?" he asked and I blinked in confusion. Heath sounded so serious. What was his problem? Since when did he care who we employed?

"This is Mia's third week I think. I –"

"Mia?" Heath looked away from her for a moment and frowned at me. "Her name is *Mia*?"

"Er ... yes, why do you–?" I trailed off as Mia's brown eyes lifted to look up at us. She only spared me a second of eye contact, which was more than she'd given me over the last week, but when she glanced at Heath her eyes widened and her lips parted. She recognised him.

"What the fuck is going on, Hea–?" My words cut off as Mia and Heath both moved at the same time. She pushed back from the workstation and sprang to her feet. He turned on his heel and strode to the door of my office. Mia glanced at me again and I saw fear in her expression. It was like looking at a cornered animal again. As Heath approached her she looked so horrified and vulnerable that I decided I'd had enough, and stalked out of the office right on Heath's heels.

Mia was moving away from Heath now – half walking, half jogging. I suspected the only reason she wasn't flat out running was so that she didn't draw too much attention to herself. That much I'd definitely noticed over the last two weeks – Mia did *not* like attention. At every turn she would try to fade into the background. When she wasn't sorting out other people's IT issues at their desks, like just now, or being forced onto reception (which Verity had put a stop to after realising Mia was about as welcoming as me) she stuck to a monitor she'd chosen at the very back of the office space, furthest away from the windows and me. Since the 'emo freak' incident last week, she'd successfully avoided me to an almost unnatural degree. Despite that, every morning there was a cup of tea waiting for me with a couple of chocolate digestives next to it, which I knew were from her. It made me feel like even more of an arse than I had before.

Even though she was jogging, Heath's legs were longer. He caught up with her easily. Yaz chose that moment to perform an expansive yoga position across the corridor, blocking my way, so I had to negotiate around the adjacent desk.

Heath touched Mia's elbow as she was moving past the creative team, but then pulled his hand back when she yanked away from him. He instead moved around her to block her path to the exit. Both his hands were held up in front of him and he was pushing them down in a placating gesture. He asked her something, which I couldn't make out, and she shook her head.

"What the hell is going on?" I asked as I approached, drawing the attention of a fair few of the junior architects around us. Heath flashed me an annoyed look.

"I just need to have a brief conversation with … *Mia* for a second," he said, the annoyance in his expression fading as he looked back at her, replaced by concern. "Just for a moment. Do you mind if we use your office, Max?"

"Do you two know each other?" I asked. Mia shook her head and crossed her arms over her chest in a defensive gesture. Heath sighed.

"Max, now is not the time to go all talkative on me, old chap. I need to speak to your employee privately in your office for a moment. It's nothing to do with her work here so it doesn't concern you." Mia's lips trembled and I felt the strangest surge of protectiveness towards her.

I stepped around to face Heath, positioning myself so I was between him and Mia, and I put my hands on my hips.

"It doesn't look to me like she wants to talk to you, mate," I said, my gaze flitting between them in confusion.

"Five minutes, Mia," he said, peering around me so he could make eye contact with her. His voice was softer than I think I'd ever heard it before. "I'd much rather we discussed this *privately*." I glanced back at Mia and saw her swallow and close her eyes briefly. Her shoulders drooped and then she gave a short nod.

"You mind, Max?" Heath asked, his determined gaze locking with mine. I looked between Heath and Mia and frowned.

"Five minutes," I muttered, starting to move aside so that Mia could pass, but then pausing before she had rounded me.

"Are ... ?" I trailed off and cleared my throat. "Are you okay with this? Because I can – "

"It's fine," she said, cutting me off with her rapid, barely audible words. She was staring at my shirt collar and I had the irrational urge to put my fingers under her chin and force her to make eye contact. Which was the last bastard thing she needed. This woman was turning me into a right nutter. "Really," she said when I didn't move to the side. "I don't mind."

Heath swept out his arm and Mia scuttled off in front of him to the office. When they were both inside, Heath glanced out at me standing in the middle of the space with my hands on my hips, and shut the door behind him.

"Haven't you lot got owt better to do?" I growled at my employees who were still watching me. They averted their gazes and restarted their conversations. With a grunt I moved over to the kitchen area to put the kettle on, all the while keeping an eye on Heath and Mia through the glass.

~

Mia

"How much function have you got back in that arm now?" Dr Markham asked me, and I sighed.

"Look, Dr Markham, I'm surprised you even remember me. You must treat thousands of – "

"Please, call me Heath, Mia ... or Helen, or whatever your name is."

"Helen is my middle name." I shifted on my feet and looked out of the glass. My gaze caught on *his*. Of course it did. Max was staring at us and scowling whilst he took a sip of what I knew would be oversweet tea.

"I will *never* forget the state you were in that night," Heath's earnest tone was roughened with emotion and caused me to blink, thankfully breaking eye contact with Max before I focused on the man across from me. "The whole department was frantic when we found out you'd left. You needed an inpatient stay, Mia. Your head injury and loss of consciousness alone would have warranted it, but combined with the rib fractures putting you at high risk of pneumonia, *and* your shoulder, which needed to be seen by an orthopaedic surgeon, it was a terrible idea to leave."

"You put the joint back into place," I said, my eyes flicking to the door of the office to make sure nobody was about to enter. "It felt fine. I–"

"Mia, the x-ray was reported as a *fracture* dislocation. If you'd have stayed in, or even given us your real contact details you would have known that, and you could have–"

"Fracture?" I whispered. Suddenly the ongoing pain in my

left shoulder was making sense. I had thought it was just because all the ligaments and muscles and stuff had taken a battering when they shoved it back in its socket.

Heath closed his eyes and let out a puff of air. "Yes, *fracture*. It's too late for you to wear a sling now, but you need proper physiotherapy – otherwise you won't get full function back. How far can you lift up your arm forward and out to the side?"

I shrugged. The answer was not far at all. I could reach stuff that was waist-height, but anything higher and I was scuppered.

Heath stepped closer. "There are people you can talk to. I've got a number ..." He started digging in his wallet then produced a small card, giving it to me. "I understand you might not want to go to the police." I flinched at the mention of police and my eyes flew from the card to Heath's.

"No police," I said, forcing my voice to be stronger than I felt.

"Okay, okay." Heath held his hands up, palms forward again. "But these people aren't police. They're confidential and they can help you."

I tucked the card into my jeans pocket and nodded. If I agreed with this man maybe he would leave me alone. One of my eyes had been swollen shut that night, but I remembered his face. His eyes had been so kind, his voice so gentle as he'd asked me what happened. After the brutality of that day I'd found Dr Markham's kindness overwhelming. I'd broken down in tears and I hadn't known how to stop, even though the salt stung the cut under my eye and the heaving sobs had been agony for my ribs and shoulder. I never cried, not normally, but I think that day I'd reached the end of my endurance. He'd wrapped an arm around me so, so tenderly, being so careful of my injuries. I never normally tolerated that level of physical contact from someone I didn't know, but that day it had been like I *needed* it. It had made me cry even harder. Nobody had touched me with any kind of tenderness in months before that, maybe even years.

"Thank you," I whispered, forcing myself to reach out and touch his arm to show him how much I meant the words. "You … you were kind. It made a difference."

Heath closed his eyes and let out a long breath.

"You're not going to ring them are you?"

I looked away.

"Would you at least have physiotherapy for your shoulder? It might not be too late to get some of the function back."

I bit my lip. My shoulder *was* restricting me. I couldn't afford to not be able to use my right arm properly. That wasn't logical and, when possible, I tried to always use logic. I nodded slowly and Heath smiled. Once upon a time, a smile like that from such an attractive man would have affected me – now I just felt … numb.

Chapter 4

You went for a walk?

MAX

"I just want t'know vaguely what it were about," I said for what felt like the hundredth time. "She's my employee – if there's owt to know you should tell me."

"Being your employee doesn't mean you own her," Heath told me as he rounded the car and waved to a couple of the guys already on the beach. "Employee is not indentured servant."

This was our weekly beach touch rugby session organised by Heath, the sociable bastard. We even had kit and a name for the team now – although both were quite frankly ridiculous: Sandbaggers was more than a little weird as a rugby team title, and frankly this kit was an embarrassment. Not to mention the fact it was too cold at this time of year for its lack of material. I jogged round to keep up with him and then 'accidentally' stuck my foot out, tripping him up and causing him to stumble to the side.

He flung his arms out angrily. "What are you? Ten?"

"Tell me."

31

"I'm not telling you shit. Leave it alone."

"How do you even know her?"

Heath drew to a sudden halt and stared at me.

"What?" I asked in frustration, my arms coming out to the side and slapping back down. "Why are you looking at me like that?"

"How do you *think* I know her, you colossal dickhead," Heath said slowly. "If I'm telling you I can't break her *confidentiality* then how do you think I've met her before?"

I blinked before my eyebrows shot up. "A *patient*?"

"All I'm going to say is stop pushing this, okay? And I know it's frightfully hard for you without a full personality transplant, but could you *try* to be marginally less of a prick to her at work."

"I'm not being *that* much of a prick." I frowned down at my trainers and scuffed the sand. "It's just–"

"She doesn't need it, Max." Heath lowered his voice and rubbed the back of his neck. "Believe me she does not need to be bullied by you on top of ... Look, I know things are difficult right now. I know you've got your own problems. But just reel in the dickhead tendencies when it comes to her, alright?'

"I'm not bullying her!"

Heath's eyebrows shot up and I tried to shove my hands in my pockets only to realise that these stupid shorts didn't *have* any bloody pockets. "Ugh! This new kit is total crap. We look like complete numpties. Did Mike have to go for neon pink?"

Heath let out a bark of laughter. "He *says* it's orange."

"Orange my arse," I muttered darkly. "And I'm not a bully. She just ... she scares easy."

A strange look passed across Heath's face before he cleared his expression.

"Can't you tell me *something*, Heath? She's working for me. Surely I should know what's going on."

Heath shook his head slowly. "Believe me, old chap. Even if I *could* tell you, you would not want to know. I promise you that."

"You ladies going to stop gossiping and play rugby or what?" Yaz shouted as she came bounding up to us, her mass of blonde hair piled high on the top of her head. She bounced twice on the balls of her feet before she punched me then Heath in the arm, hard. Her fists might be small but they packed a huge impact. When we were growing up, Mam would never believe my tiny sister could manage to bruise her much larger, much older brother. My arms would have been black and blue if I hadn't been able to keep her at arms length easily with a hand to her head – something I still had to employ on occasion, and something she still found intensely annoying.

"Bloody hell, Yaz," I grumbled, rubbing my arm. "I should have chucked you out the window when I had the chance twenty-four years ago." Yaz was eleven years younger than me having been born after Mam had remarried and we'd moved down south (mostly to get away from my father). So my sister didn't even have a Yorkshire accent like me. She was a proper soft southerner – all about yoga and New Age medicine, and in love with windsurfing and the sea.

"Hey, weirdo," Heath said, grabbing hold of her ridiculous bun and using it to move her head from side to side. "Still being a pain in the arse at our siblings' place of work?"

She slapped his hands away and gave him another punch, this time in the centre of his stomach, which caught him off guard. He let out an "oof" and had to take a step back.

"I thought you were a non-violent plant-muncher," he wheezed.

"Well, just goes to show how strong us vegans can be. You might take the piss, but not everyone has to choke back a steak a

33

day, roid themselves up and fanny about at the gym for hours to pack a decent punch."

Heath's face flooded with colour. "I do not *fanny about* at the gym. I *train*. And I certainly do not take steroids. Not everyone can afford to be a surf bum half the time and then bugger around doing weird contortionist-slash-soft-porn poses in a poorly disguised attempt at showing off to the other half."

Yaz took a step back like she herself had been punched and her smile died. "Whatever," she muttered as she spun on her heel and jogged away.

I sighed. "Jesus, mate. I know she can be annoying but what was that about?"

He shrugged and avoided my eyes. "There's no reason she has to strip half naked in your office and add to every arsehole's wank bank right in the middle of the day."

"Okay, *Dad*." I rolled my eyes. He kicked the sand.

"I bet the whole office would be more productive without her bullshit. That's all I'm saying." He jogged off towards the beach/pitch and I frowned after him. When had our office productivity become Heath's concern? He managed to distract most of my staff on a regular basis with his charm offensive. Hypocritical bastard.

"Hey."

I swung around and came face to face with a pair of brown eyes almost level with mine. The boy was growing like a weed. I smiled and brought a hand up to his shoulder but he moved away.

"You good?" I asked Teddy. "Didn't think you'd make it down. I thought you had some chemistry revis–"

"Alright, Max," he huffed, his face adopting that, unfortunately now-familiar, sullen expression – one that forcibly reminded me of his mother. "I'll just fuck off then, shall I?" The *Max* cut through me like a knife. Where had my doting, sunny little boy who loved to call me dad gone? Who was this aggravating bugger who'd taken his place?

"Hey, language, you cheeky little shit." I reached up to ruffle his hair but Teddy ducked his head down, avoiding my hand. I took that small rejection on the chin, but it still hurt. It always hurt.

"You can't tell me to stop swearing by swearing yourself, you hypocritical son of a—"

"Short stuff! You came!" Like a small, blonde missile, Yaz launched herself at Teddy and hugged him tight. The sullen expression lightened slightly as he rolled his eyes and, after only a brief hesitation, wrapped his arms around her briefly before pushing her away.

"Auntie Yaz!" he protested.

That hurt as well – why could Teddy manage to still call my sister Auntie, but I was reduced to Max?

"You *do* know you're about a foot shorter than me now, don't you?" he said. "You might have to consider switching up the nicknames."

"Hadn't noticed," she said, smiling up at him. I tried to shove my hands into my non-existent pockets again then crossed my arms over my chest. Yaz looked from my defensive posture to Teddy's face, which had set back to sullen, and she sighed.

"Come on you two." She wore a forced smile as she stepped in between Teddy and me, looped her arms through mine and then Teddy's and started tugging us towards the sand.

And, just like that, my focus was back on my newly-turned-into-an-arsehole teenage dependant and off a certain dark-haired, secretive, emo girl.

Well, at least that's what I told myself.

〜

Mia

I was so cold.

It was just my luck that last night, a night I had not been early enough to get a space in the shelter, was the coldest there'd been since I'd become homeless. A freak, cold snap in April – just my luck.

Homeless.

There was no denying it to myself now – that's what I was. Twenty-eight years old and homeless. Yes, I was getting paid in just over a week's time (I'd asked Verity when payday was. Twice.). But that didn't change anything *now*. And last night had been the worst by far. I'd slept in the alley outside the office, with the rest of the rubbish. After hauling the large bins to shield me from the road I had been sweating, but within half an hour of being huddled in my sleeping bag the shivering had started.

Now it was seven in the morning and, thank God, I'd heard somebody open the door to the office. When I was sure the coast was clear I forced myself out of my sleeping bag, which I managed to wrestle into its sack before shoving it into my back-pack. After that I could no longer feel my hands, so pulling across one of the bins to get out was a significant struggle. I thought back to the day of my escape and wished for the thousandth time that during my frantic packing I'd had the foresight to take some bloody gloves. But, then again, I'd only had one functioning arm and had been punch drunk from being knocked out cold – so maybe I didn't do too badly.

I made it to the side door, only stumbling once on my numb feet, and pushed through. The warmth hit me as I moved into the entryway. I sighed in relief and nearly tripped in my haste to get to one of the radiators. They had the fancy upright kind so I could stand with my whole body against one and my hands behind my back, sucking up at much heat as possible. Even so, the shaking continued. I closed my eyes and visualised myself sinking into a deep bath full of steaming water, every part of me surrounded with warmth. Just as everything started getting a little fuzzy and I thought I might actually fall asleep there on my feet, the air around me changed. Tension crackled through the space, and suddenly I *knew* who had opened up the office. Why was my luck always so crap? Couldn't I manage to catch a break? Just *once*?

"What are you doing here so early?" his deep voice sounded from an uncomfortably close distance. I opened my eyes and he was *right* there, only about two feet in front of me. Under normal circumstances I would have moved away – he was too close, and he was between me and the nearest exit. I'd long since learnt to never let a man cage me in or block off my available escape routes. But I doubted that even if the devil himself had materialised in front of me I would have been able to move away from that radiator. I felt like I was welded to its warmth for life.

"I-I-I n-n-needed to g-g-get a – " I broke off and tried to get my shivering under control. The adrenaline of being so close to a big man giving off angry vibes probably wasn't helping. "G-g-g-get a h-h-head s-s-s-start on ..."

"Jesus Christ, you're freezing!" he snapped, sounding even more angry than before.

"I-I-I-I ..."

He stepped forward so that he was now inches away from me. I was looking straight at his broad chest and, to my alarm, his hands reached forward for mine. My chattering mouth slammed shut and my eyes went wide as I froze in fear. I tried to keep my hands rigidly behind me, but he pulled them round with gentle firmness and then cradled them both in his large, warm ones.

"Fuck," he muttered, staring down my fingers, which were

such an alarming shade of blue they didn't look compatible with life. I gave my hands a tug to pull them back but he just held onto them more firmly, engulfing both of them in the heat of his, which, I had to admit, was about ten times better than the radiator. "You're chuffing freezing," he said, sounding even angrier as he scowled down at me. "How have you managed to get so cold on the way here? It can't be more than a ten-minute walk."

Ah – the fake address. I had to admit I was surprised he remembered my address at all. I took a deep breath and tried to slow my heart rate, despite the adrenaline pumping through my system. My head felt like it was stuffed with cotton wool, but I needed to do some quick thinking and some fast-talking to get out of this one. I was quite sure that Mr We-Don't-Need-Any-Tech-Support would *not* want an actual vagrant as an employee. If he knew I'd slept out by the dumpsters last night I'd lose my job by the end of the day. I was still in my six-week trial period. What kind of employer would want to keep on a homeless woman with a dodgy background in his classy, up-market, eco-architect set-up? But, worse, was if I told him the whole story and he decided I needed to go to the police. I could *not* speak to the police.

"I-I-I w-w-w-went for a w-w-w-walk."

He blinked and then narrowed his too-intelligent eyes "You went for a walk?"

I swallowed.

"Y-y-yes."

"You went for a walk with no gloves on, a damp coat ..."

Damn, I had forgotten about my coat – it was soaking. I'd have to dry it somehow today. It might be designer and cash-mere, but that was no bloody use to me when what I *needed* was waterproof and warm.

'... carrying a heavy backpack until your lips turn so blue

they're nearly purple and your hands look like they're going to develop frost bite?"

I bit my lip and nodded. At this point words were beyond me. And that foggy feeling was creeping back. After a freezing night, shivering on the damp ground, and having no sleep whatsoever, I found that even my fear of this man wasn't going to be enough to keep me fully awake. Max's jaw clenched as he searched my face, but then, without another word, he pulled me away from the radiator. I gave a small squeak of objection at the loss of heat at my back, and for a moment I panicked that he was going to throw me back outside into the cold. Yes, I was terrified of being trapped with him, but at that point I would have done *anything* not to be in the cold again.

"P-p-please," I whimpered, hating myself, hating the weakness in my voice. "Please I c-c-can't go back outside. N-n-not just yet. I'll only stay a few minutes longer at the radiator. You won't even know I'm th-th-there."

Chapter 5

I might be weak, but I'm not stupid

MAX

I glanced back at Mia's panicked face and my throat tightened so much I actually had to clear it before I could speak.

"I'm not going to chuck you out," I said, shocked that she would even think such a thing. Quite frankly she was scaring the shit out of me. Her skin was so blue and her hands were so cold it was terrifying. I was on the verge of calling Heath, but decided that the priority should be re-warming her.

She stiffened as I pulled her through into my office. I ignored her bewildered expression as I unbuttoned her sodden coat and threw it on my desk. Before she could protest I put both my hands on her shoulders to sit her down on my small leather sofa. When she was sitting I whipped off my puffa coat and draped it around her. It engulfed her completely. She looked tiny as she blinked up at me. I turned on my heel and prowled out of the office to grab the space heater they kept in the store cupboard for really cold days when the central heating just couldn't cut it. After I'd dragged it back into the office and set it going at full blast the room was like a sauna in only a couple of minutes.

"Thank you," Mia whispered and I moved to sit next to her, pulling her hands out from inside the folds of my coat and engulfing them in my own again. They were still cold, but not the full-on blocks of ice they'd been earlier. I was surprised that she didn't resist, but when I looked up from her hands to her face I realised that she wasn't fully *there*. Her eyelids were drooping and her head was nodding forward, her hands gradually went limp in mine – she was asleep sitting up. I took one of the throw cushions and put it at the end of the sofa, then gently moved her so that she was lying with her head on it. Her feet automatically lifted up onto the leather and she curled into a tight ball within my coat, half her face disappearing into it as well. I stood and stared down at her with my hands on my hips, then rubbed the back of my neck for a moment. Fuck it – I was calling Heath.

"What is so frightfully pressing that I have to trek down to your fancy office on the morning after my night shift?" grumbled Heath. "Have you any idea how busy the emergency department is at the moment, big man?"

I rolled my eyes. Heath had always been a whiny little bitch. "It's important, okay? Medical stuff."

"*Medical stuff* does not narrow it down. I–" Heath fell silent as we walked into my office. "Max?" he said, drawing the name out. "There's a small woman asleep on your sofa."

"Yes, I know that, you pillock," I snapped then lowered my voice when Mia stirred under my coat. "It's Mia. I want you to check she's okay.'

"Er ... why? Did something happen to her?" The note of concern in Heath's voice made my ears prick up. "Is she hurt?"

"No ... well I don't think so. She ... she's just proper nithered."

"Nithered?'

I rolled my eyes and muttered, "Southern wanker," under my breath. "She's *cold*, okay. Freezing. *Nithered*."

Heath blinked. "She's cold? You dragged me over here straight after my twelve-hour shift to show me a cold woman? Max, *everyone* is cold today. It's absolutely brass monkeys outside."

I huffed out an annoyed breath. "She's not just cold, you git – she looked almost dead and felt like ice. And once I warmed her up in the office she fell asleep sitting bolt upright. That shit is weird. Something's wrong with her."

Heath sighed but his expression softened when he looked at the small Mia bundle on the sofa.

"Okay, okay," he murmured, moving to Mia and crouching down in front of her head. "Hey, sweetheart." He kept his voice soft as he brushed some of the black hair out of her eyes and tucked it behind her ear. Her face, when relaxed in sleep and not tense or anxious or frowning, was actually ... beautiful. She had a clear, pale complexion with not a scrap of make-up to be seen. Her brows arched perfectly over her eyes, her lips – when not held in a tight line – were full and formed a perfect bow. She looked like sleeping beauty. The only jarring aspect of her appearance was how cut her cheekbones were, giving her a gaunt, underfed, unhealthy look.

I crossed my arms over my chest. Heath touching Mia was making me feel strangely annoyed. That wave of protectiveness swept through me again and I shook my head to clear it. What was wrong with me?

"Mia?" Heath called again, his voice stronger now. Slowly, very slowly, Mia's eyes blinked open. With visible effort she focused on Heath's face in front of her. After a few seconds her sleepy expression cleared and was replaced by shock. She flew up to a sitting position, the huge coat slipping off her shoulders. Before either Heath or I could say anything, she leapt to her feet. Her eyes flicked to the exit then back at us and she froze.

"Mia, I –"

Mia focused on me for a moment, but then her eyes rolled back in her head and she swayed on her feet. I shot forward and caught her before she could crumple to the floor, manoeuvring her back onto the sofa, laying her down, and cocooning her in my coat again.

"See what I mean?" I said to Heath, the snap in my tone making Mia flinch on the sofa. "Shit," I mumbled as my eyes snapped to her terrified ones. "Mia, it's okay. Heath's here to help." My attempt at a non-threatening tone came out more growly than gentle. I'd never been great at soft and gentle, however hard I tried – my body was just too big, too imposing and my voice was pitched too low.

"Mia, what happened?" Heath asked, *his* tone managing to be so gentle that I could see Mia relax just slightly, triggering that inexplicable annoyance again. Why did Heath always seem to be able to say the right thing in the right way? He made me feel like a clumsy ogre in comparison.

'Nothing ... er ... nothing happened," she said, her voice hoarse from sleep. She cleared her throat before going on. "I ... God. I'm so sorry. I must've fallen asleep."

She tried to push up to sitting again and the image of her eyes rolling back in her head ran through my brain. Without thinking I stepped forward, planted both hands on her shoulders and pushed her firmly back down into the sofa. I hadn't thought her face could get any paler. I was wrong. And now she was shaking again, not with cold this time but with actual fear. I had succeeded in scaring a woman so badly she was shaking. Did I have to be such a heavy-handed dickhead?

Heath shot me a well-deserved annoyed look and pushed me away from the sofa. I went back a step and scowled down at my shoes. I'd had to wear these bloody uncomfortable Italian leather jobs today as we had that big presentation to give for the museum refurbishment and extension. Verity had bought them for me after I'd turned up to the last one of these meetings in my scuffed, twenty-year-old loafers. I pulled at my collar, which felt too tight around my thick neck. Suits were the devil's work and I never wore a tie if I could help it. I was infinitely jealous of the green pajamas and trainers Heath was currently sporting which passed for perfect consultant-in-emergency-medicine gear apparently. The irony was that the bastard loved pretentious suits and shoes.

"Sorry about that, Mia," Heath said, his gentle tone drawing her eyes away from me. "Max didn't mean to upset you, but you probably *should* lie there for a bit. You did look like you were going to pass out. When's the last time you ate anything?"

Mia's eyes flicked to me again and she did a sweep from head to toe of my outfit.

"Oh no," she whispered. "Your presentation. That's why you're in so early. You're preparing for it. And I'm ruining everything!" She started to shift as if she was going to sit up again and I took a step forward.

"It's fine," I snapped, again not managing to gentle my tone, but it did have the effect of making Mia shrink back into the sofa away from me. At least she wasn't going to stand up again. I sighed. "Don't worry about it. Just stop being difficult and let Heath look at you, right?"

She nodded and Heath pulled out some equipment from his bag, then wrapped his hand around her wrist to feel her pulse, took her temperature in her ear, put something on her finger which flashed up some numbers and took her blood pressure.

"Okay you've warmed up now it seems," he said, smiling at her. "But the question is, how did you get that cold in the first place?" Mia repeated the *taking a walk* story she'd given me and Heath's head cocked to the side.

"Right," he said, drawing the word out in a way that stated she was not fooling anyone. "Did you eat breakfast today?"

∾

MIA

I looked into Heath's kind, concerned eyes and I felt tired. So, so tired of all the lies. I thought of my jar of peanut butter and the loaf of bread in my backpack and the fact I hadn't eaten anything other than that for the last three days.

"I ... skipped breakfast," I told him. "Look, this is all a big fuss about nothing. I'm sorry for wasting your time. I'll just get back to work, okay?"

I could see people had started to filter into the building now, all of them pausing to stare into the office until they were dismissed by a fierce scowl from Max. Having been the recipient of *many* of Max's scowls I could understand why his employees scattered so quickly. A glance at the clock showed it was after nine. Bloody hell, how long had I been asleep on this sofa?

Heath was staring at me, something working behind his eyes that I couldn't put my finger on. Max had crossed his arms over his chest and turned his scowl on *me* now. Wonderful. The last time I had showered was two days ago when I'd managed to sneak into the gym in the leisure centre down the road. Since dying my hair that god-awful colour it looked dull and grim even at the best of times, but unwashed it was even worse.

My mind flashed back to a time when my make-up was perfect, *always*. My hair used to fall in the styled, glossy waves that Nate preferred. Ponytails had annoyed him, and the one time I had had more than an inch chopped off he'd gone ballistic. After that I'd learned to keep it long and down at all times. It used to take me an hour and half every day to get ready. Cutting it all off had been one of the most freeing experiences of my life. Hair should be a woman's pride and joy, her crowning glory. But to me, it was just another weakness to be exploited. My scalp still tingled from the remembered pain.

I would never have long hair again.

But, as these two men stared down at me, I found that there was still a small spark of feminine pride that mourned the fact I looked about as far from an attractive woman as you could get. Which was ridiculous. The last thing I needed was any male attention. In fact, I'd sworn to myself that whatever happened I would *never* allow myself to be involved with another man. I'd learnt the hard way that you couldn't trust them. They used their size and their strength to bully and control. It just wasn't worth it. Maybe if an extremely short, skinny, infinitely kind, totally harmless guy crossed my path I would consider it in a few years. Maybe.

"I think you should take the rest of the day off," Heath said. "Get some proper food into you and rest."

My eyes widened as I glanced out at grey sky beyond the office and the drops of rain streaming down the windows. I started shaking my head so hard that my short hair fell into my eyes and I had to push it back behind my ears. It was time to attack it again with the kitchen scissors I had in my backpack.

"Please, please no," I begged. I hated begging, hated sounding so fucking *weak*. But I couldn't go out into the cold again. Not yet. "I'm fine now, really. I have a ton of stuff to do today. We've just had an upgrade on the system for BIM and they'll need me." I turned to Max in my desperation and his scowl morphed into a bemused expression. "*You'll* need me here. Look, I'll have a cup of sweet tea and a couple of digestives and I'll be right as rain. It was stupid to walk this morning but I just didn't think. I-I-I won't do it again."

Heath's eyes had narrowed and Max still looked confused. I'd reassured Heath repeatedly the other day that I was no longer in my ... *situation*. I'd promised him. Now I could see that it looked as though I didn't want to go home. That I was *scared* to go home. What Heath didn't know was that there was no longer a home for me to even go to. But in two weeks that would change. And tonight I'd make it to the shelter in time to get a space.

"Is everything ok in here?" Verity flung open the door and our eyes swung to her. "What's going on? Brother dearest, you know I love you but why are you here so early? Max, we've got to leave in ten. Are you ready?"

I knew an opportunity when I saw one and I was going to take it.

"Sorry Verity, it's my fault I ... I felt unwell and Max overreacted."

Max swivelled and pinned me with a furious look. Hmm, maybe that wasn't the best choice of words.

"I did *not* overreact," he bit out, moving to block my escape path from the office, but I was too fast for him. "I–"

"Anyway," I said, forcing a bright tone and even managing a smile for Verity. "Good luck today. Although, I know you won't need it.'

"Well, not with the improvements on the 3D modelling

you managed to knock up for the presentation we won't," Verity said. "Mia, I've never seen anything like it. As long as I can stop *this one* unleashing his unique brand of northern tosspot I'm pretty sure we've got it in the bag."

I'd noticed that, while Max oversaw a lot of the design side of the business, Verity was the one who dealt with clients. Apparently there had been "incidents" which had cost them some pretty big fish in the early days. It seemed that if Max thought an idea was stupid he tended to let the client know … to their faces, with swear words on occasion. So now Verity said she tried to minimise his *face time* with people they wanted to do business with. Although, when it was a big presentation and they were bidding for a job like this one, both of them had to go. Max's suit fit him to perfection. With shoulders that broad it must have been tailored to his exact dimensions. Objectively he looked stunning. However, the way he shifted in his shoes and pulled at his collar gave the impression of a big, beautiful, grizzly bear forced into a fancy suit and not being at all happy about it.

"I'll leave you to it then," I said, sliding further towards the door.

"Mia – " Max called, but I didn't look back. I could hear Verity telling him to *get his arse in gear*. Heath followed me though – right back to my terminal at the back of the office. I had a sixth sense for when I was being followed now – part of my well-honed survival instinct.

"Thank you," I mumbled at the screen as I fired up my computer, feeling him looming over me but managing not to shrink into my chair.

"Mia," Heath said softly. "If you need anything. If you need help of any kind. Like I said the other day I can put you in touch with some– "

"I'm good, fine, *great*."

Heath sighed then lowered his voice.

"I could talk to Max and Verity. They would help you, you know. If you needed some – "

"I'm *fine*," I repeated, somehow managing to add some steel into my tone. "Do *not* discuss what you know about me to my employers. Even *I* know that that would break patient confidentiality. I might be weak, but I'm not stupid."

"I never said you were weak, Mia," Heath said in a quiet voice. He rested his hand on my shoulder for a second, but removed it when I flinched away.

"You're still not moving your arm properly."

My mouth tightened but I ignored Heath and carried on logging into the system. The number he'd given me for the physiotherapy department was still in my back pocket. But I'd realised that to book an appointment they'd probably need an address and other details – stuff I didn't have. So I hadn't rung them.

"The longer you leave it the more likely you are to lose function. Listen, I know one of the upper limb physios. She can see you ... this week even."

"I can't– "

"I'll book it in and let you know the time."

My fingers paused over the keyboard and I blinked. "Really?"

"Yes. Look, give me your number and I can let you know when and where."

I closed my eyes and felt my chest tighten. After I gave Heath my new mobile number I forced myself to make eye contact with him.

"Thank you," I repeated, only this time it wasn't a whisper. This time I made sure he would know just how much this kindness meant to me. He nodded, but just as he was leaving he turned back to me.

"Why were you so cold this morning, Mia? What happened?" he asked in a low tone so that none of the other desks would be able to overhear. I looked back at my screen again and remained silent. After a long minute I felt him move away but I didn't look up.

Chapter 6

Some men did know how to apologise

MAX

I stared at the blank screen and I tried to hold onto my temper. I really did try. But the bastard *system* had lost my presentation. I'd opened up my computer, and the file just simply wasn't on my desktop. Hours of my life had been spent on that thing and now I'd spent another bloody half hour trying to find it.

Maybe if I hadn't already been in a foul mood I would have been able to remain calm. But last night Teddy had come home late *again* after ignoring my texts and phone calls. The only explanation I seemed to be entitled to, when he finally did arrive home, was a short grunt and an eye roll. It was like I was running a sub-standard hotel, which Ted was less than impressed with, but did deign to stay in at night. I couldn't even complain that Ted's grades were slipping: the bloody kid had an IQ through the roof, and sailed through all the exams, completing coursework in front of the telly that would take other students hours of concentration. The only things he struggled with were the computer science assignments, and unfortunately I wasn't very much help there.

I knew I wasn't perfect, but I didn't think I deserved the distain Ted threw my way on a daily basis now.

And then there was Mia. I'd barely seen her since her near-collapse with hypothermia. I couldn't sleep remembering how cold her hands had been. All I wanted to know was if she was okay, but she dodged me at every turn and barely gave me more than one word answers. It was beginning to piss me off.

"Where is she?" I growled as I flung open Verity's door and stalked into her office.

"Well, good morning to you too, Max," V said, sending an apologetic smile across to the junior architect sitting opposite her, looking like a scared rabbit. I put my hands on my hips and scowled down at V.

"I *told* you we didn't need that bleeding system upgrade," I said, my voice rising with my anger. "Now I've got nowt for all the work I've done in the last two days. It's disappeared into the ether."

"I'll just ..." the junior was standing next to his chair now and had started sidling out of the room. "See you later Verity, Mr Hardcastle."

I sent the guy a dirty look, which had him moving faster towards the door.

"Max, please, please stop acting like a total wanker with the support staff. You do realise where we get these people from don't you? They're not complete fuckwits I've dragged in off the streets. Most of them graduated with firsts from some of the most prestigious architecture schools in the country. A lot of them were prizewinners. There's a whole sea of talent out there and all you can do is scowl at them. You terrify them when you should be inspiring them. Young architects don't come here to work with *me* you know – it's *your* work they've seen, you they look up to and want to emulate."

"That's bullshit," I grumbled. "And I am nice, goddamn it."

Verity raised her eyebrows at that blatant lie and I rolled my eyes.

"This is beside the point. I want to know where this bloody *technical genius* you've forced into my company is so she can explain to me where the fuck my presentation has disappeared to. She avoids me like the plague."

"She doesn't avoid you. I think she's just wary since you overreacted the other day to – "

"I did not overreact!" I thundered at Verity who just crossed her arms over her chest and raised one eyebrow in response.

"Keep your voice down, you overgrown gorilla." Her calm tone spiked my anger even higher. "Firstly it's *our* company, not *your* company. I know you're the creative wonder, but you would not have any clients for whom to build your amazing structures if it wasn't for me and you know it."

I deflated and looked at my shoes.

"Sorry, V," I mumbled.

She sighed. "Now, what is the problem?'

"The problem is that an unnecessary upgrade was done to the system by an unnecessary and redundant member of staff that *you* employed, and who I can't find because she's hiding from me ... in an office made up entirely of *glass*! I mean, how is that even possible?"

A throat cleared from the door of Verity's office, and I spun around to see Mia standing at the threshold. For a moment I felt a little sick. I hadn't wanted her to actually overhear me calling her *redundant* and *unnecessary* but I pushed that aside as my annoyance bubbled to the surface.

"Finally," I said, throwing my hands up in the air. She took a rapid step back, which only served to irritate me more. "Stop edging away from me every time I even look at you." The familiar wide-eyed, fearful expression on her face melted into one that looked a whole lot like anger. Her cheeks flooded with more colour than I'd ever seen in them before, and her fists bunched at her sides.

"M-m-maybe ..." she stopped for a moment and shook her head as if irritated by her stutter. "Maybe," she continued in a stronger tone, one I had never heard from her before, "if you treated me with some *respect*. Maybe if you didn't sh-sh-shout and throw your weight around like a ... a massive toddler. Maybe then I wouldn't have to try to avoid you, and maybe *then* I could have explained how easy it is to find files in the new system I've set up. Which, by the way, has already increased productivity and wifi speed by thirty percent." By the end of her little speech she was breathing so fast her nostrils were flaring, and her hands had clenched into such tight fists that her knuckles were white. "Follow me," she snapped and stalked out of Verity's office and across to mine.

MIA

What had come over me? As I marched across the office space I could feel the blood pounding in my head and the adrenaline surging through my body. Had I really shouted at Max? Had I really called him a *massive toddler*? I was shaking as I sat down at his computer and brought his screen to life.

"Everything is in this folder. The one labelled 'Max's stuff'," I said, slicing Max and Verity, both of whom had followed me over here, a look as they stood in the doorway.

"You're such a frightful dullard, Max," Verity snapped as she swatted him on the arm. "Say sorry."

Max shoved his hands deep into his pockets and scuffed his feet on the floor. Despite his size he looked like a reprimanded schoolboy again.

"Sorry," he told his shoes. Verity nodded then swept out of the office, elbowing Max in the stomach on her way. I sighed, feeling all the adrenaline drain out of me and along with it my fighting spirit. That muttered apology was the best I could expect. In my experience men rarely apologised, so I should be grateful for what I got.

"I can set it up however you want," I told him. Even though he was still blocking the exit I found that I didn't feel any of the usual panic. Max might be grumpy and abrasive, but he was far from violent. He may have lacked charm, however I knew all too well that charm didn't mean anything. Nate was one of the most charming men you could ever meet, but his capacity for violence and cruelty was off the charts.

Max cleared his throat and scuffed the floor again with his foot before looking up at me, his green eyes alight with something that looked a lot like regret.

"Mia, I really *am* sorry," he said, and my mouth very nearly dropped open in shock. "I've been a proper dickhead. I have a temper and I'm an impatient son of a bitch but I shouldn't have gone off the deep end like that."

I blinked and then forced my mouth to close. Okay then, some men did know how to apologise.

"I, er ... that's okay," I croaked out, my throat closing over. He nodded and moved to the side so I could slip out of his office. On my way past though he reached out and touched my arm to stop me, but this time it was him that flinched back as if the contact had burned him. He cleared his throat as I paused in the doorway. "Mia, about t'other day. You've been avoiding me, so I haven't had the chance to ask but is there... ? I mean are *you* okay?"

The concern in his voice hit me in the gut, nearly winding me. I was really tempted to tell him that no, I was not okay – I was terrified, miserable and so very, very alone. But why would I trust a man who'd called me an emo freak, redundant and unnecessary, and scowled at me like I was an unwanted annoyance every time he'd caught my eye since I'd started working here?

"I'm fine," I muttered, and heard him sigh.

"If you're in trouble or anything I could ... well we'd need to know about it, right?"

I felt in that moment that he *had* physically struck me. He'd made me believe he felt some concern. But it *wasn't* concern for me that had him apologizing and asking if I was okay. It was concern that one of his employees might embarrass his bloody company. Of course, of *course* he didn't give a shit about me. I tucked my hair behind my ears and set my jaw. Humiliation, my now familiar companion, rolled through me as I met his assessing gaze. I was well aware that I looked like a heroin addict – that my cheeks were too hollow and my eyes too haunted to be considered normal.

"I'm not going to harm your business," I told him. "You don't have to worry about me being a liability."

That last bit was a lie. I could well prove to be a liability. But I was not going to reveal any of that.

"That's not what I–"

Turning sharply on my heel I stalked away from him without hearing the rest of what he had to say. I didn't breathe again until I had made it back to my desk.

MAX

I sighed and ran my fingers through my hair as I watched

her go. How had I managed to fuck that up again? Nothing I did was ever right with this woman. I had a perpetual case of Arsehole Syndrome around her. But she *was* hiding something. I *knew* it. If I was honest with myself though, if it was any other employee I would simply shrug off the nagging suspicion and get on with my life. But with Mia it was like I *needed* to know her secrets. Like I was compelled to find out everything about her. To the extent I'd pored over her employee file the other day, double checking her date of birth, as I still wasn't sure she was as old as she claimed.

I just couldn't seem to get her wide-set, chocolate eyes out of my head. On the rare occasions I could actually get to sleep, I dreamt of her. Weird dreams where she was cold again but this time I engulfed her in my arms, warming her against my body until her shaking subsided. Why on earth would I dream of her? She was so far from my usual type it was almost laughable. Rebecca had been five-foot eleven, ball-breaking, curvaceous and blonde – *not* skinny, small, make-up-free (other than badly applied eyeliner) and nervous. I needed to get a grip.

I just couldn't stand the thought of Mia keeping things from me – not my bloody company, *me*.

Which was ridiculous.

Chapter 7

Can we just forget that this happened?

MAX

"V!" I shouted as I slammed out of my office. Everyone's eyes swung to me apart from the chocolate ones that were haunting my every thought at the moment. Mia just sank further down into her chair and stared at her monitor.

"Max, what on earth?" V said as she emerged into the communal space.

I threw my hands up in the air and let them slap down on my sides. "I've bollocksed it up."

"What precisely have you *bollocksed up*, darling?" Her cool, calm collected question only escalated my frustration. Why was V always so goddamn in control? It was nauseating.

"Everything," I told her as I paced up and down between the junior architects' desk.

V put her hands on her hips over her perfectly fitted, brown leather pencil skirt and her toe of one of her sky-high stilettos started to tap.

I huffed and threw myself down into one of the free office

chairs, which creaked under the sudden impact. "It's all gone to shite. We'll have to cancel the bid. I've fucked it."

"Well, before I ring the client and tell them you've '*fucked it*', might you want to explain the problem to me and maybe we can try to *fix* it."

I scowled at her with her immaculate clothes (my shirt looked like I'd worn it for weeks) and her sound bloody logic.

"Fine, whatever," I grumbled, pushing up from the chair and glaring at the new hire next to me who quickly looked away.

"Don't mind Max," V said to the new guy as she swept past him. "He's basically on the same level drama-wise as a thirteen year old girl."

I snorted but my bloody lips twitched, damn them. V had always been able to make me laugh at myself – it was one of her unique talents.

~

MIA

I watched Max and Verity disappear into his office and let out a breath I hadn't realised I'd been holding. Max was just so ... *much*. He had a presence that filled the space and sucked all the energy out of it. Tall, muscular in a bulky way, dark – like some sort of highly strung thoroughbred, especially when he was being teenage-girl-level dramatic, as Verity put it. How she had the ladyballs to say that to his face was beyond me. I'd expected him to explode after she'd teased him again just now. But, if anything, it seemed to actually take the wind out of his sails. I'd snuck a look at his face after her comment and it even seemed like he was suppressing a smile. As if he *enjoyed* being the butt of her joke. Like he accepted he was being an idiot.

Nate would have *never* created a scene like that in public. He was always in complete control. No drama. When he was angry he didn't bluster about, he went ice cold – and the angrier he was, the more precise, more devoid of emotion his voice became. And *nobody* teased Nate. I tried to imagine his reaction if I'd compared him to a thirteen-year-old girl and shivered in my chair.

Suddenly I was transported back in my mind to a year ago, sitting in the low-slung sports car with him, trying not to crease the dress I was wearing for my cousin's wedding, and feeling the acute claustrophobia of being trapped in a confined space with Nate for two hours. But he was in a good mood. He'd told me I looked pretty. He'd even held my hand some of the way.

"The service better not be that long and there better be booze," he said, his earlier smile giving way to the beginnings of a scowl – I should have taken that as a warning sign but I'd been lulled into a false sense of security. The service was going to be Catholic and Greek Orthodox with both a priest and an orthodox clergyman.

It was not going to be short.

"Nate, you numpty, it'll take hours. You know that Tom's Cath – "

Wham.

My head snapped to the side with the impact to my face. I saw stars for a moment and blinked through the passenger window to stay conscious. As my vision demisted I looked down at my light blue dress. It was splattered with blood. I brought my hand to my mouth, pulling it away and looked at the blood on my fingers. Nate's hand returned to the steering wheel. He wasn't even breathing heavily. At the next roundabout he went all the way around and headed back in the direction we'd come from. I swallowed as the metallic taste filled my mouth.

"Don't speak to me like that." His voice was devoid of emotion. He handed me a handkerchief and I pressed it against

my mouth. Neither of us said a word on the way home. Nate phoned Tom's parents and sent his apologies. He told them I was throwing up something I ate. ("I told her not to order mussels if she's not on the coast with a direct view of the sea.")

I binned the blue dress and I missed my cousin's wedding. My sister phoned me later that day, furious with me for not coming.

"What's wrong with your voice?" she'd asked – at that stage my mouth had swollen so much it was distorting my words.

"Must be all the vomiting," I'd muttered.

Marnie hadn't believed me. She knew Nate stopped me going to the wedding and she didn't understand why I didn't stand up for myself. Why I let him separate me from my family. We got into a huge row. By the end of it my face was aching and tears were streaming down my face. That was the last time I spoke to her.

"Mia? Mia can you hear me?" I blinked and came back to myself with a jerk. My mind always felt sluggish after a flashback – as if I was hearing everything underwater and seeing everything through a thick haze. I shook my head to clear it and then noticed Verity standing by my desk.

"Sorry, sorry," I muttered. "Er ... did you need something?'

Verity paused for a moment. Her head tilted a little to the side and her eyes narrowed. "You okay?" she asked, her tone a little softer than her normal cool efficiency.

"I'm fine." I forced a small smile, blinking to clear the haze and rubbing my hands together. Fear seemed to make me cold. I was so tired of feeling so cold. "Did you need me?'

"Max hasn't *bollocksed everything up* entirely, but he does need your help with the 3D modelling again."

Bugger.

I was still managing to avoid Max quite successfully. I suspected the pickle he was in with the computer was in large part down to that avoidance and I felt a twinge of guilt. Navigating all the updates wasn't easy. Even though I knew he deserved to be ignored after insulting me again, my conscience wasn't going to allow me to make up any more excuses. I knew they hadn't won the last bid that day I'd turned up to the office half frozen, and I felt responsible for that – like maybe I'd thrown Max off his game.

"Sure, of course," I said, pushing up from my chair.

"How did you do that?" Max asked as he leaned in closer to the screen. We were both sitting at his desk side by side. My breath caught as his large arm brushed against mine. His scent – clean, male, hint of expensive aftershave – was just detectable in the air around me, his presence, as always, vibrating the atmosphere with tension and energy. He was just too much for me to handle in close proximity. I cleared my throat.

"It's ... um, I mean. It's not ...'

He laughed. "You can tell me it's easy and I'm a complete pillock if you like. I'd agree with you."

He was looking at me and smiling. When he smiled his whole face opened up. He went from just average broody-type handsome to sincerely gorgeous. He had a dimple for God's sake. I decided that was too much as well.

And now I had lost the power of speech.

"Hello? Number Five. You in there, lass? Had a malfunction?"

I dragged my eyes away from his green ones and took in a deep breath. It only served to push my arm up against his again as my chest expanded. A low twisting feeling of awareness uncoiled in my stomach, along with the familiar anxiety I had been conditioned to associate with it. As I exhaled my breath caught and I started coughing. It was the third coughing fit I'd had that day and it exacerbated the rib pain that had never quite gone away.

"Shit, Mia," Max said. "If you're ill I shouldn't have kept you late. You should've said. I feel like a reight bastad now."

"I'm not ill," I told him once I'd recovered my breath. "I *never* get ill."

"Of course you don't," he replied. "You're Number Five. Human frailty be damned."

I smiled. It felt weird – like the muscles involved had atrophied from disuse.

Then I elbowed him right in his muscled bicep.

"Christ, watch it, Five," he said and I froze. Cold fear stole through me until I registered that he still had that teasing note in his voice and that he was still smiling. Had I really felt comfortable enough with him to elbow him in the arm? How had that happened?

We'd been working on the presentation for hours now. All the others had long since left the office. At first I'd been skittish. It had taken a while before I would even sit on the chair next to his. I'd spent the first hour hovering on my feet to the side of the desk and explaining things to him from afar. When I needed to type on his keyboard I'd wait until he moved well away and dart in to do it, still hovering on my feet.

Still able to run if I needed to.

In my rational mind, I knew he wasn't going to hurt me. Even if he *was* unstable, at that time the office had been rammed. There was no way he would do anything with all those people around. But it was difficult to quieten my instincts – the instincts that had been honed to detect threats for so many years.

But after an hour, Max's anger with himself had cooled,

and his body was no longer strung tight with tension as he realised I could help him out of the pickle he'd created. He stopped grumbling under his breath and had started to relax. Eventually he'd looked up at me and rolled his eyes.

"I can't do this with you hovering there like a hummingbird on steroids," he told me. "You're making me nervous, Number Five."

Me make *him* nervous? The idea was so ridiculous that I let out a small laugh despite my discomfort.

"Number Five?" I asked.

"Yeah, you know, *Short Circuit*? Jonny Number Five? 'Input. Input.' The way you flash from screen to screen and take in all the information reminds me of him."

I didn't think that being compared to a robot from an eighties movie was a particularly great compliment, but his voice was so warm that it almost sounded like one. I'd smiled and finally sank into the free chair next to him. From then on I seemed to slowly get used to being near him, slowly settle into the small ways he teased me, even managing some smart remarks back, and now I'd actually *elbowed* him.

He cradled his arm, mock-grimacing. "Those bony things are vicious weapons. I'll have a teeny tiny bruise from that tomorrow. May have to report you to HR. Er ... Number Five? You okay in there?" Max waved a hand in front of my face and I flinched in my seat. "Mia?"

The tone of his voice was now edging towards concern. God, I had to stop behaving like such a weirdo. It was obvious he wasn't angry. There was no need for me to tense up so much.

"Fine!" I said, forcing a smile that I hoped would convince him I was a normal human and not a freaked-out mess. I cleared my throat. "Do you even *have* an HR?"

I could feel him staring at me from the side, but continued to focus on the screen.

"Ha! No. Maybe I'll give that title to Yaz?"

"Yaz?"

"It's not like she's got owt better to do. Although she kicked me in't balls a couple of months ago so I don't think she's exactly anti-violence where I'm concerned."

"She *what?*"

"Yeah. That's her idea of non-contact touch rugby. The little shit needs banning."

"You play rugby?"

I couldn't imagine Max doing anything outside of the business. He was so ambitious and focused I wouldn't have thought he had it in him.

He laughed. "Got to keep this old carcass semi-fit somehow. And it i'nt rugby it's *beach, touch* rugby."

I snuck a glance at his 'carcass'. His long sleeve t-shirt was fitted enough to see the outline of his musculature. Semi-fit, my arse. I cleared my throat and looked away.

"Beach, touch rugby. That's sounds ... niche."

He chuckled. "You'd be surprised. It's actually pretty popular. There's an annual tournament in London. They bring sand into Earl's Court and make a massive pitch there for it. We got in't semi-finals last year." I'd noticed that as it got later in the day Max's northern accent tended to get a little stronger.

"You play?" he asked.

"What?"

"Do you play team sports? It's a mixed team and it doesn't matter if you're small. It's not like normal rugby – speed's more important than strength."

If there was one thing I was it was fast. My speed and agility had rescued me from a fair few sticky situations over the years.

But I shook my head. Lack of sleep and food meant I barely had the energy for work, let alone running around on a beach. He leaned back in his chair and stretched his arms up above his head.

"Gah! We've been sitting here for three hours. You sure you don't mind staying like this? I'll make sure you get paid the overtime."

"I don't mind, honestly." I'd deal with the consequences of finding a place to sleep later – after all I needed to make sure I was useful in a crisis. I needed to keep this job.

"Want some Chinese? I'm starving."

"I'm fine, thanks," I said, but my traitorous stomach had other ideas and it took the opportunity to grumble loudly. The sound seemed to vibrate around the silent office.

"Mia ... I haven't seen you eat today," Max said carefully.

"Oh I ate lunch out," I lied. The only thing I'd managed to eat today was the Weetabix I stole from the kitchen this morning. I would have loved some Chinese food, but I could not afford to waste the money. Max frowned at me as he pulled out his phone. The order he put in was massive. No wonder he had to exercise regularly if that was the amount of food he ate.

When it arrived and he slid two containers and some prawn crackers in my direction I realised why he'd ordered so much.

"I told you I was fine," I snapped as I grudgingly took a seat at the other end of the sofa from him. He'd taken the food and laid it out on the coffee table.

"Mia, you've saved my arse by Number Fiveing the fuck out of this presentation. Just eat the damn food. Please."

I shot him an angry glare, but relented when the smell of the Chinese hit my nostrils. There was only so much will power a girl could exert when confronted by a healthy dose of MSG.

Once I started the food I inhaled it. If I'd been alone I

would have groaned in ecstasy. Max kept some beers in his office fridge and brought out one for each of us. I blamed the food and the alcohol – both of which I was unaccustomed to, and both of which relaxed me to a level I hadn't been in months – for allowing me to let my guard down.

We'd finished everything and were talking more about beach touch rugby. Max'd managed to get out of me that I'd played netball for years (until Nate – of course I didn't actually mention Nate). Max insisted touch rugby was better than 'girlie basketball'.

"Uh, I'm sorry but netball is *way* harder than your pathetic game. It's about precision and skill. We work off the ball to create space, we don't just charge about like buffalo. As for it being *girlie* – your beach touch mama's boys' game might be non-contact, but if you watched any real netball matches you'd realise it is very much *not*." Under the influence of the first bit of alcohol I'd had for a while my old attitude from years ago was starting to peek out. It was a shock to me that I could feel comfortable enough around Max to allow it, even if I was a little tipsy.

He burst out laughing and then seemed to get distracted by my hand around the beer bottle.

"Your thumbs are ridiculous," Max commented.

I blinked.

"Er ... way to deflect my direct hit at your pathetic sport with a random statement." I looked at my hand around the glass bottle and then raised an eyebrow at Max. "I fail to see how my thumbs are ridiculous.'

"Look," Max said, pulling the bottle out of my hand with one of his, then turning my hand so my palm was facing him. He then took his other hand and placed it palm-to-palm with mine. My thumb and fingers barely came halfway up his huge paws. My breath caught in my throat at the feel of his warm, rough palm against my hand. Since I'd lost weight and hadn't been able to look after myself I'd felt perpetually cold. The heat from his hand seemed to seep through into mine and down my arm.

"I mean, look at these little guys. How do you even hold stuff with them?"

He moved further into my personal space from across the sofa. For some reason, either tiredness, unaccustomed alcohol, or having a full stomach for the first time in months, I didn't pull away. In fact, as his scent reached me I found myself drifting towards him as well. His eyes went from our hands to my face and his pupils dilated.

"Mia," he whispered and I felt his breath against my mouth. His face was so beautiful this close, it felt almost over-whelming. The warmth from his palm was still seeping through me and I felt a sense of wellbeing that I hadn't experienced in years. I forgot to be scared. I forgot who he was. I forgot every-thing. It was like he was the sun and I was under his gravita-tional pull. I closed the small gap between our mouths and I kissed him. The first touch of his lips to mine sent a bolt of awareness through me so strong I was surprised that I didn't pass out. My hands moved of their own accord to his solid chest. Just as my mouth opened slightly under his, his hand slid up my arm, over my neck and into my hair.

I froze. My scalp tingled and unwanted images flashed through my mind.

"You fucking bitch." Nate grabbing me by my hair and pulling me across the kitchen; my feet sliding from under me as I scrambled to keep up with him to ease the tearing pain on my scalp; me whimpering – a pathetic high-pitched sound, which only made Nate pull harder until ...

"Mia, Mia!" Max's urgent voice cut into my mind, pulling me out of the scene. I could still hear that whimpering, and after a moment I realised it was coming from me. It cut off as I pressed my lips together, breathing hard through my nose and forcing my body to calm down. Max was back across the sofa now, looking at me like I was an unexploded bomb. My hands went up to my face to push the hair that had fallen into my eyes behind my ears. They were shaking, and after a moment I realised I was shaking too. And I was cold again. So very, very cold.

"Mia? I'm not sure what … Are you … are you okay?"

"I'm sorry," I said, my voice hoarse. He moved towards me and I flinched back into the arm of the sofa, causing him to rear back with his palms up like I had a contagious disease.

"Did I … did I hurt you?" Max's horrified expression made me want to sink down onto my knees and sob in frustration. What was wrong with me? "I don't understand what … If I hurt you then–"

"No," I cut him off. "*No*, Max. You did nothing wrong. *I* kissed *you* and … listen, it's me that's in the wrong, not you. Can we …" I broke off and swallowed, squeezing my eyes shut as humiliation crawled up my spine. "Can we just forget that this happened?"

He frowned and his hand went up to rub the back of his neck before pulling through his thick hair and down to the stubble on his face.

"Mia, you freaked out. I've never seen owt like it. I … I've got to be honest it scared the shit out of me."

"I promise it won't happen again," I told him, my tone now almost fierce. I meant every word. What was I doing kissing my boss and then having a panic attack in his office? Didn't I have enough problems without adding inappropriate behaviour at work into the mix?

"Listen," I stood up then backed away from the sofa to find my shoes, which I'd kicked off under Max's desk earlier. "You don't need me to finish the rest of the presentation. I'll just get going and–"

"I'll call you a taxi," Max said, his composure back and his bossiness along with it.

"No," I said, a little too sharply. He narrowed his eyes at me.

"It's late Mia. I've had two beers so I can't drive you, but we can share a taxi."

Seeing as there was no place for Max to actually take me to, that was not going to happen.

"You need to finish the presentation."

"I'm not letting you go home by yourself at this hour." His mouth was set in a stubborn line and his hands were on his hips.

"You are not taking me anywhere," I said, my voice going as cold as I could make it. "It would make me feel *very* uncomfortable if you took me home. I'm sure that you want to maintain our professional relationship as much as I do. I should think that after this," I swept my hand out to the sofa, "the last thing you would want to do is make me feel uncomfortable."

He blinked for a moment then recoiled from me like I'd slapped him. His expression hardened, and I told myself that was good – better that than concern for my safety and uncomfortable questions.

"Fine," he snapped, his face shutting down all expression to leave a blank mask where his unsettled expression had been before. "I wouldn't want to make you feel any more *uncomfortable* than I already have."

I gave him a stiff nod and with jerky movements grabbed my backpack off the floor. Pausing at the door I looked behind me to see Max going back to his desk and settling in his chair again. His jaw was clenched tight.

"Max, I–" I started then stopped when he looked up and scowled at me.

"Enough, Mia," he said in an angry tone then sighed. "Look, I've got a lot to do before tomorrow," his tone had lost much of its anger now, replaced by a weariness that made my chest ache. "You don't want to tell me that's fine. I think it's best if you just go home."

I nodded, but he'd already turned back to the computer screen. As I crossed the communal space I straightened my shoulders and blinked back the stinging I could feel behind my eyes. This was the reminder I needed that I had to be careful. I couldn't let my guard down. The only person I could rely on was me.

Chapter 8

Painful and wonderful

MIA

"Why did they have to come?" Max grumbled to Verity. I stiffened in the backseat, but Yaz just rolled her eyes and stuck her tongue out at him in the rear-view mirror.

"We need help with the new BIM system," Verity explained, again. "If something goes tits up Mia can swoop in and perform her magic.'

"If we hadn't updated the bloody presentation system we wouldn't need any help."

"Yes, Max. We also would not have been shortlisted, would we?"

I shrank back into the soft leather, trying to make myself as small as possible and looking out of the window to watch the countryside next to the M3 fly past. We were on the way to London to pitch for a massive eco housing project. At the last minute Verity had forced me into the car in case they 'ballsed it up' and needed me to 'save their arses'. I hadn't wanted to come any more than Max wanted me there. Panic had already set in about how I was going to get out of having, and therefore paying for, lunch once we got there. Verity had suggested they stop in at a little Italian place she knew in Covent Garden. I had been to Covent Garden, many times and had frequented way more expensive restaurants than just Verity's little Italian. I wasn't penniless then, far from it. But now, I didn't have access to any of my old accounts. Nate had always managed the money, and the only account I had access to had been a joint one. After I emptied it on the day I left, I hadn't dared access it again as he would have been able to see where I was making the transactions. Now the money I'd been relying on was dwindling. I needed to set up a new bank account but that was easier said than done when you didn't have proof of address. I'd told Janet in accounts that I was having trouble with my bank account and she gave me part of my pay in cash. The maximum she could do was £250 and I didn't want to waste any of that. It was so cold at the moment – I needed to try and stretch it out to stay in the small B&B I'd found until I could sort out the bloody bank account problem.

"Fine, whatever," Max grumbled and I tried not to take offence. I knew he didn't want me there and I didn't blame him. I wasn't exactly a good representative of the company – unless too-thin, wannabe goths were now all the rage in the architecture industry.

"And I'm hitching a lift to the big smoke, so suck it up, grumpy pants," Yaz put in.

"I thought you hated London," Max muttered.

"I do – too far from the sea. But I'm meeting up with Kira Lucas if you must know."

"Yeah, right," he said. "Pull the other one."

"She is my friend, knob cheese."

Max snorted. "As if the wife of the Prime Minster would bother being mates with you."

"You know Kira Lucas?" I asked, my eyes going wide as I focused across the backseat at Yaz.

"We've been friends for ages," Yaz told me, giving Max a one finger salute when he snorted again. "We go to the same yoga retreats and her mum runs a Wiccan rally I go to every year. Kira and I have a *lot* in common actually."

"Right." Max drew out the word. "Whatever you say. They've never actually been seen together."

"Bog off."

"Max, leave Yaz to her little fantasies," Verity put in.

"Hey!" Yaz said but V ignored her.

"You're just nervous," she continued to Max in a patient voice.

"I've never been nervous in my life," Max scoffed and I saw Verity roll her eyes in the rear-view mirror.

Max might deny it, but evidence would suggest that he was a liar. He'd been pacing the floor all morning, double and then triple checking every last detail with any of the junior architects involved in the project. I'd seen him storm into Verity's office around ten and start shouting about *light wells* and how they needed to redesign an entire wing of the project. Verity had let him rant away as usual.

I'd been sweating by the time he finished his shouting and furious pacing. Aggression of any kind now seemed to make my right shoulder and ribs ache as well – some sort of weird response to the remembered trauma. Eventually, Verity managed to calm him down, convincing him that the light wells were fine and that it was too late to pull the original design. He'd grumbled all the way back to his own office. I caught the words, 'should just pull it if it's sub standard' and 'my reputation on the line' and 'should have never entered the bloody thing at all if it wasn't right'.

Over the last few weeks it had become apparent that Max

was a perfectionist in the extreme and his own biggest critic. Whatever he was saying now, he *was* nervous about today. My presence in the situation and the tension between us after that kiss wasn't helping either.

We parked below the office building at our destination. Yaz shot off to meet Kira Lucas (or so she said – it was clear neither Max nor Verity believed her) and we made our way up to the offices. After an uncomfortable couple of minutes in the lift, we arrived at the top floor of the block and only had to endure Max's pacing for a short time before we were ushered through to a conference room. There was a panel of ten people sitting around the table awaiting the presentation. Verity did the introductions and most of the talking. I shrank into the background as much as possible, standing behind the tea trolley and wishing I could blend in with the stark white walls. As I scanned the room my eyes suddenly landed on a face I recognised, and my throat closed over. It was Nate's business partner. With my luck I shouldn't have been surprised, but London was a huge city. Did he really have to be in this meeting room in this building? I knew that there were a number of property developers interested in the project that Max and Verity were presenting, but Nate's company had never been into eco-design before.

I was barely recognisable as my former self, but when Adrian caught my eye there was a flicker of recognition in his expression, before a small frown of concentration formed in his forehead as if he was trying to place me. I looked down at my feet and let my hair fall forward to hide my face. But my heart was now hammering and I could feel a prickle of sweat at the back of my neck. Max had now taken over from Verity to describe the actual design. The model of the eco village was in front of him on the conference table and he was talking the group through it. He seemed to be in his element. Even though

I knew nothing about architecture I could see that the vision he presented was incredible. And sustainable. Yaz had told me earlier that a zero carbon eco design on this scale was virtually unheard of.

When he switched to the virtual tour of the buildings I could see a muscle in his jaw twitch as he tried to pull up the programme and project the images onto the wall. I linked my hands together in front of me and prayed. But, as per usual, my prayers fell on deaf ears. The man had a natural talent for buggering up any tech he came in contact with.

"Mia," his sharp voice brought my head up. He was scowling at me. No surprise there. "Can you sort this? Please?"

I made myself step forward, focusing only on the computer in front of Max and trying to block out the rest of the room. I took a deep breath and let my fingers fly, sorting the programme out in seconds.

"Thank you," he said, genuine relief and gratitude in his tone when the images came to life on the wall. I nodded and started to pull back but, as I straightened, my eyes caught on Adrian directly opposite. He was staring at me – that frown still marring his forehead.

"Amelia?" Adrian asked. I jerked and my hand made contact with a cup of tea on the conference table. Like it was in slow motion I saw it lean to the side and then topple over before I could catch it. Brown liquid split over the table and onto the model, marring the crisp white lines and flowing through the miniature atrium Max had just been describing.

I took a step back and my hands went up to cover my mouth. I didn't even have the wherewithal to grab a napkin from the tea trolley and mop up the mess – Verity leapt into action instead.

"I'm so sorry," I whispered from behind my hands. Every-one's eyes swung from the mess I'd made on the table to me.

Some were shocked, some were filled with amusement, Adrian's were just curious. Max shifted back in his chair and I knew I wouldn't be able to look him in the face, so I did what I do best – I turned on my heel and I left.

MIA

"Mia?" Verity's voice echoed around the large bathroom I'd found to hide in and I squeezed my eyes shut. I was sitting on the closed toilet seat in one of the pristine cubicles trying to stem the flow of my tears. Luckily over the years I had perfected the art of silent crying. Nate could never stand the sound of my sobs. It was always worse if I let him hear me cry. "Are you in here? You don't need to hide. Nobody's angry with you." She was right outside my cubicle now. When I opened my eyes I could see her heels under the door. I sighed and wiped the tears streaming down my face away with the back of my hand, then stood up on shaky legs.

"Sorry," I muttered as I unlocked the door and stepped out of the stall. Verity took one look at my tear-streaked and, no doubt, blotchy face and pulled me in for a hug. She was taller than me and more substantial so it felt like I was completely surrounded by her. She smelt of lavender and dry-cleaned clothes and she was warm. How long had it been since anyone had hugged me? I hadn't seen my mum in over a year. The only physical contact I'd had with Nate was not the affectionate kind. Verity's hug felt like it cracked something inside me. It was painful and wonderful all at the same time. More tears tracked down my cheeks as I buried my face in her neck and my body started to shake with silent sobs. It wasn't just spilling the tea – it was the shock of seeing Adrian and the massive adrenaline rush of fear it provoked.

A door opening brought me back to reality and I pulled back from Verity, who slowly released me. I started wiping my face with my sleeves, feeling like an idiot. Poor Verity probably just wanted to give me a quick perfunctory hug. She can't have been expecting me to soak her suit with my tears, or cling onto her like a spider monkey reunited with its mother.

"I ruined the presentation," I whispered.

"Bitch, please," Verity said and I almost smiled – that phrase in her posh accent was hilarious. "You didn't ruin anything," she told me, her crisp efficiency breaking through my misery. "You saved the bloody thing by being able to start the virtual tour. We would have been scuppered without that. That frightful model can be dried out and painted easily enough."

I blinked at her. "You're not angry?'

Verity stared at me for a moment, her eyes softening. "No, Mia. I'm not angry. And no, you're not going to lose your job." At that reassurance I looked down at my feet and felt two more tears leave the corners of my eyes.

"Thank you," I muttered.

"No time for that now," Verity told me, ushering me to the sinks. "We're off out for lunch to celebrate getting through the presentation without Max acting like a tit. Wash your face, darling and let's go."

"Is Max–?"

"You let *me* worry about Max." I splashed my face with cold water then peered at my reflection. My eyes were red, my face blotchy, but at least there was no make-up to run. Verity's eyes caught mine in the mirror and she made an eek face.

"Come on Bride of Frankenstein," she said, pulling open her huge bag and producing a smaller one, filled with makeup. "Let's get you fixed up."

Five minutes later, and the woman staring back at me in

mirror was from a previous time. One that felt light years away. She looked thinner than before, there was still a hint of dark circles under her eyes, her cheeks were hollower, her hair was darker but she was definitely *that* woman. For a mad moment I wanted to scrub it all off my face again, but fear of offending Verity stopped me. I closed my eyes, shutting out the reflection from my vision and turned away from the mirror.

Chapter 9

You're not angry?

MAX

"There you are," I huffed as the girls approached. It felt like I'd been waiting out here for ages. Mia's pale, horrified face had been tormenting me since she'd run out of the conference room. It had been another painful half hour before we could go after her and even then I couldn't follow Verity into the Ladies, so I'd been pacing the outside for the last ten minutes. What do women *do* in there anyway?

Verity was a tall woman, so as they approached she blocked my view of Mia, who was lagging behind. It was only when they were a few feet away that I caught my first glimpse of Mia's face. Something was different. Her eyes were larger (but the whites looked red from crying), her lips more prominent, she had more colour in her cheeks.

I took a step towards her. She shrank back from me and I frowned.

"I'm so sorry," she whispered. I had to strain to hear it above the buzz of the other people walking past us.

"Look, its fine," I told her. "I don't–"

"You can ..." she cleared her throat and then swallowed before she continued, "... I would understand if you wanted to fire me."

"Fire you?"

She took another step away. Why was she always running away from me? I tried to tamp down my annoyance. She still had that awful look on her face – it was making my chest feel too tight.

"Mia, for Christ's sake will you -"

"I wouldn't blame you," she went on. "I know how long that model took to make. I know how important that presentation was."

"Mia—"

"I won't make a fuss. I won't – "

"Listen!" I snapped, slicing my hand through the air to make my point.

That's when it happened.

Mia tracked the movement of my hand and the fear in her expression was so stark it almost took my breath away. Her own hands came up to shield her face and she ducked down, making a terrible, almost animalistic sound. She started to back up from us with short, rapid steps but collided with a man passing behind her, lost her balance, and went down to the floor. Instinctively I approached her to help her up, but she scrambled backwards away from my outstretched hand, despite the fact there were people all around us, some of whom had stopped to stare at the scene we were making. I took a step back and held my hands up in a gesture of surrender.

"I'm not going to hurt you, Mia," I said, shock at her reaction giving the words a harsh tone and causing Mia to flinch again. Verity advanced towards her whilst I hung back and rubbed my hands over my face.

"Let's get you up now, darling," Verity said. She sounded

shaken which was almost unheard of when it came to Verity. As she helped Mia to her feet a small crowd formed around the three of us.

"There's nowt to see here, you nosy bastads," I raised my voice to be heard over the low murmur of theirs. "Go on. Bugger off." Mia, who was standing now, ducked her head and tucked her hair behind her ears, her face flooding with colour.

"Let's get some lunch," Verity said, putting an arm around Mia and guiding her towards the exit. "There's a place next door that looks pretty decent."

It was nearly two o'clock so the lunch rush was thinning but we still had to wait for a few minutes at the bar for a table at the Italian restaurant next to the office building. Verity texted Yaz to let her know where we were, and then there were a couple of minutes of oppressive silence. I broke it by clearing my throat.

"Mia," I said, making a huge effort to soften my tone. "What happened? Did you think I was going to … to *hit* you?'

Her eyes flicked to mine and away again at lightening speed. "N-no of *course* not," she said, a very slight shake to her voice. I sighed.

"I'm sorry but the way you … I mean, you *shielded* your face from me. You fell on your arse you were so panicked."

She shook her head. "I wasn't panicked," she lied, her eyes staring out of the window now. "I … j-just fell. I lost my balance."

"You did not lose your balance," I said, letting frustration seep into my tone. "You were proper scared."

"No. I *told you* – I fell." She met my eyes this time, her mouth setting into a stubborn line.

"I would never hit anyone. Well, okay I did clout Tommy Barnet in Year 11, but the bugger started it *and* he was twice my size at the time. Listen, I'm not even bothered about the tea spillage. I-"

"What?" She was staring at me now and her mouth had fallen open in shock. "But I–"

"You saved my arse in there, Mia," I told her. "If it hadn't been for you I wouldn't have been able to give the virtual tour." I started to lean forward in my chair, but paused when she shrank back from me in hers. "Even if I were upset about the tea I wouldn't have said owt to you. It was a mistake. It's not like you picked it up and threw it over the model out of spite. Accidents happen. If those dullards let an accident affect their decision about using us then the buggers can shove their eco village up their arses."

"You're not angry?" she asked, pure disbelief threaded through her words.

"No, I'm not angry," I said. "I promise, Mia. And I would *never* hurt you.'

"I didn't–"

"I'd like to know why you thought I was going to though."

She looked away from me again and her mouth clamped shut again.

"Okay, darling," Verity put in, laying her hand over Mia's on the bar and shooting me a warning look. "You don't have to tell us anything now. Let's all have a nice lunch and we can discuss it later, right?"

Mia shifted on her feet and blinked at the menu board in front of her. Even more colour left her face. "Why don't I just go back and wait in conference building. Or ... or I can just wait right outside, on the pavement. I can-"

"Wait on the pavement?" I asked in confusion. "Are you serious?"

"Er ..." she trailed off as she looked back out of the window.

"We're all eating lunch together," I told her. "I'll not be left with just V and my mad sister." Is this why she was so thin? Did she not eat? The waitress came then to show us to the table. I reached to usher Mia forwards but her flinch had me backing away again.

In general women did *not* make a habit of flinching away from me. However much of a grumpy sod I could be, I had the opposite problem with them. *They* were the ones trying to convince me to eat with them. *They* were the ones I had to push away. Even down the pub with Heath they targeted me. Heath's a handsome bastard but it's always the broody ones they seem to want to sort out. Who knew being an awkward fucker could be so attractive to the opposite sex? It had been even worse since Rebecca left me. As my grumpy bastard level ramped up, so too did their persistence.

At the corporate events and dinners I had to go to for work it was almost painful. Cocktail-dress-wearing, champagne-emboldened women seemed to cut me off at every turn. One waited outside the gents for me the other month and tried to snog me, right there in the corridor.

"This is not a choice," I told Mia, hardening my tone. When I thought back over the last four weeks I couldn't recall a single time I'd seen Mia eat anything substantial other than that Chinese in my office. Yesterday she just had a slice of plain bread with a cup of tea for lunch. I had just assumed she was fussy. "You're eating lunch here and that's it.'

"I can't," she told me.

"Why not?"

"I, er ... listen this is embarrassing but I forgot my wallet, so ..."

"You don't need your wallet," Verity put in. "This'll be on us. It's business. Right, Max?"

"Yes of course," I said, frowning down at Mia in confusion. "You don't have to worry about your wallet or anything else, okay?"

Mia's shoulders drooped and relief flooded her features.

My eyes dropped to her waist. I *knew* she wore a money belt under her clothes. I'd seen her tucking change into it and caught flashes of it over the last three weeks. She didn't go anywhere without it and I very much doubted she would have come all the way to London without it either. I was surprised she hadn't dragged her backpack along as well.

We were shown through to a four-seater table and I watched Mia manoeuvre herself so that she wasn't sitting next to me. This suited me fine as it meant I was opposite her instead and could study her across the table. Yaz, never one to turn down a free meal, made it in time to order, looking between us all as she sat down and being her normal unhelpful self.

"Woah, tense atmos in here, peeps. Do we all need to do some emergency yoga? I'm sure they won't mind clearing a space for us in the back."

After reassuring the waitress that we would *not* all be lying on the floor of her busy restaurant doing some spontaneous breathing exercises, we were finally able to order. It was no surprise to me that Mia went for the cheapest option on the menu, but at least it was pasta and not a side salad.

"Steak dinners aren't really the vibe your environmentally conscious architecture firm is going for," Yaz informed me after I ordered a fillet.

By the time she started asking the waitress if the halloumi salad was ethically sourced I was on the verge of chucking her out of the window.

"Well, I think we all did jolly well in there," Verity said after the wine had arrived. "Everyone looked frightfully impressed with the whole damn thing, I must say. Good show, Max – and well saved, Mia." V raised her glass up to toast and everyone else followed suit apart from Mia.

"Mia, do you want something else to drink?" I asked, ignoring V.

"What?"

"You don't have a drink. Do you not like wine?"

"I ... no."

"You can have whatever you want."

"What about a gin and tonic?" V asked her. "They've got that fancy smancy flavoured stuff. Go on, we'll both get one."

Mia smiled for the first time that day. It was closed-mouthed and edged with anxiety, but it *was* a smile. And for some reason I was furious it wasn't directed at me.

Chapter 10

Amelia?

MIA

I should have just accepted the wine. What was wrong with me? But my memories of red wine were so poisonous I don't think I could have forced myself to drink it. My mind flashed back to the last time I thought I'd had a choice of anything in a restaurant. We'd been at one of the best in London. Way more expensive than this place. Nate and I were eating with some of his clients.

"I'm fine thanks," I told the waiter, my hand going over the top of my glass to stop the red wine from being poured in.

"Just give it a chance," Nate said, his hand coming up to grip my wrist. I winced as it felt like my bones were being compressed together and I pulled my hand back.

"Pour," Nate said to the waiter. Then, "Drink it," to me after the waiter had moved on. I knew better than to not follow that order.

"Amelia's still getting used to this sort of thing," he'd told his clients, chuckling at my expense. "It was more chip butties and beer back home, wasn't it darling?"

I'd laughed then, trying to pretend I was sharing the joke rather than being the butt of it. Then I'd forced the wine down my throat and suffered the migraine it induced later that night. Anything not to embarrass him in front of his clients. Anything not to make him angry. Anything to be perfect.

"Are you sure you want that, Mia?" Max asked me, snapping me out of my thoughts.

"What?"

"A gin and tonic – you can have a soft drink if you like. Don't let Verity bully you into drinking if you don't want to. She's just chuffed she won the coin toss and doesn't have to drive back."

He was staring across the table, his too-intelligent green eyes focused like laser beams on me, like my answer was important. Like it mattered. His attention felt terrifying, oppressive, but wonderful all at the same time.

"It's fine," I said, managing a small smile. Some of the tension around his mouth relaxed at my smile. Deep, deep down in the pit of my stomach I felt something uncoil.

We talked about the presentation.

Yaz poached a large chunk of Max's steak.

"I thought you were vegan," Max protested.

"I'm a flexatarian, you idiot."

"A flexi-whaty-what?"

"A flexitarian. I don't *choose* to *order* meat or animal products for environmental reasons, but if it's already dead and presented to me I won't let it go to waste."

"*My* steak was not presented to *you*. Neither was it going to waste. I was about to eat the blooming thing!"

"Don't you care about my iron and B12 levels?"

"No. But even if I did, I'd tell you to order your *own* chuffing steak."

"You can have some of my halloumi," she told him, and he

eyed her plate with deep suspicion. I was beginning to recognise that Max's bark was much worse than his bite. I mean, Yaz stole his food right from under his nose, and apart from an eye roll and some dry comments on flexatarianism he tolerated it.

When *my* food came I forgot myself. I forgot that I was in a restaurant, that I didn't know these people very well. I even forgot the fear of discovery, just for a moment. Because it was the second hot meal I'd had in over two months. The smell of cheese and garlic from the carbonara clicked my mind into survival mode and I fell on it like a starving animal, blocking out everything and everyone around me as I ate. When I was finished I sat back in my chair and brought my napkin to my mouth.

"Okay there, Bear Grylls," Yaz joked. "I guess you were hungry, huh?"

My face flooded with heat and I ducked my head.

"I, er ... I have a high metabolism," I muttered.

"But you don't eat much around the office," Max said. I glanced up at him and he was staring at me, his head cocked to the side, as though he was trying to work something out.

"Amelia? It *is* you!" I turned automatically and stiffened in my seat as I locked eyes with Adrian Luther. "What *have* you done to your hair?" There was a long beat of silence as I struggled to work out how to play this. In the end I decided bluffing my way through it was the only choice. I'd only met Adrian a handful of times, since he'd only become Nate's partner in the business relatively recently. And I'd looked vastly different back then. I cursed the fact I'd allowed Verity to put make-up on my face earlier. Nothing was worth the potential of discovery.

"I'm sorry do I know you?" I blinked up at him and tried to keep the fear from my voice.

"What? Yes of course you do. It's *Adrian*. I saw you just a few months ago at the Christmas do. You and Nate have had a rough time of it since then, haven't you? First Nate with the flu, and then you came down with some sort of post viral syndrome. He told me that was why you didn't make it to the client dinner in March. Never known him to take any time off before. I do hope you're feeling better."

"I really don't know what you're talking about," I said.

"But–"

"I'm sorry, but you've made a mistake." I met his eyes then and stared at him in challenge. He frowned down at me in confusion. In all honesty I felt sorry for the guy. He'd always seemed pretty decent. All Nate's colleagues were. And it wasn't as if they all knew the truth. Far from it. Most of them assumed that Nate and I were so in love that he couldn't let me out of his sight when we were out together. I'd always been clamped to his side or he'd had his hand around my arm in what must have looked like an affectionate, if a little possessive, gesture. To me, his fingers biting into my skin was just another painful show of dominance, only in public. A warning to me.

"But–"

"Adrian, good to see you again, mate," Max's low voice cut in. He'd stood from his seat to his full intimidating height and extended his hand to the other man. "Hope you liked the proposal."

"Ah, Max," Adrian replied, shaking Max's hand and tearing his eyes away from me. "Sorry, didn't mean to ignore you there. It's just I know Amelia from–"

"I think you've got Mia confused with someone else," Max said, his voice was firm.

"*Mia?*" Adrian muttered, his eyebrows going up in surprise. "I ... " Max moved to block his line of sight to me and crossed his arms over his chest. Adrian let out a confused chuckle. "Right, yes. My mistake. Well anyway, have a good lunch."

~

MAX

Mia's face was so pale she was starting to look a little green. I hadn't missed her flinch when she heard the name Amelia. There was no doubt in my mind that that was her real name. I also didn't miss the fear in her expression as she looked at Adrian Luther. Real fear. I *knew* something was going on with her. I *knew* there was more to her than met the eye. There was an awkward silence now – very unusual with Yaz in attendance. When Mia reached for her gin and tonic her hand was shaking. She closed her eyes and swallowed the whole thing in two gulps.

"That was ... odd," Yaz said after letting out a nervous laugh.

"I ... I must look like someone he knows," Mia said, giving Yaz a tight smile.

"Well, he was a frightfully persistent bugger, wasn't he," Verity put in.

"Apparently we've *all* got a doppelgänger out there," Yaz said with authority she did not have. "You should be careful. If you ever meet your doppelgänger you ... er, well I'm not entirely sure what happens. I think maybe you both sponta-neously combust or something."

"Jesus. Well we've dodged a bullet there then haven't we?" I said with a dry tone. "Have there been *many* documented cases of spontaneous combustion related to doppelgängers, Yaz?"

"Don't take the piss, knobhead," Yaz muttered. Mia gave Yaz a startled look – she always seemed so surprised when people talked back to me. When I caught Mia's eye I smiled at her and rolled my eyes. She blinked and froze for a moment before she managed a small smile back at me. At least Yaz was good for something.

Mia spent the rest of the meal glancing around the restaurant with a hunted look on her face. When the bill came she looked so uncomfortable that I nearly said something, but I knew drawing attention to her would only make things worse. Verity paid with the company credit card. Yaz didn't blink an eye, which seemed to help Mia relax. Maybe she had some sort of ethical hang-ups about company meals or something?

Yaz bumbled on about nonsense most of the drive back. I put up with it because she made Mia laugh. It was only once we made it back to the office that things got weird again.

"Get in, Mia. I'll take you home," I'd told her after the others had left for their cars. I knew Mia walked every day. Come to think of it I didn't think I'd ever seen her driving a car.

"No ... don't worry. I'm fine," she said, backing away down the pavement.

"It's not fine," I said, taking a few steps towards her as she retreated. "You've had a rough day, its dark and past nine at night. Let me drive you back home."

"No, no, no, no–," she chanted, shaking her head as her eyes went wide. Was she still afraid of me? "Honestly, I'd prefer to walk.'

I sighed. "You don't live far from me anyway. It's no trouble."

"I moved," she said abruptly. "I'm, er ... in the opposite direction to you now. So ..." She backed up a few more steps, bounced on the balls of her feet a couple of times and then ... she ran. One minute she was there, the next minute she'd gone – disappeared into the night as if she'd never really been there in the first place. I sprinted after her but she'd left no trace. Although frustrated and annoyed, my overriding emotion was concern. I couldn't even drive to her house to check on her if she'd moved as I didn't have her new address. Muttering under my breath about stubborn women, I dug out my phone and sent Mia a text.

What the fuck was that? R u okay?

The reply came through within seconds.

Yes. All good. Nearly home now.

That was it. No explanation of why she would sprint off into the darkness after the offer of a perfectly good lift. I sighed. I couldn't shake the feeling that something wasn't right. There was something I was missing.

~

MIA

Thank God I'd thought to put my phone on silent.

I watched Max through the bins in the alley I was hiding in. He stared at my reply, shook his head and put a hand to the back of his neck, before scanning the street one last time. I must have looked nuts running off like that, but I knew if I'd stayed he would have *insisted* on driving me home.

Home. Ha!

Little did he know that *home* was the sofa in his office.

Money for the B&B had officially run out yesterday.

He spun on his heel and marched away and I let out a relieved breath. Luckily he was out of hearing distance when the breath I'd exhaled turned into a cough. I grimaced and rubbed my chest, sinking down the wall of the alley to sit on the damp ground. Another coughing fit followed.

I closed my eyes and, for the first time in a long time, I prayed.

Please let Adrian forget he saw me.

Please don't let me be ill.

Please don't let Max think I'm crazy.

Chapter 11

Hottie McBusinessman

M*IA*

I froze in my seat as cold fear trickled down my spine.

Nate was here.

I felt his presence before I heard the sound of his voice. The air around me felt thick. I made a conscious effort to slow my breathing. I couldn't afford to descend into panic. Not now.

"We would have come to you if you wanted to meet," Max said. "Chuffed we're down to the last two candidates. Your partner Adrian's a good bloke."

"Yes, well Adrian spoke very highly of you all," Nate replied, oozing his standard confidence and charm. "I wanted to see the inside of the company for myself before we took the final decision."

Oh God. Now I could see why Adrian was at that meeting. This project Max was working so hard to bid for was owned by Nate's company. I mean I knew when I took this job there was a slight chance of there being some involvement with Nate's company, but my skills in BIM weren't really all that transferable, and I had thought that this would be far enough away from London. Why was my luck such complete crap?

"And there are alternative opportunities I'm exploring with the other arm of my business. I'm thinking of converting some of the luxury family hotels we own into eco hotels. I'm selling quality and that doesn't gel with tired design. Can't charge the punters twenty quid for a blob of hummus if they're not eating it in the most modern, luxurious, environmentally friendly surroundings money can buy. It needs a total revamp."

Max chuckled. "Jesus, that's a lot for some mushed up chickpeas. You must be printing your own money, mate."

"Max," Verity started to say in a warning tone but Nate laughed.

"Don't worry," he said, his good-natured charm coming to the fore. "Rich people can be difficult to separate from their money, but I'm selling a lifestyle. In the redesign I need multiple photo op points and I need them to be *Instagrammable* in the extreme."

"Of course, Mr Banks," Verity put in smoothly. "We can—"

"Call me Nate," he interrupted. "By the way. How's the whole Brexit mess hitting the business. You having to shrink the company?'

"We're doing alright. It's been a pain in the arse but we should get through."

"Still expanding are you? I always think that growth shows the health of the business. Any new hires recently?"

My stomach churned and I suppressed the urge to vomit. I couldn't see them as my back was to the entrance to the office, but I knew Nate was surveying the scene. Thank God my hair was not the same long dark blonde. I tensed in my chair. I could almost feel his eyes boring into the back of my head.

"A couple," Max said. I exhaled slowly the breath I'd been

holding and gripped the edge of the table to stop myself running away. "Shall we go through to Verity's office now?" he offered, his tone hinting at impatience.

"Sure." I heard their footsteps then the door to Verity's office closing, after which I pushed back from my desk and stood abruptly.

"You okay, babes?" Yaz asked, glancing up from the reception to give me a curious look.

"I'm fine," I whispered. "J-just got some copying to do so I'll ..." I trailed off as I sidled towards the copy room. Once I made it inside I breathed a huge sigh of relief and rested my head against the door for a moment.

Well, Nate didn't seem any the worse for wear. I should have only felt relief. But the familiar fear wrapped around me, threatening to choke off my air supply. I backed away from the door and hit my hip on the industrial printer. Moving around it I pushed into the space between the machine and the wall until my back was pressed against the brickwork. I then slid down until I was sitting on the floor. I buried my face in my knees, started singing *The Wombles* under my breath, and focused on slowing my breathing. My head jolted up when I heard the handle of the door move.

"Yo," Yaz said, her eyebrows drawing together as she saw me. Luckily she slipped into the room quickly and shut the door behind her. "So," she said, coming up right next to me and then sliding down to sit on her bottom on my other side. There was only really room for one person in the small space. She had to wiggle herself in between me and the wall. Her ever-present disregard for personal space made me smile even though I still felt sick with nerves. "What are we doing?"

"Yaz–"

"I love that tune by the way." She started humming the

Wombles tune under her breath and then singing it softly. After the first couple of lines I joined in. When the song was finished the absurdity of the two of us trapped next to a photocopier, singing The Wombles theme tune permeated and I even managed a small smile. Yaz turned to me in the enclosed space and returned it before her eyes strayed to my hairline.

"You have roots coming through, babes," she said as she started pawing my hair like a monkey would its baby. "Not sure what was up your wazzer when you decided on this super-emo look. You're a blonde, aren't you?"

"Yaz, really I don't think …" I trailed off as I heard Max and Nate's voices again. They must have come out of the office. My body froze and on instinct I reached for Yaz's hand and gripped it tightly in mine.

"Mia?"

"Shh!" I said, gripping her hand tighter as the voices and footsteps passed by the door in front of us. As they faded I loosened my hold and took in some much-needed oxygen.

"Okay," Yaz said slowly. "I love that we're bonding and all, but there's a chance I may need to get an x-ray later."

"Shit, sorry," I muttered as I let go of her hand. She shook it and then flexed her fingers before reaching over, this time taking my hand in both of hers. She gave me a smile just as the door was flung open and light from the office flooded our hiding place. Max looked down at us, blinked a couple of times, and then put his hands on his hips.

"What on earth is going on?" he asked.

"None of your bee's wax, big man," Yaz said, rolling her eyes and wiggling her bum in an attempt to dislodge herself. After a full minute she gave up.

"I think we're stuck," she told Max. Despite my anxiety I felt my lips twitching as he let out a long-suffering sigh. When I couldn't hold it in any longer I started giggling. Maybe it was the adrenaline rush of Nate coming to the office and subsequent relief of him then leaving. I hadn't laughed like this in months. "Okay, babes," Yaz said through her own giggles. "We're both going to have to wiggle at the same time. Three, two, one wiggle!" When that didn't work either, Max muttered *fuck's sake* under his breath as he leaned forward and grabbed Yaz's hand then mine, pulling us up together in one swift motion. Yaz of course sprung up and balanced on her feet with practiced ease. I barrelled up into Max, losing my balance and falling face first into his chest. Both his large hands came up to steady me against him and I felt my face flood with heat as my heart started beating double time.

But it wasn't fear this time with Max. I wasn't scared of him now. It was awareness. Awareness of his strong jaw, his hard, muscled body against mine, his smell: clean soap, maybe a hint of aftershave and undertones of pure Max. I felt drunk on it and I wanted to touch him so badly it almost felt like a sickness. I hadn't felt that way in years.

After a beat he took a big step back from me, taking his hands away when he was sure I was steady. The speed of his retreat would suggest that Max did not feel drunk on anything about me, which wasn't that much of a surprise, but it still smarted. Whatever shred of pride I still had left took a hit.

"What were you guys doing?" he asked, there were two slashes of colour high on his cheekbones which I attributed to his annoyance. He was looking straight at Yaz but avoiding eye contact with me.

"Mindfulness," Yaz said, as if it was the most normal thing in the world to be doing down the side of a photocopier. "It's totally trendy now. Mia and I were taking in our surroundings and appreciating the small things."

"Appreciating your surroundings ... in the copy room?"

"Yes." Yaz gave him a withering look. "The blank walls, the whir of the inner workings of the machine. It's all *perfect* for meditation. Aren't you up to speed with mindfulness? I sent you another memo last week."

He looked from Yaz to me and then sighed. "I haven't got time for this bullshit right now. Ladies, if you're finished *meditating* during company time would you please consider maybe doing your jobs?" I looked at him and gritted my teeth. So far today I had achieved more than the whole rest of the admin team put together.

Yaz rolled her eyes and gave Max the finger behind his back as he turned away. I smiled and was about to step out of the copy room after him when fear and paranoia gripped me again.

"Yaz," I whispered, grabbing her arm before she could flounce away.

"What's up?" she asked, stepping back into the copy room when she saw my expression.

"The man that was with Max."

"Oh yeah – Hottie McBusinessman. Clocked him big time before I came to find you."

I swallowed down my nerves. "Is he still out there?"

Yaz stepped out of the copy room and scanned the office. "Nope, Sexy Pants has vamoosed. Do you want me to chase him down and get his number for you?"

"No!" I shouted, grabbing her arm again with a little more force this time. Her smile faded and she tilted her head to the side. "Mia, you okay?" I looked down at the hand that was gripping her arm and realised it was shaking.

"Sorry, sorry," I muttered, letting her go and trying for a smile – not a convincing one if Yaz's concerned expression was anything to go by.

"Mia, can you help me? I'm making a right pig's ear out of this bollocks," Max boomed all the way from his office, making me jump about a foot in the air, such was my residual fight or flight instincts around Nate. I started moving towards him but Yaz stopped me, taking a gentle hold of both my shoulders as she turned me to face her.

"What's wrong?" she asked. "You can talk to me. I know I come across a little ... well okay, a lot ... ditzy, but you can count on me. If you're in some sort of trouble or–"

"Yaz, will you bloody well let her go so she can do her sodding job!"

"Oh, bugger off, you overgrown bed wetter," she shouted back. "We're having a moment here."

I got up on my tiptoes to look past Yaz's shoulder and saw that Max's face was turning a deep shade of red and his eyes were spitting fire. Even I felt for him with that one. Having your sister call you a bed wetter in front of all your staff was not ideal.

"I better–"

"Oh don't mind him," she told me, rolling her eyes and then taking a hand off my shoulder to give Max the middle finger again. "The roids have addled his mind.'

"I can hear you, you know," Max said.

"Well, stop being such a dick then," Yaz said, winking at me. Max looked about ready to explode.

"I'll speak to you later," I lied to Yaz and then went to duck out of her grip, but instead of letting me go she pulled me in for a hug.

"I know you won't really *tell* me anything later," she whispered in my ear. "But *you* just need to know I'm here for you, alright?" I felt a lump build in my throat and swallowed it down.

"Thanks," I whispered back and she let me go so I could walk over to an enraged Max.

MAX

Mia finally stepped into the office and I shut the door behind her.

"What was that all about then?" I asked.

She darted me a hunted look before replying. "Nothing."

I crossed my arms over my chest. "Why were you guys in the copy room?'

"Er ... like Yaz said – meditating."

"Meditating my arse," I muttered. "Why did Yaz need a moment with you?"

Mia shrugged. "I don't know. Why does Yaz do anything? So, what's the problem you need help with?"

She moved around my desk to stare at the desktop and I felt inexplicably annoyed. The reason I'd been so insistent that she come to my office was because I wanted to get her away from Yaz. She'd looked like she'd seen a ghost in the copy room and then when she was talking to Yaz a minute ago she looked trapped, hunted. Of course, it was nothing to do with me if she was having deep meaningful exchanges with my sister. How was that my business? But for some reason that hunted expression on her face had my gut churning and made my chest feel too tight. Yaz was clearly upsetting her and I wanted to put a stop to it. But, more than that, I wanted to know what was so wrong that Yaz of all people would look serious for once. I wanted Mia to confide in *me*. Which was ridiculous. As if I was any good at solving other people's problems. Look at the mess Teddy and I were in. If only I were smooth and charming like Heath. People trusted Heath. Nobody was scared of him and he didn't stick his foot in his mouth twenty times a day.

"If there's a problem at work you're better telling me than

my sister," I told her, sounding like a complete dick, *again*. What was wrong with me?

"There's no problem," Mia told me, still looking at my bloody screen instead of giving me any eye contact. Her voice was smooth and devoid of any emotion, but when I looked down at her hands I saw they were bunched into small fists and her knuckles were white. Something had rattled her. Badly.

"Do you want me to come back later?" she asked, still in that smooth, expressionless voice. I grumbled under my breath and moved around the desk to get to the computer. As soon as I was within a foot of her she practically jumped out of the way, but not before I caught a faint smell of lemons and soap. For some reason, in that moment, I found that combination more appealing than any complicated perfume I'd smelt on other women before.

I scowled at the computer and showed her some random file I pretended I was struggling with. She waited for me to move right back before she took my seat. Her fingers started flying over the keyboard. Watching her work was like watching some sort of magic. Different screens would flash up and disappear. She'd scan bits of computer code like she was reading road signs and add her own code just as fast. Within seconds she'd solved the problem I didn't even know I had. Once done she shot out of the chair and nipped around the desk.

"All sorted," she said over her shoulder.

"Mia," I called just as she had reached the door. "Er ... I ..."

Tell me what's wrong.

Tell me how I can help.

Trust me.

"You really should be available if there's an IT crisis." Is what I actually managed to get out.

She gave me a steady look.

"An IT crisis?"

Her lips twitched and I clenched my jaw, aware that I was sounding a little crazy.

"That *is* why we're employing you."

"I will endeavour to stay in your eye line at all times, poised to sprint into action in the event of other IT *crises*. Happy?"

Smart arse.

But at least she wasn't clenching her fists anymore.

Chapter 12

Model employee

MIA

"Mia, I really need to get that photo of you today," Verity told me. "You're the one that said we *have* to have staff on the website with photos, but now the only person without a photo on there is you."

Bugger. I was really hoping that nobody would notice that missing detail. What I should have done is just conveniently forgotten the fact that putting names to faces when you're choosing a business to work with is invaluable. That having a staff list with photos is essential to any business website. But my bloody perfectionist streak would not let that fly.

"Sure." I gave Verity an unconvincing smile and she studied me with her head cocked to the side and her arms crossed over her chest.

"You know you are as much a part of the team as anyone here, don't you? You should be on that staff list. You deserve to be on there."

"Of course," I said with a sense of urgency now as I saw Max approach from his office. "I'll get to it, I promise."

"You don't have to wait," Verity said. "I've got the camera here. We can do it right now."

"Oh ... wow. I just think the lighting's a bit off now. Lets do it tomorrow or ... we can–"

"What's the problem?" Max stood on the other side of my desk, his eyes flicking between Verity and me.

"Mia's being shy about the website photo," Verity told him, waving the camera in my direction. I wanted to shrink into the chair.

"You don't want to have your photo taken?"

"Look, nobody is going to care who sorts out IT for you guys. The only ones they care about are the peeps who actually design the buildings. You don't have the cleaning crew on the website."

"Don't put yourself down," Max told me, his voice edged with annoyance. "You're just as important to the running of this company as anyone else in this office. Well, anyone but Yaz. We'd probably survive fine without her."

Yaz gave him a one-finger salute from across the floor. She'd been arranging aromatherapy diffusers all over the office for the last hour. It smelt like a spa on steroids in here.

"Come on," Max said, gesturing for me to stand. "I'm not going to have some ghost working in the company. We need everyone front and centre. It looks better if we have more employees visible. Like we're a sustainable company. The photo is non negotiable."

"I will *not* have my photo on your website," I told him through gritted teeth, my anger rising.

He was so bossy!

I wasn't in the mood for this today. I still couldn't seem to get a sodding bank account. The manager in Barclays simply told me there was nothing he could do – as if I wasn't a person worth an account. Now all I had was £50 left over from my cash payment from last pay day. Mary, who sorted the finances, had already asked for my bank account details twice today for payroll. I needed that account and I needed to have enough money to stay somewhere secure. What I did not need to do was publish yet more evidence of my whereabouts on a public website.

Since Nate had visited last week I'd been in a state of permanent panic. I didn't believe in coincidences – Adrian must have told Nate that he saw me in London. It was sheer luck that I'd managed to avoid him when he'd been in the office. I wasn't leaving anything to luck anymore. Over the last few days I'd done some digging of my own. Nate was one of the potential investors for the eco village project, but when I'd casually brought up his name with Verity she'd frowned and told me he was a horse's arse. Apparently he had stipulated a lot of cost cutting demands for the project before he would invest, but his changes would compromise the carbon neutrality of the houses and she told me Max wasn't keen to do that at all. So it looked as though the company wouldn't be working with Nate after all, but I still wasn't reassured enough to let them put my picture on the website.

"You bloody well will," Max snapped. "And ... and you'll eat lunch too. It's two o'clock and you haven't left your desk all morning."

My eyes went wide and I stood up from my chair to take a step away from him. He was too close. I hadn't been this close to him since the copy room incident last week. It seemed as though he'd given up trying to extract information from me. Which is what I wanted. He was my boss. A much more appro-priate employer-employee relationship was better for everyone.

At least that's what I told myself.

But there may have been a teeny part of me that was hurt. It was the same part that still had hope that I could not only recover from what Nate did to me, but that I could be happy again. The same part that actually acknowledged the real reason Max unsettled me so much. The rest of me, being far more sensible and way too jaded by experience, knew that my attraction towards Max was ridiculous, could never lead anywhere, and was the last thing I needed.

So I was happy Max had been treating me like any other employee. At least most of me was – a good ninety-five percent ... give or take. Therefore I did not need him to invade my personal space, show concern for my eating habits again and be an insufferably bossy bastard. Not if I wanted to continue squashing that little teeny tiny five percent.

"I will *not* have my photo taken!"

It was only after the office fell silent that I realised I'd raised my voice. I was as shocked as anyone to be honest. I didn't think I'd raised my voice to another person in years. But my picture was *not* going on that website, and whether or not I ate lunch was my own damn business.

"Mia," Verity's calm voice cut through the tension. She had gone from regarding me with irritation to some concern. "Let's discuss this in private, okay?"

I glanced at Max and noticed he was looking down at my hands with a frown on his face. I forced myself to relax my fingers from the tight fists they had bunched up into.

Heat crept up my face as I cleared my throat. "Right," I said. "Good idea." Without looking back at Max I followed Verity to her office, the rest of the staff watching every step I took. It didn't surprise me that when I went to shut the door behind me Yaz barrelled in. But I *was* shocked when Max followed in her wake. Verity glanced at them both after Max shut the door. She rolled her eyes but didn't ask them to leave.

"So, what's going on?" Verity asked, leaning against her desk and staring straight at me.

~

MAX

She looked like a cornered animal again and I felt my chest clench. Over the last two weeks Mia had largely lost that look. She didn't flinch at sudden noises, her eyes weren't full of shadows like before and she smiled. Not at me, never at me, but it happened. I watched her smiles and her growing confidence from a safe distance.

"Is this because you're planning on leaving?" Verity asked, crossing her arms over her chest and narrowing her eyes. "Because if you've been in talks with a competitor, I've got to tell you that's a pretty shitty thing to do. Especially after we gave you a chance when you first came to us without even a proper CV."

"I-I-I wouldn't go to a competitor," Mia stammered, her face stricken that Verity would think so poorly of her. "Of course I wouldn't. I–"

"Well, if you won't go on the website," Verity interrupted, "then you obviously don't consider yourself a permanent member of staff. Which I think is a bit–"

"You think I would give up my job here?" Mia's stammer had gone now and her fists were once again clenched at her side. "Do you have *any* idea how much this job has meant to me?" Verity's eyes widened with shock at Mia's rising tone and she went to take a step forward but Mia held up a hand to ward her off.

"Mia, I–"

"When I came here I looked like a ... what was it, Max? A 'scrawny emo teenage weirdo'. And despite that, you employed me. I will never forget that you gave me a chance. Not *ever*." Her last words were shaky and a film of tears was shimmering over her eyes.

"Oh Mia, I–" Verity was cut off *again*. Twice in one conversation was unheard of for Verity.

"And I haven't exactly been the model employee since then, have I?" Mia's voice shook. "I spilt tea all over that model, I've refused to work on reception, I stole ..." she broke off. Her eyes closed briefly and she swallowed before continuing in a hoarse voice, "I *may* have stolen some food from the kitchen. I've lied and ..." She broke off as a small sob worked its way out of her mouth before she tamped it back down, blinking away the film of tears that had sprung up in her eyes and forcing her face into a blank expression again. The control she had over her emotions was almost eerie. Yaz went to approach her, but Mia stepped back and put up a hand to ward her off.

"Mia, stop this now," I said in a firm voice. "I don't want to hear you talk about yourself like that ever again. Understand me?"

"Max, you don't have to–"

"No, Mia, I'm serious. Do you have any idea how much value you've added to the company? Why do you think Verity's turned all paranoid about you leaving? You've sorted out the BIM for all of our recent projects. You've helped every single person in this office and saved thousands of man-hours. I don't give a fuck if you've eaten some of our food. Why are you even worried about having a cheeky bit of toast in the kitchen?" Goddamn it – now my voice was getting all choked up. I could feel my man card slipping out of my grasp.

"Mia, I'm sorry I accused you of going behind my back," Verity said softly, her voice also a little choked. "I had no idea you felt like this. You're not our indentured servant just because I gave you a chance when you needed one. I hope you know that. I hope you stay because you *want* to stay. Are you ... I mean do you need money? Are you in some kind of trouble?

We don't care about the food but if you need help then you only have to ask."

"It's fine. I'm fine," Mia said tilting her jaw to a familiar stubborn angle. I had a strong impulse to drag her across the office hold her against me, but I knew that would make me seem more than a little weird and inappropriate. "I just had some financial problems for a while, but that's all sorted now. The only thing I need is for you not to push me about the photo. I'm asking not to even be listed on the website as an employee. It won't be forever. But for now I can't have that kind of exposure."

"Okay, Mia," Verity said, searching her face. "But we're here if you need us, right?"

"Right, of course." Mia's assurance was completely unconvincing, but it was clear that she had confided as much as she was willing to us. I decided not to push her for now.

Something I would regret.

Chapter 13

Have you heard of sepsis?

MIA

The coughing was one thing, but struggling to breathe was a whole other pain in the arse that I could do without. Even walking to the kitchen had left me breathing so hard that I had to lean against the counter for a moment before I could reach up to get a cup. Distracted by another coughing fit, I forgot to use my left arm and reached up with my right hand, which couldn't even make it to the shelf the mugs were on. I swore under my breath and sensed movement in my peripheral vision.

"If you're ill you really shouldn't be at work," Max told me and I held back an eye roll. He'd come in last week carrying the viral plague so he was on shaky ground taking that line of argument.

I ignored him and switched hands to grab a cup with my left.

"It's just a cold," I said, stifling the next coughing fit with a vicious swallow. The very last thing I needed was to be sent home. I *was* home.

"You get here pretty early, huh?" Max asked, crossing his arms over his chest and leaning his hip against the counter next to me.

"I've always been a morning person," I muttered, handing him a tea, which was brewed to his exact specifications. Since I'd overheard him on the phone after I started here I'd made sure that I made him tea every day. Usually I managed to leave it in his office for him without having to speak to him, like some sort of tea ninja. He scowled down at the cup I'd just placed in his hands and I sighed. There was no pleasing some people.

"Look, I'll hide in the copy room for the day. There's loads of menial stuff needs sorting in there and I can keep my germs to myself."

"You've got a weird obsession with the copy room. You're way too talented to be stuck in there." He sighed. "Use my office. I'm out this morning anyway."

My reservations about using Max's space were quickly overridden by the realisation that I *was* properly ill. As the day went on, every breath and cough had become excruciatingly painful in the right side of my chest – like a hot knife stabbing through my ribs. And then there were the sweats. They'd been happening all day, despite the fact I felt chilled to the bone. I desperately needed a shower to warm up. I had managed to sneak into the leisure centre for one yesterday, but there was no way I was strong enough to be able to repeat that tonight. And besides, all I really wanted to do was curl up in my sleeping bag and go to sleep, which I could happily do if only everyone would just bugger off for the day. It's six o'clock people! Don't you all have families to go to? Once they were gone, I wasn't going to be cautious and wait until nearly midnight to bed down. I would curl up as soon as possible. As a precaution I'd sleep under one of the desks. Another coughing fit wracked my body and I almost collapsed with the pain.

Maybe I *should* try to get checked out? But I couldn't exactly go to the GP. They would want my address and some form of identification (something which Verity had been hounding me about lately as well). That was why I hadn't replied to Heath's text about the physio. He'd asked which GP I was registered with and I realised that in order to have any physio things would have to get a whole lot more complicated. So, no GP. No emergency department either. The last thing I needed was a curious Heath hovering over me if he was on shift.

No, it was probably just a virus anyway.

I could sleep it off.

But by the time the last person had left for the day and I had crawled into my sleeping bag, I realised I'd made a big mistake.

MAX

I shivered in the morning air as I pushed through into the building. It was after seven. Maybe I should have set up the heating to come on earlier? It was brass monkeys right now – I could see my breath in front of my face. I stopped by the boiler to make sure it was cranking up and blew into my hands as I strode through to my office, pausing as something caught my eye under one of the desks. I frowned and cocked my head to the side. Had someone left a pile of coats on the floor? As I rounded the desk I realised that this was no pile of coats. It was a sleeping bag containing a person, and that person was Mia. My eyebrows went up into my hairline and I sucked in a shocked breath.

"Mia?" I called and she stirred. Her eyelids flickered but then closed again. I crouched down in front of her and my chest seized. She looked so small lying there curled into a tiny ball. The air in the office was still frigid. I cursed myself for being too tight to keep the heating on overnight. But how was I to know that women were going to take to sleeping under desks? She'd said she had financial problems – she hadn't said she was homeless. "Mia?" I reached out and gave her shoulder a light shake. She made a small sound and her eyelids flickered again, but still she didn't wake up.

It was then I noticed that, despite the cold, her face was covered in a sheen of sweat and she looked deathly pale. I laid my hand on her forehead and swore when I felt the burning skin under my fingers. Her breathing was laboured, and as I withdrew my hand she started coughing. Goddamn it, I'd heard her coughing over the last couple of weeks. But she'd always reassured me she was *fine*. So I'd ignored it, just like she'd been ignoring me. I'd been trying to forget about her somewhat to be honest. I'd thought my preoccupation with her was unhealthy, so I'd squashed down my concern and done what I did best – bury myself in work. It was how I coped with losing Rebecca and Teddy's recent rejection after all. Burying things and working like a maniac was what I did best.

Mia's coughing was a terrible hacking sound that wracked her entire body, but still didn't seem to be enough to wake her up. I was starting to get scared now. I shook her shoulder a little more forcefully and called her name again, but still only managed to elicit that small eyelid flicker. Standing up from my crouch, one of my hands went to the back of my neck as I stared down at her. My mind ran through all of the options. I could ring Heath (but who knew how long he would take to get here and what he could actually do without any equipment?). I could call an ambulance (maybe the most sensible option, but again, how long would we have to wait?). Or I could take her to hospital now myself. Looking at her curled up like that on the floor, I went with my gut instinct.

"Max, what's going on?" Verity called from across the office. I looked up and saw her standing with Yaz, both of them staring at me and the crumpled figure at my feet. "What on earth?"

Verity's eyes widened as they approached Mia. Ignoring Verity and Yaz, I crouched down and slipped my arms underneath Mia. Trying to be as gentle as possible I pulled her out from under the desk, sleeping bag and all. Once she was out it took no effort at all the lift her up against my chest. In fact I was a little frightened by how easy it was to pick her up. She weighed next to nothing. To my relief lifting her did seem to be stimulus enough to pull her back to consciousness.

"Wh – what?" she said in a hoarse whisper. I looked down at her face and those chocolate eyes met mine. "I-I-I ..."

"You're sick," I said, for once managing to gentle my voice. I moved the arm that was around her back so that I could tuck the sleeping bag more firmly around her neck.

"I don't think – "

"You're not going to do any more thinking," I said. "Clearly your thinking about your health and welfare has been less than stellar. I'm going to be doing the thinking now. We'll start by getting you to hospital."

Despite the exhaustion I could see written all over her face, her eyes filled with panic. "N-no, I can't– " she was cut off by another coughing fit. That horrible hacking sound filled the office, her whole body tensing and bending with the force of it as she lay in my arms. After she was done she looked up at me again. Her mouth was set in a grim line and the panic in her eyes was replaced with pain. Her breathing was back to that unnatural rattle.

"Okay," she whispered as her eyelids fluttered closed again.

If anything she looked paler than before. I was starting to get really scared now and her acquiescence worried me even more.

"I'm taking her to A&E," I told Verity and Yaz. They were both staring at me with openly shocked expressions now.

"Don't you think we should call an ambulance?" Verity said. I ignored her, tucked Mia's small body closer into my chest, and strode out of the office.

~

MIA

The first thing I thought as I blinked open my eyes was that the lights were really bright. Painfully bright. And something was covering my mouth. Reaching up I felt a plastic mask over my face, and quickly pulled it down to below my chin. My left hand also felt restricted, and when I looked down I saw bandaging around it, securing some tubing. My eyes followed the tubing up to a drip-stand next to the bed I was lying on, and that's when I saw them: two huge feet, clad in boots that had seen better days. My gaze drifted up from the feet to large legs spread wide, a broad chest, stubbled jaw and finally that face in all its chiselled perfection. Max's eyes were closed, his hands resting over his flat stomach and his head at an awkward angle on the chair. In sleep, and without his perpetual scowl, he was so handsome it almost hurt to look at him. I tried to push up to sitting and the coughing started again.

"Put the mask back on," the familiar growly tone caused me to flinch on the bed. Max's green eyes were open and alert now, his scowl firmly back in place. He looked so annoyed that I decided I had better do as he asked, pulling the plastic over my mouth again, despite the claustrophobia it induced.

God, I hated hospitals.

They made me feel trapped. I associated them with pain and hopelessness.

Clawing through my memories, I tried to piece together how I'd come here. I remembered waking up in Max's car with another coughing fit. He'd been driving too fast and had kept glancing back at me as I lay with my head on Yaz's lap, which I thought was dangerous but didn't seem to have the breath to tell him so. After that, things were a little fuzzy, but I did have flashes of Max carrying me into the emergency department and shouting for help. I'd been put on a trolley and there had been what seemed like hundreds of people bustling around me – sticking me with needles, asking me questions, examining me.

I'd had a chest x-ray – that I remembered. Heath was there and had told me I had pneumonia. *Pneumonia?* He'd introduced me to another doctor – a short, efficient woman who told me she was a medical consultant and that I would be admitted into the hospital under her care.

They'd wanted to know my NHS number.

I wasn't proud of it but I faked falling asleep to make them go away. But I must have fallen asleep for real in the end because here I was.

"What's ... er, what ... what are you doing here?" I asked, annoyed by the mask muffling my speech.

"You've gone and got pneumonia," Max told me. His voice sounded accusing, as if it was *my* fault I was ill.

"Well, yes but ...'

"So, when I told you to take time off. When I told you to go to the doctor, you probably should have bloody well listened to me." He sounded really cross now.

I closed my eyes to block out his scowling face. I didn't have the energy for Max right now. Max was a very exhausting person. In that moment, I didn't seem to have the energy to cope with much more than breathing. When I tried to clear my throat, another coughing fit was set off. I sat forward with the violence of it, trying to hack up whatever seemed to be lodged in my chest. Tears streamed down my face and I felt a large hand come to rest on my back.

"Okay, love," he murmured in his low voice. "You'll be right. Everything's going to be fine." He was rubbing circles around my back now and the sensation was oddly calming. When the coughing subsided he helped lower me back onto the pillows and then wiped the tears from my cheeks before I could reach them. His expression had gone from anger to intense concern within the space of seconds.

"I'm sorry," he said, still using that low, soothing voice. "I can be a right bastad when I'm worried. Brings out the worst in me."

There he was again – apologising for just talking sharply to me. Something he'd done out of worry. It just wasn't what I was used to. I didn't know what to say. I glanced up at him with a frown and then looked away quickly.

"I ... er, it's fine. You're fine. There's no need to–" I broke off as the doctor from yesterday came into the cubicle.

"Mia?" she said. "I'm Dr Firth – the consultant in charge of your care.'

"I remember," I said from behind the mask.

"You'll have to stay a little while with us," she told me. "Have you heard of sepsis?'

"Er, I think–"

"Sepsis is the body's response to overwhelming infection. Your pneumonia set up that response. You've been very unwell. Often we can treat chest infections in the community with oral antibiotics, but you're going to need intravenous treatment for at least the next forty-eight hours. I–" She broke off and glanced up at Max. "Are you her partner?" Something was off about the way she said it – there was an edge there, as if she was angry. But that didn't make any sense.

"No I–"

"He's my boss," I put in.

"I'm Max, a friend of Heath's. I brought her in."

"Ah, right. Max, of course. Heath's mentioned you before," Dr Firth said with obvious relief. That angry tone left her voice and some of the tension around her mouth relaxed. "Okay, Mia. I need to speak to you *alone*. Is that okay?"

Max's large hand had enveloped mine since the coughing fit and for some reason I felt ... safe. I knew I shouldn't. I knew I should send him away but I was just so exhausted.

"Can Max stay?" I asked in a small voice and he squeezed my hand. Dr Firth looked surprised.

"Well, yes but ..." Dr Firth paused, glanced at Max again and then sighed. "Mia, it's not normal for someone of your age to come down with pneumonia so severely."

I stiffened. Where was she going with this?

"Unless ... Mia, unless they are malnourished and under-weight. *That* can put them at risk of pneumonias and other infections."

"Ah. I–"

"Mia, do you *know* you're underweight?"

"Well–"

"Heath told me about an incident a few weeks ago. You were hypothermic? He had concerns at the time and he has some ... ongoing concerns."

She'd sat on the edge of the bed now and I could tell where she was going with this by the expression on her face.

Pity.

She *knew*.

Suddenly it didn't seem like such a good idea for Max to be here with me.

"Your chest x-ray didn't just show a pneumonia, but you know that. Don't you, Mia?"

My eyes shot to Max who was frowning in confusion at Dr Firth.

"On second thoughts, I'd really prefer to speak to you alone, Dr Firth," I rushed out before she could go on.

"Of course," she told me. "Max, would you mind?" Max looked between me and the doctor, a muscle ticking in his jaw and concern in his expression.

"Max?" Dr Firth prompted when he didn't move.

"Okay, okay," he muttered. "I'll – I'll go and get a coffee." He squeezed my hand again before letting it go. "I'll be back soon, love."

When the door closed behind him Dr Firth turned back to me and her voice softened.

"So, the old rib fractures you have there aren't a surprise I'm guessing?"

"No," I whispered.

I looked away from her kind face and over at the tap in the corner of the room. It was dripping. Surely taps in hospital rooms shouldn't drip like that?

"Mia, I talked to Heath about your previous admission as well."

I nodded. I should have expected that.

"We're going to need your *real* name. You know that, don't you?"

I nodded again. I was tired of fighting all the time. Fighting to survive, fighting for my freedom, fighting to just *be*. I'd always hated lying, but Nate had slowly, insidiously, made my entire life a lie until it became almost second nature.

"My name is Amelia. Amelia Banks."

Chapter 14

I just hate hospitals

MIA

A wave of dizziness came over me as I stood underneath the steady spray of the shower. It was so strong that I had to hold onto the soap dispenser to stay upright. I nearly pulled the damn thing off the wall.

"You alright in there, pet?" Carol called from the other side of the shower door, and I closed my eyes as I slid down the tiles to sit on the floor of the shower. Slowly the tunnel vision resolved and the nausea receded enough for me to speak.

"I'm fine," I called, but my voice was too weak to be heard over the shower, and before I knew it Carol had let herself into the small bathroom.

"Oh, sweetheart," she muttered as she pulled back the curtain to see me in a pathetic heap on the shower floor. "You should have called me." She shut off the water and, with the efficiency of a nurse with decades of experience under her belt, wrapped me up in two hospital towels and helped me to my feet. Before I had any time to be embarrassed, she'd dried me off, changed me into my clothes and helped me back into bed.

"Thank you," I said, and she smiled at me as if it was nothing. I'm sure her days were filled of these small acts of heroism, and I'm sure she never realised how important they were.

"Your young man was here whilst you were in the shower," she told me as she bustled off to hang the towels up in my ensuite.

"He's not my young man, Carol," I said for what felt like the eleventy-billionth time. "He's my boss."

"Of course he is, dear," Carol said, giving me an indulgent smile as if I was a child denying my first crush.

Carol was the nurse I'd spilled all my secrets to on my third day of admission. The one who had given me the number of the local domestic violence team. After not telling anyone anything for so long I ended up telling this woman *everything*, and not just about Nate, but all about Max and how he'd been such a grumpy bastard to work for, but then so unexpectedly kind. About how confusing I found it that he was visiting me in the hospital. Carol had let me talk. After I finished, when I thought she might phone the police, she'd hugged me instead and told me everything was going to be alright. That I didn't have to be homeless. That there was help for people in my situation. All it took was a little trust. I had thought that my quota of trust was used up, but the prospect of more nights on the street in my current weakened state changed my mind.

I wished I'd taken Heath's advice and contacted the domestic violence team sooner. I was just so scared they would make me go to the police. But all they wanted to do was help me and offer me advice. Everything was about my choice. The worker that came to see me at the hospital told me that the local women's refuge didn't have any rooms left, but there was a small bed and breakfast nearby which I could stay at whilst I waited for one to come available. So, today I'd decided that that was where I was heading. I couldn't stay in hospital any longer. Apart from my aversion to them (the smell and the clinical atmosphere brought back too many painful memories) I was not going to let Max pay for another night here. Somehow he'd had me moved into a private room after my stay in the high dependency unit, muttering something about *employee health care*. I knew that we did not have private health care included in our contracts. Max was paying for it out of his own pocket.

"Mia, why is your bag half-packed?" Carol asked. "I didn't know you were being discharged today."

I shrugged.

"I'm not sure that's the best idea, pet," she said her voice full of concern. "You're still weak as a kitten."

"It's fine. I'm *fine*," I told her, keeping half an eye on the door in case Max came back.

"Look, I think you should wait until the ward round. Really it's not–"

"I have to get out of here," I said in a fierce whisper. "Please, Carol. I *can't* stay here any longer."

A buzzer went off in the corridor and she frowned.

"Damn," she snapped as she stood up from the bed. "Listen, wait a minute ok? I'll be back in a sec and we can talk about it. Just ... hold on. Don't move." She gave me a wary glance and pointed at me before she left. I leaned back against the pillows and closed my eyes in defeat. Carol was right. I needed help. Maybe ...

Making a split second decision before I could think any better of it, I picked up my mobile from the desk and dialled the number I knew by heart, but hadn't dared to put into my new phone in case the temptation to ring it became too much.

"Hello? Who's this?" I closed my eyes as my sister's voice washed over me. She sounded like home.

"Marnie," I whispered into the phone.

"Mimi? Mimi, is that you? Where are you?" her voice was rising now. She sounded frantic.

"Marnie, I'm in trouble." I darted a look towards the door of the room I was in. There was only one other patient in the unit, but Dorothy had such severe dementia that the only real communication she ever embarked on with me was popping her head in and asking for her mother or a cup of tea (the tea was doable … her mother, seeing as Dorothy herself had just celebrated her own ninetieth birthday, not so much). So, even though there was little chance of being overheard, I knew I didn't have much time. "I … I think I need your help."

"Anything, Mimi," Marnie said. "You know that. Please, just tell me where you are." She was crying now and I closed my eyes as the familiar guilt washed over me. Marnie was only two years older than me but, even with a small age gap, she'd always been very protective. Always wanting to fight my battles for me. Nobody messed with Marnie's little sister … until Nate that is.

"Please don't cry, Marnie." My voice was tortured. Why didn't I listen to my family six years ago? Why didn't I let Marnie be the big sister she'd always wanted to be?

"I knew something was off when that evil fucker came sniffing around," she spat. Anger had replaced the tears now. I froze on the bed and my eyes shot open wide.

"Nate came to see you?"

"Asking if you'd been in contact. Said you had a 'little tiff' and that you'd 'flounced off'."

Images flashed through my mind – *me crawling away from him with only one arm working, hearing his footsteps and then feeling the tearing pain in my scalp as he dragged me back across the floor by my hair into the kitchen; my head flying to the side as he backhanded me, then my eyes fixing on the knife lying next to the chopping board …*

Then it was me running from the house, clutching my back-pack and hurtling straight into Nate's head of security (I'd always got on with Brian, we'd shared the odd cup of tea at the house. He reminded me of my dad); registering the shock in his faded blue eyes as he took in my beaten face and blood-splattered shirt; my stomach turning over as he ushered me outside to his car and asked me whether the blood on my hands was mine.

"No," I'd replied, my voice hoarse from shouting. "Not mine."

He'd smiled then. A wide, deeply satisfied, slightly scary smile.

"Good," he'd said in a fierce tone, his eyes locking with mine, full of fire. "Good, Amelia."

He knew whose blood it was and he was glad. It wasn't the first time he'd seen me sporting an injury. He bundled me into his car and took off. Each bump in the road had jarred my shoulder. I'd tried to hold in my small winces of pain but he noticed and his lips had tightened.

"I hope he burns in hell," *he'd muttered under his breath and my blood had run cold. What if Nate was dead? There'd been so much blood. What if I'd killed him? That was when I made Brian call the ambulance to the house we'd left behind. I couldn't have Nate's life on my conscience.*

We'd deliberately driven for over two hours to the coast, to a hospital far from my home. Before he took me in he grabbed both my hands, ignoring the copious amounts of blood now dried onto my skin, and he looked into my eyes, that fierce look back in his own.

"You go in there, young lady," he said. "You get fixed up and then you run. Don't ever look back. Run away and keep running. Do you understand me?" *He'd given me all the money he had in his wallet and ushered me through to the triage desk.*

So, *little tiff* and *flounced off* weren't altogether accurate terms. And Nate wasn't burning in hell – but he *was* looking for me.

"Mimi? You there, hun? Talk to me, *please.*"

That was when I realised that as much as I wanted to, I couldn't go to my sister now.

I swallowed. "I'm fine. I just wanted to let you know I'm ok."

"Mimi! Tell me where you are. We can sort everything out from there. Just tell me wh-"

"I've got to go," I whispered as Max's large frame filled the entrance to the bay. "I promise I'll call you soon.'

"Mimi, don–" I took the phone away from my ear. My hand shook as I pressed the screen to end the call. I could still hear my sister shouting on the line before I cut her off. Max came to a stop by the side of my bed, shoved his hands in his pockets and frowned down at me.

"Hey," he said, his voice gruff.

"Hey," I replied, managing a small closed-lipped smile as I started to grab the meagre amount of stuff I had left in my side cabinet. I'd already filched one of the hospital towels – it was shoved down into the depths of my backpack. When I had some more cash I'd donate something to the hospital to replace it. Still – I was a thief and it wasn't the first time. There was probably a special place in hell for people who stole from the NHS, but for now I couldn't bring myself to care.

Max looked down at the half packed bag on the bed and then up at my face.

"You going somewhere?" he asked.

"I'm being discharged today," I lied as I zipped my backpack shut.

I had been on the high dependency unit having intravenous antibiotics for the first two days until my chest improved. I'd

been out on the general ward for three days now. I was definitely on the mend. Sort of.

"Hmm," he muttered. "Just a minute – I've, um ... got to
make a call. Business stuff." He strode out of the room, pulling
his phone out of his back pocket. I continued to gather together
my meagre possessions, which took longer than it should with
my breathing still so laboured. When I'd finally finished I sat on
the edge of the bed, trying to catch my breath. Max chose that
moment to appear at the doorway again and it had the unfortu-
nate effect of triggering another of my coughing fits. They were
less frequent now, but I was aware I still sounded like a
seventy-year-old man with emphysema. As my body convulsed
with the force of the coughs and tears ran down my cheeks, I
felt Max's huge hand rest across the back of my chest, splaying
to almost its entire width. The feel of his warmth grounded me,
just as it had all the other times he'd done it over the last five
days. I felt calm despite the coughing and after a few more
hacking sounds the fit subsided.

"You alright, lass?" His voice was low and gentle and his
scowl had faded into that slightly panicky, concerned look that
he had been prone to recently. Why he came to visit I had no
idea. In the HDU I hadn't really been up to talking so he'd just
stood next to the bed with his hands shoved in his pockets,
before demanding a progress report from the staff. I think most
people were under the impression he was my boyfriend. An
assumption that was so far from reality that I had trouble
getting my head around it.

At the time, I didn't see why Max was so interested and
doubted he'd stick around for that long anyway, so it was a
surprise when he became a daily visitor. So far I'd been too out
of it and sick to really question why he was doing all of this.
Maybe he got this involved with any staff member that was

sick? Maybe there was some sort of weird HR policy that had him visiting the hospital?

Yesterday he'd brought Yaz and Verity with him. Yaz gave me an amber necklace meant to draw out all my negative energy from my chest. Verity, being on the slightly more practical end of the spectrum, brought me fruit and books. Max hadn't brought me anything, other than the private room of course. I hadn't had the energy to argue over that either.

"I'm fine," I muttered, and his hand dropped away. For some reason the loss of his warmth made my stomach tighten. I straightened and wiped the tears from under my eyes before tucking my hair behind my ears. It had grown to almost shoulder length now. I was desperate to cut it again, but didn't trust myself not to do another hatchet job in the process. My funds definitely didn't extend to going to the hairdresser. Although, that would change soon. The domestic violence team told me I could open a bank account at HSBC without a permanent address. Apparently it was one of the only places women staying at the refuge could open an account, as you weren't allowed to give out the refuge address. Once I did that, I could finally give Mary a place to deposit my salary. I was about to pick up my bag when Max stepped forward, his large hand closed over one of the straps and he swung it up onto his shoulder.

"Where are you going?" he asked again.

I looked from my bag to his face and it was my turn to frown.

"I've been discharged. My chest is getting better now with just the tablet antibiotics. I don't need to be here anymore."

"Right."

"Right." I reached for my bag on his shoulder only to have him take a step back.

"Uh, so I kind of need my bag."

"Do you have somewhere you can stay?" he asked, his too-intelligent eyes assessing me now. And that was when I realised.

He knew.

I closed my eyes and pressed my lips together, hoping that if I wished hard enough Max would disappear and I would not have to have the inevitably humiliating exchange we were about to have. Of course, with my current luck, when I opened them he was still there, but now his arms were crossed and he was sporting a stubborn expression.

I cleared my throat and shoved my meagre toiletry supply back into its small bag, as I felt my shoulders tense up and rise towards my ears in a defensive gesture.

"Of course I do," I told him, risking a glance up at his face. His expression was calculating now.

"Okay," he said slowly. "I'll drive you."

"N-no!" His eyebrows flew up and I realised I was shouting. I clenched my fists at my sides and made a concerted effort to calm my voice. "I mean, thanks, but I don't need a lift anywhere. So ..."

He shrugged. "It's Sunday. I'm not doing owt. No sense in you getting a taxi."

"Oh, all packed? That was quick."

Shit. Carol again.

"I really think you'd be better staying so that-"

"I'm leaving, Carol."

Carol sighed and crossed her arms over her chest. "I can't stop you leaving but you do know you've got to take things easy for the next few weeks, right?" Carol asked, shooting Max a quick smile.

Carol liked Max. "Just like my Barry," she'd said yesterday. "Gruff and hard on the outside, but inside – marshmallow and kitten fur." That had made me think of Nate. His exterior was so smooth and charming, but there was no warning of the ice beneath. "Nice arse too," she'd added, and I'd rolled my eyes.

"Yes Carol," I said through gritted teeth. "I'll be fine."

"Regular meals wouldn't go amiss either," she put in, narrowing her eyes at me. Turns out pneumonia was a killer on the appetite. Combine that with the previous weight lost and you had my current near-skeletal form. Not the best look. And to top it all off some of my *hair* had fallen out in the shower yesterday. I was turning into some sort of mangy, underfed dog. I was about to reply when the door banged open again.

"Hello Mia, Max."

Bloody double shit. I couldn't catch a break around here.

"Hi, Dr Firth," I muttered, hoisting my bag onto my shoulder in preparation for my getaway.

"Call me Becky," she said as she pulled my chart off the nightstand and studied it.

"No fever in two days, CRP and white cell counts coming down. Good stuff. I just—"

"Great," I cut in, taking a small step towards the door. "I mean, thanks. You really didn't have to come in on a Sunday. I'm sorry I—"

"I know I didn't need to come in. There's an on call team. But Max gave me a ring and I was on my way to Homebase anyway."

I paused before taking another step.

"Homebase?"

"It's on the industrial estate just past the hospital. I need some compost and some slug pellets."

"You called her?" I asked Max and he shoved his hands back into his pockets.

"You hadn't been given the all clear to leave. I didn't think we should take any chances. Heath and Becky are mates so he gave me her number."

What was happening? Max didn't think 'we' should take any chances? Since when were *my* problems *his* problems? I opened my mouth to speak but was cut off by Dr Compost and Slug Pellets.

"I'd be happy for you to leave, Mia," she said softly. "If you have someone at home to keep an eye on you. Otherwise I really, *really* think you'd be better staying in for another twenty-four hours at least. Carol told me about the shower incident."

Traitor. The unrepentant Carol gave me a wide smile.

I took in Dr Firth's sincere, caring expression and then let my bag slip off my shoulder and onto the bed. She was right. I was too weak to look after myself properly. I *did* need another day at least of meals I didn't have to forage for myself and proper rest. The shower incident was proof of that.

"Okay, okay," I muttered, suddenly feeling really silly for causing all this fuss on a Sunday. "I'll stay another night.'

MAX

I watched Mia sitting on the bed next to her pathetic ruck-sack, a look of complete dejection taking over her expression.

"I-I'm sorry to cause all this hassle. I didn't mean for ..." she trailed off, looked down at her shoes and tucked her hair behind her ears. "I just hate hospitals," she whispered. I felt something shift in my chest, almost like it was cracking open.

"She's coming home with me," I said, my gruff voice making it sound more like a threat than an offer of help. Mia's head snapped up. Carol beamed at me.

"Ah, well that changes things."

"Okay," Becky Firth said slowly, her eyes flicking between Mia and me. "You *will* feed her won't you, Max?"

131

I rolled my eyes. "I can cook, and I have a spare room." In fact I had three spare rooms but Becky didn't need to know that. I shrugged. "It won't be a problem."

Mia was still sitting on the bed, but her wide eyes were fixed on me now.

"You don't have to do that," she muttered. "I can stay here ... or I can speak to my-" She broke off and bit her lip.

"Your ...?"

She shook her head. "No, sorry I wasn't thinking straight. I ... look I'll just stay and then ..." she broke off again and her face flushed bright red. "Oh bollocks," she muttered. "You're paying for the bloody room. I almost forgot."

"The *business* is paying," I lied. It was totally me, but I didn't want to look weird. "And it's fine. It's ... uh ... tax deductable."

"Wh–"

"But you don't like it here and you don't have to stay here." My voice was rising. Watching Mia hooked up to all those drips and machines just days ago and now seeing her so dejected at the prospect of staying in this place was getting to me. "I have a huge house. Loads of spare bloody rooms and a fridge full of food. Of course I can–"

"What's your security system like?" Mia asked, her expression carefully blank.

"My security? Well ... I have electric gates with a tannoy, an alarm system which I activate with a code. And an Alsatian."

Her eyes were wide again for a moment, but then, to my shock, she smiled.

Chapter 15

She can stay

MIA

Screw the refuge and screw the bed and breakfast.

I was going to stay in a house with a goddamn gate, an alarm system *and* a motherfucking Alsatian. Then maybe the sick fear I'd been carrying since Nate's visit to the office would recede. I couldn't go to my sister. Nate would find me there easily. I knew I should tell Max the whole situation, but I just needed a *break*. Once I was stronger, just a *little* stronger, then I would tell him. If he kicked me out then I would still have a chance at the refuge. With my strength back and my wits about me I'd be much more likely to be able to evade Nate. To be honest, I knew that in reality I'd have to move on again soon, especially now that Max was involved in one of Nate's projects. But I also knew how hard it was to set up a life in a new area with next to no resources. It was not an option I was over keen on at the moment.

We stopped outside some stainless-steel gates, which opened automatically. I leaned forward as we drove into the drive and blinked up at the beautiful structure in front of us. It was set back from the road and the top floor had glass from floor to ceiling. The building was clad in some sort of weathered wood and as I got out of the car I realised that the multilevel roof was covered in moss, grass and wild flowers.

"Wow," I breathed the same time that Max muttered, "Bugger."

He was staring at another small electric car in the driveway.

The size of Max's car had been a bit of shock to me. I was surprised that he managed to fold his huge frame into it at all. Max turned back to me and his large hand went to rub the back of his neck.

"Listen, Teddy's here. I thought he was staying with a friend tonight. I haven't told him you're coming so ..." He sighed. "He can be a bit–"

"Who's Teddy?" I asked, peering around Max to look up at the front door. Another sigh.

"Teddy is my ... well he's *kind of* my stepson."

That statement hit me like a solid blow to the chest.

Max had a *kind of* stepson.

He probably had a wife in there too.

I took a step back but noticed the gates behind me were closing again.

"Your stepson?" I asked, my voice coming out in a squeak. Disappointment washed over me like a familiar blanket. Which was ridiculous.

"Max?" A deep voice called out from the house. I could see the doorway was now open and almost entirely filled by a massive, male figure with a large, black dog at his side. The dog emitted a low growl and I fought the instinct to take another step back.

"Hey, Ted," Max said, turning from me and jogging up the steps to the hulking *man* in the doorway. "Listen something came up and I ... I mean we've got a houseguest for a bit." I'd never heard Max sound so hesitant. "Uh ... Mia, come up here and meet Teddy." The dog growled again as I took a tentative step forward. "Don't mind Roger. He's fine once he gets used to you. Keep sudden movements to a minimum though." As I got closer I could see that part of Roger's ear was missing. "He's a rescue," Max explained. "The people at the centre think he was beaten by his old owners, so he's a bit skittish."

"It's Ted, not Teddy," the large boy-man put in with a sullen voice as he crossed his arms over his massive chest and continued to block the doorway.

Okay, so not a child then.

"Hi," I said from behind Max. "I'm Mia."

"You've brought a woman back to stay here?" Teddy's voice rose and I took a small step back. "Nice one, *Max*."

"Would you try not to be so bloody rude and stop with this 'Max' bollocks. You used to–"

"Whatever," huffed Teddy, shouldering past his stepfather then giving me a wide berth as he made his way to his tiny car. Roger started to follow him but Teddy waved him back. The great dog settled at Max's feet to have his ears stroked. "Don't ask *me*. It's not like I've got the biggest exams *of my life* coming up or anything. As per bloody usual nobody really gives a shit about *me*." Ted folded himself into the car in another feat of large-men-folk-human-contortion. Before the door slammed shut I heard him mutter, "*Arsehole*". He shot Max another foul look before he started the engine.

When the gates were closing behind him Max sighed again.

"I'm not sure that–" I began.

"Don't mind Teddy," Max cut in. "He's being a little bastad to *everyone* at the moment. Believe me."

Little? The boy was well over six foot. I hitched my bag up higher onto my shoulder and tore my eyes away from the closing gates.

"He does seem a bit cross," I said as I followed Max and Roger into the house. Max let out a bark of laughter as he led me through to the kitchen.

"Ha! Yes, a bit cross doesn't quite cover it I'm afraid. For the last six months he's been like an aggressive Eeyore on steroids. Sorry, I should have warned you about him. But to be honest he's either up in his room, or eating everything in my fridge in under five seconds, so you won't have to see much of him anyway." He led me up the stairs, which appeared to be floating in midair through the centre of the house. The living space was double-height, with the first floor landing looking down on the kitchen-living area. It was so bright in there. Light poured in from the glass walls and even from light wells in the roof above, bouncing off the clean, white, almost clinical interior.

"I didn't know you were married," I said as I followed him up onto the first floor landing. "Is your wife–?"

"Rebecca and I never married, but we were together for eight years. She left 'bout a year ago now." He shrugged. "Had enough of me, I guess. Headed up t'London. Always was a bit boring for her down here to be honest." Before I could ask why Teddy wasn't in London with his mother, Max stopped in the corridor and pushed open a door into what most would consider a lovely room.

"This okay?"

I ignored the king-sized bed with fluffy duvet covered with white cotton sheets and I focused on the glass. Floor to ceiling windows. I would *not* be able to sleep in here.

But I managed to force a small smile onto my face.

"Wow," I said, hoping I'd mustered as much enthusiasm as the room deserved. "This is great."

Max was frowning at me again.

"The remote for the telly is on the side table. There's an en suite with towels in. Yaz stocked it up with some stuff – I hope you like essential oils."

His sister stocked the guest room?

"Er ... is there anyone else–?"

"It's just me and Teddy."

"Right."

He opened his mouth to say something, shut it again and then spun on his heel to leave, muttering something about sorting supper.

MIA

"Hey, lady?"

I heard a muffled voice just beyond the wardrobe door and flinched. Somebody was moving around the bedroom. Some-body with very heavy footfalls. I gripped my book tightly in my lap, dropped the phone I had been using as a light to read the pages and froze. Before I could react the door was wrenched open and light poured in, blinding me for a moment.

"You're reading," a deep voice told me, and I blinked against the light to focus on the large figure's face. Fear was clogging my ability to speak. "In a wardrobe." I blinked again and managed to adjust my vision enough to see it was Teddy. My hands relaxed their death grip on the book and I let out a slow relieved breath.

"Hi," I said once the silence had become uncomfortable. Teddy was frowning down at me, but the sullen expression from before had been replaced by open confusion. I guess anybody would find a woman choosing to sit in a dark wardrobe and read with artificial light from her phone when she had an entire massive bedroom at her disposal weird.

"Why are you in a wardrobe?" he asked.

Susie Tate

"I like the quiet?"

Teddy opened the door wider. "Yeah, cause it's absolute bedlam out here," he said. "Ram jam." He tilted his head to the side and lapsed into a deliberate silence, during which I heard one faint bout of birdsong and one car passing in the far distance. I pushed up from the small nest of pillows I'd made on the ground and another head rush hit me as I made it to my feet. I had to hold onto the doorframe for support.

"Shit," Teddy muttered, his hand moving to catch me should I fall and then withdrawing when he saw I was okay. He was looking less and less hostile and more unsure of himself now. "Whoa, you ... er, are you alright?"

I gave him a small smile. Maybe he acted like 'Eeyore on steroids' most of the time, but I was willing to bet there was a sweet boy buried under the layers of teenage arseholdom.

"I'm fine. Thanks though."

He moved away from the door to let me pass, scuffing his feet and shoving his hands into his pockets. "Dad ..." He shook his head in a jerky motion as if to clear it. "I mean, *Max* says you've been sick."

"Yes, I have but I'm getting better now."

Teddy glanced at my pillow nest in the wardrobe then back at me. He didn't look convinced.

"Well, he sent me up to tell you supper's ready. I *did* knock on the door, but you didn't answer so ..."

That explained the coming into my room.

"I wouldn't have let myself in, but all the doors are so insulated they keep any noise out. And Max said you needed to eat." He looked down at me then quickly looked away. "No offence lady, but I think he's right."

"It's Mia."

"What?"

"My name is Mia. And thank you for coming to get me,

138

Teddy. I appreciate it." He flicked another glance at my pillow nest, then back at me before blanking his expression and turning to leave. I laid my copy of *Jane Eyre* carefully down into my backpack before following after him.

As I made my way down the floating stairs I heard muffled angry voices coming from the kitchen.

"Just please try not to be such a pain in the arse for once, Ted," Max grumbled as a couple of pots were slammed down on the granite.

"What am I supposed to say? That I'm happy you moved a random weirdo into the house without even asking me?"

"She's had a rough time, mate," Max said in a low voice. "She needs help for a bit. I know you're still upset that your mum couldn't come to–"

"Don't talk about Mum!"

Real pain filtered into Teddy's previously indifferent tone now.

"Ted," Max's normally low voice was even more gravelly now. "I'm sorry. *I* thought you were proper champion in the regionals. She missed out. It's her loss, lad." I peeked around the banister and saw Max put his hand on the back of Teddy's neck. For a moment Teddy leaned into Max, but then the moment was gone and Teddy jerked away.

"Don't bring *Mum* into this. She might be an uncaring bitch, but at least she would want me to concentrate on my exams."

I decided that I should probably give them a bit more time and took a step back up the stairs. But when I turned I came face-to-face with Roger's black eyes. His ears went back and he bared his teeth, a low growl rumbling from deep in his chest. I jerked back and collided with an upright lamp, which wobbled for a second before crashing to the ground before I could catch it. Roger gave me a disgusted look before he took off down the stairs.

"Crap," I muttered, trying to right the stupid thing – it was bloody heavy. Luckily it was only the massive light bulb that had shattered. Bit of a strange lamp – no lampshade or anything, just a huge copper pipe angled in the middle with the massive, now shattered, bulb at the end. I heard noise on the stairs and looked down to see three sets of eyes staring up at me. "Er ... sorry," I called. "The *random weirdo* might have knocked over a lamp. But I think it's just the bulb that's broken so ..."

"Ever heard of an exposed filament LED bulb?" Teddy asked.

"Shut *up*, Ted," Max snapped.

"Er ... a what?'

"That bulb cost more than my allowance for a year."

"Oh my God." My hand went up to my mouth and I felt my face drain of colour. "I'm so sorry."

I saw a twinge of regret in Teddy's expression before he dropped his gaze to his shoes. "Don't get too worked up. Max is a tight git so my allowance isn't that much."

"Teddy, for Christ's sake," Max snapped. "Listen Mia, don't worry about the bleeding light.'

"I'll just tidy it up so that ..." I flinched as a sliver of glass pierced my finger. Blood was now dripping onto the otherwise immaculate tiles. Max took one look at the blood then bounded up the stairs taking them two at a time. When he got to me he made a grab for my hands and on instinct I snatched them away from him. He took a step back and held both his hands up in front of him.

"Mia?" he called softly. "It's okay. I was just going to put some pressure on it so it stops bleeding."

"Yes, yes o-of course," I stammered. He approached me again, this time keeping his movements slow and deliberate.

Once he'd pressed a tissue into my hand, he withdrew again to let me put the pressure on the wound.

"Teddy can you get a dustpan and brush to sweep up please?" Max asked. I heard Teddy sigh and shuffle off. Max hovered as we went down the stairs like I was some sort of invalid.

"Sorry about the light bulb," I said once we were in the kitchen. "I can pay you back." I thought about the tenner I had stashed in my backpack. It wasn't like I was going to be able to save up a security deposit for a flat anytime soon. I still had to open another bank account for goodness sake.

"It's fine," Max said, pulling out a chair at the kitchen island for me, which I hopped up onto whilst still pressing the tissue to my finger. "Ignore Teddy."

"Standard," I heard Teddy mutter as he moved through the kitchen with the dustpan and brush. Max rolled his eyes. I made a mental note to look up how much exposed filament LEDs cost and decided to drop it for now. Max was pulling out large bowls from the cupboard. Two pots were bubbling on the stove.

"So ..." I paused as I looked up at the exposed beams and bare light fittings on the ceiling. "You're having some work done?"

"What?"

"Er ... you're having some building work done. Looks like it's all nearly there."

Max paused in his draining of a rather alarming amount of pasta and stared at me. "I'm not having anything done."

"Oh ... but what about the, er ... the ceiling and stuff?" Above me a large cable wound its way up a rough beam and then hung down with a bare light bulb at the end.

A loud burst of laughter sounded from behind me and I jumped a little in my seat.

141

"Ha! I love it!" Teddy said, still laughing. "*Looks like it's nearly there.* Classic."

"What?" I frowned at him. Up until now I hadn't been sure Teddy could smile, let alone laugh like that.

"That light fitting you're pointing at cost over a grand," Teddy said. "It's Max's wanky industrial look. He paid through the nose for that shit. This place was featured in magazines. Okay, Max. I've changed my mind. She can stay."

Chapter 16

Daniel-son

MIA

I was beginning to think that the streets would have been a less stressful option.

After staying with Max and Teddy for the last two days, I really wasn't sure I could take much more tension. Teddy was *not* a pleasant human most of the time. And, despite his joy over me insulting Max's décor, he was really not a happy teenager that I had invaded his home. I'd been in the kitchen yesterday when he got back from school, and had offered to make him a cup of tea. He'd looked at me like I'd offered to inject heroin into his eyeballs and said:

"Er ... *no*, seeing as the caffeine would, like, *stunt* my growth."

I'd bit my lip to stop myself from commenting that perhaps his growth could do with a little stunting. He'd then looked me up and down and raised his eyebrows as if to say – *See, short-arse? This is where caffeine gets you*. I'd scuttled off to my room with inhuman speed as soon as my own growth-retardant poison was ready.

Susie Tate

Luckily, I hadn't been conscious an awful lot for the last two days. Pneumonia had definitely taken it out of me. I'd slept ... and slept ... and slept. In between bouts of sleeping, I'd been force-fed by Max. He gave me such a huge bowl of pasta yesterday I only managed about a third, which had earned me a hard stare and a grunt of disapproval. Both mornings he had presented me with a fry up. The only upside to this was that feeding bacon and sausage on the sly to Roger seemed to have secured his undying devotion. At least *one* of the living beings in the house liked me. During all our meals, Teddy bolted his food down whilst scowling at his stepfather and me, then stalked out of the kitchen to either go to school, up to his room, or out with mates – ignoring Max's request of a time to expect him back. Max might be in control at the office, but it was clear that he was way out of his depth on the home front.

I'd offered to cook yesterday, but Max had told me I wasn't strong enough. He had everything delivered and there was a truckload of food in the house (unsurprisingly, seeing as Max and Teddy consumed a massive amount between them) so there was no point in me going to the shops – not that I felt brave enough yet to go out on my own. Yesterday I'd started to clean the downstairs bathroom and nearly screamed the house down when a middle-aged lady interrupted me mid toilet scrub. She'd introduced herself as Mandy, Max's cleaner, and told me Max had asked her to check on me and that I was *not allowed* to do anything around the house. So I went back to bed and slept.

Now it was late afternoon, and Roger's insistent barks had woken me up. He'd been lying next to me on the bed when I went to sleep – something I doubted was allowed, judging by the furtive looks Roger had been giving me when he got up here – but there was no way I was ordering this 80-kilo dog around, and I was tired of sleeping in the wardrobe. Having

Roger on the bed made me feel safe. But now I could hear barking from what sounded like outside.

Panic that I'd left a door open and let him out induced a mini coughing fit as I got out of bed. The barking continued, but with it I heard a thumping sound coming from the garden. Curious, I opened the slats of one of the blinds and peered through. There was Teddy in shorts and a t-shirt punching and kicking a large bag suspended from a hook on one of the trees. He had that teenage, long-limbed gangliness, but already I could see his musculature start to develop. His build was so similar to what I imagined a young Max's would have been, and their mannerisms were so similar that it was sometimes hard to remember that they weren't actually related. Teddy's movements were fluid and fast, the impact he was making on the bag revealing the power behind his fists and feet. Roger was loving it and gave a bark for every contact Teddy made with the bag.

For a moment I let myself imagine driving a fist into Nate's face then kicking him in the balls with that amount of power. I felt a small smile tug at my lips before my mouth set into a grim line of determination. The blind fell back into place as I retrieved a hair band and shoved back my now shoulder-length hair.

～

"C-can you teach me that?"

Teddy spun around at the sound of my voice. Roger, who'd been patiently watching his master in exchange for the occasional head stroke, trotted over to me and then sat on my feet. I scratched behind his ears. Teddy narrowed his eyes at us as if I was petting his dog with nefarious intent. He lowered his hands, which were raised in combat position, and stared at me.

"Teach you what? Taekwondo?"

"I ... er, well. I really just want to be able to kick and punch like that."

His brows drew together. "Lady, aren't you like, sick or something? Why d'you wanna learn how to throw down now?'

"Look, you seem to know what you're doing with this stuff.'

"County champion, so *yeah*."

God, he was so arrogant. Again, just like Max.

"Okay, *county champion*. So you can teach me how to hurt someone, right?'

"Taekwondo is not just training to *hurt people*. It's about developing character, personality, and positive moral and ethical traits. It's about peace."

Whoa. Who knew this teenager had hidden depths or that he could string so many words together at once?

"Okay, Mr Miyagi. I'm *all* about the peace. Believe me. But I *need* to know how to defend myself as well." I couldn't believe I hadn't thought about this before. Of *course* I had to learn self-defence. Nate was alive and well. I couldn't hide forever. If he found me ... "I have to be able to hurt somebody if ... if I need to."

He crossed his arms over his chest and narrowed his eyes. "Who d'you need to hurt?"

Ugh! He was a too-curious son of a bitch, yet another characteristic in common with Max. I closed my eyes for a moment before making a decision.

"Teddy, I don't want to get into the details, but you'd honestly be doing me a massive favour if you just showed me a few things. Only a couple pointers that I can practise on my own. I ... I wouldn't ask if it wasn't important."

"You're small," he said, and I blinked.

"I am aware of that.'

"If someone attacks you, you need to *run away*. Not fight them. You run away and you get help."

"Teddy, I'm not an idiot. I would run." All I seemed to do was run at the moment. "But if I'm cornered ... it's not ... it's not always easy to get away."

"Get away from who?" he asked, some concern now threading through his words.

"Hypothetically, I mean. Get away from somebody *hypothetically*."

"It doesn't sound particularly hypothetical to me," he said in a sceptical tone. "Perhaps Max should–"

"Max has enough sh – I mean stuff going on, Teddy. *You're* the one who's county champion, not him."

A bit of ego stroking definitely helped. Teddy stood up a little straighter. But he was still hesitating.

"I'll pay you."

That did the job. When it came to teenagers, cash was really all it took in my experience. His eyes lit up and he gave me a short nod.

"I think I may die," I said as I fell back onto the grass for what must have been the eleventy billionth time. Turns out that high kicks are not as easy as they look – especially not high kicks with power behind them.

Teddy grinned at me and offered his hand, hauling me up to my feet again.

"I actually felt that one Daniel-son. Less of a slight tickle and more a nudge," he told me, back to bouncing on the balls of his feet again. After some bag training he'd decided I should kick him in the ribs instead to see how much power I was putting behind them. Turns out, not a lot. He'd started calling me Daniel-son half an hour in. "You even have the same hair," he'd joked.

Susie Tate

"Hey, this self-defence thing is a blast. I'm used to Sensei Trenton ordering *me* about. It's fun the other way around. Maybe I should suggest that Jenny and I—" He broke off and snapped his mouth shut. I smiled.

"Jenny, huh?" I said as I tried another kick, this time managing to stay upright for once. Annoyingly he didn't even seem to notice the impact to his ribs at all, he was quite obviously more concerned about my newfound Jenny-knowledge. Seems I might have stumbled upon this kid's Achilles' heel. "Don't stress yourself, Romeo. Your secrets are safe with me."

"S'not a secret," he said, shrugging his shoulders. "She's just a friend. She doesn't want-" He broke off and his face went red.

"Okay, no more Jenny chat," I reassured him. "I didn't mean to embarrass you, Teddy."

"I'm not embar-omph! Hey that wasn't bad!"

I'd managed to get a kick in that he actually acknowledged. I smiled then felt a familiar catch in my throat before breaking into a coughing fit. It caught me off guard and was so violent that I had to double over with the force of it. Teddy, in an obvious panic, had hovered over me and given my back a couple of ineffectual slaps. I wiped my eyes and straightened up.

"Sorry about that," I said, my voice hoarse.

"I don't reckon this was the best idea, Daniel-son," Teddy said, that concern back in his voice.

"I'm fine," I said, trying to catch my breath. "But maybe that's enough to be going on with." I moved to my backpack, which I never let out of my sight. "Here you go," I said as I pulled out a tenner and handed it over to him.

"Thanks," Teddy said, his concern dissipating in the face of ready cash. I watched one of my last lifelines disappear into his back pocket.

"What did you just give him?" Max's voice thundered as he ran out into the garden, ignoring Roger's enthusiastic greeting.

"I–"

"You just handed my son something," Max said, coming to a stop directly in front of me and cutting off my view of Teddy. "I want to know what it was."

"Max, chill!" Teddy said, trying to move forward but Max's large arm blocked his way. "I gave her a Taekwondo lesson and she just paid me. And I'm *not* your son."

Max turned to Teddy and crossed his arms over his chest.

"Empty your pockets," he ordered and I felt heat hit my cheeks. What did he think I'd given Teddy?

"Max!" Teddy snapped. "You're being a major dick. She didn't give me anything dodgy. What is your problem?"

"Empty. Your. Pockets."

Max's back was to me now so I took the opportunity to start sidling away towards the house.

"Stay," Max said. Both Roger and I froze where we were.

Teddy rolled his eyes and then turned the pockets of his shorts inside out. The tenner I'd given him fell to the floor. Max picked it up and then looked around the area. He cleared his throat as he gave the money back to Teddy.

"You know I wouldn't do drugs with my training schedule, Max," Teddy said. "Anyway I thought Mia worked for you. What makes you think she'd be giving me something dodgy?" Teddy humpfed in disgust and stormed back into the house.

"Why would you think something like that?" I whispered. Roger came and sat next to me, leaning against my legs and I stroked his head.

Max groaned, running both his hands through his hair. "I saw you hand him something. He looked shifty as he took it. His behaviour lately ... I just ..."

"But why would you think *I'd* have anything to do with–"

"Mia, you're underweight, you contracted pneumonia, you have financial problems, your behaviour can be erratic. In that moment, when I saw you handing something to Teddy it all seemed to ..." He shrugged. "I'm sorry but I can't take any chances with him. I've made too many mistakes already."

"I have never taken drugs in my life," I told him, shaking with anger. "Teddy did me a favour and I was paying him, that's it."

"Okay, I'm sorry. It's just ... it always feels like you're hiding something, and I -" Max paused and then frowned down at me. "Why do you want to learn Taekwondo all of a sudden?"

I looked away from his piercing stare. My heart was still hammering with the adrenaline spike of my anger and I didn't trust myself not to give anything away.

"Listen, I'll stay away from Teddy from now on so you don't have to worry." I took a step back towards the house but he came after me, his large hand encasing my forearm to halt my retreat.

"Why Taekwondo, Mia?"

"It's none of your business," I yanked my arm out of his grasp and took another two steps away from him.

"Mia, I can help you if you'd–"

I had had *enough*.

"*Nobody* can help me," I said, my voice hoarse with pent up anger. "You think you know what you're talking about but you have no idea what I'm up against."

"That's because you *won't tell me*."

It would be so tempting to unload everything onto Max. But if he knew it all there was no way I'd be staying in his house. No way I would have a job in his company. If he knew everything *I'd* done he would want me as far away from him as possible and I *needed* this small piece of respite before I moved on.

I kept my mouth shut and fled back into the house.

It was only when I was in the safety of the wardrobe that I let myself cry.

Chapter 17

Safe from what?

MIA

The realisation that Max thought I was capable of supplying drugs to his stepson galvanised me into action. My cough was improving and I'd managed a full night's sleep, albeit in the wardrobe (I still wasn't fully happy with the exposure of the windows – the confined space felt safer). So, now that I was stronger I had decided it would be best if I found somewhere else to stay. Teddy was right – the last thing he needed was a strange woman in his home when he was trying to revise for his exams. I'd already phoned the refuge and been told they had a room. They asked if I minded that it was 'a bit basic'. After living on the streets, *basic* was the least of my worries.

I'd written Max a note thanking him for everything and left it on the kitchen counter. The only problem with my plan was that I'd realised I couldn't work the electric gates or set the alarm, so I resigned myself to waiting for Teddy. When he arrived home, I resisted the urge to run out of the gates like a madwoman without explaining anything to him – he thought I was weird enough already. I waited in the hallway, one hand stroking Roger's soft head and ear fur to calm my nerves.

"Hey!" I said with a forced smile when the door opened. Teddy gave me one of his trademark scowls and a chin lift.

"I'm leaving today," I blurted out as he stalked past me in the direction of the kitchen. Every day, Teddy consumed an entire loaf of bread after school, either as toast or in sandwich form. I caught him drinking tea with it too, the 'tea-stunts-your-growth' lying toad. He paused outside the kitchen door and turned back to me.

"Oh? Max never said.'

"I haven't *exactly* told Max," I said. "But I think it's best all round. I get the feeling I may have outstayed my welcome just a touch."

Teddy shifted on his feet looking uncomfortable for a moment.

"You don't have to go," he muttered.

"It's fine, Ted. You've both done me a massive favour, but I'm stronger now so really it's right that I move on."

"Maybe I should call Max–"

"No," I cut him off. Max didn't believe I was even strong enough to make scrambled eggs at the moment. I doubted he'd approve of me moving out just yet – even though I knew it would be a massive relief to him. "All I need to know is how to open the gate. And I didn't want to leave without setting the alarm. I can call a taxi."

"I'll drive you," offered Teddy. He'd dropped down to give Roger a rubdown whilst the dog licked his face as if they'd been separated for months. Roger might tolerate me now to a reason-able non-growly level, but he *loved* Teddy.

"It's fine. Honestly, don't worry. I–"

"Da– I mean, Max – would bloody kill me if I didn't drive you," he said as he straightened up and fixed me with a stubborn expression that reminded me forcefully of his stepfather. "Go and pack. Call me when you're done and I can carry your stuff down."

I looked at Teddy, glanced down at the backpack at my feet, then back up at him again.

"Er ... this is it," I told him, picking up my backpack and slinging it over my shoulder. His eyebrows shot up.

"Whoa, you travel light for bir ... I mean, for a lady."

"Yes." I forced another smile and avoided direct eye contact.

"Okay then." He cleared his throat before skirting round me back to the front door. I sighed, but if Teddy was anything like his stepfather then I was not going to win this battle. May as well let him drive me and be out of his hair as soon as possible. I dropped to my knees to give Roger a full-on hug. He licked my face when I pulled back, which I considered a high compliment. For some reason it caused a lump to lodge in my throat. Bloody hell, was I so starved of affection that even the canine kind could make me blub? Blinking fast to force back the tears I stood up and followed Teddy out of the house and into his electric car.

"Postcode?" he asked, once I'd slid into the passenger seat.

"Ah, hold on," I said as I dug out my mobile and opened my texts.

"New place?"

I glanced up at him from the screen to register his openly curious expression.

"Hmhm," I murmured, biting my lip. Max and Teddy must not have discussed my situation. I wasn't surprised – they didn't seem to be too hot on the old communication front. Once I'd pulled up the text from my key worker, I typed the postcode into Teddy's SatNav.

When we pulled up in front of the refuge, Teddy peered

across me at the non-descript building. Women's refuges aren't signposted. Most of the women staying there don't want to be found.

"Okay," I said, trying to adopt a bright tone and failing miserably. "This is fine here. Thanks for everything, Ted." I flashed him a brief smile and then scrambled out of the car. Once on the pavement I had to pause for a long moment to read the text again so I could actually find the entrance, which was down the side of the building. The only problem was it didn't say *which* side. I walked over to the right, peered around the corner but only saw brick wall and a fire escape, so I doubled back on myself to check out the other side, letting out a small sound of surprise when I found Teddy blocking my path.

"Is there a problem?" he asked. He was frowning down at me with his head cocked to the side. "Don't you live here?"

"Yes, of course I do."

"So why don't you know the way in?"

I sighed. "Look Teddy, it's complicated."

"I'm in the top set for further maths. I can do complicated."

I rolled my eyes. Yet again his ego was matching his pseudo stepfather's perfectly.

"I do live here. At least I will live here once I ... er, register and stuff."

"Register?"

"Teddy, look," I said softly, moving forward and putting my hand on his arm. "I'll be fine. Honestly you don't have to waste your time. I'm safe here, I promise." I pulled my hand back and backed away towards what was hopefully the building entrance.

"Safe?" Teddy asked. I glanced behind me to see he was now following me to the entrance I'd finally spotted. "Why *wouldn't* you be safe?"

Bloody hell. Me and my big mouth.

"Go home, Teddy," I said through gritted teeth as I reached up to ring the buzzer next to the door.

"Yes?" a voice came through the speaker.

"Hi, I'm Mia. Helen sent me."

"Come through," the voice instructed and I heard the automatic locks on the door turning. As I shouldered my way in I turned back to see Teddy frowning at the intercom.

"Bye, Teddy," I said as I started to close the door behind me. His hand shot out to stop me and he stepped into the corridor after me.

"I'll see you in," he said, his tone so firm and unflinching that he didn't sound like the seventeen-year-old boy I knew him to be at all. He sounded like Max.

"Oh, hello," the voice from the intercom said, now coming from the woman in a floaty skirt who'd emerged from what looked like an office on one side of the corridor. "Mia, so lovely to meet you. I'm Nadia, the staff manager. Helen's told me all about your case." Nadia then looked at Teddy and her brow furrowed. "And you are?"

"Mia's been staying with me and my stepdad," Teddy said. If he was surprised by me being described as a *case* he recovered quickly. "I'm helping her move in."

"I told you about Max," I said to Nadia. "My boss who let me stay with him after I was sick. This is his son."

"Ah, right. That's kind of you to help, young man," said Nadia, eyeing my small backpack and then giving Teddy a slightly baffled smile. "How old are you, love? Men over eighteen aren't allowed in, see."

Teddy glanced at me, then back at Nadia. "I'm seventeen ... here." He pulled his wallet out of his back pocket and gave her his driver's licence.

"No problem," she said, handing it back to him. "Right then. Let me show you to your room." The floor of the corridor was covered in old lino that was ever so slightly sticky. Some of the paint was peeling off the walls and there was absolutely no natural light. It felt a little like how I would imagine a prison to feel. "I'm afraid you don't have your own bathroom. It's a bit of a bun fight as there's only two for this corridor."

"That's fine," I said as she pulled out a key and opened one of the doors.

"And the room may be a wee bit on the small side," she said, giving me an apologetic smile as I moved into the tiny space and sat on the bed. I returned her smile and slipped my back-pack off my shoulder.

"I don't exactly have much stuff. This is great."

"There's a communal kitchen – I'm afraid that's a bit of a bun fight too. I'll just pop and get the rest of the paperwork." She gave Teddy another baffled smile as she retreated up the corridor to her office. Teddy was *not* smiling.

"What the fu– I mean, what's going on?" he asked, looking around the tiny room with a disgusted expression on his face. "Jesus," he added as he moved into the room. "Is that damp?" He reached up to the top corner near the low ceiling to feel the peeling wallpaper. "There's black mould up here. Doesn't this room have any ventilation?" He attempted to open the window, which was obviously welded shut. There were even bars on it for good measure. "What *is* this place? I thought I was taking you home?"

I sighed and closed my eyes for a moment. When I opened them he was staring down at me, his arms crossed over his chest.

"This is a women's refuge, Teddy," I said softly.

"A what?"

"A women's refuge. It's for women who ... it's for women who need a little help."

He blinked.

"But there's no sign outside or anything. I never knew anything like that was on this street."

"Teddy." I bit my lip, trying to choose my words carefully. "It's not easy to find women's refuges because the women that stay in them often don't *want* to be found."

His face drained of colour.

"You don't want to be found?"

"No, Teddy, I don't," I whispered.

"You said you'd be *safe* here. Safe from what?"

"Right," Nadia opened the door. She had a clipboard in hand and another bright smile on her face. "This won't take too long to fill in then you're all set. I just-"

"She's not staying," Teddy said.

"What?" asked Nadia, her eyes bouncing from between Teddy and me.

"She can't stay here. She's recovering from pneumonia and there's mould on the ceiling. She'll get sick again. My uncle is an emergency doctor – he's always on about mould not being good for my asthma." Right on queue I started coughing. I'd forgotten how exhausting coughing fits were. By the end of this one there were tears streaming down my face. Teddy's face had regained too much colour now. His cheeks were bright red and he actually looked on the verge of tears himself. "She's not staying here." He grabbed my backpack and stormed out of the room.

Chapter 18

Maybe you should try taking advantage for once!

MIA

"What's up Ted?"

I blinked in confusion at the kettle when I heard Yaz's voice coming from the front door.

"It's complicated," Teddy mumbled. I heard the front door shut and footsteps coming down the corridor. Then Yaz appeared in the kitchen.

"Hey, Mia," she said, rushing forwards to envelop me in a big hug. "How are you, hun? Your energy's all wonky. Do we need to do some emergency meditation? How about a sea swim?"

"You could try not squeezing her to death," Teddy said in a dry tone, and Yaz scowled at him then gave him a sharp punch in his bicep. "And she's had pneumonia Auntie Yaz – the last thing she needs is a sea swim."

"Shut your face, squirt," she snapped, and I almost smiled at her referring to a human almost twice her size as *squirt*. "You and your dad need to get on board with the healing powers of the sea. Anyway, what's going on?"

"I'm sorry, Mia," Teddy said, turning to me and rubbing his arm. "But I don't know anything about women's refuges or … well, *any* of that stuff. Yaz is the only old woman I knew to ask to come."

"Thanks, Teds," Yaz said in a dry voice. "I *am* only twenty-five you know. But nothing like an ego boost from my favourite nephew."

"Your only nephew." He then shook his head and frowned. "And I'm not really your nephew either."

"Semantics, little man. And you can cut that crap out with me. It might work with your dad–"

"He's not my-"

"But it won't work with your *Auntie* Yaz."

Teddy sighed, but Yaz turned back to me.

"So, what's all this about a women's refuge? And why aren't you answering your texts? Getting info from Max is like getting blood out of a stone. I've been worried. And the bossy bastard told me to let you rest."

I bit my lip as I dropped Yaz's hand. "Sorry. I just haven't really got around to engaging with my phone," I lied. The truth was that I was embarrassed. Embarrassed that they knew I'd slept on the floor of the office. Embarrassed that they now knew my limited wardrobe and my backpack weren't just little quirks but necessities. One of the times Yaz had come to see me in the hospital and I'd pretended to be asleep. I'd heard her talking to Max in hushed tones by my bedside about my situation and I'd died a little inside at the pity in her voice.

"So what's got Teddy's knickers in a twist?" she asked her gaze flicking between her pseudo-nephew and me. I sighed.

"Really it's nothing. I–"

"It's *not* nothing," Teddy said, he sounded shaken and upset now. In the background I could hear the front door opening again and I suppressed an eye roll. The last thing we needed was Max arriving home. But Teddy was too caught up in his recount of events to notice. "I thought I was taking her to her *home*, but when I dropped her off it was at this weird building with no house number or anything. She didn't know the way in, and I ... it didn't feel right."

"You did *what*?" Max's large frame filled the doorway to the kitchen. His hands were on his hips as he looked at all of us in turn.

"I thought I was taking her home, Da– I mean, Max," Teddy said in the smallest voice I'd ever heard from him. "But it was–"

"It was a women's refuge and it was *fine*," I said, giving Teddy what I hoped was a reassuring smile. Max opened his mouth but Teddy cut him off before he could speak

"It was *not* fine," Teddy said, his face going a little red and his demeanour not reassured in the slightest. He was starting to look very young indeed now. "The room was like, *tiny* and there was *mould* on the wall. You couldn't even open the window." He looked at me. Guilt flooded his expression. "I didn't mean to make you feel you had to leave. I just ... I'm sorry for being a dick when you arrived. I-I didn't know that–"

"Teddy," I cut him off in a firm tone. "This is your home. You should have a say in who stays here and invades your space."

He huffed. "This house is *massive*. I have all this and you ..." He sniffed and then swallowed before blinking rapidly.

"Hey, hey," Yaz said softly, moving to him and putting her arm around his waist – she was too short for it to go over his shoulder. He opened his arm and she tucked under it into his side. "You always were a sensitive little chap, just like your ... Max."

Teddy snorted. "I'm *not* sensitive," he said, but the slight wobble in his voice gave him away. What surprised me was that Yaz would put Max in the sensitive category as well.

"Both of you are bloody idiots," Max snapped at us. "You," he pointed at me, "are not well enough to stay anywhere on your own, let alone a women's refuge for Christ's sake. If you didn't want to stay here you should have chuffing told me and we could discuss it like rational adults instead of you going behind my back."

"It's not like I didn't want to stay," I said, my long-dormant temper rising at his highhanded approach. "But I was imposing Max. It's not fair on Teddy *or* you. I don't want to take advantage of—"

"Maybe you should try *taking* advantage for once!" he said, his voice rising. "Maybe if you had asked for help just *once* over the last two months you wouldn't have been living on the streets and you wouldn't have almost bloody well *died*."

Silence fell in the kitchen. I glanced at Teddy and watched a tear slide down his cheek. Yaz was staring at Max, open-mouthed in shock.

"And you," Max said, pointing at Teddy, too lost in his anger to realise how shaken Ted was. "You should never have agreed to drive her anywhere. You know she's in no fit state. I thought I taught you better than—"

"He didn't do anything wrong," I said, slamming my hand down on the kitchen counter and surprising myself as much as anyone else. "I was going to call a taxi, Max. He offered to drive me because *that's* the kind of man he is. I don't blame him for not being over keen on having a random woman invade his space. You should have asked him if it was okay that I stay here before you brought me back."

There was a long minute of silence, broken only by the occasional sniff from Teddy.

"He didn't have to ask me," Teddy said in a wobbly voice.

"Max doesn't owe me anything. I'm lucky he even lets me stay here. He could have kicked me out when Mum-"

"Teddy stop," Max was frowning at Teddy, but his expression softened as another tear slid down Teddy's cheek. He moved to Teddy and gave him an awkward pat on the back before cautiously putting an arm around his shoulders, as if he was bracing to be shrugged off at any moment. "This is your home, son. You've lived here since you were nine years old. You mean the world to me, mate. You know that. Don't you?"

Teddy just sniffed in response, giving a small shrug.

"She's right. I should have asked you. I'm sorry."

"S'okay," Teddy choked out as he scrubbed the tears away in fast movements, his face flooding with colour.

"Teddy, please don't upset yourself," I said softly. "I'm sorry I put you in that position. I should have insisted I took a taxi."

"You shouldn't have been going to stay there in the first place," Max told me and I sighed.

"I can't stay here. I-I'll sort something else." I didn't quite have a deposit for a flat sorted yet but I could stay at B&Bs until I did.

"Mia, you're either staying here or with me in *my* flat." Yaz's voice was firmer than I'd ever heard it before. Her tone clipped.

"She's staying *here*," Max bit out. "Your flat is tiny, Yaz."

"Hey!"

"And it's not as secure as this house. Mia stays."

"Yes," Teddy put in. Two sets of eyes were turned on me now, both lit with equal amounts of determination. I sighed and self-preservation kicked in. Max was right – if I wasn't going to stay at the refuge then this was the safest option.

"Thank you," I whispered, leaning towards them to emphasise how grateful I was – how much this meant to me. Teddy's cheeks pinked up as another guilty expression took over his face.

Max for some reason almost looked angry.

"Christ," he said under his breath as he turned and marched over to the other side of the kitchen to put the kettle on.

Chapter 19

I need it shorter

MIA

"Who cut your hair before, hun?" Lila, the hairdresser asked as she pawed through my scalp. "It looks like it was hacked off with a pair of shears. Hatchet job."

"Er ... I–"

"We'll have to sort the colour out first. What possessed you to go this dark? You're a blond, right?"

Yaz squealed from behind me. "Ah! Dye it the same as mine. We'll be hair twins!"

"Yaz, why *are* you here?" Verity asked from the chair next to mine. "This is supposed to be relaxing and you are *not* a relaxing human."

"How very dare you! I'm super chill. Look, I'll show you – just do these breathing exercises with me whilst you're-"

"I've told you before," Verity gritted out, her left eye twitching. "I do not like to be told when to breathe. *My* respiration is *my* business. Kindly bugger off."

"Yeesh, you toffs are so uptight. I'll just leave this rose quartz here." She put a crystal on the small shelf in front of

165

Verity and gave her a wink. "That'll readjust your aura." Verity eyed the pink stone, her eyelid twitching again.

I knew why Yaz was here. She'd caught me earlier staring into the mirror at work, fingering my horrific hair. Now that I hadn't had the chance to dye it for a while and the blonde roots were starting to come through I looked truly scary. She'd sidled up to me and I tried to give her a smile, but it had come out as more of a grimace.

"I used to have such pretty hair," I'd said to her. "You wouldn't believe that now, would you?" Yaz's mouth got tight and she gave me another of her full body hugs.

I'd noticed her in Verity's office later that morning and the next thing I knew Yaz and Verity were dragging me off in my lunch hour to Verity's hairdresser.

Yaz was here because she was kind, and she was worried about me.

"I don't want to go too light," there was no way I wanted to risk returning to the light blonde Nate preferred, "but I can't go on like this I guess." I fingered a clump of black hair. "And I do want it shorter."

"Mia, no," Yaz said, standing between the mirror and me with her hands on her hips. Her own hair falling in long, blonde spiral curls down her back and over her shoulders. "Layer it up but leave some length." She pulled my hair forward over my shoulders to frame my face. "Don't have it all shorn off. It's so thick and gorgeous. You'd be mad to go too short."

"Okay, okay, let's have a think," Lila said, moving back into position behind me and laying her hands on my shoulders. "She might be right you know. We'll do it in stages and you can see."

I shrugged, unwilling to get into a battle of wills with Yaz.

Yaz might seem all peace, love and spiritual energy, but I

was discovering that underneath that relaxed persona there was a will of iron. After refuge-gate she'd been spending a lot more time round at her brother's. Each time she came over she brought another bag full of clothes. My wardrobe had quadrupled. Yaz claimed they were 'cast offs' that she was trying to get rid of, but, seeing as they all seemed to fit my shorter, less well-endowed frame, I doubted that. I tried to protest but she just waved me away saying:

"I've got no chance getting that lot over my t and a, hun."

She was right of course but I doubted *any* of it had *ever* fitted over her chest past the age of thirteen. She'd bought it for me. And I knew Yaz wasn't exactly rolling in it – her flat was tiny and she didn't just work for Max. For someone whom Max and Verity had clearly labelled as flaky, she seemed to be working a curiously large number of jobs. On top of running reception at the office she was also a windsurfing/kitesurfing instructor, as well as a Pilates and yoga teacher. Strangely she very rarely mentioned this. Max was fairly dismissive of it all which I thought was unfair. He called it 'buggering about on the water' and said she was 'obsessed with the bloody sea'.

"If you don't want it I'll bag it up and take it to Oxfam, but it'll be a pain in my arse."

So now I had an extensive Yaz-based wardrobe: surf t-shirts and vests, distressed jeans, and jumpers with overlong sleeves and wide necks. I knew I shouldn't accept her kindness, but I loved everything she gave me – it was all so different to my old wardrobe. But it wasn't just Yaz adding to my clothing collection. Last week Verity had given me a super warm, olive green coat with a fur-lined hood, which she claimed was 'so last season'. Yesterday I'd seen a picture of the Duchess of Sussex wearing the *very same* coat in Canada. The article listed its price as over £300. I highly doubted that anything one of the world's leading fashion icons wore could be considered 'last season', but the damn thing was so warm and I'd been cold for so long that I didn't have the heart to give that back either.

"We'll see," I told Lila.

When Lila pulled off the towel after my hair had been recoloured I stared at my reflection for a long moment. It wasn't nearly as light or as long as it had been before, but it made a huge difference. My complexion didn't look as pasty and unhealthy.

"Right, so I'll take some off and then you can see what you reckon."

I nodded and gave her a small smile. She worked on my hair for twenty minutes and then stepped back.

"There, perfect for your face," she said. My hair hung to my shoulders and she'd chopped layers into the front. Yes it suited me but ... I ran my fingers through it and then twisted it around them, gaining a secure hold.

"It's great, really. But I want it shorter," I said, letting my hand drop down.

Lila frowned at me. "Listen, let me dry and style it. It'll come up once it's dry and I bet you'll change your mind."

"My God, Lila, you're a genius," Yaz said, moving to stand in front of me and then squeezing my cheeks together. "Look at this face," she said, tilted my head from side to side. "You are one sexy little beast."

I smiled at her. "You're not so bad yourself."

"Okay, so let's pay and get out of this joint. Smoothie bar? I'm buying."

"I'm not drinking charcoal again, Yaz," Verity said as she pulled off her gown and patted her newly styled hair. "Most of the stuff they serve there is not for human consumption."

"Says you who eats dead animal flesh and –"

"Lila, I'm sorry," I said, causing Yaz to break off her rant and turn to me. "But can you cut it shorter?" I stared at the mirror as I ran my fingers through my hair again.

"Trust me – this is the length you want. It would–"

"*Shorter*, please." I caught her eye in the mirror. She must have read the determination in my expression because she gave me a brief nod.

"Okay, if you really want to go shorter then I can make it work. Er ... it'll be cute."

Yaz and Verity hovered behind me and tried to convince me otherwise, but I wasn't going to back down. I had more pressing concerns than how attractive my hairstyle was. But as I watched the hair float to the ground I did feel my stomach clench. I was still vain enough to care.

"There, now that's short but still–"

"Shorter." My voice hoarse with stupid emotion. Why was having my hair cut getting to me like this? I blinked and managed to keep tears at bay.

Yaz moved forward, her eyes on mine in the mirror. "Mia, I really think you should–"

"Shorter," I repeated, my voice stronger now.

"Er ... okay," Lila said, moving forward and starting to cut again. "Well ... um, we can still make this cute. It'll be great, in fact." She made a show of cutting, but there was very little length actually taken off. My hand crept into my hair after she'd finished. I could *still* twist the strands around my fingers.

"Shorter," I whispered to a now perplexed Lila.

"Mia, I think that's short enough," Yaz said, her normally sunny smile had dropped and she was looking at me with the beginnings of concern.

I shook my head. "Shorter," I said, making my voice as firm as I could manage.

"Honestly, Yaz is right. You don't want to go any shorter. It would–"

"You don't understand," I cut in, my voice rising with the pent-up emotion that I normally kept brutally in check – squashed down deep where I put all the memories I didn't want to think about. The customers, including Verity next to me, and hair stylists in the small salon fell silent at my rising voice, but I was too worked up to notice. My hair, my once beautiful hair was lying around me and it still hadn't been enough. I took both of my hands and pushed them into the strands, pulling my scalp back on both sides. Then my right hand went to the side of my head. I wrapped my hair around my fist. "I want it short enough so that nobody can do this." I pulled the hair, yanking my head to the side. "I don't want anyone to be able to get a grip on my hair. It's really important."

I didn't hear the gasps around me. All I concentrated on was the feeling of tension at the roots of my hair and the familiar panic it evoked.

"I *need* it shorter." My voice was thick now and to my horror a single tear fell down my cheek. I wiped it away furiously. I didn't have time to cry. I needed to make them *understand*. With the tears gone I let my hands fall to my sides and sat up straighter in my chair.

"Please, just cut it," I whispered. When Lila didn't move to pick up the scissors I looked up and it was then I noticed her horror-struck expression. She was frozen behind me, staring at me in the mirror. I looked over to Yaz and saw there were tears swimming in her eyes and her lips were trembling. The whole salon was deathly silent. The normal babble of chat and background noise of hairdryers wasn't there and all eyes were on me.

"Mia," Yaz said in a choked voice. Before I knew it she had flung herself forward and was hugging me in the chair.

"I ... um," Lila cleared her throat, her own eyes were now filled with tears and I could hear a few other sniffles from the other women in the salon. "Cutting it shorter is not the answer, Mia. It's *not*." Her voice was rough with emotion.

"No," Yaz said fiercely, drawing back from me so that she was in front of me with her hands on my shoulders and her face inches from mine. "The answer is that you tell me who the fuck has pulled you about by the hair so that I can *fuck them up*."

Peace-loving, chilled surfer chick Yaz had officially left the building.

"Yaz, please," I said, coming back to myself and realising what I had revealed. "It's fine now. Honestly, you don't have to fuck anyone up."

That was when I noticed that Verity had stood from her chair and was crouched down in front of me. "There are people that can ..." Verity paused for a moment and swallowed, her eyes wet as well which was really shocking as Verity was very much a stiff-upper-lip-type person, "... help you. We can-"

"I'm fine," I told her, turning in my chair and taking her hand in mine. "Please," I addressed this to all the curious onlookers in the salon, "I'm sorry to worry everyone. I didn't mean ..." my voice broke as more stupid tears filled my eyes and I took in a deep shuddering breath.

"Right, enough of this," Verity told me, lifting me up off the chair, taking my hand and dragging me to the front desk – all cool efficiency and purpose. "You will not have *any* more of that *beautiful* hair chopped off today. Nobody is ever going to exploit that weakness ever again. Not on our watch."

∽

MAX

"This isn't something you can bluster about fixing, Max," Yaz said to me, keeping her voice low so that Mia, who'd retreated upstairs, wouldn't hear her. "You need to give her space. There's things you don't ... look, I can't break her confidence but tread carefully okay? You've upset her enough as it is."

I shifted on my feet and shoved my hands into my pockets. Yaz had a point – I did tend to put my foot in it with alarming frequency where Mia was concerned. But I was itching to do *something* about whatever it was that was going on. Yaz and Mia's eyes had been red-rimmed when they came back from town. When I asked Yaz what happened she told me they'd gone to the hairdressers. How did getting your hair done make you cry? I got my hair cut every month at *Bob the Barber*. Bob was sixty-five, bald and had a large beer gut. It was not an emotional experience.

"I can't exactly give her space when she's living here," I muttered, fishing out some sandwich fillings from the fridge. "She, er ..." I dropped my voice to a whisper and leaned closer to Yaz, "Teddy said she's sleeping in the cupboard in her room unless we let the dog sleep upstairs, which of course is now standard. That's ... that's *not normal*." I stared at my sister as her eyes started to fill with tears and her mouth set in a firm line. A couple of tears fell but she swiped them away, glancing up to check Mia hadn't come back down the stairs yet.

"I don't even *know* anything concrete," Yaz said, her voice a little choked with her tears. She cleared her throat before continuing. "But I know enough. That woman needs to be handled with care. Above all she needs *friends*."

"And a few chuffing good meals."

Mia was still too thin. She didn't have nearly enough weight before the pneumonia and that had only exacerbated the problem.

Yaz gave me a small smile. "Well, you're the expert on that at least. You love cooking. Feed her up – it's a start at least."

"She eats like a bird," I grumbled. "I think Teddy and I make her nervous."

"Well, that's okay then 'cause I've seen you feed up *actual* birds. Remember that pigeon with the broken wing? The one you hid in your room? And that's only one example."

I rolled my eyes. "Mia's not a pigeon or a woodland creature. She's a human woman who's had a shit time."

"My point is, I know how kind you are under that hard shell, how gentle. I know you can help her. But, if you're not up to it then she can stay with Verity or me. We can–"

"She stays with me." The absolute conviction in my tone was a surprise, even to me. But in that moment I realised that I didn't want Mia anywhere else. I wanted her here. I wanted to know she was safe.

"I love my big brother," Yaz said in a wobbly voice before she launched forward, throwing herself into my arms and giving me one of her fierce hugs – the same type of hugs that she'd been giving me since she was a baby and I was ten years old. The ones that convinced ten-year-old me that maybe, just maybe, the screaming, snotty, poo machine Mam had brought home wasn't altogether a pain in the arse. I wrapped my arms around her. "I don't really know what to do if I'm honest, Maxie. I've never dealt with anything like this before."

I sighed and gave her a squeeze. Then I did what I had been doing since I was eleven – I reassured my little sister. "We'll work it out, Midge. It'll be okay."

Chapter 20

It's not nothing to me

MIA

"Hey." I gave Max a small wave as I took a tentative step toward the kitchen island with Roger at my heels. After we arrived back from the salon he'd followed me up to my room and pushed his way in before I could shut the door. I'd spent a good half hour crying into his fur then we went and sat in the wardrobe together for a while. "Is Yaz ... ?"

"She's gone to pick up Teddy from the tournament. He sent me home from it earlier 'cause apparently I'm embarrassing. Little git." Roger rounded the island and sat next to Max who slipped him a piece of beef from the sandwich he was making.

I took one of the kitchen stools opposite him and sat down. Max sliced a massive sandwich in half, shoved it on a plate and then slapped it in front of me. I looked from the sandwich back to Max, who was now assembling another monstrosity for himself. I tentatively lifted one of the massive slices of crusty bread to peer at the hunk of beef, mass of melted cheese and very token leaf of salad balancing on top of it all. A cup of tea was pushed my way as well.

"Thanks," I muttered. How was I going to eat this thing? I looked and watched Max shove his own equally massive sandwich into his mouth, taking a huge bite out of it. It was like watching a lion sink its teeth into a gazelle.

"Eat up, love."

My head jerked up at yet another casual endearment. Max paused chewing to give me a small closed-mouthed smile. Warmth spread out from my chest through to my fingers. Nate had always called me 'darling'. I'd thought it was dead posh when I started seeing him. It wasn't until much later that I realised how cold, empty and possessive that word really was. Towards the end, calling me darling had almost seemed like a threat. By contrast 'love' in Max's warm, Yorkshire lilt was the complete opposite. I blinked rapidly and cleared my throat.

"Your hair ... " Max said out of nowhere as I tried to take a bite out of the sandwich, only managing a small corner of the bread. He shuffled on his feet and rubbed the back of his neck before he spoke again, his voice a little gruff. "It looks right nice, it does."

"Oh." I fingered the short strands at my nape. After all the drama it ended up more of a layered bob than anything. I gave Max a small smile. "Thanks."

With the help of a steak knife I managed to dissect the rest of the sandwich whilst Max emptied the dishwasher, glancing back at me every so often like some kind of food police.

"So, I'll see you later," I said after I'd finished as much of the sandwich as I could and put the rest in the fridge under Max's disapproving glare and muttered comments of "not enough to keep a mouse alive". I started edging towards the door. This had been my pattern since I'd moved in. I didn't want to crowd Max and Teddy so I'd made myself scarce as much as possible.

"Yer can stay," Max blurted out. It sounded more like a command than a suggestion. My feet stalled. "I've got Netflix." He pointed to the large comfy sofa and the widescreen telly it was pointed at. "You don't have to hide in yer room."

"I'm not hiding."

"Right." Max drew out the word as he made his way to the sofa and flopped down on it, his t-shirt pulling tight across his expansive, muscular chest.

"I'm not."

Max flipped open his laptop and started typing. I was still paused at the bottom of the stairs, debating whether or not to scamper up to my room and hide – just like he was accusing me of doing. "If you're not too busy standing there confusing my dog, you could come and help me with this chuffing 3D programme for the museum design – I can't make head nor tail of it." I gave the stairs a fleeting look and then my eyes flicked back to Max who was staring at me with one eyebrow raised. "Or I could just continue to press buttons randomly until something-"

"Stop!" I flew across the room and skirted to a halt next to where he was sitting. "I spent ages getting that programme up and running." Without thinking I sat down next to Max, making a grab for his laptop. My arm brushed against his and I felt heat hit my face. Once I had control of the computer I scooted a foot away. It took me a few minutes to put right what he had blundered about doing. He had to lean into me as I explained how to use the programme properly. I could smell his crisp, masculine scent all around me. It was almost over-whelming.

"Thanks, Number Five," he said after we'd finished the piece of work he needed to alter. I nodded and was about to scurry off when I paused. Teddy still hadn't come home, and I needed to take the opportunity to talk to Max without him here.

"Is everything alright with you and Teddy? I mean ... you didn't fall out over what happened with me did you? I know I added a lot of tension and–"

"Mia," Max interrupted, turning towards me but not in a sudden movement. He did everything slowly, gauging my reaction, giving me time to move away or flinch. I felt a lump in my throat that he was making that sort of effort for me, checking himself when I knew his normal spontaneous movements were anything but slow. "Teddy's been acting like a shit since his mum left. It has nothing to do with you. I ... he's ..." he trailed off and then shrugged. "Listen, if anything, having you here has helped bring the situation to a head. At least now Ted's admitted how he's feeling. I know now that he's worried I won't give a toss about him anymore. His mum ... she ..." Max trailed off and then sighed. "She wanted to take Ted to London with her when she left, but he decided he'd rather knock around here. All his mates and his school are down here after all. He's not really into big cities."

"And she just left him?"

"She wanted out of this kind of life. We moved the company down here five years ago and Rebecca never adjusted to living 'in the sticks' as she called it with 'the backwater weirdos'. I think the reality of life with a boring northern bastad like me who's not *actually* on the telly and whose idea of a night out is a pint down the pub wasn't enough for her. Not her cup of tea. City girl through and through. I'd been with her for eight years, since Teddy was nine. She did our PR for the company at the time. She was a force to be reckoned with," Max went on, and for some reason I felt a pang of jealousy.

"Sorted out the company publicity wise. Sorted me out.

Navigated all the bullshit for me – God she lived for the bull-shit. Could work a room like nothing you've ever seen. Glam-orous, urban, nothing like me at all. Shocked t'shit out of me that she wanted to give us a go. Then I met this skinny little nine-year-old boy she had in tow and that was it. They moved in within three months. Ted's father's never been involved, and Ted and I – we used to be right close. I was the one that got him into Taekwondo. We went fishing together. I coached his kids' rugby club. He used to look at me like … like I had all the answers, like I was a superhero – totally infallible. After a couple of years he started calling me dad." He shook his head. "Now he looks at me like I'm just some twat he has to live with and only barely tolerates."

"Oh, Max," I said, the anguish in his voice when he spoke about Teddy, a boy he wasn't even related to but one that he obviously cared about like a son, was heartbreaking. "I'm so sorry. He'll come around."

"Christ, listen to me – a right Moaning Myrtle." He broke into a smile. "You've got enough of your own stuff going on. You don't need t'be listening to my family drama."

His smile, together with the green of his eyes, short circuited my brain for a moment. He was so handsome. It felt like I was being drawn into him, as if my body couldn't help but move closer. Without realising I'd turned fully to face him and our faces were inches apart. Embarrassed I cleared my throat and broke eye contact to glance down at my lap. "Uh …" I started to say, my voice coming out a little higher than it should. I cleared my throat again. "No, no it's nice to think about someone else's problems for once. And … well, it's nice to know that you've got your own shit going on. It gets tiring being the only fuck-up in the room. And I love that you just referenced Harry Potter by the way."

He laughed and that sound went right through me down to

my toes. Relaxed and laughing, Max was almost too much charisma to handle.

"I read all of them with Ted. Thought it was a load of cobblers when I started, but I was a right Potterhead by the last book."

"I'm sure Teddy knows you care about him. He probably just –"

"He misses his mum. Not ideal being stuck with a crusty old bugger like me."

"You're not a crusty old bugger. He's lucky to have you."

Max shrugged. "His schoolwork's stressing him out as well – the bastad's smart. But he's finding his computer science A level harder than he thought. He keeps swearing at the screen. I thought he was going to throw his MacBook across the kitchen yesterday."

"I could help him," I blurted out then bit my lip.

"You would do that?"

"Sure."

"That would be great. I know he's got the potential, but his self confidence is ... he just has to ..."

"... believe in himself," I finished his sentence and his eyebrows went up.

"Exactly," he said, his voice firm as he stared at me with a renewed intensity.

Max turned his hand and closed his fingers around mine, giving them a light squeeze. And for some reason it didn't feel intrusive. It felt ... right. It was like I knew Max down to his soul. Knew that he would never hurt me. Which was bizarre – I'd only known him a few weeks and he wasn't the most outwardly gentle man. But then again, I'd take his gruff, abrasive, brutally honest way, over charming and disingenuous – I'd had enough of that to last a lifetime. That crackle of tension buzzed between us again. Max leaned forward, his eyes taking on a slightly glazed look. Our lips were a hair's breadth apart and I could feel his breath on my mouth when the front door crashed open.

"Whoa!" Yaz said, dropping her bags to cover her eyes with one hand then searching blindly with the other to shut the door. "I do not need to see my brother doing the dirty on the sofa, thank you very much."

At Yaz's explosive entry I sprang back from Max until I was practically sitting on the arm of the sofa. Max broke eye contact with me reluctantly to level his sister with an exasperated look.

"It's okay," she said, not taking her hand down from her eyes as she stumbled through to the kitchen area to dump her keys and purse. "Teddy's staying with a mate overnight. Don't mind me. Continue with the dodgy sofa action. Don't let me throw off any of your energies at this crucial stage."

"Yaz," Max snapped. "Stop being a drama queen, shove some of those bloody crystals off the spare chair and watch some telly.'

Yaz gingerly took her hand down from her eyes both of which were scrunched up closed. She opened one eye then the other, baring her teeth in an eek face as if anticipating the immediate incineration of her eyeballs. You could have poached an egg on my face by this stage.

Max glanced at me and frowned. "You're embarrassing Mia," he told her as if this was akin to drowning small puppies for kicks. Yaz looked at my red face and gave me a smile.

"Sorry, hun. You know I love you but I'm not sure I can survive seeing you and my big bro Netflix and chilling. I'm not surprised you're finding your mojo though – that crystal you're holding is an orange carnelian."

"Er ... this?" I lifted the stone I'd been fiddling with for the last hour.

"Yeah, orange carnelians recharge the energy of the sacral

chakra, enhancing sexuality and restoring vitality to the female organs."

I blinked in horror at the orange crystal I'd been innocently holding and then placed it on the side table next to the sofa as if it were an unexploded bomb.

"Yaz, why do I have a stone for recharging vaginas in my house?" Max asked, which I thought was a reasonable question.

"I put that there six months ago. Figured that if you ever *did* get around to bringing an actual lady home again I wanted her vagina to be super-powered. I've got your back, brother mine." Yaz flopped down into the spare chair. "I'm sure your foof is in tiptop health, Mia, but it never hurts to get a little extra help from the universe. Now, what are we watching?"

"Yaz, stop putting sex stones in my house – it's weird. And I asked you to *stop* embarrassing Mia."

"What do you mean?" she said, lifting her mass of wavy hair up off her neck and holding it on the top of her head. "How is discussing Mia's foof embarrassing her?"

"It's fine," I put in, willing the heat to leave my cheeks. "At least now I know not to handle the crystals without protective clothing. I'm not sure my sacral chakra would appreciate any revitalising at the moment."

"Everyone's sacral chakra needs a good recharge," Yaz told me, snatching up the remote and proceeding to flick through Netflix. She put on a documentary about veganism, telling Max to suck it up. He muttered 'my bloody house' and 'bossy little shit' under his breath but, as I was coming to expect from Max, he gave in to his little sister. Max got up halfway through and retrieved more food from the kitchen (this included pork scratchings and earned an eye roll from Yaz). The man was obsessed with me eating. As I settled back into the sofa, Roger jumped up and lay on my feet with his head in my lap. More muttering from Max including 'untrained bastad', but he moved closer so he could stroke Roger and scratch behind his ears. It was becoming more and more clear that Max was just a big softie.

I let the easy banter between the siblings and the warmth of the dog on my legs wash over me. My eyelids started to get heavy as Arnie came on the screen talking about how many eggs he used to eat. I sank further into the cushions, feeling safe for the first time in months.

I FELT GENTLE FINGERS TUCK MY HAIR BEHIND MY EAR, and blinked my eyes open. The telly was off and the lights dimmed in the room. Max was hovering over me, but instead of the instinctive fear I would have expected I felt weirdly reassured.

"Hey," he rumbled. "Sorry, love, but it's late and I've got to take this one out." Roger was still lying on my legs, his head resting next to my stomach.

"Whoa," I breathed, feeling a head rush as I sat up. "How long was I asleep?"

"Yaz has buggered off, thank God. You're lucky – she made *me* watch *another* bloody programme about bean eaters. Painful."

I smiled and rubbed my eyes. Max was trying to pull Roger off my legs – the dog gave a groan of protest and settled further into me. I snuggled into his neck for a moment then pulled back to plunge both hands into the fur behind his ears and lift up his huge head.

"Come on, gorgeous," I said to his face. "We can't lie here all night." Roger responded by licking from my chin to my forehead with his huge tongue. I pulled back, giggling and wiping my cheek. My laughter cut off as I caught Max's eye. He was staring at me with an expression I couldn't decipher. It was soft and hard at the same time, and for some reason it made my stomach hollow out and that warm feeling spread from my chest. He broke eye contact to pull Roger off me. The dog gave another grunt of protest before complying. Once my legs were free I planted them on the carpet and pushed up to standing. Max still hadn't moved from his position in front of me. We were standing nearly toe to toe. He searched my face, that soft look intensifying.

"You're right pretty, mind," he whispered, then blinked as if he hadn't meant to speak out loud. He cleared his throat, two flags of colour appearing high on his cheekbones. I was frozen in place, staring up at his beautiful face. The air around us crackled with that tension and energy from before. I was both equal parts terrified and exhilarated. His hand reached up to brush a lock of my hair behind my ear with a feather-light touch. A trail of fire was left in its wake as though he'd left a mark there. Roger, not happy to be ignored, chose that moment to give a soft woof and nudge Max's leg.

"Christ, sorry. I shouldn't've ..." He snatched his hand away and shoved it into his pocket, breaking the spell between us as he took a small step back. I let out a breath I hadn't realised I had been holding and took my own step back, only to come up against the sofa. I teetered for a moment and Max's large hand grabbed mine to steady me – the warmth shooting up my arm like a bolt of electricity. He looked down at our hands for a moment, blinked, then let me go. The loss of his heat made me feel strangely alone.

"Okay," I said hoping my falsely bright tone would cover the slight tremor in my voice. "Thanks for all the food. In future maybe remember I'm not a six-foot-two teenage boy as far as calorie requirement goes."

"No, you're not," he said, his voice dropping lower as his

gaze fell to my mouth. That bolt of awareness shot through me again and I took a sharp breath in.

"Anywho."

Yes, I said 'anywho'. Like a weirdo. Could I make the situation any more awkward? "I'll just ..." I lifted my arm and pointed my thumb back to the stairs.

"Night, Mia."

I paused in my backward scuttle and looked over at Max. He'd turned away to take Rodge to the backdoor. Taking a deep breath and squaring my shoulders I made my way back to him.

"Max," I called when I was only a foot away. He turned and fixed that assessing green gaze on me again. "I really *am* grateful to you for letting me stay here." I didn't bother trying to offer rent again. We'd been over that particular conversation too many times. Apparently, as I had become ill in Max's building, he was liable to pay for my recovery, despite the fact that, one – I shouldn't even have been sleeping in his building in the first place and, two – I wouldn't dream of suing him or have a leg to stand on if I did.

He closed his eyes for a moment, when he opened them again his expression was almost pained. "Please don't thank me again. It's nothing. Honestly."

"It's not nothing to me," I whispered. Before he could answer I fled up the stairs.

Chapter 21

Let the poor girl go home

MIA

"What am I doing?" I muttered under my breath as I approached the beach. My steps slowed to a crawl when I saw the large group of mostly men running at each other and chucking a rugby ball between them. Yaz was the first to notice I'd stalled. She spun on her flip flop (it was the first time the flip flops had made sense to me) and grabbed my hand.

"You look like we're dragging you off to be a human sacrifice," she said, giving my hand a firm tug and pulling me forward in her wake. "It's just rugby!"

"Rugby is one of the most dangerous sports you can play," I told her, coming to a halt again. "I googled it. You guys are mad."

Yaz rolled her eyes as she jogged back to me, her mass of curls pinned on top of her head and a rugby top falling off one shoulder. She was wearing the same orange and red top as the men had on, apart from, whilst theirs were skin-tight and reached their waists, hers was baggy and fell halfway down her thighs. The wide neck and the sleeveless element meant that most of her sports bra was showing.

I'd chosen the most conservative active wear outfit I could find from the extensive selection Yaz had given me – but even that seemed to be showing an uncomfortable amount of cleavage and there were panels cut out of the leggings with black see-through material instead of opaque lycra. I hadn't felt so exposed in months.

"It's touch rugby, you muppet," she said as she drew up next to me and took my hand to pull me along.

"Where is the girls' pitch?" I asked, looking up and down the beach.

Yaz bit her lip. "Okay, don't kill me."

"Yaz." I drew out her name and stopped in my tracks.

"You wouldn't have come if I said it was all blokes. Come on, Mia. Just try it. For me?" I sighed and allowed her to tug me forward.

"I thought you said it was non contact," I muttered as two of the men slammed into each other and went down together onto the sand.

"Oh that's just them mucking about like toddlers," Yaz told me dismissively. "They're just warming up."

They did not look even remotely like *toddlers* to me – they looked huge and intimidating with their tight sleeveless tops stretched over broad chests and showing off a fair amount of arm muscle porn. I was about to melt into a puddle of pure lust or pure fear into the sand. What I was not about to do was get out there amongst them.

I was making progress, but this still might be a step too far. After my scene in the hairdressers Yaz and Verity both talked to me about counselling. Verity even offered for the company to pay for it privately. But I remembered the number the refuge had given me and decided to try there first.

I nearly didn't go into the first session, as I just did not think anybody was going to be able to help me, let alone a man. But Ismal was kind and patient. He practised something called eye movement desensitisation reprocessing therapy, which, he explained, used the technique of directing a person's eye movement while encouraging them to relive past events. He said it was often used to treat trauma and would help me to talk about what had happened to me. Gradually he eased me into it. Last week I was able to tell him about one of Nate's attacks. During my recount of it, he encouraged me to focus on my fear and my powerlessness, whilst at the same time watching his hand moving side to side in front of me. Somehow, after doing that, the incident just seemed to lose power. The fear lessened. He also taught me a technique called 'tapping', which helps to ground someone during a flashback or with intrusive, negative thoughts. Just as when I watched Ismal's finger, the physical stimulation of tapping one finger on the top of my other hand took me out of the terror – focused me on the present.

Since that first session I went to see Ismal every week. As well as the tapping and desensitisation therapy, he helped me practise rationalising negative thoughts, and stopping myself from going down the black hole into anxiety.

It had given me hope. Nate *hadn't* broken me. Not yet. And with hope came courage. But did I have the courage for this? I doubted it.

"Yo! Willy wavers!" Yaz shouted as she jogged onto the beach and punched the nearest man on his impressive bicep with her tiny fist.

"My God, she's totally nuts," I whispered, staying firmly where I was.

"Listen up, Y chromosomes!" Yaz shouted again. "We've got a newbie, so can you try to behave less like frustrated gay men trying to cop a feel of each other, and more like *actual* sportsmen."

"What about the *actual gay* sportsmen?" one of the guys piped up.

"Tim, as an actual gay man whose husband is watching, you especially might wanna tone down the man cuddles."

"S'okay," an attractive man in a checked shirt called from his position sitting on a wall next to the beach. "Tim can touch other boys. I'm good with it." And he did look very good with it. His smile was huge. I noticed there were a fair few other people standing and sitting with him, mostly women and some kids. They all looked very okay with the on-pitch action. I was guessing I wasn't the only one who'd noticed the arm porn and tight outfits.

"Hey, Mia." A large red and orange chest filled my field of vision. I looked up to see Heath's open, smiling face. "Max mentioned you were going to join the madness."

I gave a nervous laugh and started to inch backwards. "This may have been mis-sold. I'm actually a netball player, so maybe I'll just ..."

"Bollocks, mate," Yaz said, giving me a small shove forward. "Same skills just different shaped ball."

"Er ... I don't know whether-"

"Number Five!" Max greeted me as he jogged up to us, a huge smile on his face. "I'll sit this one out with you and explain it all."

Before I could tell him that I'd decided to make my way home and that rugby did not look like my kind of thing, he'd enclosed my hand in his big, warm one and was pulling me along to where the others were standing at the side. He introduced me to a few of the women and to Tim, the gay partner, who had an adorable small baby strapped to his chest. They all sent our still-joined hands curious looks. Most were friendly, but a couple of the women shot me some fairly strong side-eye when they thought I wasn't looking. Being as watchful as I was had its advantages, but knowing when people were talking about me behind my back wasn't one of them.

We stayed on the sidelines for two games. Max explained the rules whilst intermittently cheering for Teddy who was on the pitch. Teddy was as tall as the others, but he hadn't quite developed as much bulk. Luckily this didn't seem to matter for touch rugby. What mattered was speed. That was where Teddy had the advantage. He could outrun most of the other men and didn't even seem out of breath – the joys of being a teenager. Yaz also had speed on her side, and her small size seemed to work to her advantage – she slipped past and jinked around the larger men, even at one stage going through a set of legs to score a try.

"Come on, Number Five," Max said after a half hour of watching. "Give it a chance."

"I don't think so," I said, refusing to move as he attempted to tug me forward. "I'll just stay over here. You go back and–"

"Ah, I see," Max said, dropping my hand and nodding to himself. "It *is* a lot more complicated and fast paced than *netball*. I can understand how you might find it intimidating." He grinned at me. I knew what he was doing. I knew he was trying to goad me into playing. It didn't stop the reflex flash of anger going through me at his words. Netball was all about speed and agility. At my peak I could run rings around these guys whatever the shape of the ball.

"Fine," I grumped, jogging past him onto the sand. I dropped my voice to a whisper. "You and your misogyny can kiss my arse."

"That's the way, sister!" shouted Yaz, high fiving me as I ran past her. "You stick it to the patriarchy!"

I gave her a weak smile as I took up a position on the field.

Max was still grinning as he moved to the opposing side. I rolled my eyes at him but focused on the ball. As I realised just how big the men surrounding me were I felt a low flutter of fear in my chest. Before I had time to launch into a full-blown panic attack the whistle went and the ball was flying my way. Despite being distracted I somehow caught it, but it took a minute to remember that, unlike netball, you could actually run with this ball.

Over the next hour I started to get a feel for the game. I kept forgetting you couldn't pass forwards, stopping with the ball, being in the wrong place at the wrong time, but I was slowly getting it – I was holding my own. But then I realised that was an illusion. Of course I was holding my own because they were letting me – not tagging me as much, not seeing me as a threat.

Making me a charity case.

Again.

I'd had enough of being a charity case. So, during the last game, as soon as I got hold of the ball I swallowed down my fear and ran straight for the two men directly in front of me. They were both smiling at me like I was a dog learning to walk on its hind legs rather than a fellow sportsman. Somewhere, deep down inside, my competitive spirit, which had been squashed for so long, began to unfurl. When I was feet away from the guys I feinted to the left but at the last minute jinked right to skim around them just out of arm's reach. I looked back, saw Heath was ready, and passed to him. Once he had the ball he made a run for the line. I knew he wasn't going to make it. I screamed his name as he was tagged, keeping my position on the far side of the pitch. The ball sailed over the other players towards me. I thought it would be impossible to reach but I jumped into the air, extending my left hand to just manage to tag it with my fingertips and bring it back to the safety of my right. As soon as I had possession I made a run for it and scored a try just before Max tagged me.

"Brilliant!" Yaz shouted as she pulled me up out of the sand and into a hug. "Bloody brilliant!" She swung me side to side then pulled away to shout at the rest of the field. "Take that sausage smugglers!" She turned back to me and smiled big. "Finally, a girl that can play."

"Lucky fluke, Number Five," Max's deep voice sounded from my other side and I disengaged from Yaz to scowl at him.

"Whatever you reckon, rugby boy," I said, picking up the ball and spinning it on one hand – a trick I'd perfected with a netball, but one that I could still pull off with an oval ball. There were some whoops from the people on the pitch around us on the pitch and even from the sidelines.

"You just got burned, Max," a smiling Teddy said, slapping Max on the back. Max reached up and rubbed Teddy's hair before pushing the side of his head.

"Okay people, let's get ready to rumble!" shouted Yaz, jumping on the spot with her high ponytail flopping from side to side on the top of her head.

"Jesus, Midge," Heath complained. "You've blown my eardrum. Only bats can hear you now you realise." He grabbed her and put her in a headlock. She laughed when he let her up, but it didn't escape my notice that her face was bright red and her eyes were a little too bright.

Heath looked at me. "Great play, Mia," he said.

"Uh, thanks."

Heath had let Yaz up now and was staring at my right shoulder. I realised that I had been rolling it and rubbing it to try and ease the ache that had started up during the game. This wasn't the first time I'd noticed Heath watching me either, often with a frown on his face which didn't seem to be typical for him.

"You coming for a drink?" Yaz asked as we walked away from the pitch. My smile fell a little. I still wasn't completely comfortable in busy bars and restaurants. They sparked my claustrophobia and flashbacks. I associated them with all the enforced socialising I had done with Nate. I still couldn't shake the feeling of being trapped in the endless small talk hell that was my social life with him – of standing by his side whilst he banged to his posh friends, clients or other *contacts* as he called them. After a while it had felt like being social just wasn't my forte. Like I was somehow dysfunctional and had imagined the carefree teen I had been before Nate came along.

"You're man of the match – you've got to come."

"I'm ... not, er ... I don't think that–"

"Yaz, you're so pushy," one of the women from the sidelines said, approaching our group and sidling up to Max. "Let the poor girl go home." She turned to Max and started swiping sand off his bicep. "Bloody hell, Maxie. You're covered." Max didn't seem to mind a female human sand-removal technique that involved extensive muscular forearm strokeage, but for some deranged reason I did.

That's why I was now standing in a pub nursing a pink gin and tonic, feeling awkward and no way sticking it to strokey arm woman.

Chapter 22

You've been preying on my mind

MIA

Within fifteen minutes of being here it was clear this had been a bad idea. The warmth, the banter, the casual teasing – stuff I vaguely remembered from before Nate – was so alien that I couldn't really handle it. I felt like a small child out in the cold, watching these people through a foggy window with my nose pressed up against the glass but not being able to reach them. Max, Yaz, Verity (who'd met us after the rugby) and Heath stayed close and made gentle attempts to include me, but I just didn't know how to behave.

With Nate there had almost been a script I was expected to follow. We were always in cold, clinical, uber-posh bars or restaurants, not cosy little pubs with the odd dog wandering around (Roger was sitting on my feet as I stood in the circle which I found oddly comforting). I had known what was expected of me and I had had a mask of full make up and designer outfits on to hide behind. Now, I was standing in the middle of a crowd of people with no make-up, partly covered in sand, my hair a windswept disaster and wearing a dodgy borrowed lycra outfit with a way-too-big sleeveless rugby top over it. The way these people interacted made my heart ache. It brought home how much Nate had taken away from me over the years I was with him.

"Mia," Heath said from my other side and I held back a sigh. I tried to avoid Heath if I could – he always asked too many questions.

"Heath!" Yaz said, then turned bright red when silence followed her semi-shouting his name. "Er ... can I get you a drink?'

"I'm okay thanks, Midge," he told her, holding up his full pint and giving her a bemused half smile.

"Right, yes of course," she mumbled followed by an out of character nervous giggle.

Heath gave her a lightning quick but dismissive smile and then turned back to me.

"Mia, can I talk to you for a minute?" He wasn't smiling now.

"Oh." I bit my lip. Twice before he'd made a vague attempt to speak to me on my own but I'd been able to dodge him pretty well. "Er ... I-"

"What's up?" Max asked, moving in closer to me so that the side of his body was almost flush with mine. Under the intense gaze of Heath and so close to Max I started to feel the familiar pull of claustrophobia. It was ridiculous – Heath's eyes were awash with concern, and who wouldn't like being this close to Max? But I felt scrutinised, trapped.

"Excuse me," I muttered. "I've ... er, just got to nip to the loo."

I put a considerable effort into not running away from the group, and managed to slip out of the circle of people before breaking into a light jog. Roger, bless him, followed me, staying glued to my side as I weaved my way through the crowd and finally made it to the Ladies. Once inside the cubicle I sat on the closed toilet seat and put my head between my legs, trying to slow my breathing and tapping on my wrist. After a couple of minutes I felt more in control, and like a bit of an idiot. I pushed open the cubicle door and stood over the sink, staring into the mirror. These people had been nothing but kind to me. If I wanted to start living again I had to try and get over my anxiety. I had to try to remember who I'd been before and get back to that woman. I squeezed my eyes shut, gripped the side of the sink for a moment and then looked back at myself.

"Snap out of it," I whispered. "You're safe here. Just try. *Try* to be normal." Filled with new purpose I walked back out of the toilets to a waiting Roger, but just as I'd finished giving him a head scratch Heath appeared in front of me.

"Mia, I don't mean to be a creepy bloke who waits outside the ladies' toilets, but I really wanted to speak to you on your own."

"Oh," I said. He was blocking the corridor, directly between me and the rest of the bar. Short of running around him and cementing my reputation as a freak I didn't have much option but to talk to him. Given the concerned looks he'd levelled at me over the last month and the disapproving vibe I often seemed to get from him I was guessing that he wasn't too happy with his best friend's new choice of charity project. "Why do you-?'

"You're still not using your right arm properly."

"What?" I asked, my eyebrows going up at his random statement.

He sighed. "You're right handed. But every time you reached to tag the ball in the air during that match you used your *left* hand to bring it down."

I shrugged. "Wh–?'

"You didn't see that physio, did you?"

I bit my lip and tucked my hair behind my ears in a nervous gesture.

"My arm's fine." The last thing I wanted to be reminded of is my injuries. The ones that meant I couldn't even bloody well reach up to get a coffee cup down from the cupboard at work with my dominant hand.

"It's not fine," Heath snapped, in an uncharacteristic loss of patience. He took a step forward and I took a corresponding one back. Roger moved with me and I put a hand into the fur of his head to calm my nerves. "You had a fracture dislocation, Mia. It needed rehab. Your shoulder movement could be permanently restricted. Why are you being so stubborn about this when–?"

"What's going on here?" Max's annoyed voice sounded from behind Heath in the corridor.

"I'm just talking to Mia, Max," Heath said.

"I can see that, arsehole," Max replied as he shouldered Heath out of his way to come and stand next to me. "I can also see that you're stressing her out."

Heath threw up his arms and, damn it to hell, I flinched. Both men froze and stopped glaring at each other to look at me.

"It's fine. I'm fine," I said, forcing my body to relax. I *had* to stop being this frightened rabbit the whole time and grow a pair.

"Gi'over. Yer not fine," Max said, his accent stronger than normal – likely as the result of his beer consumption. "E's blockin' yer way which you hate. Your hand's in't fur of dog 'cause yer stressed and ..." He paused, glanced at Heath then at me before tilting his head in the direction of my hands. I'd been tapping against my wrist without even realising I was doing it. He turned back to Heath.

"I don't know what you're playing at, but you need to move out t'way and let Mia pass."

"Shit," Heath muttered, moving back at lightning speed and looking horrified that he might have done something to upset me. Great. Freak-level weirdness achieved. The man was just trying to have a simple conversation with me. He was trying to help me. "I'm so sorry, Mia."

"Look, honestly its *fine*," I told him. A couple of women chose that moment to squeeze past us to get to the loos. "Let's at least go to the bar." I managed a weak smile and then led them out into the open. Once out of the corridor but still separate from the rest of the crowd I came to a stop. Roger sat back down on my feet.

"Max, wipe that thunderous look off your face, you grumpy article," I told him in an effort to lighten the mood. The last thing I wanted was to cause problems between Heath and Max. "Heath's trying to help me, okay. He didn't mean anything by it. He doesn't know I'm a bit ... weird about stuff."

"You're not weird, lass," Max snapped, scowling down at me. "Don't you dare say that." I rolled my eyes.

"Someone who can't have a couple of simple conversations in a pub without verging on a panic attack is a little bit weird," I said, dropping my voice to a near whisper.

"Mia, I didn't mean to make you feel boxed in. I would never–"

"I know!" I was losing patience with this whole situation. "It's fine, please, please don't worry about it. You were only trying to help."

"Help with what?" Max asked, his eyes flicking between Heath and me. Heath clamped his lips together and looked away from us to the bar beyond. I remembered what he'd said before about patient confidentiality and I sighed. I was putting him in an impossible situation with his friend.

"I hurt my shoulder six months ago and Heath treated me in the emergency department."

Max's eyebrows shot up. "How did you hurt your shoulder?"

"I ... um, I fell.'

He narrowed his eyes at me. "And what did this *fall* do to your shoulder?'

I swallowed past the lump in my throat. Max deserved to know some of what happened. I was living with him at the moment for God's sake.

"Heath you know the details. I give permission for you to tell him. About my injuries." Heath searched my face for a moment and I gave him a short nod. He turned back to Max.

"Mia sustained a fracture dislocation of her shoulder, a couple of broken ribs and extensive facial bruising.'

"What the fuck?" whispered Max, his face had drained of all colour and his mouth had fallen open. I felt the back of my throat burn, but I bit back any tears.

"The reason I wanted to speak to Mia is that I set up some physio for her to rehabilitate her shoulder after I saw her again at your office and she never attended."

"Why does she need rehab?" Max asked, frowning at Heath.

"Mia," Heath said, turning to me with a patient expression on his face. "Lift up you right arm please."

I scowled at Heath and then lifted my right arm up to waist height and then quickly down.

"Above your head, Mia," Heath told me. I managed to get it to about ninety degrees but it wouldn't go any further. "When Mia tagged any of the high balls today she used her left hand, but she catches with her right. She didn't have any proper rehabilitation on the joint. Shoulders can be bastards if you don't do the physio after that kind of injury."

He shook his head and looked pained for a moment before he turned to me. "I'm sorry, Mia, but you've been preying on my mind." He rubbed a hand down his face. "The state you were in ... we see a lot of shit in that emergency department, but everyone – even the most hardened A&E workers – were upset by your case. And the fact that you self-discharged before we knew that your shoulder had fractured as well as dislocated, and without any family support taking you home ... The number you gave us didn't work ... I just ... Mia, I feel like we let you down after your ..." he paused and glanced at Max before continuing, "*fall*. We let you slip through our fingers and I just want to make sure you have the treatment you need now."

Chapter 23

I love the Pig and Whistle

MAX

"Excuse me," I said, my voice tight. Everything felt tight – my throat, my muscles – like I was a bow pulled to maximum capacity. "I'll be back in a minute." Mia and Heath both gave me curious looks as I turned to stride down the corridor. I didn't stop until I got to the Gents, threw open the door walked straight up to the built-in metal condom machine and punched it ... hard. It groaned and the metal collapsed in, leaving a massive dent. A string of condoms fell out of the bottom.

"Whoa!" a guy said as he emerged from one of the cubicles. "Jesus dude, I applaud you for the safe sex and all but that's a little aggressive for The Pig and Whistle on a Thursday night. Just saying."

"Sorry, mate," I mumbled, leaning over the sink to splash water over my face. For a moment I actually thought I might throw up.

It hadn't been a fucking fall.

I didn't need Heath's subtle emphasis on the word to know that. Bloody hell, how could anyone think of hurting Mia? She was a scrap of a human, totally defenceless. I closed my eyes for a moment, willed the nausea back down and took a deep breath. The last thing she needed was for me to go all *Hulk* on her at this stage. I also didn't want to talk about it in front of Heath.

Oh yes, I'd be talking to fucking Heath, no doubt about that. But now wasn't the time to get into the old best-friend-withholding-important-information-about-the-woman-I'm-becoming-obsessed-with thing. When I was sure that I was back in control of myself I pushed away from the sink and back out of the door. Mia and Heath were still talking by the bar. Heath said something to Mia and she laughed. She *laughed*. After learning what I'd just learned, Mia laughing with Heath just didn't compute. The last thing I wanted to do in that moment was crack a smile.

"Message me the physio details," I said to Heath as I barrelled up next to them both.

Heath, who was still smiling, looked at me then at Mia before frowning in confusion. "Er ... what?'

"Max," Mia said, her hand going to my overly tense forearm. "Are you okay?"

Was I okay? This woman had sustained a fracture dislocation of her shoulder plus God knows what else, and she asks *me* if *I'm* okay?

"What? I'm fine."

"It's just you ... er, you look a *little* intense right now."

"Yeah, mate," Heath says. "You've got your serial killer eyes going on and that freaky muscle in your cheek's ticking from clenching your jaw too hard."

"I'm fine, *mate*," I say to him through gritted teeth. "I just need the details of the physiotherapist, so I can set something up for Mia *tomorrow*."

Mia gave my arm a light squeeze and I looked down at her

upturned face. She gave me a small smile. "Max, I don't think that the NHS works that way, you know. You can't just demand an appointment the next day. It's not an emergency. I'm fi-"

"Mia," I snapped, hating myself at her small start, but I really felt that if I didn't get my point across somehow that my head might explode. "You won't be seeing the physio on the NHS. You'll be seeing a private physio and you'll be seeing them *tomorrow*."

"Max, I can't–" Her words cut off as I took her hand gently and pulled her away from Heath. We wound our way through the pub and out of the front door where I came to a stop under the Pub sign (a large plaque with a painting of a pig standing up, wearing a tweed suit and holding a whistle in its mouth – below the painting were three rows of text: *no food, warm beer, poor hospitality*).

"Okay," she said slowly, looking up and down the street. "What are we doing out here?" I took a deep breath in before lifting both my hands slowly, so as not to startle her, and settling them under her jaw to tilt her face to me. I closed my eyes and rested my forehead on hers for a moment then. Her hands came up to my forearms but she didn't pull me away.

"We're out here so that you don't feel trapped or boxed in when I talk to you."

Her breath left her in a soft whoosh, fanning my face.

"Right. Well, I'm going to ask you again – are you okay?"

"No," I told her truthfully. "No, Mia. I'm not okay. Not after hearing how badly you were hurt just weeks before I met you." I pulled back a little to look into her wide brown eyes. "Not after I remember how I treated you when you started working for us." I laughed briefly but without humour. "I like to think of myself as this principled man, as a voice for the underdog. When I met you, you were *hurt*, and I treated you like dirt."

Those beautiful eyes looked up at me and she swallowed. "You couldn't have known. I went out of my way to make sure nobody knew. It wasn't your fault."

"Please don't make excuses for me, Mia," I told her, my voice strained again. "Please, please don't do that. Not tonight. Not after what Heath just told me."

"Okay," she whispered.

"You didn't fall, did you?" I whispered back.

There was a long pause and a swift intake of breath from her before she answered. "No." The whisper was so quiet I had to strain to hear it. "No, I didn't fall."

I cleared my throat, trying to dissipate some of the urgency I knew would leak into my voice. "Could you tell me what happened?"

"Max, I–"

"Mia, I really need to know what happened and who was responsible."

Hmm.

I was trying not to sound too intense but may not have achieved that aim. *Maybe* demanding names at this stage was a step too far. Her eyes darted away from mine; she took a step back and bit her lip.

"I can't," she said.

"Mia, please." The strain in my voice was still making it gravelly and I couldn't seem to unclench the fists that had formed at my sides. "I need to know how you've been hurt. I'm sorry I've been such a massive dick in the past but please, please believe me – I care about you. I can't bear to think of anyone-" I broke off and took a steadying breath. The thought of some-body hurting her was making me want to punch the window I was standing next to and, although the Pig and Whistle's land-lord, Fergus, did not give one shit about the décor, I'm not sure he'd be overly happy with a fist shaped hole in his murky glass.

Mia's eyes darted back to mine and she took a tentative step forward before laying her hand on my chest. She must have been able to feel how rapidly my heart was beating. Something flashed in her eyes as she stared up at me, something almost like wonder, like hope.

"I'm sorry, I can't tell you more, Max. Really I am." I let out a long breath but then gave a short nod.

"Okay. I'll leave it for now." She visibly relaxed, relief flooding her expression. As I searched her face I realised how tired and pale she looked. I was pushing her too hard. "Look, Mia. You don't have to stay at the bloody Pig and Whistle. I'm sorry I made you come out. I've got to stay with Teddy, but Yaz can take you home and-"

"I *love* the Pig and Whistle."

"What? Nobody *loves* the Pig and Whistle."

"Well, I do." Her voice was steady and her eyes still looking up at me, shining with something I couldn't quite put my finger on. "So I don't want to go home now. Now I just want to be with you and your friends for a little while. I know I'm an outsider and ..." she shrugged, "... well I just haven't been around people like this for so long. The warmth between you all ... I just would like a *little* more time on the outskirts of that."

I swallowed past my now tight throat. "You're not an outsider," I told her once I could speak without sounding choked.

"Max-"

"You're not and I'll prove it to you."

I took her hand again and led her back into the pub. As we made our way back to the others the bell rang for last orders. Yaz gave me a curious look then beamed at Mia, dragging her into the group saying, "Welcome back from the longest wee in history! Now tell us about this Bitcoin malarky again. I've decided I'm gonna get me some."

I knew for a fact that Yaz was not interested in crypto currency. Yaz wasn't really interested in any currency of any kind. But my sister was kind and she wanted to include Mia. And if that meant asking about blockchain and Bitcoin then that was what she was going to do.

"I'll be back," I whispered into Mia's ear before striding to the bar.

"Fergus?"

"What?" Fergus, the landlord, snapped, looking supremely pissed off that a paying customer would dare speak to him.

"How long is it since we did a lock-in?"

Fergus lost his grumpy expression at that, and his craggy face slowly broke into a broad smile.

~

MIA

"I'm gonna be a miner!" Yaz shouted, arms straight up in the air. I was laughing so hard that I nearly choked on my drink.

Heath snorted. "I hardly think that your career progression so far, including pissing about on the water and pissing your brother off in his office, is really preparation for mining bitcoin, Yaz," Heath said, and as always when Heath teased Yaz, there was just a little undercurrent of meanness about it – it was like he was talking to *his* little sister and not Max's. Yaz scowled at him.

"You'll be laughing through your arse when I've mined all your Bitcoin, posh boy."

"Laughing through your arse is not a saying, Midge."

"I know what I said, arsehole." Yaz paused to take another huge swig of her beer. "We can't all do *terribly serious jobs* saving lives left, right and centre. Some of us mere mortals just want to chug along doing what we enjoy. Anyway, I help peeps too."

Heath rolled his eyes. "Sure you do. I'll call you next time somebody's bleeding out in A&E and you can come and give them an emergency bit of rose quartz to hold, or teach them to windsurf. Sure that'll do the trick rather than all the pesky emergency surgery."

Yaz's face flashed with hurt for a moment before she masked it with a laugh.

"She's helped me," I put in, wanting to wipe that hurt expression off Yaz's face. Unfortunately, given how uncharacteristically loud my voice had been, my outburst drew the attention of the majority of the table.

We were currently at a lock-in.

I'd never been to a lock-in before, but two hours ago grumpy Fergus had shut all the doors with us inside the pub and the alcohol started flowing freely. The posh restaurants and bars I was used to didn't do lock-ins and they certainly didn't have grumpy, slightly smelly landlords who sat at your table drinking dodgy cider.

I was five rhubarb gins in. By that stage I bloody loved Fergus.

"She gave me some aromatherapy oils and they help with …" Oh bugger. Drunk me hadn't thought this through. Yaz's oils helped with my anxiety. I didn't want to be banging on about that at a lock-in though. "I-I can … sometimes I get worried about stuff – they help with that." I was receiving a lot of curious glances now. Yaz reached under the table and squeezed my hand.

"That's great Mia," Heath said, his kind eyes making my chest constrict.

"So you'll block my chain, Number Five?" Yaz asked, giving me a lopsided smile. "For realz?"

I laughed. "Yaz it's called *the* blockchain and you can't just–"

"How do you know *all the stuff*?" Yaz asked and I shrugged.

"I don't know *all* the stuff. I'm good with numbers and computers so I-"

"Do you own Bitcoin?" Heath asked.

"No, I … er." *I* wasn't the one that owned the Bitcoin. I was just the mug that mined it and converted it for my complete prick of a husband – making him millions in the process. "I don't own any."

"When are you going to start taking Bitcoin, Fergus?" Max asked.

"You can take yer' fuckin' Bitcoin and shove it where the sun don't shine," Fergus replied. "Gimme a tenner and be done with it."

"You could *maybe* start by thinking about getting contactless," Heath said, smiling into his beer, well aware of the fuse he'd just lit. Fergus exploded into a long, mostly incomprehensible, rant about 'city wankers' and their 'fancy fucking ideas' buggering up his pub.

It was brilliant. I loved Fergus. In fact I loved everybody. I had a warm fuzzy feeling about all the humans around the table. I'd already told Heath that he was Bournemouth emergency department's answer to George Clooney, Yaz that she was a beautiful healing water goddess with superpowers and Verity that she was a power-dressing awesome powerhouse boss lady with a heart of gold.

I sat back in my chair and listened to Fergus' rant, letting the warm feeling of being with these people wash over me. Maybe they weren't my friends, maybe this wasn't really my life – but I was here *now*.

Chapter 24

That's your big secret, isn't it?

MAX

"Rugby boys, they play one,
They think sex is just for fun.
With a scrum down, line up, get into a ruck,
Rugby men aren't worth a –"

"Okay, okay ladies," I interrupted Mia, Yaz and Verity's second rendition of a rugby song I hadn't heard since my uni days – instigated of course by Yaz. "I think we've heard enough dirty songs for one night. Fergus needs to get t'bed." Fergus was indeed fast asleep on his chair, snoring away happily. "We need to clear out."

"Home!" shouted Yaz. "I *love* my flat.'

"I love your flat too," slurred Mia, her eyes glassy as she put her arm around Yaz's shoulders. "There's all this ..." she trailed off, disengaged her arm from Yaz's shoulder and made waggled her fingers in the air, "Beautiful funky stuff everywhere. Like a magical little cave."

"Hmm," Yaz's eyes were closed now and she was wearing a

small smile as she leaned back against the booth. "My magic cave."

Teddy sniggered and I punched the little shit on the arm. Okay, so it wasn't a school night, but I was pretty sure calling your teenage stepson to come and pick you up at two in the morning on a Saturday was still *not* stellar parenting. Although Teddy seemed to be chuffed to bits I'd asked it of him.

"Don't laugh at your aunt's magic cave."

Heath was laughing now as well.

"Whasso funny?" Mia slurred.

"They think they're funny," Yaz said. "You're just jealous of my flat, you pricks."

"It's so messy. I love it."

'S'not messy," Yaz grumbled. "I just have a lot of stuff and its all on display like ... like a museum."

"The Museum of Yaz."

"Awesome," Yaz whispered, her body was slowly going more and more slack where she was sitting.

"Are we still talking about Auntie Yaz's magic cave?" asked Teddy.

"Christ," I muttered under my breath. I'd had enough experience with my sister to know when she was about to pass out. "Yaz," I said, raising my voice. "Don't you bloody dare fall asleep there, you useless sod. I'm not carryin-"

"Uh oh," Mia muttered, leaning over Yaz and peering at her sleeping face. "She is outters."

"Bloody bloody hell," I muttered as Yaz slowly crumpled down into the booth with her head landing in Mia's lap.

"Yaz?" Mia whispered, pushing Yaz's hair out of her face and then giving her shoulder a gentle shake. "We gotta go home now. Yaz?" Mia looked up at me with wide, glassy eyes. "She's sleeping."

"I'm aware of that," I told her.

"S'my fault," Mia slurred.

"Mia, you didn't pour rhubarb gin down her throat," Heath said as he came up next to me to stare down at the crumpled Yaz. "She's just useless."

"Hey," Mia cried, pointing at Heath in a rare show of aggression. "She s'not useless. She's bloody lovely. She only stayed for *me* – so I could have this." Mia threw her arms out to indicate the dilapidated, beer-stained interior of the Pig and Whistle.

"Number Five ..." I paused and rubbed the back of my neck. "I think that statement proves you're rat-arsed as well. Nobody in their right mind covets this place."

"I do," Mia said, her voice now fierce as she slapped her hand to her chest. "I love it. Even jus' for a lil' while." Her voice trailed off and her eyes became unfocused. It wouldn't be long until she was in the same state as Yaz.

"Right then," I said. "Heath, can you get Yaz? I'll help Mia."

Heath made a face. "Do I have to? Last time I took your sister home she vomited all over my shoes, and these are new trainers."

"Pick her up, you selfish git," I told him. He rolled his eyes but did bend down to pull Yaz out from the booth.

"Mia?" I asked and her eyelids flickered until she focused on my face.

"Hi," she said, smiling up at me with a goofy grin, the like of which I'd never seen on her face before.

"I'm going to take you home now, okay?"

"Hmmhmm."

If it were Yaz I would have put my shoulder in her stomach and hoisted her up in a fireman's lift – no nonsense. But I instinctively knew that Mia wouldn't want to be carried. It would make her feel trapped. I took her hand and helped her to stand. She swayed for a moment and then grabbed onto my arm, leaning her weight into me.

"I'm putting my arm around you now, Mia," I warned her so she didn't freak out. She looked up at me and gave me another crooked smile.

"'k."

We made our way out of the pub with me taking most of her weight so I was practically carrying her along side me. Heath, Teddy and I managed to wrestle Mia and Yaz both into Teddy's car. By the time we got home they were asleep. As predicted when Heath hefted her out of the car Yaz vomited. Most of it was in my flowerbed. His shoes may not have come away completely unscathed. This time I *had* to carry Mia up the stairs, but, as unconscious as she was, I doubted it would trigger a panic attack. We put them in the spare bed together, both fully dressed apart from their shoes. I didn't think Mia'd wake again but as I was pulling the covers up to her chin her eyes blinked open and she focused on my face.

"That's your big secret, isn't it?" she said.

"What's that?"

"You – you're kind. You're a good man. *You* would never hurt me."

"No, love," I said softly, searching her face and pushing her fringe back from her forehead. "Not ever."

"I really, really like you," she said, giving me so much direct eye contact it was like a punch to the gut.

"I like you too, Mia," I told her, my voice rougher than normal and my chest feeling tight.

"'s not real," she whispered, as her eyelids fluttered closed.

"What?'

"'s not for me," she said, her voice so faint it was a struggle to hear it. Her body went completely lax then and her eyes drifted shut.

Chapter 25

I want to help you get it back

MIA

"Oh my God. Kill me."

I blinked open my eyes. On the pillow next to me all I could see was a mass of curly hair above the duvet that was pulled over Yaz's face. The low, constant groan from underneath sounded like an animal in pain. I lifted my head off the pillow and pushed up onto my elbows. Yaz's hand came up and pulled the duvet down so she could look at me. Her eyes were bloodshot, her skin tone decidedly green.

"What happened?" she groaned, rubbing her hands down her face. "And why am I at my brother's house?"

I sat up bolt upright with a start and my mouth fell open as a stream of images from last night filtered back into my consciousness.

"Oh no," I whispered. Max had carried me. It was bad enough that he had to support me so I could walk out of the pub but I knew, I just *knew*, that when we got to his house he *carried* me. I could still smell his aftershave. Bloody hell! I'd told him I liked him. Really, *really* liked him. Why didn't I have the ability to forget drunken behaviour like Yaz?

"Hey, you okay?" Yaz asked, sitting up next to me and reaching out to touch my forearm. Like always her touch was calming. It helped me breathe through my panicky thoughts. There was a sort of peaceful, warm energy about Yaz (even hungover Yaz) that settled my mind.

"I'm good," I said, giving her a shaky smile. "I mean, apart from the badger mouth and nausea."

"Jesus," Yaz sighed, flopping back down onto the mattress again. "How did Max get us both home?'

"Heath carried you. Don't you remember?"

"What?" Yaz shot bolt upright again only to have her face drain of all colour. Her hand went to her mouth and she scrambled off the bed to lurch towards the bathroom. I heard her retching and then groan like an animal again before the bathroom tap went on. She emerged five minutes later looking pale and very small, her hair a crazy mass of curls sticking up in all directions. "Okay, be honest. Was I sick on him?"

I bit my lip. "You weren't sick on him *exactly*.'

"Mia," she said in a warning tone.

"Well, you *were* sick in Max's geraniums. Heath may or may not have held your hair back while you chundered." She groaned and leaned over to put her head in her hands.

"Why do I always have to make such a dick out of myself in front of Heath? This is the first time I've been drunk for *ages,* but it always seems to happen when he's around. He always sees me at my worst."

"Oh Yaz," I said softly, crawling over the bed to where she was sitting so I could rub her back. "I'm sorry, hun. I thought you might have a bit of a crush on him but-"

'What!" she said in a horrified voice, taking her head out of her hands to stare at me with wide eyes. "I hate his guts, Mia.'

"Oh, right. Yes." I suddenly regretted mentioning her thing for Heath. She looked humiliated. But how could she not realise it was obvious? "Of course you do." I crossed my fingers behind my back as Yaz let out a shaky sigh.

"Hey," Max's voiced sounded from behind the door, making me start on the bed. "You ladies alive yet?"

"No," said Yaz in a dejected voice. I scrambled off the bed and went to the door as she flopped back down again.

"Sorry I –" My voice cut off as I flung open the door to be confronted by a freshly showered Max in jeans and bare feet. Don't ask me how a man's bare feet can be sexy but Max's were gorgeous. I felt like I couldn't breathe for a minute, he looked so utterly and effortlessly handsome. I was suddenly very aware of the fact I was still wearing the oversized Sandbaggers' top and leggings. One of my hands went up to my head and yes, yes of *course* half of my short hair was bunched up in a tangle at the side. I cleared my throat. "I'm so sorry about last night. You must think that-"

"I *think* that I organised a lock-in at the Pig and Whistle and my sister got you pissed on rhubarb gin," he said, taking in my dishevelled appearance with half smile and a twinkle in his eye. "You have nothing to be sorry about." He turned to Yaz. "You on the other hand owe Heath *another* pair of shoes. Fancy ones too."

"Bugger off and die," Yaz said, bending her arm at the elbow and shaking it at him. In return he bit his thumb and flicked it towards her.

"Okay well, I'll be out of your hair in a sec. I just need to-"

"Feed. Me." Yaz shouted and Max bit his thumb at her again.

"You can feed yourself, Midge. I'm feeding this one." Then, to my surprise, he reached forward and took my hand in his warm, dry one, tugging me out of the bedroom. I shook my head.

"You don't have to feed me," I told him.

"Quit yer mitherin. It's Sunday. Every bugger gets bacon on a Sunday. Well, apart from Yaz – she'll have a mushroom or something." He shuddered. "House rules. You need to eat."

"Really Max. I–"

"Mia," he cut me off and turned to face me, one of his hands going to the back of my neck and curving around below my hairline. It should have felt intrusive, provoked anxiety, but for some reason all his touch did was make me feel safe, and warm, and triggered a strong wave of awareness to spread down from my neck to my toes. I let out a shaky breath and looked up into his intense gaze. "You're going to eat some bacon and then I'm going to take you to see a physiotherapist."

"Wh-what are you on about?" My head was throbbing now as I sat down at the kitchen island. As he turned to the kettle Yaz pulled out the stool next to me.

"I wouldn't bother arguing with him," she said, slumping forward onto the counter once she made it up on the stool. She rested her head on her hands and her puffy bloodshot eyes looked up at me. "He's a bossy bastard. I should know. I grew up with him."

"Hey, you're alive."

Yaz's eyes shot open when she heard Heath's voice accompanied by his heavy footfalls as he walked into the kitchen.

"Kudos both of you for not choking on your own vom. Hashtag winning." He held his hand up to me and I gave him a weak high five. Yaz's face flushed a deep red colour. One of her hands went to her out-of-control curls, which, after a night of drunken sleep, looked way more Side Show Bob than ruffled surfer chick.

"Why aren't you working?" she asked accusingly, searching

her wrists for a hair band, which wasn't there. "You're *always* working."

"I do get the occasional day off, Midge, and it *is* a Sunday," he said, moving towards the kettle after it was clear Yaz was going to leave him hanging. A plate landed in front of me loaded with bacon, sausage, beans, toast, even black pudding was on there. I blinked.

"I'm not a massive breakfast eater," I told Max something he knew and he shrugged.

"You can't afford to carry on missing meals, Mia."

"See," muttered Yaz. "Bossy."

Max faced me across the counter, lifted one eyebrow and crossed his arms over his chest. The bacon did actually smell pretty good. But I couldn't bring myself to pick up the fork. I felt anger trickle through me, strengthening my spine.

"Don't tell me what to do." My voice didn't even sound like my own. It was cold and harsh. Max's face lost the arrogant expression and he frowned, uncrossing his arms to rest his hands on the counter. I pushed off the stool and took a step away from the kitchen island.

"Mia," Max said slowly, the rest of the kitchen was silent. "It's okay if you don't want to eat that breakfast. I just think you should have *something*. You're hungover. The only thing that will make you feel better is food. I'm not *telling* you to do owt, I'm asking. I'm sorry if it sounded like an order but the truth is I bark out orders all day long to these buggers, most of which get completely ignored. It just becomes a habit. I'll be more … careful in future."

The tension drained from my body and I felt my shoulders relax. My cheeks felt heated as I took back my position on the kitchen stool.

"I may have overreacted," I muttered into the plate. "You're right. I do need to eat." I lifted one of the rashers of bacon off the plate and took a small bite. Max pushed a cup of tea tentatively across the kitchen island towards me as if he was offering it to an angry badger. I wished now that I could claw back my words. The last thing I wanted was for Max to be *careful* with me – to treat me differently. Despite my churning stomach, after a few mouthfuls and a few sips of tea (half a sugar and lots of milk – just the way I liked it) I started to feel better. Funny, but in all the years I was with Nate, he never learned how I took my tea. I offered Yaz a slice of bacon but she groaned and shook her head.

"I'm gonna make a smoothie," she said, slipping off the stool and grabbing some fruit on the way to Max's Nutribullet. Instead Heath snatched it out of her hands and shoved it into his mouth.

"Nothing you can Nutribullet is going to cure your hangover like bacon, Midge," Heath told Yaz. "Whilst you're crying about the poor piggy wiggies the rest of us are feeling bloody brilliant, having restored the required salts and protein needed for alcohol poisoning recovery."

"Bugger off, Heath," Yaz mumbled, her face still a bright shade of red as she ducked her head to make her smoothie.

"Well, aren't you a delight the morning after the night before. You should go and stand outside over Max's raspberries – scare off all the birds."

"Ha, or provide them with a ready-made nest," Max chipped in. Yaz stopped what she was doing, turned on her heel, and power walked out of the room. I didn't think I'd ever seen Yaz do more than just amble, when she wasn't on the rugby pitch that is, so her power walking was vaguely alarming.

"What was that about?" Heath asked in a bewildered voice after Yaz had made her exit.

"I think you hurt her feelings," I told him, keeping my eyes on my breakfast.

"But I *always* take the piss. That's what little sisters are for."

I was about to tell Heath that Yaz wasn't *his* little sister, and that maybe he should be a little less clueless and open his bloody eyes to see the way she looked at him, worshipped him. But I bit my lip. Yaz would be humiliated if anyone pointed out how she felt about Heath to Heath himself.

"Well, I don't know what's crawled up her arse this morning," Max said, sipping his coffee. "Yaz can normally take a joke."

I bit my lip again. I was sure that Yaz could take a joke in normal circumstances, but after having vomited (for the second time) on the shoes of the man that I was now convinced she was secretly in love with, then seeing that man the morning after when she looked like she had been dragged through a hedge backwards, in *those* circumstances, a little teasing – the type that was good natured but had just an edge of cruelty – that type of teasing would be tough to take.

"So, Mia," Max said. "You still love the Pig and Whistle after last night? Got to say I've never heard anyone wax lyrical about that shithole and its grumpy old bastard of an owner like you did."

I laughed and took a sip of my tea. "I stand by everything I said last night." My smile dropped a little after I caught Max's eye and remembered how *much* I'd said. The smile he gave me was smug this time. I'd never seen him so pleased with himself.

"Not a wine bar, Michelin star type girl then?" Heath asked. Images of the bars and restaurants I'd frequented in my former life and the utter desolation and loneliness I'd felt there clashed with my warm memories from last night and I shuddered.

"No, I fucking *hate* places like that." The vehemence in my voice caused his eyebrows to shoot up in surprise.

'Er ... okaaay," he said slowly. "Hope you're taking note Maxy Boy – no *nice* places for this lady. Strictly sawdust on the floor and no toilet paper in the bogs type of girl. Right up your street, you stingy northern bastard."

"I'm going to call an Uber," a slightly less dishevelled Yaz said from the door of the kitchen. She'd managed to find her hair band and controlled her lion's mane, but a few wayward curls still stuck out at random angles. She turned to Heath. Her face was pale and her eyes a little red rimmed. My heart ached for her. "I'm sorry I threw up on your shoes ... again." Red stains appearing on her pale cheeks before she turned and made a swift exit, pulling her phone out as she went.

"Yaz," said Heath, jogging around the kitchen island to catch up with her. "Don't be a numpty. I'll drive you home. You don't have the money for an Uber."

Max and I listened to them argue all the way to the front door and until it closed behind them.

I took another sip of tea before breathing in deeply through my nose and out through my mouth.

"Max, listen," I said as I put my cup down on the counter and looked up at him. Holding eye contact wasn't easy for me, but it was time I stopped being such a wuss. "I know you want to help me and I really appreciate it. But honestly you don't have to take me to a physio today. My arm is fine, whatever Heath says."

Max huffed out a frustrated breath and closed his eyes for a moment before making his way around the kitchen island to stand in front of me. The stool was high so my face was more on his level than normal, but I still had to tip my head back as he moved into my space. He lifted his hand to my shoulder then it stilled before making contact.

"Is this okay?" he asked, his eyes flicking down to his hand then back to my face. That was when I realised that I hadn't tensed at all at his approach. Hadn't felt even a shiver of apprehension. In the back of my mind, I know I had thought that maybe I'd stay broken forever. That maybe I'd never be normal again. For the first time in a long time I felt hope, unfamiliar but strong, blooming in my chest. I smiled tentatively and gave a quick nod. With hope came bravery. So, as he swept my hair back behind my ear, I reached up to his face. I ran my hand along his strong jaw line – smooth but rough after his shave that morning. The stubble would be back in full force in a few hours. I traced up behind his ear and into his thick hair, my eyes flying to his when he took in a quick draw of air.

"I know I don't *have* to, Mia," he said, his mouth a hair's breadth from mine. "None of this is about *have to*. Don't you see that yet?"

His eyes were burning green fire, his expression was almost fierce. Two slashes of red appeared high on his cheekbones as his pupils dilated. And because I felt brave and hopeful and whole for the first time in years, because I felt like I was burning from the inside out with the need to be close to him, because I trusted him and because it would have been impossible to stop myself, I closed the minuscule gap between our lips and pressed mine against his in a feather-like kiss. He sucked in a sharp breath and his head jerked back just slightly so he could read my expression. After a moment's pause his lips fell back onto mine.

This kiss wasn't gentle. It was firm, insistent and accompanied by a low sound from the back of his throat. One of his hands slid under my jaw, the other rested on my hip – not closing me in, not pushing for more. But as I slid my fingers from his hair to the nape of his neck, arching my body into his, and sliding my other hand up his back, I could feel the trembling of his body as he held himself back from me – worried, even now in the grip of his desire, worried that he might crowd me, that he might overwhelm me.

I loved that this big, abrasive, gruff man cared about me so much that he tried to contain all that fierceness so as not to scare me or push me too far. But at the same time I hated that he felt he had to do that. That he thought I was so fragile. I wanted unedited, disinhibited Max. The rough, unapologetic Max. I didn't want him to be careful with me, not now. So I opened my mouth under his, allowing his tongue to sweep inside. Still he didn't let his big body relax into mine, still I felt the tension in the muscles under my hands. I pulled back enough to whisper against his lips.

"I'm fine. You won't scare me. I want the real Max. My Max. Be *real* with me, please."

"Your Max," he whispered back before scooping me up off the stool and lifting me so that my legs went around his hips. His hard body finally falling into mine and that low growl back in his throat. "I've wanted you for so long," he breathed against my neck as he kissed the skin at the base of my throat. "I felt like I was going mad with wanting you." He lifted me up and put me on the granite of the kitchen island, his mouth fusing back with mine and his hips pressing against me. My breath caught, the high of having him so close almost too much to take. His large hand found the hem of my t-shirt and then splayed across my ribcage under my breast. I followed his lead to feel the smooth skin of his back under his shirt, stretched tight over his taut muscles. Need, sharp and biting, welled up in me and I let out a noise I'd never heard myself make before. A quiet but desperate moan that felt like it was ripped from my soul. Max stilled. It was a good few moments until I realised his phone was ringing.

"Bollocks," he muttered, moving back enough to look down at me. He was breathing heavily and his expression was still saturated with need but there was guilt there too, and more than a little concern. He didn't answer his phone, just continued to stare down at me, searching my face for something. "I'm sorry, love. I didn't ... I mean I didn't mean to rush things like that. I know you need to be comfortable with me. Attacking you in my kitchen when you're weak with a hangover is not in the plan."

"Okay," I said, trying to get my own breathing under control. "What is the plan then? And why are you the only plan maker?" I grinned and moved my hands up his back to encircle him, hugging him to me and laying my head on his chest, still high from those hopeful feelings and the fierce desire I felt for him, coupled with the ability to act on it without becoming a terrified mess. My counsellor had told me that PTSD didn't have to rule my life. That I could go on to have real relationships, but, if I was honest, I hadn't really believed him. And anyway, I had thought that if I ever *was* brave enough to give a man that much power over me again, he would be physically much weaker than Nate ever was – nothing like Max who could squash even Nate like a bug.

But it wasn't just a matter of physical strength, was it? You could be the strongest, most lethal man in the world – that didn't mean you weren't gentle and caring with the people you loved. With real strength comes the integrity not to use physicality to control others, or emotional abuse to chip someone down to a shadow of their former self. Real strength means helping to build someone up so that they can be a real partner, an equal. A narcissist like Nate didn't want a partner – just a pawn, someone he could keep in 'her place' – subservient, reliant, broken down

"The plan is I take you to your physiotherapy appointment now, then-"

"Max." I cut him off, highlighting my point by bringing my

hands up and onto his chest. "I can't afford a private physio and I-"

"You're an employee. If you need to see a physio for an issue that was affecting your work, the company, *my* company will fund it."

I rolled my eyes. "My shoulder is not affecting my work performance. The only thing it affects is my ability to get a mug off the top shelf."

"I've seen the way you inhale coffee in the morning, Number Five. It's like the plutonium in your Dolorean, the Sky Net in your Terminator. I would argue that your cup-reaching ability is *crucial* to your work performance." His grin was so smug that I tipped my head back to look up at the ceiling and let out a short laugh. "Mia, you are going to this appointment today. It's already paid for so I'll be spending the money whether or not you show up."

"Max–"

His smile dropped and his hands cupped my face to tip it down from my contemplation of the ceiling and gain eye contact. "It's your *right arm*, love. Your dominant arm, and you haven't got full use of it. Something has been taken from you, and I want to help you get it back."

I paused for a beat, taking in his stubborn expression. "Okay," I said softly. "Okay I'll go. And Max ..." I leaned into him, my hands moving from his chest to his wrists below my jaw, "... thank you." I swallowed a lump in my throat. My next words were a little choked with emotion but I managed to get them out. "I *mean* it. For last night, and for this. Whatever happens between us I'll always be grateful."

He groaned. "Bloody hell, Number Five," he said in a pained voice. "Didn't you listen to anything Verity and I said last month? It's *us* that's grateful to *you*. And please don't thank me for setting up a lock-in in one of the grimmest pubs in Dorset – that makes me feel like a right tight-arse."

"I love the Pig and Whistle – give me that over the Ivy any day."

"You've eaten in the Ivy?" he stared at me in that assessing way he had.

"You know – figure of speech."

He narrowed his eyes at me. "Right," he said slowly. "Anyway – plan is physio now. Then later in the week I take you somewhere that's not the Pig and Whistle and we talk, right?"

"What physio works on a Sunday anyway?"

"One that wants to get in Heath's pants."

Chapter 26

Do your worst

MIA

"Eyes, nose, throat and groin," Teddy told me as I kicked the training bag again. Roger lay on his back, basking in the sunshine of the garden and letting his humans do their bizarre punching. It was two days after my first physio session and my shoulder was already feeling like it had a little more range of movement. "You've gotta go for the vulnerable areas, because you're going to be smaller than most people out there – *and* weaker."

"Gee, thanks," I said to him, aiming a punch at his bicep, which he didn't even flinch at.

"Case in point," he said with a smug expression, pointing from my fist to his arm and back again. "I barely felt that. I don't even have to wear the training pads when we practice punching."

"What? You don't normally just hold your hands up for peeps to punch?'

"If I did that with my training buddies I would have

multiple fractures and trips to the emergency room. Your punches – not so much."

"Fine, fine, Mr Miyagi: eyes, nose, throat and groin. Got it."

"So, groin kick is one of the best. Palm heel strike to the vulnerable areas. Combination of the two. Once the attacker's down, you run. Whatever you've got on you, you can use. Got any keys?"

I turned to my rucksack and fished out my house keys.

"Okay, so hold them like this." Teddy showed me how to grip the keys so they were sticking out. "Show me a hammer strike with the keys." My arm sliced down forward through the air to plunge the keys into an invisible foe. "That's it. Now, using your elbows is important, especially if your attacker is at close range and you can't get enough momentum to throw a punch or a kick. So, elbow strike." Teddy demonstrated and I copied him. Then Roger jumped up and ran towards the house, barking and tail wagging.

"What's going on?" Max was walking from the house towards us, frowning at me and giving Roger a distracted rub down as I did a series of elbow strikes into heel palm strikes.

"Mia asked me to teach her some more self defence."

Max stared down at me and put his hands on his hips. He was still wearing his suit from earlier, but his tie was askew, a five o'clock shadow was darkening his jaw and some of his thick hair was curling around his nape.

"*More* self defence? When did you ..." I saw the memory came back to Max of me and Teddy in the garden before. "Ah, right. I remember." He shifted on his feet for a moment. "Sorry about that again, by the way," he added in a low voice.

"You were only worried about Teddy," I said, dropping my hands and taking a step towards Max. "You were just protecting him."

Teddy snorted. "He was just being an arsehole."

"Teddy!" I snapped but Max grinned.

"The kid's right," he said, giving Teddy a slap on the back. Teddy shook his head but there was a small smile on his face. Ever since refugegate and then the late pick up from the Pig and Whistle, Teddy seemed to have softened towards Max. He was less hostile. There was more light-hearted banter between them, which was how I suspected their relationship was before all the upheaval with Ted's mum. It wasn't completely without tension – there was still something underlying their interactions which I couldn't quite put my finger on. Teddy seemed almost watchful, as if he was waiting for something, bracing for it even. "I'm an arsehole. But a curious one. What are you teaching her then?"

"Eyes, nose, throat, groin," I chanted, showing him some kicks and heel palm strikes.

He frowned. "It's all very well punching the air, but with a real human, things are a bit different."

I nodded and shrugged. Believe me, I knew how different things could be.

"You know you should run away if you can, Mia," Max said. "Don't try to fight someone if you can get away from them."

I nodded again and held back an eye roll. If there was one thing I knew how to do, it was run away.

"Of *course* I told her that," Teddy said, clearly miffed. "I'm not completely useless. Right, I'm off to training."

"Hey," I said, skipping after Teddy as he turned to leave and laying my hand on his arm. "Thank you for taking the time with me. I know you didn't have to. I appreciate it."

His cheeks went a little pink and he shrugged. He might try to hide behind a teenage mask of indifference, but I could tell he was chuffed he was helping me.

"You don't have to thank me, alright? I-I ..." He paused

228

and glanced back at Max who was still out of hearing distance. "Listen, I'm not stupid. I know what a women's refuge is, right? I know why people have to go there. If you want to be able to defend yourself then I'm going to help you."

"Okay, honey," I said softly, resisting the urge to pull him in for a hug, which I could tell would embarrass the hell out of him. His jaw tightened and I saw him swallow before he jerked his chin up and strode away back into the house.

I walked back to Max and there was an awkward pause. Neither of us had mentioned the kiss in the two days since it happened, but you could cut the tension between us with a knife. "He's a good kid," I said, breaking the silence.

Max snorted. "He's a punk." He looked at my expression and smiled. "Okay, so when he's not being a teenage arsehole I guess he can be a good kid. Sometimes. Did he show you how to break a hold?"

"Er ... what now?"

"Break out of a hold – you know if someone grabs you from behind."

I shook my head.

"Good – cause he's a teenage punk. Bad – cause that's one of the most important things to learn. I-" He swallowed and cleared his throat. "I can show you if you want?"

I nodded. Max was right – if I wanted to learn to defend myself I had to actually deal with a human.

"Do your worst," I told him, bracing for impact. He chuckled.

"Mia, I'm not going to attack you. Look, stand with your back to me." He stepped up in front of me took both my shoulders and spun me around so I was facing away from him. "I'm going to put my arms around you from behind very slowly, alright?"

I tensed. My right index finger started tapping onto my left wrist, centring me in the moment. I took a deep breath.

"Okay," I said on the exhale. He'd moved closer – I could smell his aftershave mixed with fresh soap and underlying Maxness. His arms came up around me slowly. Roger, sensing the tension, gave a short bark. His ears were forward and he was watching me.

"You tell me to stop anytime you need, Number Five," Max told me. "I'll drop away my arms any time you say, alright."

"Right," I said in a high, choked voice. "It's fine. Go on." His front pressed against my back and his huge arms came up around my waist, pulling me into him.

Max

She was shaking.

I could feel the fine tremors as her soft body moulded back into mine. Her breathing sped up and all her muscles tensed. I held still for a minute, waiting for her to tell me to release her. But my brave Number Five, she did that tapping thing on her wrist again and the shaking subsided ... almost. Her hair smelled of strawberries. I had to conjure up an image of my nan making marmalade naked to will my body into relaxing. I gave it a few seconds but she was still too tense and her breathing too erratic so I let go and stood back.

"What was that?" she asked, turning to me with a confused expression.

"Have a break," I said. "Take a breath. There's no rush." She wasn't going to take anything in if she felt trapped and terrified. She blushed, probably guessing that I could tell how anxious she'd been. After a moment she shook her arms out, turned her back to me and told me to go for it again. I put my arms around her twice more, each time waiting a little longer before I let go. On the third time after I stepped back she turned to me with a frustrated expression.

"Are you actually going to teach me or what? I don't think most attackers are going to just let me go."

"Mia, I'm *not* an attacker," I said in a gentle voice. "You've got to be relaxed to take it in – not scared to death."

"I'm fine. I-" I raised an eyebrow and her eyes went to the side, before focusing back on me again. "Okay, but I *will* be fine now. Try it again."

This time when I enclosed her in my arms she didn't tense and she didn't need to tap.

"Okay so lean forward over my arms." She did as I asked which pushed her bottom into my groin and I almost had to step away. "Bring your elbow up. Now, swing round and elbow strike me to push away." Her elbow strike was completely pathetic but I let her go anyway.

"I did it!" she said and I stifled a laugh.

"Mia, I let you go again."

"Oh."

"You've got to *go* for it. Really smash me in the throat or nose. You won't hurt me." We tried it twice more. She gradually put more effort into her elbow strikes but they still didn't make me release her.

"Okay, you need to get your *rage* on," I told her. "There's got to be some real anger behind your attempts. Forget who I am, okay? I'm not Max for the moment. I'm someone you've *got* to get away from. Someone you want to hurt." She stared up at me and I saw her eyes fill with determination, her mouth set in a hard line before she turned her back to me again.

"Right, I'm ready," she said, her voice low and steely, her fists clenched by her sides. As soon as my arms trapped her she jerked forward violently over my arms, nearly throwing me off balance, then her small elbow came up and slammed into my throat, forcing me to let her go. She shot forward as soon as my arms dropped and then turned to me with a huge smile on her face.

"I did it!" she shouted, bouncing up and down on the balls of her feet. Roger bounced around her as well, barking his head off with excitement – never mind that his master could barely breathe. "Elbow strike, motherfucker!" she crowed.

I would have laughed but I was too occupied with trying to suck air in after the blow to my windpipe. "That's great, Number Five," I managed to get out in a choked voice once I could inhale enough air to survive on.

"Oh no," she said, her eyes flying wide as she rushed to me. "Max, are you okay? You said I couldn't hurt you."

My breathing started to ease. One of my hands went to my neck to rub my throat. I could feel my eyes watering.

"Underestimated you," I said, my voice no more than a pathetic croak now. She reached out for my hand that wasn't clutching my throat and I took hers, giving it a squeeze.

"I'm so sorry," she whispered and I rolled my eyes.

"Stop apologising all the time. I told you to really give it some beans and you did. I'm proud of you: *Though she be but little, she is fierce.*"

"I didn't know you could quote Shakespeare."

"I might be a bit rough around the edges but I did English Lit GCSE like everyone else. Right, come on. I don't think I can manage a curry now after you've mullered my throat, but there's a chippy round the corner."

Her face lit up like fish and chips was the finest dining available. "I'd love that."

"Christ, you're easy to please," I told her, tugging her along and into the house.

"There's nothing better than a chip butty."

"You sure you're not from up north, lass?"

I swept up my wallet from the side, shoved it into my pocket and then slung my other arm over Mia's shoulders to walk to the front door. Pulling her into my side was instinctive. It was only when we were making our way down the driveway that I realised what I'd done. Up until then I had tried to make slow approaches as far as physical contact went. I worried that this was a step too far and loosened my grip. But instead of moving away from me or putting distance between us, Mia tentatively put her arm up around my waist and let her body relax into mine. By the time we made it to the chip shop I had such a huge smile on my face that I freaked out Brian behind the counter (he was used to me being a surly bastard most of the time – the blatant display of my teeth seemed to unnerve him. He couldn't get us our battered haddock quick enough).

Mia paid. She insisted, and when I objected she pulled back from me, laid her small hand on my forearm and looked up at me, her brown eyes serious. "Let me do this Max. Just once, let me be the one getting *you* something you need." How could I say no to that? I couldn't go over how much she'd done for my business again – I was beginning to sound like a stuck record.

We ate straight out of the paper, sitting up on the harbour wall, watching the sunset and drinking slightly warm Sprite. We talked about Teddy and how he seems to be coming around slowly. How my sister has a huge crush on my best friend – Mia refused to comment on that one but her silence was deafening. I informed her that it's been the worst kept secret ever since Yaz was ten years old so the confidentiality ship had sailed long ago anyway. After we'd binned the paper I decided I couldn't put it off any longer.

"Mia, are you ready to tell me how you were hurt?"

Mia had been laughing after I'd told her the latest string of Yaz-related work demands – my sister wanted me to allow a mass yoga session during working hours. She also wanted me to import a full-size tree into the middle of the office space to improve air quality and, yes, so that employees could hug it at regular intervals. Actual tree hugging – the woman was a walking cliché.

Mia's smile dropped at my question and she looked away. I noticed movement in her lap and when I looked down she was tapping on her wrist again.

Chapter 27

Maybe if she just tried a little harder

MIA

I sighed and looked out at the sea, closing my eyes and letting the sun warm my face. I know he must have guessed a fair amount of my story. But he probably thought I was just the victim in the narrative. He didn't know what I'd done. But I could trust Max, couldn't I? He'd proven that. Even if it was with just part of the story. I could trust him with that much.

"There was a teenager called Amelia." If he thought it was odd that I was telling the story in the third person he didn't say anything. For some reason it was easier for me this way. I felt so remote from the person I used to be then. "She was lucky. She had everything she ever wanted. Her parents were loving, her sister was a pain in the arse – aren't all big sisters?

"But, Amelia liked expensive things. What she did *not* like was her parents' run down old Ford Fiesta, or their small terraced house, or the holidays they had in their caravan in the UK. Amelia thought she was better than that. She didn't want fish fingers and peas and the odd bit of stolen cider with the local kids – she wanted to be eating in swanky places, drinking champagne.

"She was always good with computers. When she was eighteen she went on work experience at a large company and she met a man – *the* man, the boss. Let's call him Mr Big Cheese. Mr BC was very rich, very good-looking and very interested in Amelia, which she couldn't *believe*. He made her feel special and he gave her expensive things. He was a lot older than Amelia and Amelia's parents weren't very happy. They didn't care how much money Mr Big Cheese had. Amelia's dad said he just didn't like him. He said Mr BC was too charming, too slick, too controlling. He thought that Mr BC had a bad vibe and a cold look in his eyes. Amelia loved her dad but she didn't really want to hear any of that, not when Mr BC was showering her with new designer clothes and expensive jewellery, or whisking her away to the Caribbean when she'd never even been on a plane before.

"So, Amelia went to a university Mr BC chose, and she didn't join in with student life. Why would she need to? She wasn't going to sit in a student union drinking cheap beer when she could be eating at Michelin star restaurants with celebrities. What would be the point? Mr BC's friends became Amelia's friends and when Amelia finished uni she worked at Mr BC's company. They got married in a huge wedding that made Amelia's dad massively uncomfortable as he couldn't afford to even cover the alcohol bill. Amelia's sister refused to be a bridesmaid – she said she didn't trust Mr BC, and that Amelia was too young to get married. Amelia's mum cried during the ceremony, but not because she was happy. Amelia's family didn't fit in at the reception and left early. Amelia was glad when they left." I looked up at Max then and felt my eyes fill with tears. "She was embarrassed of them. Her mum was in a boxy M&S suit, her dad was asking for a pint instead of drinking champagne, her sister's latest boyfriend was telling people he was a plumber. Amelia wanted them to leave. She was a selfish, materialistic *bitch*."

"Oh Mia," Max muttered, reaching to brush a tear away from my cheek and then taking my hand in his. I sniffed and turned back to the sun.

"None of Amelia's school friends were invited as she'd long since lost contact with them. It was only towards the end of the reception when she looked around the room and saw only Mr BC's friends or business contacts that she started to have just the tiniest of niggling doubts. After the wedding Amelia and Mr BC moved into a huge house which Amelia didn't have to clean. She didn't even have to choose the furniture – all of that was done for her. Never mind that she might *want* to choose something. That idea was just funny. Didn't she know she had bad taste? Didn't she realise that their house needed to be somewhere Mr BC could entertain and not feel embarrassed? Better leave it to the professionals.

"Amelia worked at Mr BC's company. At least *that* she was good at – even Mr BC had to agree with that. She knew that she was creating updates that made the company revenue, but she never seemed to see any of the money. Mr BC said that she wasn't very good with money. That he should manage all the money. After all, wasn't he generous? He got her racks of designer clothes that he liked. Make-up tutorials with famous make-up artists. Appointments at the best hair salons. And Amelia was grateful. She supposed her hair *had* been a bit dull without all the highlights he insisted on. Her skin *was* a bit pale without the spray tan and she *did* look more polished with professional make up.

"So what if she didn't really have contact with her family anymore? When she went to see them, or they came over, or even if she just talked to them on the phone, Mr BC would be cold to her for days. She'd become scared of this new, hyper-critical, cold Mr BC. Maybe if she just tried a little harder he could be like he used to be with her again. After all, she *was* infuriating, she made his life difficult, she didn't understand how hard he worked, she wasn't interesting enough company for his friends, her make-up was never quite perfect enough. If she could just be *better* then maybe he'd change back. Maybe then she wouldn't have to admit to her family that they were right and she had been wrong. She wouldn't have to go home with her tail between her legs.

"It's just the harder Amelia tried, the more difficult Mr BC became to please. She began to feel stupid, worthless and even maybe a little crazy. He made her doubt her decisions. If she cried or reacted she was 'hysterical' and 'unstable'. Then one day, when they were driving somewhere and they got lost, Amelia tried to lighten the mood by teasing him about his sense of direction. He didn't shout or scream at her, he just raised his hand and brought the back of it down on the side of her face. She was wearing a blue dress. The blood looked so shocking against that pale blue. Mr BC was sorry. It was an accident. She shouldn't have distracted him when he was driving. But a line had been crossed and that's when the real fear started."

"Oh my God, Mia," breathed Max. I looked back at him again and his eyes were burning with a mixture of fury and sorrow. "I'm so sorry, love." He reached up to brush the tears I hadn't even realised were falling down my cheeks away then pulled me into his chest as if he just couldn't bear having any physical distance between us. "How long did he hurt you for?"

I sighed, giving up on the third person thing.

"After that first hit I stayed another year," I told him and his arms tightened around me. "But something had snapped in my mind. Any love I had for him was gone. Before then I hadn't really wanted to sleep with him, but I made myself do it because if I didn't he would be unbearable. It was just easier to go along with it. But after he hit me I literally *couldn't* do it. He never forced me, but he just descended more and more into this quiet fury. Every so often he'd snap.

"A few times he dragged me around by my hair, sometimes yanking it out from the roots. I had long hair before – it was halfway down my back. He could wrap it around his fist easily." I sighed. "I'd never realised before how many of the trappings of femininity make you weak. High heels mean you can't run as fast, long hair makes you vulnerable to being grabbed, tight skirts are less easy to manoeuvre in. It's like we're physically weaker anyway, but then, just for good measure, society decides we need to be hindered even further."

"That's why you keep your hair short? Why you don't wear heels or skirts?"

I nodded against his chest.

"What happened? How did you leave?"

"I left work early one day – told everyone I had a headache and took the tube home. He always drove me to and from work so that was my only opportunity. Anyway, it must have got back to him that I'd left, because he came home before I'd finished packing my backpack. I was in a pair of my old jeans from before we were married and my ratty trainers. He knew as soon as he saw me what was going on. I tried to run but he grabbed my ponytail, threw me to the ground, and then kicked me in the ribs. When he was finished he twisted my arm behind my back and used that to yank me to my feet again – I felt it come out of its socket and my scream must have shocked him because he let me go for a second. Then ... I, er ..." I bit my lip, trying to decide how much to tell Max. He gave my shoulders a squeeze, urging me to go on but I just couldn't do it. I couldn't completely ruin his impression of me – it was bad enough he now knew what sort of person I really was, without letting him know what I was actually capable of. My voice lowered as I whispered my half lie. "Then ... then I ... managed to get away. One of the security guards helped me."

"Why didn't you go to the police?"

I shrugged, my throat feeling thick with the weight of guilt weighing down on me. My mind flashed back to the blood on my hands. I swallowed and closed my eyes tight.

"Max ... I-I can't go to the police."

"Mia," he pulled away from me and then faced me on the wall, taking my shoulders in his hands to turn me towards him. "You can't just hide from him forever. You'll need to get a divorce and–"

I shook my head vigorously. "No, no. He doesn't need to know where I am to get a divorce. The workers at the refuge told me all about that. And I can get legal aid if I can prove I'm a victim of domestic violence." The thing was I hadn't just been a victim, had I? "I'll do all of that when I'm ready but–"

"What if he hurts somebody else, Mia?" Max's soft voice almost brought tears to my eyes. I pressed my lips together to stop them wobbling. "He's dangerous. You know that. And he deserves to be punished for what he did to you."

I bit my lip and looked away. Nate wasn't the only one that deserved to be punished. I *would* tell Max everything – I just needed more time. A little more time to be happy.

"What if he tries to find you?"

I shook my head again. "As long as I stay away from my family, for now, I don't think he can." I didn't tell Max about seeing Nate's business partner in London or Nate coming to the office. If Max knew that Nate was one of his biggest potential clients I didn't know what he would do. The situation was impossible. I'd have to leave eventually. But for now I just wanted to be with Max.

"I'd like to meet *Amelia's* sister and her parents," Max told me, jumping down off the wall and holding my hand as I did the same.

"I'd like that too." My voice hoarse with longing. I missed my family so much. But, if I was honest it wasn't just the need to hide that kept me away from them. It was a little guilt, a little cowardice, and a lot of shame. How could I have let Nate separate me from them? How would they ever understand?

"Is Amelia your real name?" he asked. "I don't have to use it – I just need to know your real name."

"Yes, but my family call me Mimi. I didn't completely lie about that. *He* only ever used Amelia though."

But right now, as I walked hand in hand with a man that – whilst being more a stingy, grumpy northerner rather than a charming, extravagant smooth-talking Londoner – *was* kind, *was* gentle. A man who did make my heart skip a beat, who cared about a difficult, surly, lost seventeen-year-old boy enough to treat him more like a son than his own mother did, who looked after his staff like they were family, who cared about his sister. Right now I was more worried about how this difficult, awkward, gorgeous, scruffy wonderful man was going to feel about me once he learned the truth.

Chapter 28

I know what I want

MAX

I had to calm down. The fury running through me as we walked back from the chippy was making me a little insane. I knew I should be level-headed and gentle with Mia. The last thing she needed was an angry man on a rampage to kill her husband.

Husband.

Mia was married. The thought made me feel a little ill. I wished I could meet eighteen-year-old Mia, before that sadistic prick got his hands on her. Before she was ground down with gas-lighting and emotional abuse leading to actual violence. How could anyone hurt something so wonderful? What kind of monster wanted to take a bright teenager and grind them down into a shadow of themselves?

But I had *this* Mia with me now. Maybe she wasn't as naïve and outgoing as she had been back then, but she hadn't let him break her. She was strong, my Number Five. Strong and stubborn and funny and kind and beautiful, with an edge of insecurity and fear. But, given her strength, I knew she could fight her way through the latter two. She'd been coming out of herself more and more over the last few months. A wave of guilt hit me when I remembered what a judgemental, surly twat I'd been to her at first – she'd dealt with that when she didn't even have a place to sleep, when she was still *hurt*. As we made our way into the house and I closed the door behind us a lump formed in my throat. For a moment it felt a little hard to breathe.

I stopped in the corridor and turned to Mia. Anger was battling with immense guilt and I couldn't go any further without letting some of it out. What I was feeling must have reflected in my expression because Mia frowned as she looked up at me.

"Whoa. Max. Are you okay?"

"No," I said in a tight voice. "No, I'm not okay, Mia. I'm very fucking far from okay, but that's not your problem."

"Wh-?"

"I am so sorry for how I treated you when you started working for me," I told her and her frown deepened. "The only shitty, shitty excuse I have is that somewhere, deep down, I was drawn to you. Teddy's mum had let him down for another visit and he was being the biggest shit in the world to me – testing me as it now turns out – and I was feeling like a bloody idiot for trusting Rebecca to come through. I didn't want to be attracted to someone not much older than Teddy, or so I thought, someone who was hiding things. Someone I couldn't trust. I'm afraid my trust had been broken so thoroughly by that stage that it changed me into someone I didn't even recognise. I wish I could go back and have the curiosity and backbone to find out why you were so secretive. Maybe if I'd been a little less blind you wouldn't have got sick. That's on me. I accept the responsibility for that. If I'd come down from my high horse I would have seen how desperate you were."

"Max, no. I–"

I moved into her space, facing her, took both of her hands in mine and leaned down to rest my forehead on hers.

"Let me take that, Mia," I whispered. "Let me live with that guilt. It's mine. I won't have you letting me off the hook. I will never forgive myself for not helping you when I could."

"You *did* help me, Max." Mia reached up with her small hand to feel the stubble at my jaw. "That job saved my life. *You* saved my life when you found me that day. It's not your fault I was in the situation I was in. It's not even *my* fault – my counsellor has helped me see that. It's *his* fault. I won't let you take any of that blame, Max. I won't."

MIA

"Stubborn," he muttered, pulling back a little to smile down at me. Max's smiles close up were so magnetic, made his face so blindingly handsome, that I almost felt light headed. I blinked up at him for a couple of stunned seconds before going up on my tiptoes and pressing my lips to his. My body was on some sort of automatic pilot, driven by a Max-smile-induced hysteria. I felt as though I would die if I didn't kiss him right now, if I couldn't be closer to him. His face jerked a little in shock under my hands after my lips brushed his. He took a moment to study my expression before he dipped his head down and then he was kissing me.

One of his hands went to my waist and the other into my hair at the back of my head. My mouth opened under his and a low sound vibrated through his chest before he slid his hand up the back of my shirt to the skin of my back. The contact sent a shiver up my spine and suddenly I couldn't seem to get close enough to him. A side of myself that I thought was lost forever surged to the fore. I *needed* this man. I was tired of waiting for him, tired of him treating me like I would break. I gave a small hop and wrapped my legs around his waist so that our mouths were more on a level. He pulled back a little to read my expression, concern cutting through the desire on his face. His pupils were so dilated that there was only a small rim of green around the outside and his jaw was clenched tight.

"Mia–"

I put my fingers to his mouth to cut off his words. "Don't ask me if I'm okay," I said softly. "Don't treat me like I'm fragile. I know what I want. Let me have my autonomy back."

His too-intelligent eyes glittered down at me and another low almost-growl came from deep inside his chest. Then he started moving. His long strides ate up the distance between the front door and the stairs, which he jogged with me still wrapped around his middle. The extra weight didn't seem to bother him at all. I knew I was still too skinny, but I'd been working on my arse with regular chocolate consumption, so jogging up the stairs as if I weighed less than a feather was nothing to be sniffed at. He shouldered open a door at the top and then we were in Max's bedroom.

Everything was white apart from the wooden frame of the bed and the industrial light fittings hanging from the ceiling. It smelt of washing powder with the subtle undertone of Max's aftershave. Now that we were in the bedroom Max's pace slowed. He walked to the bed and lowered me down onto the pristine white sheets, hovering over me, but not letting me take his full weight. A small furrow formed between his brows. I could see his mind whirring behind his eyes. He took a breath, and I knew he was going to ask *again* if I was okay.

I could understand his concern – I'd had panic attacks with him a few times now – but I just didn't want to hear it, not like this. I didn't want the reminder that I wasn't *quite* normal. So instead of letting him speak I leaned up from the bed and closed my mouth over his, one of my hands going to the back of his neck and the other up, around and under his t-shirt to feel the tensed muscles of his back under the smooth skin.

He made another low sound in the back of his throat and gave me more of his weight, and, rather than feeling trapped, I revelled in it. I felt like it was somehow grounding me in the present – similar to the tapping but on a much larger scale. I could feel him hard against me, and my heart rate picked up, not with anxiety for once, but with a fierce, almost feral *need* that was burning through me. I rocked against him and tugged at the hem of his t-shirt. He pulled back a little so that he could yank up my shirt over my head in one swift movement and throw it to the side. He froze above me then, his eyes trailing over my torso. My underwear was the most expensive set of clothing I owned. When I left Nate, I only had nice underwear to take so I grabbed a load. It was the only trapping of my former life I'd kept hold of. And as Max's eyes fixated on my intricate white lace bra and two slashes of colour appeared high on his cheekbones, I was very glad that I hadn't chucked that as well.

"My God," he breathed, one of his hands coming up to my neck, shaking slightly as it traced its way down to the skin below my collarbone until finally closing over my breast. "You're so beautiful."

My back arched and I pushed into his hand. A needy sound fell from my lips. It was like my body had taken complete control of the situation. Cautious, worried, scared Mia was no longer in charge. Desperate, hungry, Max-crazed Mia had taken her place and was pushing to get what she wanted. His chest was all hard planes of tanned skin with a dusting of hair across it down to his defined abs. Nate had taken care of his body, but he had nothing like the bulky musculature of Max. I swallowed as my fingers traced over his shoulder and down to the hair of his chest before skating the ridges of his abdomen to his belt buckle. One of his hands went down to cover mine at his belt and he stilled their attempts at removing it. That look was back on his face again as he searched mine. The questioning, concerned look that was warring with the absolute raw need I could feel in the tension of his body, and see in the way his jaw muscles were ticking as he gritted his teeth.

"Please," I whispered and he closed his eyes as the red on his cheekbones heightened. One of my hands came back up to rest flat over his heart. I could feel it hammering in his chest. His desire for me was like a tangible, thick presence in the room, boosting my confidence and hardening my resolve. "I *need* you, Max."

As soon as they left my mouth those whispered words seemed to snap something in him. He fell forwards into me and kissed me more deeply and with renewed desperation. As he was kissing me his hands ran down my chest and then over my stomach to my jeans. He made quick work of the button fly and then finally he was where I needed him to be. His hand moving in the exact right rhythm again. I let out a muted scream as I moved with him. With him hovering over me and his skin against mine I started soaring. But I didn't want to go there alone.

"No, Max," I whispered and instantly he stilled, ready to pull back. "No, I mean, not without *you*. Please."

He groaned and kissed me again, this time working his way down my neck to my breast as he pulled off my jeans and then his trousers before reaching for a condom in the bedside table. Once we were both naked and he was pressing against me he hesitated again. Both his hands came up and pushed my hair away from my face.

"Tell me you're okay," he whispered in my ear. This beautiful, strong man was shaking with need above me, but he had held himself back to check *again* that I was right here with him. That this was what I wanted too. I felt my eyes fill but I blinked the tears back as I nodded. Max must have seen the wet because he froze. Then I moved, arching against him. He let out a low growl and surged forward, and finally I was filled with Max. The overriding feeling was overwhelming relief, as if not connecting in this way with him had been causing a previously unacknowledged physical pain. And then the desperation set in, the acute need for more. I moved under him again, feeling the tightness of the muscles of his back as he held himself still. His jaw was clenched and he looked almost in pain.

"Are you okay?" he asked me and I almost burst out laughing.

"No, Max," I said and he tensed even further. "I won't be okay until you *move.*" He groaned as his mouth fell on mine and finally, finally he was moving inside me. I could feel the tension build low down in my stomach. We climbed together until his rhythm became erratic and desperate as he became impossibly harder. When I crested the wave and burst into a thousand pieces Max kept on moving, wrenching aftershocks from my body until he finally followed me over the edge. When I could register my surroundings again, Max was lying on his back and he'd pulled me over onto his chest. He was stroking my hair and every few seconds he would kiss my forehead, my hairline, my eyes, sometimes my lips, reverently – like he almost couldn't believe that I was there with him. I slipped an arm around his waist and gave him a squeeze. In response he pulled me even tighter into his side. I felt as if I were floating on a cloud, as if nothing could touch me.

For the first time in years, I felt safe.

Chapter 29

Getting somewhere

MAX

"Her hair colour was different, lighter," I said into the phone as I looked out of my office at Mia's back. She was leaning over Yaz to help her with something on the computer but then had started laughing. Yaz could be a pain in the arse, but in that moment I had not one single regret about keeping her in the office. Anyone who could light up Mia's face like that was worth their weight in gold.

Over the last month Mia had been laughing more. I don't think I'd seen her crack even a small smile in the first few weeks I'd known her. The change had been gradual, but, compared to the woman she'd been back then, she was almost unrecognisable. She still wore barely any make-up, just a touch of mascara and occasional lip-gloss, but there were no longer dark circles under her eyes. The emo clothes had been replaced (I was not sad to see the back of her one and only pair of scuffed black shoes) by a lot of Yaz's surfer stuff, but she had also bought some new items of her own. The rate limiting step of setting up a bank account had been resolved with HSBC, who had a scheme for people without permanent addresses. I offered for her to use my address but she'd flatly refused. In fact, after we slept together she informed me that she felt like she was taking advantage of me. *Her* taking advantage of *me*! As if I wasn't wracked with guilt that it was the other way around. Once her bank account was set up she decided she should move out, but before she could look for somewhere to stay Yaz had offered her a spare room at her flat. Her friend Dee had moved out and she needed the money. I'd helped Mia move in last weekend.

To be honest I would have preferred to keep her at my house, but I knew that really *would* have been taking advantage and I didn't want to stifle her growing confidence. She was coming to realise how important she was to the company, that she did have value to add in meetings, and that people respected her. Outside of work I could tell she still struggled to square away how people saw her and how she saw herself. It helped that Yaz and Verity were persistent friends. Beyond what Yaz shared after the hairdresser incident I wasn't sure how much they knew, but I'd caught each of them looking at Mia in that careful way more than once – watchful, concerned. Yes, they knew a fair amount, maybe even more than me, but I didn't want to betray Mia's confidence to ascertain what. Because in the bid to win Mia's trust, I knew I had to tread very carefully.

Physically, things were amazing between us. We couldn't get enough of each other. She was like a fever in my veins – I wanted her constantly, thought about her incessantly. When I was with her I couldn't stop touching her – holding her hand, resting my hand on the small of her back, pulling her into my side, kissing her temple, tucking her short, soft hair behind her pixie ears.

"It's the same deal as your thumbs. How do these things

even work?" I'd teased her last night after I'd nuzzled the shell of her tiny ear. "They're ridiculous, Number Five."

"Just cause I don't sport giant elephant ears there's no need to be a cheeky bugger. I can hear out of these bad boys just as well, if not better, than you can out of your oversized face flappers."

"Right, that's it," I'd growled, moving on top of her in the bed and rubbing my ear against her mouth. "Lick the normal sized ear lobe and accept the superior hearing." I'd tickled her until she'd given in and declared my hearing superior and my ears perfect, manly specimens.

The fact she felt confident enough to tease me, that there was no flicker of fear even when I'd held her down to tickle her, said something about how far she'd come. Tickling led somehow to clothes being shed, and, in a rush of blood to the head, I'd told her to hold onto the headboard, and not let go until I said so. She'd blinked up at me, and for a moment I thought I might have pushed her too hard. I could be dominant in bed, but with a woman like Mia that might have backfired. But then her eyes had lit with desire, and she'd licked her lips as she reached up and gripped the slats above her head, and I knew I had her. I'd stayed mostly clothed as I kissed down from her mouth to her neck then breasts, sucking her nipples into my mouth as she squirmed underneath me. I moved down further, kissing along her stomach and tracing the soft skin with my fingertips before finding her centre, causing a low moan to sound in the back of her throat. When I replaced my fingers with my mouth, she'd arched off the bed and plunged her hands into my hair.

"Hands," I'd growled up at her and then I'd smiled when she actually complied. I built her orgasm slowly until pushing her over the edge with my tongue and she screamed, thankfully into the pillow. Afterwards, when I'd gathered her in my arms,

I was a little concerned again that it might have been a bit much, but she wasn't having any of it. She pushed me to my back in a rare show of confidence, tore my shirt open and started her own attack, her soft mouth making its way from my neck down my chest and stomach, then ending with her lips closing around me. She'd then taken me right to the edge, but I didn't want to go there without her, so I pulled her up and flipped her onto her hands and knees, entering her from behind in one smooth thrust. The sex that followed was completely uninhibited – wild and totally out of both of our control. I came so hard I still thought I could hear the ringing in my ears.

After it was over and I realised that I hadn't exhibited the normal restraint I used with her – my normal tenderness and caution, I had frozen with my head buried in her neck, waiting for her to stiffen with fear. But she'd been like liquid in my arms. When I'd collapsed with her onto the bed, pulling her into my arms to study her face, there was no trace of anxiety. Only a goofy half-smile and a soft, sated look in her eyes.

"Wow," she'd breathed into my mouth. "You're pretty good at that."

I'd rested my forehead against hers and let out a long exhale, beyond relieved that I hadn't pushed her too far and terrified her. From that moment it was clear to me that, in the bedroom at least, she trusted me. It was *outside* the bedroom where her walls were still up, hence my phone call to the private investigator. I was giving her time and space to let me into all her secrets, but I knew she was still scared. Still watchful. I justified the invasion into her privacy as a measure to secure her safety.

I'd researched domestic violence and emotional and physical abuse since Mia had revealed that glimpse into her past. I knew that an abusive person was at their most dangerous when they felt that their victim was slipping from their control, and

Mia was most definitely *not* in that arsehole's control any more. So yes, I could justify it with concern for her safety ... but I also knew that wasn't the only reason. The pure, unadulterated *rage* boiling inside me when I thought of someone hurting her was almost overwhelming. I needed to know who this bastard was and I needed him to pay for what he'd done to Mia. She said no police, and I knew there was something she wasn't telling me. Something else had happened. Something that made her ashamed – fearful of my reaction. Sometimes I could see indecision flicker over her features as she hesitated before speaking.

She was deciding whether to trust me with the whole truth.

But I knew it would be a while before she did. She was only *just* starting to trust me with small truths – her favourite takeaway for example. That information had taken Teddy and I over an hour to obtain. At first Teddy had just thrown his curry order at me from his position at the computer with Mia, who was helping him code for his latest school assignment. I'd told him he was a selfish brat and maybe he should check with Mia what she wants before he barked out his requests. Teddy had rolled his eyes, but when Mia jumped in saying she didn't mind what we ordered – that we shouldn't feel like we *had* to include her anyway, that she was probably imposing and should go back to Yaz's, that Teddy probably needed his space etc etc – Teddy then stopped coding and narrowed his eyes at her, his mouth setting into a familiar, stubborn line.

"You're not going *anywhere*," he'd told her. "How can you be imposing when you've saved my arse with this computer bollocks? Max likes you here – he's less of a grumpy bastard with you around. You should stay." When she agreed to stay but insisted curry was "*fine*" it was like she'd laid down a personal challenge to Teddy. After much wheedling and the equivalent of the Spanish inquisition she'd finally admitted that Thai food was, in fact, her favourite.

So yes, she was getting there with the trust, but it was slow work and I needed results just that bit quicker.

"Her first name is Amelia," I told Sam Clifton, the boss of the security firm I'd hired to dig up Mia's past. When I'd originally contacted him two weeks ago, he'd told me he didn't have any space in their schedule for another case. That didn't surprise me – he came highly recommended for a reason. But then I told him her story. Mr Clifton *found* space after that conversation. In fact, he took on the case himself. But without her real name he'd been getting nowhere. "I'm still not sure of her surname but I *do* know that her husband owns or is CEO of a large company. She worked for him and she's something of a computer genius."

"Right, noted," Sam's deep voice sounded in my ear. "On it." He disconnected. I had noticed that with Sam he didn't waste words unless completely necessary. I lowered the phone and watched as Mia rounded the desk, still laughing. She caught my eye as she sat down. Unlike before when she would duck her head and wipe any expression off her face when our gazes had met, now her smile actually grew, her eyes danced and a light blush spread to her cheeks.

Yes, I was getting somewhere.

At least, that's what I thought.

Chapter 30

Such an interesting way to treat an aubergine

MAX

"Hey there!" Roger's ears picked up at Mia's call from the front door and he shot off down the hall to find her. The dog was totally besotted. It might have been something to do with the copious amounts of bacon she fed him under the table when she thought I wasn't watching, but at the moment Mia was his favourite human. I had even heard the beast give a low growl when Mia cuddled into me on the sofa, the furry, possessive maniac.

"Oh hey there, baby boy," I heard Mia say in that ridiculous voice she reserved for my dog. You didn't speak to Alsatians as if they were precious fluffy little fur babies. Roger was eighty kilos of killing machine, not a Maltese terrier. "How's my gorgeous puppy. Yes, yes you're a good boy. Yes you *are*."

"Thanks and I know," I told her as I watched her being licked and nuzzled on the floor of the corridor by a frantic Roger. He'd only seen her yesterday for fuck's sake. Where was his self-respect? And why was I letting a dog get in the way of

255

my woman. If she should be nuzzling anyone it was me, dammit.

Mia rolled her eyes as she straightened from the floor.

"*You* don't need any positive reinforcement," she told me, leaning down to pick up two huge shopping bags packed to the brim with stuff. She hauled them up with difficulty but only got a couple of steps before I whisked them out of her hands and put them back on the floor. I then stepped into her personal space, slipped my arms around her waist and kissed her, light and sweet on the lips. When I pulled back I saw she was wearing that dazed expression again. It was the way she looked at me whenever I gave her some unexpected affection, or when I listened to her opinions and ideas, or when I asked her what *she* wanted to do, what she wanted to eat. It was full of wonder – like I was a rare discovery that she never believed could exist before.

Of course I liked that she looked at me that way. It made me feel fantastic – like a God among men. But then I would remember *why* she didn't know that normal affection for your significant other wasn't something to be dazzled by, that simple kindness and caring wasn't the seventh wonder of the world. When I thought about *that* my blood would start to boil again and I'd have to squash it down or I'd be too angry to speak.

I frowned down at the bags with Mia still in my arms.

"How did you haul all that from shops?"

"Oh, I got the bus.'

"The bus ... but there isn't a bus stop anywhere near here. You must – "

"It's only a ten minute walk, Max."

"Try *twenty* minutes and you're carrying half a tonne of stuff. Why didn't you call me?"

Mia had been more confident about being out in public over the last month. More nights out to the Pig and Whistle, more lunches with Yaz and Verity. But strangely, as her watch-fulness diminished, mine seemed to be ramping up.

She rolled her eyes and then stood on her tiptoes to kiss my cheek. "I didn't want to put you out. Anyway, I'm here now; so let me get set up. I want everything to be sorted by the time your parents get here."

I frowned down at her. "All this is for my parents? I told you we'd get a takeaway. They don't expect me to cook."

She shrugged and looked away. "I know but I'm happy to and ... well, it might help me make a good impression." A flicker of worry flitted through her expression and her body tightened with anxiety. I sighed and rubbed her back.

"You don't have anything to worry about, love," I told her, wishing I could absorb all her pent up insecurities and stress. She was getting there, she was slowly coming out of herself but there was still a long way to go. "My folks will love you."

I was regretting letting Mam and my stepdad pop down now. From the worry lines on Mia's forehead I could see that what I viewed as an innocuous visit she saw as some kind of test.

"Yaz, Teddy and Heath will be here too."

I had hoped that reminder would reassure her, but she was still going into herself – her features tightening with stress. The last thing I wanted was for her to cook. Not that her cooking wasn't the dog's bollocks, because it was. She'd cooked for us loads now, and although the food was incredible (lamb for me and Teddy last week, fried halloumi steaks when Yaz came over a few days ago), I still couldn't enjoy it.

Mia was a nervous cook. Too nervous.

She measured ingredients as if her life depended on the exact quantities and bit her lip the whole time until it was nearly bleeding by the end. By the time she served up she was too stressed to eat any herself – picking at her food and glancing at our faces as we ate ours. It was unnerving. It had taken an hour of mindless telly after the last time for her to calm down and relax into my arms on the sofa. In my mind the stress of it all wasn't worth it. But as she pushed away from me and started gathering up the bags with a look of determination on her face, I decided to let her do what she needed to do for now and pick up the pieces later.

Not my best idea as it turned out.

M*IA*

"You're not an architect, Mia?" Max's mum, Fern, asked me, her green eyes, so like her son's, lasering me across the table.

"Er ... no, I'm not exactly a creative person."

"So what do you do in't office?" she asked, raising her eyebrows.

"I told you, Mam," Max's annoyed voice cut his mum off. "She works with computers."

"Oh, I see," Fern said, her tone suggesting that she in fact did not see, at *all*.

"It's actually a really important role, Mam," Yaz put in. "It's made a tonne of difference to how Max's company is run and how the projects are presented."

"Yaz. No offence, love – but you know absolutely bugger all about running a successful business or about computers." Fern laughed as she took a sip of her wine. "My daughter is more into the sea, crystals and auras than anything grounded in reality. Not sure where she gets it from, but there we are." Fern was a science teacher. She came across as an almost fiercely pragmatic lady. I'd learnt from Max that she got her teaching qualifications after leaving Max's father. Aubrey, Max's stepfather and Yaz's father, was a GP. I liked him instantly. He had a quiet manner and kind, brown eyes, just like his daughter. Fern's eyes were exactly the same shade of green as Max's. It was a little unnerving having two sets of sharp, green, too-intelligent eyes focusing on you when you tried to answer a question.

Yaz's face was red as she looked down at her plate. Heath, not picking up on Yaz's discomfort, let out his own chuckle.

"Oh no, she's into acupuncture as well now, aren't you, Midge?" he said and she gave him a forced half-smile and small nod. Any hint of acknowledgement from Heath seemed to light Yaz up like a set of Christmas lights. It was almost painful to witness. Then he went on, "You do know that acupuncture has been proven now not to work according to the usual standards of medicine."

"That study was flawed," Yaz mumbled into her food. "And benefits are difficult to measure so—"

"How on earth would you know if a scientific study is flawed or not, love? You've never looked at one in your life." Fern said, laughing again. It didn't seem like she was being deliberately cruel – but just treating Yaz like a child who's just a little bit dim and needs things explained to her.

"That's not—" Yaz began, but Max cut her off. "Can we not talk about science and medicine at the table for *once*."

"This is great, Mia," Teddy said on a near shout, shocking everyone at the table into silence. I blinked at the unexpected compliment – praise in any form was a rare event with Teddy. When I looked over at Teddy I could see him scowling at Max's parents. Whether it was in Yaz's defence or mine I wasn't sure, but it did surprise me. From the moment they arrived it was obvious that Fern and Aubrey doted on Teddy.

"Thank you, Teddy," I said just above a whisper. Those eyes all came to me again and I shifted uncomfortably in my chair. It was frustrating that I found this so difficult, that I couldn't relax, but Max's parents were too intimidating for that.

"Yes, thank you, Mia," Fern said, giving me a stiff smile. "Such an interesting way to treat an aubergine." I wasn't an idiot. *Interesting* did not equate to *good*. "How long have you been a vegetarian?"

"Er ... *I'm* not a vegetarian," I said, shooting a confused glance at Yaz. The reason I'd cooked this menu was because Yaz was vegan. Surely her parents knew this?

"Mia cooked it for me, Mam," Yaz muttered into her food.

Fern rolled her eyes and Aubrey chuckled. "Oh that's right in't it, love," he said through his amusement. "Hard to keep up with these fads of yours."

"I've been vegan for ten years, Dad," Yaz said. She was gripping her fork so tightly now that her knuckles were white. I'd been silent all meal but I couldn't just let these comments go by. Not when I could see how hurt and embarrassed Yaz was in front of Heath.

"A study published in the *Journal of the American Medical Association* showed that vegans have substantially lower death rates than meat eaters. You know, er ..." I cleared my throat, suddenly feeling a little uncomfortable with being the focus of the table, "... since you like research papers so much. Also, um, eating a vegan diet could be the single biggest way to reduce your environmental impact on earth. Which is also good since we only have twelve years to reverse global warming so ... er, there's that as well." I caught Yaz's eye and she smiled at me. Max grabbed my hand under the table and gave it a squeeze.

"Good points, Mia," said Aubrey, giving me an encouraging smile, no doubt pleased that I did in fact possess the power of speech. Fern's mouth was pressed into a thin line, but she did manage to give me a tight, close-lipped smile of her own. I felt a trickle of sweat down my back just as the smell of burning wafted from the kitchen. My eyes flew wide and my back shot straight as the panic set in. Amid all the Yaz bashing I'd forgotten about the pies in the oven. And goddamn it there *was* a meat one as well as a vegan one, but now they were all likely ruined. I pushed my chair back from the table in a sudden move that almost had it toppling over and then I ran to the oven to turn it off. When I flung open the door a small amount of smoke came out and I could see the burnt edges of both of the pies.

"Shit," I muttered under my breath as I pulled on oven gloves and grabbed the first pie out to dump it on the side. In my haste to grab the second pie it slipped and burnt my forearm before I could put it down.

"Ow, bugger," I muttered as I inspected my forearm, but the smell of burning distracted me from my pain so I pushed it to the back of my mind and went to work on the pies to see if they were salvageable. My heart was racing and sound around me started to become muffled. I could feel the panic closing in as I tried to scrape away the blackened edge of the pies, which I'd spent ages painstakingly preparing earlier. I'd wanted something ready to go that I could put in the oven and forget about, which is precisely what I'd bloody well done. My hand was shaking so badly now that it was difficult to keep hold of the knife I was using. My vision had become blurred with tears. Only the throbbing in my arm grounded me in reality.

Chapter 31

I have a surname

MIA

"Mia? Mia?" I could hear someone calling my name as if from very far away, but it wasn't until his hands curled around my upper arms that I realised how close he was. That was when it happened – I cringed away from him and a small fearful noise made its way from the back of my throat.

All I could process in that moment was that I was in a kitchen, I'd fucked up big time and a large man had me in his grasp. I *knew* this scenario. I'd been taught what to expect in this situation.

"Mia?" He loosened his grip to turn me in his arms so he could look at me. On instinct my elbow flew back to connect with his face. He grunted and let go of me completely, giving me the opportunity to scuttle back from him until I came up against the fridge.

"Baby, calm down," Max was facing me now and talking in a soft voice. His hands were both held up in front of him, palms up. "Let me look at your arm, okay?" I shook my head violently. Adrenaline was still coursing through me. I swiped my eyes so that I could unblur my vision and search for the exit. That was when I registered that all the diners were now gathered in the kitchen behind the island. Teddy's face had gone white.

"Great elbow strike, Number Five," he told me in an unsure voice, giving me a wobbly half smile. My eyes flew back to Max who was moving towards me very slowly. I shook my head again and held my hand up. I heard Yaz suck in a shocked breath and looked down to see the burn on my forearm had started to blister.

"We've got to get that under water, Mia," Heath's calm, practical voice distracted me from Max. He had rounded the island and was focused on my arm. "I'm going to turn the cold tap on and I want you to move there now and hold your arm under it. We'll give you space, honey. But I'm sorry you *have* to do that for me now or the burn will get worse." Heath skirted around me quickly to turn on the tap.

I blinked and everything started to come into more focus. Nobody was shouting at me. There was no anger in the kitchen, only concern and worry.

"I-I'm sorry," I stammered. "I don't know what I was ... I can't even ...'

"Mia, please," Max said in that soft voice again. "Please, love. Can you put your arm under the water for me? Okay?"

I gave a short nod and felt heat rise to my face as I moved to the tap and put the burn under the cold water. I hissed as the searing pain, that I hadn't even noticed until that moment, was relieved.

"What's wrong with her?" I heard Fern whisper to Yaz and the heat in my face intensified. Yaz shushed her. They moved out of the kitchen and there low voices talking in the hallway.

"Mia?" Max's voice again, still sounding unsure and a little shaken. "Can I touch you now?"

My vision blurred with tears again and I gave a short nod,

not able to look at his face. How could I have thought he would hurt me? How could I have lost sight for one minute of the kind of man he was, after all he'd been to me in the last few weeks? I hadn't had a panic attack in *ages*. Why did it have to happen in front of Max's parents? They must have thought I was crazy. Max's hands came to my waist and slowly his arms encircled me until he was hugging me from behind as I held my arm under the water. The warmth of his body seeped to mine and the fine tremors in my hands gradually subsided.

"I'm sorry," I whispered, but he shushed me against my hair and kissed my temple.

"You don't have owt to be sorry for," he told me, his voice so firm it was impossible not to believe him. "Mia, is there something about cooking and ... well, about the kitchen – something that upsets you? Because you know you don't have to cook for me and my family. Just you being here is enough and I-"

"Everything had to be perfect," I whispered.

"What, baby?" he replied, his tone confused. I turned to look up at his green eyes, alive with concern.

"He was particularly fussy about meals. It was bad enough when it was just the two of us but when the Banks' reputation was on the line – if he had clients or his friends over then ..." I trailed off and closed my eyes, hoping to block out the painful memories but of course it had the opposite effect. It also meant that I didn't see or notice Max's eyes go wide at the name Banks or the way his entire frame locked in shock. "It was rarely violence," my voice dropped to an even quieter whisper and Max had to dip his head to hear me. "But he was cruel ... the things he said to me ... I-" I took a deep breath in and ran my tongue over my incisors. "But once, with the guests still in the other room, he slammed me into the granite and I chipped my tooth." When I opened my eyes Max was frowning down at my mouth. I tapped my second incisors with my free hand and gave a small shrug. "The tooth survived. It's only a small chip from the bottom but I ... "

"Oh Mia," Max said in a tortured voice. "I'm so sorry, love. You should have said something. I would have never-"

"I *wanted* to cook for you," I told him, frustration leaking into my tone. "And I wanted to make a good impression on your parents." I shook my head. "Never mind," my voice was back to a whisper. "It doesn't matter now.'

"Mia, please. You don't have to try to make a good impression." At the back of my mind I was aware that more people had filed back into the kitchen, but there was something dark and painful building in my chest. Something I wasn't fully in control of. "All I want is you here. It doesn't matter if you can cook or –"

"How about speaking, Max?" I said, pulling my arm out from under the stream of water and tearing away from Max to back up into the middle of the space. "How about functioning on some sort of normal level? How about not embarrassing you by behaving like a complete freak!"

"Mia, stop this," Max snapped, taking a step towards me, the concern still there in his eyes but also mixed with anger. The anger should have scared me, but that dark, painful feeling in my chest was swamping any fear I might have felt.

"No, *you* stop it!" I shouted. My hands went into my hair and I pulled at it, nearly yanking it from the roots. "Stop with this. Stop with *me*. What's the matter with you? How can you possibly ... argh!" I scrubbed my hands down my face. Max made a move towards me but I held out my hand, warding him off. "Don't you see it?" I shouted. "I'm damaged goods. You should be with someone good and brave and right and ... *clean*." My voice broke on the last word. "You shouldn't have to settle for a coward who can't even cook a meal without having a full-blown panic attack. Someone who *hurts* you. Someone who's just a beaten down used up shell of a human." I started sobbing openly now. "I-I hurt you." I didn't have the strength to ward Max off when he moved to me then. I was tired of fighting. I let my body collapse into his and my tears soak into his shirt.

"You are not a coward," he growled as his arms locked around me tight. "You're the bravest woman I know. And you're *not* a shell. What he did to you does not make you unclean – that's *his* burden, that's *his* cross to bear. Not yours. Never yours. You're smart and kind and funny and intelligent and beautiful. You help my son with his schoolwork even when he's being an obnoxious shit to you. You helped me with my business even when I was doing the same. *I'm* the one that doesn't deserve you – not the other way around. And I hate to break it to you, but your elbow strike is still a bit pathetic – you didn't hurt me."

"There are loads of women out there with way less baggage than me. You could be with anyone you wanted. You could-"

"Has it occurred to you that I'm not, Mia? Has it occurred to you that I've reached the age of thirty-six and I'm not with anyone else. I want to be with *you*."

I pulled back a little and blinked up at him. My mouth opened then shut. I was at a loss for words.

"Right." I startled in Max's arms when Fern's voice filled the kitchen as she marched over to us. Her face was a little red and her eyes were bright. She drew to a stop next to the kitchen island brandishing a large first aid kit, which she slapped down on the granite. "Arm back under the water *now*, Mia," she told me, bustling around to us and then reaching for my arm. Max moved back to let her through and I opened my mouth to speak, but then she took my hand and gave it a gentle squeeze with one of hers whilst the other cupped my elbow to move my arm into the stream of the water. "Oh dear, that'll need dressing alright," she said, her tone going from bossy and clipped to gentle and soft when addressing me. When she raised her eyes from the burn to mine I saw that they were soft as well. "We'll get you fixed up, pet," she said, giving my hand another squeeze. I nodded and she turned to the rest of the room. "Aubrey!" she shouted, making me jump. "Don't just stand about like a great lump – get the iodine and a burns dressing ready for Mia. Between you and Heath I'll expect her to be made good as new."

"There in't a burns dressing in 'ere," he muttered.

"Then *go* and *get* one from your medical bag in the car," she said, rolling her eyes. "Now, Heath, you're the most quali-fied for this," she continued to boss. "You sort out Mia's dressing and I'll sort the pies." Heath nodded and moved to the kit on the granite. Anyone would agree with Fern when she was using that voice. "Now, pet," she said, looking at me and using that softer tone again. "You let Heath sort you out." I nodded and felt my eyes sting at this formidable lady's unex-pected kindness. A tear fell and she reached up to wipe it away. "Those pies look right lovely. All they need is a bit of a trim. You've nowt to worry about." Her voice sounded a little shaky at the end and to my shock I could see her eyes were just a little wet. She blinked and cleared her throat, squeezed my hand again and then let me go to let Heath take her place. "Don't just stand there, boys," she snapped as she bustled to the counter. "Aubrey – where is that dressing? Max? Get me a sharp knife. Teddy? Get the kettle on for the veg and, Yaz – go and hold Mia's hand."

After a few more minutes under the tap I was moved to the kitchen table. Yaz settled in the chair next to mine and took my hand as Heath started to clean the burn. I was too shocked by Fern to feel any pain as he doused it with antiseptic. When I glanced at Yaz she gave me an encouraging smile. My gaze moved to Heath and I could see a muscle working in his jaw. When he looked up his eyes were burning.

"If I ever get my hands on that bastard he'll have more than a fracture dislocation of his shoulder and a few broken ribs to worry about," he said, his voice vibrating with anger.

"I-I'm fine now, Heath," I told him.

"No, you are *not*," he said, looking back down at my arm. "But you will be."

"Mia?" Teddy had made his way out from behind the kitchen island and was standing in front of the table across from us. He looked pale and a little shaken but he managed a small smile. "We'll work on your elbow strike, okay?"

It was slow and it was wobbly, but I managed to give him one in return.

~

MAX

"Mr Clifton?" I muttered into the phone as I pushed up from the bed. Mia was sleeping now. Her arm bandaged and her face still tear streaked, but she was finally peaceful. I pushed out the memory of the tortured look on her face as she told me how she was *used up, damaged, unclean*, and tamped down the rage I felt in response.

"What time do you call this?" Sam's voice rumbled down the line. "You nearly woke up my wife." For some reason I couldn't picture the big ex-special forces man with a wife, but I shrugged off my surprise.

"Look, I'm sorry," I said as I moved to the ensuite bathroom and closed the door behind me. Mia was too worked up earlier to realise what she'd let slip. I didn't want to risk her over-hearing me now. "But it can't wait. I have a surname."

Chapter 32

She's been through enough

MIA

"I'll go, Verity," I said, pushing the stubborn woman back down into her seat. "It's raining and you'll ruin your make-up."

"What about *your* make-up?" she asked and I raised my eyebrows.

"Stupid-naturally-thick-eyelashed bitch," she muttered and I smiled at her. It was pouring outside and *I* was the one with unstyled hair, no make-up and a waterproof coat. Verity's hair was straightened into sleek chestnut sheets, her eye makeup was flawless and she had on the highest, thinnest heels I'd ever seen in my life. Her coat may have been Dior, white and fabulous, but it was not exactly weatherproof.

"Anyone want anything from the café?" I didn't need to ask Max. He always had the same – I'd long since learnt Max was a creature of habit.

"I am happy to go you know," Yaz told me from her downward dog position in the middle of the office – it was Yoga Madness Monday – much to Max's exasperation.

"The café is 200 yards down the street. I think I can make it that far without falling in a pothole." After taking another order from Abdul, one of the junior architects, I headed out.

The problem was that in the last few weeks I'd started to forget.

Spending time with Max and allowing myself to fall into a safe cocoon of happiness and normality, I'd let all my fear slip into the background. I'd forgotten that there was a *reason* to be afraid. That life, at least my life, wasn't all about good men who were patient and kind, and all kinds of hot in the bedroom. About friends who valued you and supported you. About teenagers who slowly lowered their defences around you. About watching telly curled up to a beautiful man, arguing good-naturedly with his beautiful stepson about whether or not he could tolerate another weird Netflix documentary.

No.

Life was dangerous. It was precarious. I should not have forgotten that. Maybe then I wouldn't have been caught with my defences down.

"You look like shit."

I flinched and whirled around on the pavement at the sound of *his* voice and there he was: tall and imposing in his tailored suit and Italian leather shoes, his hair styled to perfection, his stubble artfully sculpted rather than the messy, unkempt look I had grown to prefer. He looked at me with that familiar disgusted expression on his face, as if I was an insect beneath his notice.

"What the fuck happened to your hair?"

I froze for a moment, stumbling to a full stop in my tracks. It was as if the fear just completely shut down my synapses and I was unable to move. All those months of fear and dread and now here he was, feet away from me. Coming out of my frozen stance I glanced around. The street was bustling with people who were now skirting around Nate and me on the pavement. I took a deep breath in and let it out slowly. He couldn't very well snatch me away in broad daylight. I had to show strength. Nate would pounce on any weakness and use it to destroy me.

"It's none of your business what I do with my hair or anything else now." I tried to keep my voice strong, hating the thread of fear I could hear in it.

"You're always going to be my business, Amelia." He was smiling at me, but his low voice was laced with menace. "You're my goddamn *wife*." I glanced around at the busy street again before turning away from him and walking as fast as I could. He easily fell into step with me. When his arm brushed mine and I scuttled to the side he reached for my elbow and held it in that punishing grip. A man coming in the opposite direction frowned as he saw me give my arm a violent shake to try and dislodge Nate's hand.

"Make a fuss and your northern bit of rough's business sinks like a stone," he hissed at me, his smile still in place. I stopped struggling and my heart skipped a couple of beats.

"W-what are you talking about?" I said as we drew to a stop outside the café I'd been heading for. It was obvious Nate had known where I was going and what time I'd be going there. I always suspected he would have me watched, but the realisation that it was true made my skin crawl.

He dropped my arm and stepped back, a smug expression on his face, which made the feeling of dread in the pit of my stomach intensify.

"I've been branching out a bit, investment-wise. Found this great new architecture firm to work with - few hotels here. Eco village or retreat there. Museum or two. Eco project visitors' centre. It's a growth area all this tree-hugging hippy shit. *Really* great way to make my money work for me."

No. I screamed in my head, trying to keep from my face the

271

despair I was feeling. I had known that Nate was involved with the eco village project, but had been reassured by Verity that they weren't moving forward with Nate as an investor. I didn't know that there were other projects involving Nate's company. No, no, no.

"But ...but it was only the eco village and that –"

"I don't always advertise my investments as you well know, Amelia," he said with a smug smile. "Once I found out that you were working at Hardcastle and Markham I managed to insinuate myself in all sorts of their projects. Then I bided my time. You know how I like to come at things from a position of power. And you should know, *I* am the one in a position of power here, Amelia. It's such a shame when one of the investors in these big projects loses faith in the architect that's been commissioned. One loss would be difficult for a fledgling firm to take, even if they do have that 'hot architect off Dream Homes'. Three losses would put them in real financial difficulty. Enough that they wouldn't be able to pay their staff. Companies like that live month to month with their outgoings."

"What do you want?" I said through gritted teeth, and his smile grew even wider before he stepped into my space and leaned down until his face was an inch away from mine.

"You thought you could just waltz away from me? Did you forget who you are? Did you forget who *I* am? Nobody walks away from me. Not until *I* say. You walk away from me now and I go straight to the police – something the hospital said I should have done at the time. They were quite insistent actually. I might have refused, but that didn't mean I declined having it all documented in case I were to change my mind. It would be a shame if you went to jail and your boyfriend went out of business."

That's when I felt myself shut down. All my emotions simply evaporated, leaving a shell of a human behind.

"Just tell me what you want," I said. The lack of fear in my voice made his eyes flash and a muscle tick in his jaw. I could see his hand twitch and I thought for a moment he was going to hit me, right out here in public. I almost wanted him to. But after a few seconds he was back to wearing a cool expression, his eyes only communicating indifference again.

"I knew you'd see reason," he told me and then he smiled.

MAX

"Where is she?"

"Max, for the millionth time I don't know, alright?" Yaz said on an eye roll.

"She must have said something about where she was going?"

"I've told you already. She decided to visit her family. Apparently she hasn't seen them for a few years and it's a tricky situation. That's probably why she didn't want to involve you. Cool your jets will you? She'll only be gone a couple of days."

I huffed out an aggravated breath and crossed my arms over my chest. Mia had been acting right weird since she'd come back with my bacon roll yesterday. The lack of eye contact was the first thing I noticed. She'd gone back to her desk and focused on her screen like her life depended on it. At the end of the day when she was due to come back to mine so we could finish watching *Stranger Things* with Teddy, she'd told me she had a headache and needed to go home.

Looking back on it now, I can remember her hands were shaking. I'd assumed that it was something to do with her head – but what kind of headache made your hands shake? And she hadn't looked into my eyes once. When I gave her a hug she was stiff in my arms, only briefly squeezing me back, which just wasn't Mia. Maybe it was the stress of anticipating seeing her family? I knew how she believed she'd let them down and how worried she was about their reaction to her now. But I couldn't shake this bad feeling. Deep in my gut something didn't sit right.

"And you have no idea where her parents live?" I asked. Yaz sighed.

"She didn't say. Listen, I'm sorry Max, but I wasn't supposed to even be telling you this much. Let her sort out things with her family by herself. There's nothing that any ... hey! Max!"

I had walked away without looking back and fished my mobile out of my back pocket. Interrogating Yaz was getting me nowhere.

"Clifton."

"Tell me you have something."

"Amelia Banks," Sam said and I closed my eyes in relief. "Wife of Nathanial Banks." My eyes snapped open and I pulled in a shocked breath.

"*The* Nathanial Banks?"

"Property developer, CEO of the biggest online estate agent in the country? That's the one."

I stopped walking and stared into the middle distance, taking this new information in.

"Jesus Christ," I breathed. Mia's violent ex-husband part-owned three of my biggest projects. The bastard practically owned *me*.

"I have his address."

"Uh ... yeah, great," I muttered.

I blinked as I forced my feet to keep moving then sat down heavily in my office chair.

"Do you have the contact details of her family?" I asked, trying to focus on the immediate problem and not how I was going to beat the shit out of a man that held my future in his abusive hands.

"Right, so I ... yes, but ..." Sam never seemed unsure about anything. I frowned.

"What's the matter?'

"Well, it's just that you might not need *their* address."

"Sam, I do need their address. She's gone to them. I just want to make sure she's okay."

"Listen, the thing is, I might have sent a more junior member of my team to see them and he might have fucked up. Just a bit."

Just then the doorbell went, followed by a long banging on the door.

"What do you mean?" I asked as I pushed up from the office chair and made my way into the hallway.

"He was a bit obvious. Seems that Mia's sister doesn't miss much. She made him almost instantly. He ended up giving her *your* address. Apparently the sister was quite ... insistent."

Before I could say anything Yaz had opened the front door. Teddy poked his head out of his bedroom and caught my eye.

A blonde woman with a striking resemblance to Mia stood on the threshold to my house, flanked by an older couple. The blonde woman looked furious, the older couple nervous.

"Where is my sister?" the woman shouted at me as Yaz stepped back to let her through. "I can't *believe* another one of you wankers sent people to spy on my family. How does Mimi *find* these dickheads?" She strode up to me and poked me in the chest, hard. "I'm not afraid of you, mate. Now, go and get my sister. I'm taking her home."

"Er, yeah," Sam muttered through the phone that was pressed to my ear. "Sorry about that. Look I'll send over the file on Amelia Banks. Everything's there."

"Okay, great," I said, my gaze fixed on the small blonde in front of me with the all-too-familiar dark brown eyes.

"A warning though, Max," Sam said, his voice having dropped in pitch. "It doesn't make for easy reading. Understand what I mean?"

My chest clenched. "I understand," I said, my voice wooden with shock. "You'll get the rest of what I owe you tomorrow."

"No further charge," Sam said, his voice firm.

"But – "

"No," he snapped. "No charge. And if Mia needs our help going forward there'll be no charge for that too." I closed my eyes slowly. Bloody hell, what was in that file?

"Thanks, man," I said to my feet before I disconnected the call and let the phone drop to my side. When I looked up the small blonde was right in front of me with her arms crossed over her chest. The older couple were hovering a few feet away, looking very uncomfortable and staring around at the vast hallway and glass roof in awe.

"Mum, Dad," the blonde woman snapped. "Stop standing there like a pair of scared mice and looking around as if we're in Buckingham Palace. Any monkey with a few bob can buy a house like this. He –"

"He designed it actually," Teddy chipped in, having come out into the corridor. "Built it from the ground up."

Her eyes flashed but stayed focused on me. "Oh *fancy*, Mr Dream Homes. Well I don't give two shits what you designed. All I want to know is where my bloody sister is, you arse. And if you've hurt her – "

"I would *never* hurt her."

"The last time I spoke to my sister she could barely talk and she sounded like absolute crap," the blonde snapped back at me.

"When was that?" I asked.

"Four months ago."

"Oh, well that was when she was in the hospital so – "

I didn't get the chance to complete my sentence. At the mention of hospital, all hell broke loose in the corridor. The older gentleman who had *seemed* fairly mild mannered, suddenly launched himself at me and shoved me hard in the centre of my chest. I had a good few kilos on him, but the surprise of it did cause me to stumble back a couple of steps.

"What the–?"

"How *dare* you hurt my daughter!" the man shouted, his face twisted with rage. "She's been through enough!" He made another lunge towards me, but the blonde girl and the older woman both moved to hold him back, and Teddy moved to block his path, flanked by Roger who was growling. The older man struggled for a moment then seemed to come back to himself. The anger drained out of his expression leaving deep sadness. "She's been through enough," he repeated on a broken whisper as his body sagged forward.

"Dad, calm down," the blonde said in a worried tone. "You know your heart isn't up to this kind of upset."

"My dad would never hurt anyone," Teddy told them, bristling with indignation. I blinked. Teddy hadn't called me *Dad* in over a year. "He looks after people. It's just what he does. He looked after Mum when she let him, he looks after me, he took in Roger and now he looks after Mia as well. He wouldn't hurt a fly."

"Mia?" The blonde frowned as she took in the massive, ugly, scarred dog and scruffy teenager.

"I think maybe we should all calm down," the older woman said, her soft voice a sharp contrast to the animosity in the atmosphere. She turned to Yaz, who she must have thought looked the most reasonable human at that moment (which was saying something as Yaz had her most slouchy surfer chick outfit on – a distressed peace sign t-shirt paired with frayed cut offs, flip flops, multiple shell necklaces and her hair was piled up on top of her head complete with a couple of braids threaded with bright colours). "Do you have any tea, dear?"

Chapter 33

Nobody is going to hurt her

MAX

A couple of character references later (to be honest the one that seemed to hold the most weight was from Roger, who, since the perceived threat to my person had not left my side), and the Suttons had calmed down enough to sit around the kitchen table with a cup of tea. Stiff, awkward introductions were made, and Marnie (Mia's sister), Sid (her dad) and Ann (her mum) started to explain why they'd barged into my house.

"We've been through so much with Mimi," Ann said in her quiet voice. When I made eye contact with her I almost flinched at her haunted expression. "And it's not the first time we've been followed. To learn that *another* man was pulling the same trick was ... upsetting."

"I'm so sorry," I told her, wishing I'd known what I was getting myself into when I set up the account with Sam. "I didn't mean to invade your privacy. I just really needed to ..." I sighed and looked up to the ceiling for a moment, searching for the right words. I didn't want to come across as just another controlling arsehole. "I care about your daughter. When she came to work for me she was ..." I broke off again and glanced at their drawn, worried faces. The last thing I wanted to do was upset them more, but they needed to hear the truth. "Listen, I'm sorry to tell you this, but she was in a right state. I didn't know it at the time, but she was still recovering from some pretty severe injuries."

Ann's hand closed over her husband's, and Marnie's eyes filled with tears.

"She was underweight, had dyed her hair nearly black. To be honest she looked like a teenager and ..." I swallowed and one of my hands went up to the back of my neck, "I made some stupid assumptions because she ... well let's just say I was wrong. I don't want to upset you more than you already have been, but she was sleeping rough for a while. We didn't realise until she came down with pneumonia and had to go into hospital." Marnie was openly crying now. Ann was gripping Sid's hand so tightly that her knuckles were white. "After that, Mia and I, we ... we became closer and I–"

"Dad looked after her," Teddy cut in, obviously still smarting from the perceived insult to me. "She was really sick and he looked after her. Even when I was behaving like a spoilt brat and didn't want anyone else staying with us because I'm selfish."

"Okay, Teddy," I said gently. "You can stand down, big man." I patted him on the shoulder to soften my words. He gave a huff but sat back into his chair. "She stayed with me for a short while but then moved in with Yaz."

Yaz cut in. "Over the last few months she's been getting better. She's put on weight. She smiles now."

I heard a small noise from Ann and noticed a tear was now rolling down her cheek. "She used to smile all the time as a child. I haven't seen a real smile on her face in over eight years."

Yaz reached across the table and put her hand over Ann's

free one. "She's having counselling as well. Honestly, she's not all the way there yet, but things are getting better."

"Why didn't she come to *us?*" asked Sid in a choked voice. "We would have looked after her. She didn't have to sleep on the streets." His voice broke at the end as if even the idea of Mia homeless caused him physical pain.

"Look, I don't know everything, but I do know that she felt she *couldn't* go to you," I told him in a low voice. "Banks would have found her. And for some reason she doesn't think she can go to the police either. But I know she cares about you, misses you."

"But why couldn't she go to the police?" asked Sid. "If he hurt her badly then ... I know they haven't helped in the past and I know he's a powerful man, but why didn't she go this time?'

"There's something she won't tell me," I said. "Some reason she didn't think she could go to the police. It stopped her going after she was attacked. She left the emergency department without being formally discharged. Gave a false name. She won't tell me why." I let out a frustrated breath. "She wouldn't tell me specifics of her background and identity either and I just ..." I rubbed both my hands down my face, wanting to explain myself without coming across as too full on. "I wanted to make sure she was safe. That's all. That's why I sent the investigator. I promise I wasn't trying to control her. Not like that. But I'm not sorry I did it. Not now, after I haven't seen or heard from her for two days. I'd be completely at square one if I hadn't acted earlier and gone behind her back."

"Y-you mean she's not here?" Marnie said, looking confused. "I thought she was living down here in this area now?'

"She's still living with me," Yaz said. "But she left the day before yesterday. She said ... she said she was going to reconnect with her family."

"It's not like her to just go off and not give us any notice at work," I put in. "She's never taken any time off. Even when she had pneumonia we only managed to keep her away for a couple of weeks. You should know she's transformed the IT system at my company. We'd be sunk without her."

"And I'd be failing my computer studies A level without her," Teddy muttered.

"She always was a computer whizz," Ann said through a watery smile. "Part of the reason he wanted to control her. She made him millions, that ungrateful bastard."

"How did she make him millions?" Yaz asked.

"She developed new programmes for that online estate agency of his. Coded everything. Made it efficient. Made it the most innovative one on the market. Of course he claimed all the credit. She was always just in the background."

"He won't have wanted to give that up, will he?" Yaz said into the silence that followed. "I mean, he doesn't sound like the kind of man to just let her go."

"And if she's not with you, then where is she?" I asked.

"He's got to her," Marnie whispered. "It happened before. She came to stay with me two years ago. I was angry with her because she'd been ghosting me whilst going off to all these fancy parties in London, but I'd known as soon as she arrived on my doorstep that something was wrong. She told me she couldn't stay with Nate anymore. That she'd made a mistake. I heard her crying in my spare room for hours every night. Then, a week into her stay she was gone. Just packed up and left one day without even leaving a note. When I went to their huge house in Putney – I fucking hate that place – I had to argue my way through their security system. Massive gates, state-of-the-art alarm system, security guards on the street. Eventually I managed to see her. She barely looked at me. Told me to go away and that everything was *fine*. Snapped at me, told me I was interfering. That she didn't need my help. Told me to go back to my 'small, sad life' and leave her alone. I'd just had a new baby at the time and we'd been struggling financially with me being off on maternity leave. What she said *hurt* me. So I left. I just left her there. I didn't even ..." Marnie broke off as fresh tears rolled down her cheeks and she choked out a sob. Yaz moved from her seat to go to her and put an arm around her shoulder.

"Shit," I muttered at the table. "So, she's probably with him."

"Well, we just need to go and get her back again," Teddy said with misplaced teenage bravado.

Marnie shook her head. "You won't be able to just waltz into Nate's house *or* his company. They're both like Fort Knox. He's kept us from her for the last three years and we're her family."

"We're her family now too," Teddy said, puffing his chest up with more of that teenage overconfidence.

"What do you–?" Sid started to say, but I cut him off.

"You should know – Nathanial Banks is an investor in three of the largest projects my firm has taken on in the last six months. I had no idea who he was to Mia when I made those deals, but I suspect he's been deliberately targeting our company for a while. He's not someone I should make an enemy out of. But sir, I'm in love with your daughter." All eyes swung to me. Mia's family wore shocked expressions. Yaz and Teddy looked unsurprised by this information. "No billionaire psychopath is going to keep her from me, and nobody is going to hurt her. Not any more." I pushed back from the table, pulled my phone out of my pocket and dialled the last number in recent calls.

"Clifton," Sam's voice sounded in my ear.

Chapter 34

I keep what's mine

MAX

"No, I don't have an appointment," I said through gritted teeth to the lady at reception. If I was honest, I could understand her hesitation – I hadn't shaved in a day or so and I was in jeans and a ribbed thermal (quite the opposite of the slick business attire of everyone else in Nate's building). But I wasn't giving up. Not until I saw him. "But I'm the main architect on a number of projects this company is funding. I've been here before. It's urgent I see him today."

"I'm sorry, sir, but I ... sir! You can't just go through there. He's in a meeting. Sir!"

I strode past the reception desk. I'd been waiting for two fucking days and I couldn't just stand around in some swanky office with only a couple of doors separating me from that dickhead. After making my way through a glass door then down a corridor I pushed open a set of double doors into the large room. A bunch of suits were sitting around the long table. The bald chap who'd been midsentence as I pushed open the door broke off when I slammed into the room and rounded the table in a few long strides.

"Mr Hardcastle," Nathanial Banks' smooth, unaffected voice said into the silence. "Always a pleasure, but we are in the middle of a fairly–" I slammed my hand down on the table in front of him and even *his* next-level urban sophistication slipped enough for him to flinch.

"Where is she?" I growled.

He pushed away from the table and stood up with the chair between us. Not so brave with someone more his size it seemed.

"I don't know what you're –"

'Your *wife*," I said, pushing the chair out of the way with a flick of my wrist. There was another crack in Banks' smooth exterior when he flinched again as it shot back on its wheels and slammed against the wall. "Where is *Mia*?"

Banks took a step back and let out a small laugh.

"Now, see here, young man," one of the old duffers Nate had been talking to stood up and scowled across at me. "We're in an important meeting. I don't think this behaviour has any place among civilised–"

"It's okay, Jeff," Banks said, giving the man a smooth, unruffled smile then turning back to me. "*Amelia,* my *wife,* is at home and she's perfectly fine. Now if I could ask you to –"

"Was she *perfectly fine* when you beat her so badly that you broke several of her ribs?" I asked, eliciting a few sharp intakes of air from around table. Jeff's annoyed expression morphed to shock and he sat back down heavily into his chair. "Or when you yanked her around so hard that you dislocated her shoulder?" Banks' face flushed red with anger and his hands curled into fists at his side.

"Ladies and gentleman," he said, his unruffled manner sounding forced now. "This is, of course, all a misunderstanding, but for the moment I think it best we end the meeting there. Molly at reception will be happy to reschedule." There was some shuffling of papers and stowing of laptops before everyone filed out through the double doors. Low murmurs were exchanged and some frowning looks directed at Banks, but they left without confronting either of us – a mark of Banks' power and a reminder of how impossible Mia's situation had been.

"Tell me where she is and I won't smash your annoying face in – at least not today."

Banks' colour had receded and his expression was back to the carefully blank one from earlier. A subtle twitch in his left eyelid was the only evidence that he was at all affected. He cleared his throat.

"Why don't you take a seat?" he said. Moving to the opposite side of the table from me to sit down, and then gesturing for me to do the same. I squeezed the back of the chair in front of me until my knuckles turned white as I stared at him.

"I don't want to take a fucking seat," I said, my voice still coming out with an undercurrent of growl. "I want to see Mia."

Banks leaned forward in his chair, resting his forearms on the conference table and linking his hands together as if we were engaged in some sort of goddamn business negotiation.

"You can bark orders as much as you like, Mr Hardcastle," he told me smoothly. "But if anyone has the advantage here, it's me. I hold the fate of your company in the palm of my hand. For you to come storming into my place of business like a bull in china shop is the height of stupidity. I can't think that you would–"

"You didn't think I would challenge it, did you?" I asked, my eyebrows going up in shock. "You didn't think that I'd come after her, not when I found out who she was married to. You thought I'd just let her go."

Banks stared at me, his expression stayed the same but there was a subtle flare behind his eyes that told me I'd hit the nail on the head. There was no way he thought I confront him like this.

"I'll admit you have ... surprised me. Not many people surprise me, Mr Hardcastle."

I snorted. "You mean most of the people you know are amoral wankers like you."

He shrugged. "In my experience it is unusual for a man to risk his business, for any reason."

"All I want is Mia. My business will survive losing your poxy contracts. With the amount of corners you want to cut, I doubt I'd want my name put to them anyway."

He shrugged, but a small smile played across his mouth. "You can bluff all you like, Max, but if you could afford to walk away, you would have done it by now. I know exactly how close to the edge most architecture firms are financially. Even you, with your *Dream Homes* reruns bolstering business every few months, your awards and your Royal endorsements. Even *you* feel the pinch. Losing my business would be catastrophic for you."

"I don't care about–"

"And, let me ask you this: do you really *know* the woman you're risking it all for? Do you know what *poor, defenceless* Mia is capable of?"

"Whatever you–"

"Would you like me to show you?" A horrible smile spread across his face as he unbuttoned his suit jacket and lifted his shirt, revealing a long scar, which traversed from his chest down to his stomach. With another short wound next to it.

Suddenly all of Mia's worries made sense. *You don't know what I've done*, she'd whispered.

"She left me for dead," he said through a smile. "Did you

know she was capable of that? Of leaving a man to bleed to death?"

I looked up from his scars and narrowed my eyes at him. "I know the results of what *you* did that day. She still can't use her right arm properly. You beat her to a bloody pulp. You're twice her size. If I had been her, I wouldn't have stopped stabbing you until I could see the life leave your eyes for myself. If you think this will stop her pressing charges you're wrong. Once the police see all the evidence you'll be completely fucked. Do you think a jury is going to convict a woman for giving you a little scrape on your side –"

"It's hardly 'a little scrape'," he spluttered, his composure slipping. "That bitch stabbed me. Twice!"

"You nearly killed her!" I said, my voice rising. Banks flicked a wary glance towards the door.

"Can you please keep your voice –"

"Anybody looking between you and Mia, with the knowledge that you beat her badly enough to break three ribs and fracture-dislocate her shoulder, is not going to hesitate to convict you. No matter what she did in self defence."

The corner of his left eye twitched again, before he pushed back from the table and stood up.

"Whether or not a jury would convict me is a non-issue," he said, his hand pushing up his shirtsleeve so he could check his expensive watch. "*I* won't be going to court as *Amelia* won't be going to the police. And if you've got any sense you'll lose interest in the situation." He placed both hands on the table and leaned forward towards me, his eyes locked with mine and lit with a fierce determination. "Forget about her, Max. Don't throw away everything you've built for a woman that doesn't even want you anymore – for someone who would walk away from you at the slightest provocation. Don't go down that rabbit hole – believe me, I know how badly it can end."

I stood up and opened my mouth to speak, but the door to the conference room opened. Two large security guards made their way inside, flanked me and looked towards Banks for further instructions.

"Gentlemen," Banks said, smooth as silk. "Mr Hardcastle and I have concluded our business for today. If you could show him the way out of the building I would appreciate it."

One of the men reached for my arm but I threw him a murderous look and he dropped his hand.

"This isn't over," I snapped across the table at Banks. "You can't keep her from me forever."

"On the contrary, Mr Hardcastle, I've found in my life that I can largely do what I want ... and I keep what's mine."

Chapter 35

Did he just throw her?

MIA

"My mother's been ill," I said by rote, for what felt like the hundredth time. "I've been spending some time with her, but she's getting better now. It's so nice to be out with Nate again. I've felt like a bit of a hermit over the last few months." The death grip Nate had on my elbow eased somewhat as I repeated the excuse I'd been coached to say again. There would be bruises on my arm by the time the night was over.

"Oh really?" Adrian asked, his assessing eyes flicking from Nate to me and I stiffened. "That's odd. I could have sworn I saw you out and about in London a few weeks ago. You had a sort of emo look going on if I remember correctly."

Nate let out a forced laugh. "Emo look? Adie, you crazy bastard. With Amelia's penchant for designer labels I doubt she'd ever go *emo* on me."

The other people in the circle we were standing in were looking between the three of us with curious expressions. Nate's grip tightened again and I had to work hard not to flinch.

I lowered my hands as much as possible so I could start tapping on my wrist to ease my anxiety.

"Hmm, my mistake then," Adrian muttered. "So you're back at work are you, *Amelia*?" He stressed my name and I managed to maintain my fixed smile with some effort.

"Still taking some time off," I said through the gritted teeth of my smile. Real pain was now spreading out from my elbow under Nate's too-hard grip.

"Well, you look fantastic," Adrian's wife put in, in an obvious effort to ease the bizarre tension. "Sorry about your mum though."

"She's doing much better, thanks," I said softly, hating all the lies Nate was making me spew. "And I love your dress, Sophie."

"Ugh, this old thing? I look like a overripe blueberry."

"Now, see here," Adrian cut in. "I think you look smashing, darling."

"Oh put a sock in it, Adie," she replied, rolling her eyes at him. I always liked the way she stood up for herself with him. "What you know about fashion would fit on a postage stamp. Mine's nothing compared to Mia's. Is that a Stella McCartney, Mia?"

"Er ... I ..." I gave a helpless shrug. "I'm not sure to be honest. Nate took care of it."

Nate had *taken care* of everything. He'd had a whole rack of dresses sent in, a hair stylist, make-up artist, beautician. I'd been buffed and polished to within an inch of my life, and then forced into this uncompromising sheath of a dress which fit me like a glove from my neck to the floor – a wide slit up the side and a low back the only skin it revealed, and that skin was perfectly tanned and shimmered. The dress itself was off-white with a rim of gold around the edges. My hair had gold combs holding back the sides and was also now back to the lighter blonde tones that Nate preferred. I was back to perfect and I hated it. The urge to rip out the combs, scrub off the make-up and tear off the stupid dress was almost unbearable. All I wanted to do was unperfect this version of myself. Because unperfected Mia was happy. Unperfected Mia smiled real smiles, she laughed, she wasn't terrified all the time.

"Oh God, he really spoils you, doesn't he?" Sophie gushed. I kept my smile in place and gave her a short nod. Spoiling wasn't quite the term I'd go for. Manipulated, controlled and terrorised were much more fitting. I hated this formal get-up and the palaver involved. I hated the fact that I'd been standing on these four-inch heels for the last three hours making forced small talk with these people. I'd much rather be lounging in a booth at the Pig and Whistle, arguing about whether watching *Love Island* made you a div or not. I'd prefer to be served by grumpy, craggy old Fergus than the immaculate waitresses that swept away my empty glass and replaced it with a full one with me barely even noticing. It was sterile, fake and stressful, but at the same time unbelievably boring.

But this was the deal I'd struck with Nate. I would come to these things with him. Show my face to everyone. He'd promised me that after a couple of months *he'd* dump *me*. Publicly, so that it would look like he'd been the one to walk away. He'd keep his pride and I'd get my freedom. Given the evidence he had against me (he'd made damn sure to document the stab wounds – I'd been shown the photo evidence and the hospital report. Despite the urging of the police he hadn't reported me ... yet) and the hold he had over Max's company, leave alone the threats he'd made against my family, I didn't have much choice.

All evening I'd been stared at and admired by Nate's competitors, envied by their wives and girlfriends. Like some sort of trophy, he'd paraded me around the charity function. I'd been too nervous to eat any of the canapés circulating, and besides, a white dress plus finger food was too risky. Nate wanted perfection and I knew better than to give him anything less. But I'd barely slept the last two days and I was bloody starving. If we didn't leave soon I'd collapse in a heap at his Italian leather shoes and really bugger everything up.

"Excuse me," I said to the crowd around us. "Just nipping to the bathroom. Nate, darling, do you mind?" I held out my champagne glass to him and he reluctantly released my elbow to take it. Flashing everyone what I hoped was a genuine looking smile, I turned around and made my way through the crowd. Once I was far enough away I let out a long breath, put my hand to the back of my neck and flexed it to get out the crick that had settled there with how tense I was. I needed one of Yaz's massages. Just as the crowd was thinning, my heel caught on the back of my dress and I stumbled forward. A pair of strong arms caught me before I could go down and a familiar, clean, masculine scent engulfed me.

"Max," I breathed as my eyes flew from my shoes to his face. Relief fierce and strong was the first thing I registered. He was here. Somehow my Max was here, like a bright candle in the darkness. I smiled and my hand went up to touch his face, but then I remembered where I was. I remembered who I was. And I remembered that, in *my* life, nothing was ever this easy. My smile fell and I pulled away from him. He was supporting me under my lower arms and for a moment he kept me in his hold. It caused pain to shoot through my bruised elbow and I winced. He frowned and then gently, as if I was made of finest bone china, he tilted my arm around to look at the finger mark bruising I knew was there. His expression darkened to one of absolute fury.

"Jesus Christ," he snapped. "What has he done to you?"

I pulled back, and this time he let me go immediately, likely worried he might hurt me again.

"Max, you can't be here," I whispered urgently, glancing behind me to check Nate wasn't on my tail – he'd been known to follow me to the ladies room when he was feeling particularly suspicious and stalkery.

"What's going on Mia?" Max's eyes travelled from my perfectly styled hair to my strappy gold high heels. "You look … I-I've been searching the crowd for you for the last hour. Your hair it's so … I–"

I'd never known Max lost for words. But then he'd never met *this* Amelia. The cool, controlled, perfectly groomed, untouchable Amelia. I'd managed to thoroughly unperfect myself by the time he'd met me at that interview so many months ago. He looked like he barely recognised me now.

"Listen, love," he said, moving into my space and cupping my face with his big hand. I desperately wanted to lean into his touch, but forced myself to resist the impulse. "Come with me now. I've got a car outside. We can be back home in a couple of hours." I took another step back from him and blanked my expression.

"Max, you have to leave. You can't be here. How did you even get in?" This was a high profile function – Prime Minister-in-attendance high profile. The security was unreal.

"I couldn't get to you any other way," he said, moving a step towards me. I took a corresponding one back and he frowned. "Listen, your family's waiting to see you, Mia. They've been so worried. We've all been so worried. Just come with me and everything will be okay, I *promise*."

I closed my eyes as my heart made its way up into my throat. All I wanted was to collapse into Max and have him carry me out of here. Of course he'd found my family. Of course he wanted to give them back to me. Max would always put my needs first – he'd bend over backwards to give me what I wanted. The contrast between someone as loving, generous and kind as Max, and a narcissist like Nate was stark. But I'd made my bed when I chose Nate over my family all those years ago, and again when I did what I did a few months ago. There were consequences to actions, and these were mine. Besides, only a little longer of this then I'd be free. At least that was what Nate had promised, and he wasn't the only one who'd kept evidence. I also had an extensive catalogue of the results of his abuse which the domestic violence team had helped me compile, and it had come in very useful in my negotiation with Nate. If he touched me, if anything happened to me all of that evidence would go to the press. We were effectively in a stalemate, both of us having the ability to destroy the other. It was exhausting.

"I'm fine," I said, forcing any emotion out of my voice – *this* Amelia, Nate's Amelia couldn't afford it. "You need to leave me alone. This is a big night for Nate."

"Fuck Nate," Max growled, attracting some attention from the people around us who were shooting us curious looks.

"I'm his wife, Max," I said, my voice cold as ice. I had to make Max believe that I wanted to be here, to make him hate me – it was the only way I knew he'd leave. "I made a commitment to him and he gives me …" I glanced away and then swallowed, "he gives me what I need."

"He stopped being your *anything* when he dislocated your fucking shoulder, Mia," Max's raised voice was really concerning me now. Most of the people around us had paused their conversations to listen.

"I don't know what you're talking about," I said in a tight voice that I kept carefully lowered. I shot a polite smile to some of the onlookers to try and make them lose interest.

"Mia, love," he said, his voice dropping now and his hand

coming up to hold mine. It was stupid but the feel of his large, warm hand around my smaller frozen one was so blissful that I didn't have it in me to stop him. "You don't have to do this. Whatever he's threatened you with, whatever you've done or you think he can do to me – none of it matters. All that matters is that you're safe and away from him." I allowed myself a moment to bask in the intensity of his green gaze, knowing that he wasn't going to let me go, not unless I really hurt him – like I'd hurt my family, like I'd hurt my friends in the past. I wrenched my hand from his and blanked my expression.

"Do you really think that I want to come back to the arse-end of nowhereville and work at your pathetic little company?" I asked him, my lip curling and my voice full of sneering conde-scension. "Going to the local pub, putting up with your shitty kid who's not even yours, tolerating your pathetically aimless little sister and living in her tiny hovel of a flat. Do you think I'd really give up all *this* for that? Get over yourself." Max blinked. He opened his mouth to speak then snapped it shut. I watched as his green eyes flashed with anger and two slashes of red appeared high on his cheekbones. I'd deliberately struck at him in a way that would hurt the most, using the same reasons as Rebecca for leaving him – and it worked.

"Have it your way," he said, his voice now devoid of all emotion. "I hope you like your fancy clothes and lifestyle," he looked me up and down and this time his expression was less awestruck and more disgusted, "God knows you've paid enough for them." He turned and walked away. Within moments he was swallowed by the crowd. I felt my eyes start to sting but swallowed down the emotion. Nate would go nuts if I ruined my make up and embarrassed him. But for a full minute I was just frozen in place, unable to move.

"Amelia." I stiffened at Nate's voice, the annoyed edge to it putting me on high alert. Right on cue I felt his grip on my bruised elbow again and flinched at the pain. "Will you stop that goddamn tic you've picked up." He manoeuvred us so that he was standing in front of me, still holding my bruised elbow in one hand and using the other to enclose my other wrist and pull my hands apart.

"W-what?" I asked, looking down at his fingers around my wrist and feeling disorientated and a little fuzzy. No food and an emotion-filled few minutes were catching up with me.

"That thing you do with your hands. It's driving me nuts and it makes you look like a mental patient."

I hadn't even realised I'd been tapping again. Over the last few days Nate had made his feelings about my coping mechanisms and how much they annoyed him very clear.

"Right, yes sorry," I muttered as my eyes slid to the direction I'd just seen Max disappear in. Nate gave me a small shake and my gaze snapped back to his furious expression. "I'm warning you, Amelia. Put some effort in tonight or our deal is off and I'll hang you and your boyfriend out to dry."

"I'm doing my best," I said through my teeth then pulled on both my arms, tugging them out of his grip. "And stop hurting me. You promised – no violence. You know what will happen if you go back on that."

He rolled his eyes. "I've barely touched you. Rein in the drama, Amelia, and keep your fucking voice down," he hissed.

"When can we leave?" I asked, not bothering to argue with him or point out the bruises he'd already inflicted. The rules were that I would come out to public appearances with him, but he wasn't allowed to hurt me or in fact come anywhere near me when we were alone. I hated his prison of a house in Putney, but at least it was large enough for me to stay out of his way, and so far he'd stuck to his side of the bargain. But I had a bad feeling tonight. I didn't like the high colour in his cheeks or the slightly maniacal gleam in his eyes. Plus he'd been drinking and that always made things worse.

"Hello there." The band had stopped playing and a voice came over the sound system. Nate and I turned to the stage and saw the Prime Minister, Barclay Lucas was at the microphone. "I'm sorry to interrupt tonight but I have an announcement to make at the bequest of her Majesty the Queen." The room fell silent and all eyes turned to the stage. This was the biggest industry, political event of the year. As well as the Prime Minister, the Duke of Cambridge was also in attendance. It was typically the event at which the winners of the Queen's Awards for Enterprise would be announced. Nate hand shot around my waist and he clamped me into his side. When I looked up at his face I saw his eyes were shining with anticipation and a small smile was playing on his lips.

No. He couldn't have?

"The first category is one close to my heart as you all know and that is the Award for Sustainable Development. The winner of this award is making zero carbon homes the norm and allowing eco-homes to be the future, not just for the chosen few in society that can afford them – but for all."

A ringing had started in my ears as I realised what was about to happen.

"I'm pleased to announce Nathanial Banks as the winner. Nate, would you please make your way up here."

Of course, Nate would be on first name terms with the bloody Prime Minister – his power and influence were spreading everywhere like a cancer. I pulled away from him to allow him to go up on his own, but he grabbed my hand and towed me along behind him. Before I knew it we were up on stage, he'd shaken hands with Barclay Lucas, and was making a speech into the microphone. I was frozen in place beside him, staring out at the crowd. A crowd that was honouring this man.

Honouring this hideous excuse for a human being. And I was standing there encouraging it, complicit with it. Nausea welled in my stomach and I could feel acid work its way to my mouth.

I knew for a fact that he was involved in elaborate tax avoidance schemes. That he was trying to cut as many corners as possible with the building of his ecohomes and hotels. That he squashed complaints from buyers with ruthless efficiency. That he didn't care about the environment – he only cared about lining his pocket. That it was only because of Max's tenacity that the houses might stay true to the designs he made for them.

"... and, finally, I'd like to thank my wife, Amelia. Without her support none of this could have been possible." I looked up at him. He was smiling down at me – smug, blissfully happy with his victory, totally self-assured. My lips pressed together in a flat line as I made my decision. His smile faded a little and a small frown formed on his forehead. Before he could stop me I grabbed the microphone.

"No," I said into it in a clear, firm voice. "Just *no*. Not this man. Not today." Nate snatched the microphone back and let out a forced laugh.

"See how funny she is," he said into the shocked silence of the hall. "Always ready with a joke."

"Prime Minister," I said, leaning into the mic to make myself heard. "You're making a mistake." Nate made a grab for the microphone, grappling with me for a few moments before he enclosed both my upper arms in his large hands and literally threw me backwards across the stage. I could feel my shoulder joint protesting on my weak side as I flew through the air and a collective shocked gasp came from the audience. Hands at my waist caught me to stop me falling to the ground and I glanced behind me to see Barclay wearing a confused expression as he stared across at Nate. His bemused eyes came to my face and I mouthed "Sorry", before launching away from him towards the steps from the stage.

Without looking back, and trying to ignore Nate wrapping up his acceptance whilst making excuses for my 'crazy sense of humour', I zigzagged through the people towards the exit. A low murmur was spreading through the crowd. I caught snatches of conversation as I hurried past. Things like 'Did he just *throw* her?' and "What was that?' and 'Did she look scared to you?'. A couple of people caught my eye and some tried to speak to me, but I broke into a light jog until I made it out through the double doors and into the empty corridor.

Chapter 36

Throat, eyes, balls

MAX

"Dad, what the fuck are you doing?" Teddy snapped as I walked towards them. My ears were still ringing with Mia's words. Yaz, Teddy, Heath and Verity rushed forward.

"Where is she?" Yaz asked, frowning up at me. "Why haven't you brought her out?"

"She didn't want to come with us, Yaz," I said, my voice tight with anger. "She's made her choice and it wasn't us."

"Ugh!" Yaz shouted, surprising me with a punch to my arm, her fist was small and sharp and, just like when we were kids, surprisingly effective. "You are such a total knobhead! She doesn't have a choice. Are you blind?"

"She wants what he can give her," I told her. "Limos and houses with security guards. You didn't see her in there. She didn't even look like our Mia.'

"Of course she's still our Mia," said a furious Teddy. "Have you completely lost it? You need to go back in there and get her."

"She said she couldn't be bothered with 'my shitty kid who's not really my kid', Teddy," I replied, then turned to Yaz. "She basically called you a loser and your flat a tiny hovel. She doesn't care about us."

"For fuck's sake she didn't mean any of that, you stupid sod," Yaz shouted. "And I *am* a loser. Who cares? You were supposed to take her away from that abusive arsehole. Tell me something, Max, was she tapping in there? When you watched her before you approached did she seem happy and relaxed? Or was she wearing a fake smile and *tapping*? Things you know very well she only does if she's distressed."

"But ..." An image of Mia standing next to Nate flashed into my brain. Perfect, beautiful, untouchable in that long white dress but, yes, she was tapping two of her fingers on her other wrist, there may have been a smile on her face, but it looked fixed and it didn't reach her eyes. Another image of her upper arm covered in finger mark bruises intruded and I felt my heart clench in my chest. "Shit," I muttered.

"She's not Rebecca, Max," Yaz said and I closed my eyes, letting out my breath in a short exhale. "She loves you. You know she does. She doesn't care about any of this other stuff."

Yaz was right. I'd let Rebecca's rejection colour how I viewed Mia's. It was as though Mia telling me I wasn't good enough had propelled me back to the bad place I'd been in when Rebecca left me – brought back all of that insecurity. Then I remembered what Marnie had told me, about how Mia had said the most hurtful things she could to her sister, just to make sure she left. To make sure she stayed safe. Christ, I was an idiot.

"We've got to get over her leaving us, Dad," Teddy put in. He was staring at me now with a steady gaze. "I can't go around being a tosser and trying to push everyone who actually cares about me away anymore, and neither can you. We've got to get our shit together."

I put a hand on his shoulder, gave him a shake and then a slap on the back as I nodded.

"Bloody hell, look at this!" Yaz cried as she passed me her phone.

"Yaz, for Christ's sake I'm not sure now is the time to–"

"Watch it!" she snapped.

"Oh my God," Teddy breathed out as he stared at her phone. I snatched it from her and frowned in confusion at what was playing on the screen. Nate was on stage with Mia and the bloody Prime Minister. He was accepting an award then thanking Mia. I stiffened as I watched what unfolded next. Mia saying "No' into the microphone, Mia being wrenched backwards by her bad arm by that arsehole and literally *thrown* to one side before running off the stage.

"When was this filmed?" I demanded, tearing my eyes off the screen to look up at the exit from the building.

"Just now. It's a video of the event online from just now that's going viral."

I shoved the phone back at Yaz and took a step towards the road which separated us from the event venue. Cars were streaming in both directions. I was about to launch myself into the middle of the road and stop traffic when the double doors were flung open on the building opposite and Mia shot out down the stone steps.

"Mia!" I shouted and she paused mid step to look up. When she caught sight of me her face melted into relief and her hand went up to the centre of her chest. I moved forward, waving my arms to stop the oncoming car, which screeched to a halt in front of me. When I was in the middle of the road, a large limousine pulled up in front of Mia. She glanced down at it and frowned, taking a step backwards just as Banks appeared out of the building behind her. I managed to stop the cars again and ran across the road. But by the time I reached the pavement, Banks had got Mia. He grabbed a fistful of her hair at the back of her head, wrenched open the door of the limousine, and threw her in. I made it to the passenger door of the limo just as it was pulling away. The windows were tinted and I couldn't see inside. I slammed my hand against the glass but it glided out into traffic and away from the curb.

"Fuck!" I shouted, both my hands going to the back of my neck as I bent forward at the waist. "Fucking hell!"

"Quick," Yaz cried, grabbing my arm. "Come on. This way." She was dragging me back towards the building

"Yaz, what are you doing? I've got to go after her. We've got to call the police."

"Did you see the look on that dude's face?" asked Teddy. His face was pale and for the first time in ages he looked like the little boy I used to know.

"She'll be fine, Ted," I told him, pulling back from Yaz to flag down a cab.

"She will if you *listen* to me," Yaz said. "We won't catch up to them if we travel normally. We need to cut through the traffic.'

"And how do you suppose we do that?" I asked, trying to shake her off my arm.

"With them," she told me, pointing at the four police motorbikes surrounding the Prime Minister's car.

～

MIA

"How dare you embarrass me like that?" I heard Nate's ice-cold voice as if it was coming at me down a dark tunnel. My vision started to narrow, and small dots danced in front of my eyes as I clawed at his hands which were wrapped around my throat. The soundproof partition was up between us and the driver so even if I could have called out for help it would have been useless. "You're my wife. I gave you everything," he hissed, "Did you think you'd be able to walk away again? That I'd *ever* let that happen?"

I realised then that deep down I had known he wouldn't have ever let me go. That our agreement had been a fantasy. I think I'd always known that someday it would come to this. In public, Nate kept a handle on his violence most of the time, but it was always lurking there, under the surface. Being urbane, sophisticated, and charming served him well in his rampant pursuit of power. Having me on his arm fitted into that as well. He might control me, hurt me, beat me down, but he wouldn't normally do anything to jeopardise his handle on power. However, I always knew that if I pushed him far enough he had the potential to shed all that urbane sophistication and go fully murderous on me. Just as he was finally doing now.

His hands tightened around my throat, and I felt my vision start to fade. At least now it would be over. No more nightmares. No more hiding. I would be at peace. But, just as I let that acceptance wash over me and felt my hands, which had been clawing at Nate's, start to go weak, I had flashbacks of a different kind:

Yaz, testing her reflexology out on me – telling me that she was cleansing my kidney as she put pressure on my insole then rolling her eyes when I burst out laughing (my feet were always ticklish).

Teddy's eyes, shining with happiness last week after he'd received his acceptance to Cambridge for computer sciences – sweeping me up in a tight hug and swinging me round, whilst telling me how he would never have been able to answer the interview questions without me practising with him.

Verity, picking up my peanut butter sandwich with the tips of her fingers like it was contaminated with toxic sludge, binning it and then dumping a latte and a fancy patisserie roll in front of me.

Heath, lecturing me about my physio exercises for my shoulder. Demanding he see the range of movement in the pub every week after rugby. Muzzing my hair on the top of my head with his large hand, and smiling down at me when I regained a few inches of extension with it.

And then Max ... Max lifting me up in his arms when I was ill. Max realising when he was blocking the exits in a room and moving so that I felt more comfortable. Max pulling me into his side gently on the sofa, always checking that I was okay, that I didn't feel enclosed or panicked. Playing with my hair as we watched Stranger Things, hating Love Island but watching it anyway. Cupping my cheek and kissing me – always one light brush of the lips first before searching my face to check it was okay before he deepened the kiss. Max's kindness, his smell, his strength, his loyalty, his humour, his honourable nature, his sense of justice, his genuine love for the environment and his desire to make it better, and the way he cared so deeply about his family, his friends, his dog.

It wasn't so much my *life* flashing before my eyes, it was what made my life worth living *now*. I'd survived. I'd even managed to be happy. The abyss wasn't better than the life I'd built. I wasn't going to go quietly into the night.

If you're pinned and there's no way out, go limp, Teddy's voice filtered into my brain. It went against all my instinct, but I did it. After a moment, the pressure around my neck eased. I was desperate to start gulping in air again but forced myself to resist the urge. The dots inside my eyelids faded away and I felt the strength return to my arms. The car was slowing and for some reason I could hear sirens outside, but I focused on my survival.

Repeat after me, Teddy's voice continued. *Throat, eyes, balls.* I clenched my hand into a fist at my side as Nate's fingers loosened even further. Then I moved. My arm shot up in between his and I throat punched him. As he was choking I brought a knee up and in sharp contact with his groin. Just as he let out an inhuman noise of pain the car ground to a stop. I scrambled to turn around and managed to get the door open.

"You fucking bitch!" Nate choked out as I flung myself out of the car, landing hard on the road surface on my hands and knees. There were blue and white flashing lights everywhere, and multiple headlights blinding me. I blinked into the brightness and pushed up onto my knees, but before I could manage to stand my head was jerked back violently by the hair and I was pulled towards the car.

"Let her go!" My eyes flew to that familiar voice, and I saw Max running towards us. Nate's hand tightened on my hair. I glanced back at him. His eyes were crazed and he was snorting like a cornered bull. My vision was adjusting to the headlights and I could see that they were coming from police motorbikes.

Surrounding us were at least eight police officers, *armed* police officers. And Nate still had my hair in a death grip. There were trained men pointing guns at him and telling him to let me go and he still carried on hurting me.

He was such a dick!

A stupid, self-centred, narcissistic excuse for a human. And I wasn't enduring a second more of him and his bullshit. A policeman had caught up with Max and was trying to hold him back, but a 15 stone, rugby-playing Max was a difficult beast to control. He broke free and started towards us again. I made a decision in that moment. Nate wasn't going to touch *my* Max. He was never going to touch anything I cared about ever again.

I bent my good arm into a tight unit, drew it up and back across my body and then put my full body weight into an elbow strike, right into the centre of Nate's face. I heard his nasal bones crack and he fell back from me, releasing my hair. Then I ran. But I'd forgotten about the fucking heels Nate had made me wear and I tripped after a couple of steps. So of course, of *course* my Max caught me. Just like I knew he would.

Chapter 37

You. Are. Wrong

MIA

"Thank you," I said in a hoarse whisper to Kira bloody Lucas. Because, turns out, apparently Yaz *is* friends with the Prime Minister's wife. All those times we'd taken the piss and she'd been telling the truth. They were such good friends that Yaz could convince Kira to not only commandeer her husband's police escort to chase after me, but also bring the Lucases along for the ride.

And now Kira and Barclay Lucas were standing next to my hospital bed at three in the morning. It was a few hours since I'd escaped from Nate under the glare of the police headlights, and I was still in a state of shock. After I fell into Max's arms, Nate had made another frantic lunge for me but the police had been there to pull him back. When it became clear that I'd been strangled and the driver (a man who was very shaken and clearly not in the mood to cover for his psycho boss) told them what he'd seen, Nate was arrested. I had no idea what happened to him after that as the paramedics arrived and I was hooked up to oxygen and taken to the nearest hospital.

"Don't thank me, you wankpuffin," Kira said. "I've never been in a *real life* car chase before, and we've never been able to get the boys to turn on the flashing lights. That was the most fun I've had at one of those yawnfests for a while."

I blinked at her and without realising it my hand went to my throat to trace the swelling there.

"Ki Ki," Barclay Lucas, the actual Prime bloody Minister said. "I'm not sure that's the most tactful thing to say to Mia. She most likely does *not* think tonight was much fun."

Kira's face flushed red, her eyes went wide and her hand came up to cover her mouth.

"Buggering badgers, I'm so sorry. You must think I'm the most terrible cockwomble." I could actually see why Kira and Yaz were friends – they were both as off-the-wall as each other. "I make jokes when I'm nervous. I didn't mean – "

"It's fine," I forced out, the strain on my vocal cords causing me to wince in pain.

"Mia, love," Max said from my other side, giving my hand a squeeze. "The doctor said to rest your voice. Can you *please* try to do that."

I turned my head to look at him. He was focusing on the bruising around my neck again and his eyes were flashing, that muscle in his jaw ticking with anger. Yaz had reluctantly given me a mirror after the doctors had finished examining my neck and shoulder. I was not a pretty sight. The eye make-up, that had been so perfectly applied earlier in the evening, now gave me the appearance of a drunk panda. The whites of my eyes were bloodshot in the extreme (one of the effects of the strangulation) and dark bruising was blossoming around my neck. The previously pristine white dress was now covered in dirt from the road and a heavy smattering of Nate's blood from when I'd broken his nose.

"I think that's our cue to leave, Ki Ki," Barclay said gently to his wife and she nodded.

"I really didn't mean to be an insensitive wankpuffin," she whispered to me, giving my free hand a squeeze. I smiled at her and squeezed hers back. "I hope you get better in time for the summer solstice," she said. "My mum runs a festival in the New Forest. Yaz told me *ages* ago to count you in. It's properly bonkers. The Ferret's Testicles play every year and we dance naked around the fire pit."

"There you go, Mia," Barclay said in a dry voice, completely unfazed by talk of his wife naked fire dancing in the New Forest. "Something to look forward to." He smiled at me and I thought that the news reports didn't really do this man justice. Up close he was almost as attractive as Max. Almost.

When Kira and Barclay left, Teddy came back in with teas for everyone. He hadn't said much since arriving at the hospital and he looked shaken and pale. I gestured to the laptop next to Max and he handed it over.

I did all the moves you taught me, I typed then turned it around so Teddy could read it. He looked down and bit his lip as he read.

You saved my life, I added below. This time when I looked up I saw his eyes were filled with tears, his chest puffed up in an effort to keep them in.

Thank you.

He gave me a stiff nod and shoved his hands into his pockets, but one of his tears spilled over onto his cheek.

Can I have a hug?

Both cheeks were wet now. He hesitated for a moment, before launching forward to me on the bed and sobbing into my neck as his big arms enclosed my body.

"Ted, mate," Max said, pulling back on his shoulder a little.

"Careful of her neck." Teddy immediately started to draw away, but I shot Max an annoyed look and put my hands up to hold Teddy's face near mine.

"I'm going to be fine," I told him in that broken whisper. "And that's down to you." He nodded and scrubbed his cheeks, holding my eyes for a moment before he drew himself back to standing.

"Will you please *stop* talking," Max ground out and I rolled my eyes, mouthing the word bossy to Teddy and earning a smile which eased some of my worry that he'd been scarred for life by this bad experience.

I took the laptop again.

I'm sorry I didn't believe you about Kira. Thank you for everything tonight, I wrote, and turned it to Yaz. She smiled down at me.

"Everyone always underestimates me," she said.

True that. I typed, then added several exclamation points for good measure. Yaz took my hand and gave it another squeeze.

"You know," Teddy said in a tight voice, interrupting the silence of the room and causing all eyes to swing to him, "Well ... what I want to say is that Dad and I ... we won't let anything like that happen to you again, right? And ... and I think you should move in with *us* now. Auntie Yaz's place is too small, and I think ... well I think you belong with us."

"Of course she'll be staying with us, Ted," Max said. I glanced between the two male faces set in determination, and mouthed 'bossy' again, this time to Yaz, who rolled her eyes and gave me a small smile.

Later, after everyone had left and it was just Max and me, I reached for the laptop again.

Thank you for coming for me, I typed.

He stared at the screen for a moment but instead of replying he turned it towards him and started typing.

I would go anywhere for you. I love you, he typed.

I blinked up at him as exhaustion dragged me under until the room faded to black. He smoothed the hair back from my face and then traced his thumb over my eyebrow and down my cheekbone. There his fingers moved under my ear into my hairline and his thumb continued to stroke my cheek.

"I love you too," I managed to say in hoarse whisper. I felt his lips brush mine.

"If you really love me then you'll stop using your voice," he whispered against my lips and then rested his forehead against mine.

"Bossy," I mouthed without sound and registered his low chuckle.

Then with the comfort of his smell surrounding me, and his light, rhythmic touch, even after all that had happened, even after all the trauma of the day, I fell into a deep sleep.

"Mia?"

I blinked open my eyes, and Max's face filled my field of vision. His five o'clock shadow was progressing into a full on beard, and his gorgeous face looked drawn with fatigue, but he was still so beautiful. I smiled up at him and lifted my hand to stroke the side of his face.

"You stayed," I croaked, and then winced as the forgotten, searing pain shot through my throat. My hand went to my neck to rest on the tender flesh and I gritted my teeth, willing the discomfort to subside. Whilst Max watched all this play out, his tired but affectionate expression turned grim.

314

"Please, *please* don't try to speak, Mia," he said. "You promised me, remember?"

I nodded and blew out a sigh of frustration. It was typical that the one time I had so much to say I had effectively been gagged.

"Okay," Max said, moving to sit on the side of my bed and taking my hand. "I've got to talk to you about something and–"

I cut him off by gesturing at the laptop.

"Mia, can I just … okay, okay," he protested as I opened my mouth to speak. "Hold on. I'll get it."

As soon as I had hold of the laptop I shuffled up to sitting and typed.

Did you stay here all night?

"Yes, but Mia that's not really –"

My eyebrows went up and I ignored him to type more.

Where did you sleep?

He sighed. "Mia I really need to –"

I tapped on the laptop to cut him off and he rolled his eyes.

"I slept a bit in the chair. Now Mia – "

NO. I typed. *No sleeping in the tiny chair. Sleep in bed. You look tired. I'm worried about you.*

Max blew out a huff of frustration through a reluctant laugh as he leaned forward to plant the softest kiss ever on my lips, which I'm pretty sure was a calculated move so that I would be too dazed to object as he removed the laptop from my fingers.

"Of course you would be worried about *me*. Of course," he said, his face still hovering inches from mine. "*You're* the one in a hospital bed, but me missing a couple of hours of sleep is obviously the priority. You're impossible."

I shook my head and opened my mouth to speak, but he put a finger on my lips.

"You promised," he said and it was my turn to huff out a frustrated breath. "Mia, honestly, this is important. There are some police officers outside the room."

I stiffened on the bed and my eyes flew to the door. As I looked back at Max I could feel them stinging with tears. They'd come for me, just like Nate said they would. I should have known this would happen. Nate had all the power, all the connections. I never won against him. I didn't stand a chance.

"I'll be right here with you the whole time, okay? They only want to speak to you for a minute. You've got to use the laptop though, right?"

I blinked away the weak tears that had formed in my eyes and set my mouth into a grim line before giving Max a stiff nod.

"If there was any way around this I'd make it happen," he told me, watching my face carefully. "You haven't anything to worry about though. They just want to speak to you."

I gave another stiff nod, but my eyes wouldn't meet his and I knew my expression must have remained grim. I felt his gentle touch on my cheek. He put pressure on it so that I turned my face and my eyes were looking up into his. The green was lit with determination so fierce it almost took my breath away.

"Do you trust me, Mia?"

I blinked up at him and sighed, but then nodded my head in agreement.

"You have nothing to worry about. You have my word.'

I closed my eyes for a moment and bit my lip. He might think that now but he didn't know what I'd done. He wouldn't have stayed with me all night on an uncomfortable hospital chair if he did.

"You'll see," he whispered before giving my hand a squeeze and then leaving me to let the police into the room. It was a man and a woman. Neither were in uniform. The woman looked to be in her late forties, the man a little older with greying hair. The woman's hair was dark blonde and tied back at the base of her neck. She was attractive, in an efficient type way.

"Hello, Mrs B–" the lady paused, her eyes flicking to Max for some reason then back to me, "I mean, *Mia*. I'm Detective Hargreaves and this is Detective Finch, but you can call us Lucy and Mike, okay?"

"Hi," I croaked. "I–"

Mike held his hand up to stop me.

"Mia," he said, "We've been briefed ... at length," his eyes also flicked to Max before softening on me, "that you're not to speak. If you wouldn't mind typing out what you need to say to us that would be great.'

"We know you've been through a lot, Mia," Lucy told me. "But this won't take long. Would you be able to type your responses?" After a moment I nodded.

"Mia," Max said. "If you want me to wait outside then I can, okay?'

NO. I typed. STAY. He nodded and one of his hands reached up to push my hair behind my ear. "Okay, love. Whatever you want."

"I'd like to start by saying I've read your file, Mia," Mike said. He was staring at me. "You gave leave for all your medical records to be released." I nodded slowly. Mike was all business and efficiency, but there was a flash of something in his expression I couldn't quite catch. "We also have an account of the incident a year ago which led to your attendance in hospital, from your husband."

Max let out a disgusted sound but Mike continued.

"He has some documentation of the injuries *he* sustained at the time. His account is that you stabbed him twice and that the injuries he inflicted on you subsequently were in self defence."

I closed my eyes slowly as I let this information wash over me. Of course this was the way Nate would twist things. With the amount of power he wielded, and the no doubt insanely good legal team he'd probably hired, I would be toast. The fact he'd tried to kill me *twice* would be inconsequential. A familiar feeling of powerlessness swept over me, and my hands started to pull back from the keyboard. What was the point of fighting him? But my eyes flew open when an unfamiliar hand caught mine during its withdrawal. Lucy held it for only a moment until my eyes met hers then she let go but moved closer to the bed.

"Mike?" she gestured to the recording device. Mike nodded, turning it off before Lucy continued. "When we say we've read your reports it means we've read *every word.*" Her face was no longer impassive and efficient – her eyes were lit with anger and her body was tense with it. "I've spoken to the admitting doctor from that incident and I've spoken to your husband's security staff – or rather ex-security staff. There *are* cases where we have to let victims know that we'll be unlikely to win. The burden of proof lies with us, and there's not always enough to secure a conviction. This is *not* one of those cases."

She lowered her voice even further before continuing. "If you think that *son of a bitch* can get away with throwing you across a stage in front of the world's media, and then strangling you in his goddamn car, you are *wrong.* If you think anyone will believe for one second that what he did to you a year ago was *self-defence?* You. Are. Wrong. I don't care what kind of resources the prick has access to, or how slippery he is. That abusive bastard is going down. Do you understand me?"

Lucy turned back to Mike and nodded for him to switch back on the recording device.

"Mia," Lucy's voice was all business now, cleared of the anger from before as if it had never happened. "If you could type your version of events including dates and times that would be much appreciated." I blinked at her and then looked down at the computer. My fingers had made their way back onto the keys without any conscious thought. Then I started typing.

I thought it best to start at the beginning. Years of abuse spilled out onto the page. Seeing it in black and white made me feel ill. All that time wasted with Nate. Even worse was when the laptop was shifted over so that Mike could read it out loud for the benefit of the recording device. Max's fingers closed so tightly around mine that I had to wriggle them slightly to get him to relieve the pressure. I frowned up at him, worried about his reaction to everything I'd put in there. He looked down at me and gave me a small encouraging smile, but his eyes were burning. When it came to the part where Nate dislocated my shoulder Mike broke off for a moment and I glanced at him. His voice had been steady and emotionless as he read what I'd written, but I noticed then that his hand that was resting next to the laptop was bunched into a fist so tight his knuckles were white, and his nostrils were flaring as he clamped his mouth shut, letting his eyes close just for a moment before he released a slow breath and carried on reading – still in the same emotionless monotone.

After it was done, I was exhausted. When they turned off the recording device before they left, Mike was still looking murderous. Lucy rested her hand on my shoulder before she said, "Don't worry about that piece of shit. We are going to nail his balls to the wall."

I was fairly sure that calling subjects of investigations 'pieces of shit' and telling people that you were going to 'nail their balls to the wall' was not protocol, but it made me feel better all the same. I managed to give her a small smile.

"I'm fine now," I whisper-croaked. "Honestly." Max started

muttering about using my voice, but Lucy gave my shoulder a squeeze and her expression softened.

"No you're not," she whispered back. "Not yet." She glanced up at Max who was looking cross after my voice-usage and then back at me, giving me a small smile in return. "But you will be."

Chapter 38

Something's wrong

MIA

"This place is the nuts," my sister told me with a laugh in her voice. "It's more of a dive than the Nag's Head and you *always* turned your nose up at that when we were teenagers."

"I was an entitled little snot as a teenager," I told her, something she already knew. "But don't worry, I've had that knocked out of me now." The moment the words left my mouth I regretted them, and my sister's stricken face made me feel even worse. "Shit," I muttered. "That came out wrong. I didn't ... I just mean-" Marnie cut me off by grabbing my hands and pulling me towards her.

"I wish we had tried harder to get to you," she told me in a fierce whisper. "When you left I was hurt and ... if I'd have known what was going on I-" Her eyes filled with tears and she pressed her lips together to stop them wobbling.

I squeezed her hands. "Hey," I whispered back. "You've got to stop this, honey. I'm the one who swanned off to a 'better life'. I'm the one who left you all in the first place. You couldn't have known-"

"Mia, I'm your big sister. I gave Tommy Saunders a wedgie in Year 4 cause he dropped a slug into your lunch box. I 'accidentally' kneed Sam Barnet in the balls when I caught him boasting to all his friends in the Year 12 common room about how he'd fingered you, when I knew all he'd managed to get was a cheeky snog. That's what big sisters do. I should have been able to protect you."

We'd been over this already. Many times, starting on the last day I was in hospital. Mum, Dad and Marnie had come to see me after the police left. I'd been so worried about seeing them again, so concerned that they might hate me for ignoring them for so long. My own guilt had eaten away at me so much that I hadn't stopped to consider theirs. They all felt that they should have protected me more. They knew something wasn't right, but they hadn't been able to get to me and didn't know what to do. Nate was so powerful that it didn't seem like there was a lot they *could* do. But now they were convinced that they didn't try hard enough – just like I was convinced *I* didn't try hard enough to get away sooner, and to prioritise my own family. We were at a stalemate. What we *did* agree on was that we loved each other and we would never let anyone stand in the way of that again.

"There was nothing you could have done," I told her, not for the first time. "I had to save *myself*, Marnes. You know that." Marnie was about to answer, but I felt a tug on my leg and looked down to see a serious little face staring up at me.

"Mi Mi carry," Cece said, stretching up her chubby little arms. I bent down to pick her up. Once I'd settled her on my hip she fixed me with a frown (her favourite expression). "Max, Teddy," she said to me with an imperious tone that I recognised from my sister. Genetics were strong with this one. It was uncanny – like a miniature, slightly more pissed off version of

Marnie. Over the last few months I'd got to know my niece slowly. She wasn't a smiley, friendly child. In fact, she more often than not sported a resting bitch face. But once she was used to you, she gave the best hugs. And the night after the court case had finished – when I'd been crying with relief with my family at Max's house – she'd sat on my lap and offered me her slightly soggy giant cookie, all the while staring at me with those serious, concerned brown eyes. She was the best toddler ever, resting bitch face and all.

"I'm not sure where they are, Squidget," I told her and her eyebrows lowered even further.

"Max. Teddy," she said again, this time patting my cheek for emphasis.

Marnie sighed. "Cece, you can't just demand humans to be brought to you. This is Max's party. I think he's pretty busy." Cece gave her mother a withering look and, I swear, despite being only three, she raised one eyebrow at her perfectly, before turning back to me.

"Teddy. Max," she said again, her brown eyes boring into mine.

"You called, my lady," Teddy's voice sounded behind me and I turned to look up at his smiling face. He must have grown a good three inches over the last six months. It was a little frightening. And his voice had become deeper. The rapid growth had even thrown out his balance in Taekwondo, but he was still winning at the Nationals.

"Turn the frown!" Cece shouted, a barely-there smile on her lips as she stared up at Teddy's face. He laughed, snatched her out of my arms and flipped her so her feet were over his shoulder.

"Upside down!" he said, tickling Cece with his other hand and eliciting a rare giggle from her.

"Hey," my brother-in-law, Paul joined our group and grinned at Cece and Teddy. I'd always liked Paul. He'd been with my sister since they were teenagers. He'd hated Nate from the start. Paul had *never* been fooled by Nate's charm. Paul was a pint-of-lager-and-a packet-of-pork-scratchings type guy. He owned his own plumbing business. He was *not* into champagne, posh restaurants or swanky bars, but he *was* into anything that made his wife happy. He would have tolerated Nate and the lifestyle Nate inducted me into gladly if he hadn't got what he called a 'bad vibe' from him.

Paul's judgement of Nate had angered me at the time. Who was he to criticise this new relationship that I considered myself lucky to be a part of? In those days I was just hoping my family didn't embarrass me. When it came time for Marnie and Paul's wedding, Nate offered to pay for all the booze. I thought my parents would be grateful, but Mum had been hurt. Paul had just been plain furious. He and Marnie got married at the local church and had the reception in a barn outside the village. They'd bought kegs of beer and people sat on hay bales. Nate had spent most of the reception eyeing the kegs of beer with a look of disgust and muttering about how they should have accepted his offer. We'd left early. I should have been embarrassed of Nate, not of my family. Looking back now, their wedding was way more fun than mine, or any of the ones I went to subsequently with Nate – apart from Nate's grumbling and refusal to stay late that is. What was I thinking back then?

Over the years, as I'd drifted from my family, Paul had been angry, but that anger soon merged to concern. He'd twice been removed from the house by Nate's security in the second year we'd been living together. Eventually I rang Paul and told him I was fine. That I didn't have time to deal with my family fussing. I was busy now. Busy with *important* people, doing *important* things. Paul couldn't possibly understand. After that conversation there were no more tussles between Paul and Nate's security. No more contact full stop. And that was on me, *not* Paul. But Paul, being the man he is, didn't see it that way.

"I left you to him," he'd whispered the first time they visited me in the hospital. I'd started typing to tell him it wasn't his fault but he covered my hands with his own. "I don't care what you say Mimi – I'll never forgive myself for that." And he hadn't. So now he watched Max with a suspicious elder brother vibe and made sure that he and the family were very much all up in my business. No more distance. No more relying on phone calls. Hence a small party in a local pub prompting a Sutton family invasion. This was beer and sausage rolls rather than champagne and caviar. My family was here. My new friends were here, but still I couldn't shake this bad feeling.

"I thought you were watching her?" Marnie said, elbowing him in the ribs.

"Chill your boots, *boss lady*," he muttered, kissing her temple and pulling her in for a side hug, most likely to prevent further rib elbowing. "I could see you taking a trip to Serious Town and I thought Cece would lighten the mood. This *is* a party. Isn't that right, Mimi?" He put his other arm around me and gave me a brief squeeze before letting me go. "Alright mate?" Paul said to Teddy before tickling his daughter's tummy as she was still suspended upside-down in Teddy's arms. "Want me to get you a beer?"

"Paul! He's only *just* turned eighteen," I scolded. Since Paul had found out Teddy taught me self-defence, he had developed a huge amount of respect for the teenager. No doubt he thought Teddy could handle his booze, but the last thing I wanted was my family plying Max's son with alcohol.

Paul rolled his eyes and grinned at Teddy. "He's built like a brick shit house, Mia," he told me. "Think he can put away a pint and be none the worse for wear."

"Paul!" shouted Marnie at the same time as a delighted Cece shouted, "Shit house!" Teddy flipped Cece right side up, settled her on his hip, gave her a huge grin and then he and Paul moved off towards the bar.

I smiled after them before catching sight of a pair of green eyes staring at me from the opposite side of the bar. With his height, Max was easy to spot in a crowd. He broke off his conversation with Heath (something I knew would wind Heath up beyond measure), and gave me a wide smile (Heath called this Max's freaky serial-killer smile – he said that after years of Max's facial expression being set to various levels of pissed off, the smiling was a little weird). I saw Heath punch Max on the arm to get his attention back. My own smile felt strained. I broke eye contact and looked down into my drink. Sounds around me faded away as I stared at the liquid.

"Mimi?" my sister called, and I tore my eyes away from the half empty glass.

"W-what?" I asked, blinking as the scene around me came back into focus. Yaz was standing next to Marnie now and they were both frowning at me.

"We've been calling you for the last five minutes," Marnie said.

"Mia?" Yaz said softly. "Is everything okay?"

I looked up at the two women who meant everything to me. Both of whom I'd let down. Both of whom I didn't deserve, and I did what I'd been doing for the last three months.

I lied.

MAX

I watched as she blinked at her sister and mine, giving her head a slight shake as if coming out of a trance, then I watched her lips move to form the word *fine*. If I heard that word one more time from Mia I was going to lose it. She was not fine. Not even close.

"Something's wrong with Mia," Heath told me.

"I know," I muttered, taking another sip of my beer as I watched Yaz place both her hands either side of Mia's neck and rest her forehead on Mia's in one of her *energy transferences*. Standard Yaz mumbo jumbo, but it did put a genuine smile on Mia's face, so I approved.

"Is her shoulder getting –"

"The physio's still working with her." I sighed. "She'll never be able to lift her arm above her head, but at least she can still use it. I'm *told* it could have been worse." That rough angry quality had leaked into my voice again. It was something I tried to keep a handle on when I was with Mia, but with Heath I let it out.

"Hey, old chap," Heath said. "You might want to ease off on that pint glass – it'll shatter in a minute if you're not careful." I glanced down at my death grip on my drink and made a conscious effort to loosen my fingers as I placed it on the bar beside me. Once both my hands were free I raked them through my hair and tipped my head back to look up at the ceiling.

"That bastard got off easy," I muttered. "I hope someone fucks his shit up in prison."

"You could get your wish there," Heath said. "I don't think they're frightfully keen on woman beaters in prison. Given how high profile the case was he'll have a target on his back from day one. And now he's lost the business, even when he does get out his life will never be the same again." An image of Mia lying in her hospital bed, deep purple bruising around her neck, broken blood vessels high on her cheekbones and in the whites of her eyes, wincing as she swallowed her own goddamn saliva popped into my mind and I felt my fists tighten at my sides.

"You can't let this eat away at you, Max," Heath said, glancing at my fists. "She's safe now. You've still got a business to run. Thank God that guy Adrian is actually a decent bloke. You would have been screwed if the company had withdrawn the funding from all those projects."

"I don't give a fuck about-"

"I know you don't, mate," Heath cut off my furious tirade before it could get going properly. "But you might if your business had gone under and you couldn't pay for Teddy's uni or to keep Mia safe and give her what she deserves. She works for you too, you muppet."

I snorted. "Mia's had offers from three different tech companies since this whole thing blew up. She'd been fine without me."

"She would not be fine without you," Heath said. I looked down at my boots, but after a moment's pause I nodded. Sometimes Mia looked at me like she couldn't quite believe I was real. Every time I did something for her like bring her a coffee to her desk when she was deep in the Number Five zone, turn the telly over to *Poldark* (okay, so I'd rather be killed slowly than admit it, but this was one bit of crap telly that had sucked me in – I mean that bloke can really swing a scythe), order the Thai takeaway she likes instead of the curries she knows I prefer, hold her in my arms after we make love (sex was something that hadn't been affected by recent events – weirdly it seemed to be the only place Mia's eyes weren't shadowed, the only time she really seemed free. Which was awesome of course. But did throw into stark contrast the reserve she still maintained the rest of the time) she'd get this look in her eyes – reverence, awe, wonder, love, but also for some reason, behind it all there was worry. And the worry wasn't getting better with time. In fact, the closer we became the more apparent the anxiety. But all I got was *fine*. God, I fucking *hated* that word.

Yes there was something wrong with Mia.

And problem solving was a skill of mine.

Or so I thought.

Chapter 39

Otherwise they win

MIA

"Hey," Max said softly as he joined our group, put his arm around my shoulders, and pulled me into his side. He ignored both of our sisters to stare down at me, his eyes warming as he searched my face. "Maybe we should head off in a bit, love? If you've had enough I –"

"No, no it's fine," I told him. For some reason his eyes narrowed at my "fine" and he clenched his jaw.

"Mia," Verity said as she joined our group. She was frowning down at her phone. "Why have I just had an email asking whether we could release you early from your employment contract?"

"Released from your contract?" Yaz asked, frowning across at me in confusion.

"Are you looking for a new job, Mia?" Marnie put in.

Max didn't look at me, he was staring at Verity. "Who's the email from?"

"Starlight Systems in London."

"London?" Yaz said, her voice rising. "Mia why are you looking for a job in London?"

"I haven't been looking," I said. "I ... they ..."

"Mia's been headhunted," Verity said, keeping her tone neutral but I could tell she was angry. "By multiple firms. I just didn't think she would go for any of the offers."

"But ... but you love it here, Mia," Yaz said, turning to me. My chest constricted as I saw the hurt expression on her face. "You're happy here ... with us. Aren't you?"

"Mia, can I speak to you in private for a minute," Max asked, his voice so studiously polite it was cold. I looked up at him and noticed all the warmth had fled his expression.

"Sure."

Max nodded and put his hand to the small of my back to guide me gently where he wanted me to go, which was over towards the seating area where it was a bit quieter. Unfortunately it was also where his parents were sitting with mine a few feet away.

"You're going to London?" Max asked, taking his hand away from my back and then taking a step away from me before he crossed his arms over his chest in a defensive gesture. "Did you think you might want to let me know that at some stage? Maybe before you agree to sign a fucking contract?" He was furious. The anger was vibrating through him. I knew Max had a temper, but he'd been so careful with it around me over the last few months I'd forgotten how formidable it could be. I wrapped my arms around my middle and shuffled back a little. His eyes narrowed. "I'm not him, Mia," he clipped. "I'd never hurt you."

"I-I know that," I said, my voice small and I felt pathetic. But then I *was* pathetic. I wasn't normal. Not anymore. Normal people didn't shrink away from the slightest perceived threat that to anyone else would have been recognised for something completely innocuous. Normal people could handle anger and irritation from their other halves without crawling into their shells to protect themselves. And that's why I had to leave, why I'd allowed the head hunters to interview me.

"Don't you think I deserve to know that you're moving? Wait ... were you even going to tell me? Or were you just going to leave?"

I closed my eyes to block him out and try to get it together. I couldn't *think* with him looking at me with that hurt expression on his face.

"I haven't taken the job yet," I said, my eyes still closed. "It was just something I was ... exploring."

"But why, Mia?" Max asked, the anger leaching out of his voice and leaving only the hurt. "Please look at me, love," he whispered as I felt his large hand gently cup my jaw to tilt my face to his. "Are you unhappy here, with us? Is it something I've done? Talk to me."

I felt the frustration, the fear, and the repressed anger all bubbling up to the surface. After keeping such fierce control over my emotions for so long it felt like all of that was slipping away. Like a monster inside of me was being unleashed. I yanked away from Max's touch, slamming into Heath and Teddy who had emerged from the crowd to stand behind me and spilling some of their beer. But none of that registered. I was breathing hard and black spots were dancing in front of my vision. I *had* to make Max understand. Everything was building and building. I felt like I was going to explode.

"Don't you see?" I shouted. The loud clamour of the pub quieted around me, but I remained oblivious. "Don't you understand why I should move away? Why I should get another job? You deserve someone *normal,* for Christ's sake. And it's not like I just broke a bone – something quantifiable, something definite, something you can fix. I'm broken in a thousand small ways, tiny little jarring bits of twisted psyche all coming together to make me entirely *fucked up!*"

"Mia," Max said, his eyes now so soft they were liquid. "Come here," he lifted his hands up towards me but I backed up another step and shook my head in a jerky movement side to side.

"Don't you realise I can tell how *careful* you're being with me?" I said, unable to turn down the volume of my words. I threw out my hand wildly, causing Heath to duck to protect his beer again. "How careful everyone is? Aren't you all exhausted by it? Exhausted by me? Don't you, Max, want to be with someone who isn't waking you up with her nightmares? Who doesn't have to have a clear path to an exit in any given space? Who doesn't *flinch* when you're trying to have a normal goddamn conversation with her?"

"Mia, please, baby, come to me," Max said, his voice low and his eyes still soft but now his jaw was clenched with determination.

I took another step back and tore both of my hands into my hair, feeling some of it rip out at the roots. The pub was completely silent now. All our friends and families' eyes were on me. But I didn't seem to have it in me to care.

"I can't do this," I said in a rough, tortured whisper. "I just – " Max reached for me in that moment and I couldn't take it any more. I turned on my heel and I ran. As I pushed through the crowd I registered their shocked expressions. Some people moved to let me by, a few tried to hold me back or catch my hand but I shook them off. I'm pretty sure more drinks were spilled. But I needed to get away. As soon as the pub's doors closed behind me, I took a deep breath in of the crisp night air and let it out in a rush. Then I disappeared into the alleyway down the side of the building. I'd always been fast and the time

I spent on the streets meant I knew all the shortcuts like the back of my hand.

~

"Mia?"

I started in surprise at the sound of Max's mum's voice. "Come out of there now, pet. This isn't a game of hide and seek and I've already stepped in what I'm quite sure was a puddle of urine. These heels may be from M&S but I don't want to test their limits of durability unnecessarily." Her voice was so brisk and no nonsense, so commanding and firm, that I took a step out from the shadows towards her.

"Ah, now that's better. We can't have you lurking around alleyways. Not right proper at all." She stepped towards me and I held my ground. When she reached me her eyes scanned my tearstained face and they softened, just like her son's – it was the first time I could actually see the resemblance properly. "Now then," she said, reaching to push my hair back from my face and then producing a handkerchief from the depths of her cavernous handbag. "Let's tidy you up and get you back t'Max. He's tearing the whole of Bournemouth apart looking for you right now."

"How did you find me?" I asked, my voice hoarse from the shouting I'd done earlier.

"I saw you disappear down here after you darted away. I'd been on my way to the Ladies and so was nearest the door. I didn't tell Max or the others because I thought you probably needed a breather after all that drama in there. And anyway, it didn't seem like he was dealing with it right well in my opinion. I thought it might be better if you spoke to me first and I sorted you out." She was now swiping away happily at my tear streaked, and no doubt mascara streaked, face. "Much better, pet," she muttered under her breath and stowed her hanky away.

"I'm sorry I made such a scene back there," I said, feeling heat creep into my cheeks. I shouted the pub down and ruined that party. "You must think I'm mental."

"Of course you're not *mental*, love," Fern told me. "And you're not *broken in a thousand ways*. You young people – always with the drama. You've nowt to be worried about. My boy loves you. He's had it rough, my Max. His dad was a hard man and then that vapid bitch Rebecca left him high and dry. Him *and* his boy, they don't need some pampered southerner in their lives. They need a strong lass. A lass that escapes a murdering bastad with a broken shoulder then finds another life for herself. You're not broken or flawed. You're the toughest southerner I've ever met."

"You don't understand," I whispered. "I'm not sure I'm capable of ... he needs someone that's ... that's whole and clean and right. Not-"

"Don't you *dare*," she said, her voice dropping and her eyes flashing as her hands shot out to my shoulders to give me a gentle shake. "Bad people do bad things t'good people. That's the way of t'world. I know this, right? Love, I'm saying I *know*."

I looked into her green eyes and pulled in a soft breath. The fury in her expression was pouring out of her. Yes, bad things did happen to good people. I could see that Max's mum knew this beyond a shadow of a doubt.

"I didn't leave Max's dad for an easier life. I left him because there was no other choice and I was worried that I couldn't protect Max from it any longer. It might have been that long ago, but it marks you," she told me. "It marks you and you carry it with you. You'll never be as quick to trust. You'll never forget that type of fear or the knowledge of how ugly folks can be. But you're *not* broken. You're stronger in lots of ways *because* of your experiences. Your ex fella he can ... well he can *bugger off*!" She bit her lip and looked to the side as if to check that she wasn't going to be caught by the swearing police.

Despite how wrung out I was, Fern's expression when she said a mildly offensive swear word did force a small smile to my lips. At my smile her angry expression switched to relieved amusement. "Bugger him!" she shouted. "Bugger, bugger, bugger."

I giggled – another miracle given the circumstances – and she pulled me in for a hug. "Do you know what says *'bugger you'* more than anything? What really sticks it to the bastads? It's living a good life, despite what's happened to you before. It's letting yourself be happy. Otherwise, love ... otherwise they win. Otherwise you let *him* win." Her voice dropped to a whisper as she pulled back and held my eyes with hers. "I'll not let those ... those ... in the words of my grandson – *mother-f-words* win. I'll not. And you're not going to either."

"I'm sorry you were hurt," I whispered and she closed her eyes slowly.

"Don't talk 'bout it much, love," she said. "Harpin' on 'bout these things was seen as weakness in my generation. My Aubrey knows nowt other than I had to leave. Max knows enough not to see his dad, but not–"

"I won't say anything," I cut in.

"Course you won't, love," she said, patting my cheek and giving me a soft smile. "Right then. You finished being a daft article? Reckon we could all use a brew and a nice digestive."

"Mia?" We both turned at the sound of Max's voice from the road at the end of the alleyway.

"You have to choose to be happy and to make my son happy, love," Fern whispered. "You have a *choice*."

I froze for a few seconds, then spun on my heel and ran. This time it wasn't away from Max. I was so tired of running away. No, I ran hell-for-leather towards him. He made a soft "oomph" and went back on one foot as I collided with his solid body and wrapped my arms around his waist.

"I'm sorry," I sniffled, feeling the tears soaking into his shirt. "Your mum's right: I *am* a daft article."

"Y'alright lass," he murmured into my hair, his arms coming up around me and hugging me into his chest. "Y'er not daft."

"Mia?" I looked up and saw Teddy standing a couple of feet away and eyeing me like I was a wild animal that could flee at any moment. Behind him stood the rest of our families and quite a few friends. "You've come right now?" he asked, and for the first time I could detect his father's northern accent in his voice. "Dad's made it right?"

I managed to smile at him as my hand shot out and closed around his, pulling him towards us and into a group hug. Max tousled his hair like he was still a boy and enclosed us both in his arms.

"Yes Teddy," I said, my voice a little choked but still clear enough. "Yes, your dad's made it right.'

Epilogue

You're going to live

MAX

"Mr Hardcastle, would you agree that your houses will revolutionise the postmodern era of environmental design, combined with affordable housing? Was that your intention?"

I pulled on my shirt collar. The damn thing was choking me.

"Folks need houses," I said with a shrug. "I make sure they don't cost an arm and a leg. Not exactly a revolution."

"Er ... yes but typically this kind of zero carbon design was costly to– "

"The buggers that need zero carbon are the same ones need affordable housing. Helps to pay for food if your gas bill don't cost owt."

"*Yes*, but you're the first to really take that and make it on a massive scale and at an affordable price. You've changed the face of modern architecture.'

I rolled my eyes and Verity gave me a kick in the shin.

"It were just common sense. Any bugger can see that-"

"Yes, we're very proud of the project, thank you Dermot,"

Verity put in, cutting me off. My tie was still choking me again. I huffed and pawed the bloody thing off so I could undo my top button. "Max," Verity hissed.

"What? It was choking me, V. Listen Dermot, mate. Would me wearing a tie make you any more likely to hire me to design a chuffing building?"

Verity groaned next to me, but Dermot McWilliam laughed.

"No, Max. I don't suppose it would."

"Oh my God," groaned Verity, her face going into her hands. "Can we restart this interview?"

Dermot laughed again.

"I am grateful you're giving this interview," Dermot told me. "I know that even though you're the creative force, you leave most of this stuff to Verity. The award acceptances being a prime example."

"V's better at this stuff than me," I mumbled. "She says I come across as a bit of a grumpy, northern bas –"

"Thank you, Max," Verity said on a forced laugh, "your eloquence as always breaching the cultural divide." She turned to Dermot. "Max isn't exactly a people person I'm afraid. He's more of a nurse-a-pint-in-the-back-of-the-Pig-and-Whistle than give-a-coherent-interview-on national-television type man. But he is frightfully talented and the new housing communities are all his design."

"You must be relieved that everything was still going ahead after Nathanial Banks was arrested. I understand that was a tense time."

I shrugged. "Water under t'bridge now."

"Mr Banks is serving a ten year prison sentence for attempted murder, and has subsequently been stripped of his assets after it was discovered he'd been embezzling money from the company and committing tax fraud."

A slow smile spread across my face at Dermot's words and I looked straight at the camera. "Don't reckon on them liking woman beaters in prison. Do you, Dermot?'

There was a pause for a moment. "Er … *no* I don't suppose they do." When I didn't say any more Dermot cleared his throat. "Well, you're working with Adrian Luther who was a partner in Banks's company, but has now taken full control. Is that business relationship less … er, fraught?"

"Adie's a good lad," I said.

"Always a bonus to work with someone who's not a raving psychopath and who isn't attempting to murder one of our employees," Verity put in, in a cheerful voice. Dermot's mouth fell open and his eyes went wide.

"Right, yes I suppose that is …" he cleared his throat again. "Amelia isn't just an employee now though, is she? I understand you're living together, Max?"

"Well, she's the old ball and chain now. Would be a bit daft if we weren't living in the same house."

"She's … er, what?"

"Max and Mia are married," Verity explained and I felt my chest puff up with pride.

"Oh, really?" Dermot's eyebrows' were raised. We'd shocked him again. The media attention after Nate's arrest had been fierce. Mia had become the reluctant poster child for domestic violence. The fact that he'd assaulted her on national television, directly before kidnapping her right outside the event had dominated the headlines for weeks. The clip of Mia being thrown across the stage and Barclay Lucas catching her up had millions of views on YouTube. The fervour surrounding the story was not helped by the footage that emerged of Mia breaking Nate's nose and then running to me. The Prime Minister and his wife plus their whole security team in the background of the video had only added to the drama.

Two years later, the press interest had still not died out completely. Luckily, Mia and I were boring. We stayed in, had mates over, went to the Pig and Whistle – not much there for even the keenest pap to take an interest in.

"Doubt you would have seen owt about it in the papers, Dermot," I told him. "We had the reception at our local. Just a few sausage rolls and some beers. Champagne n'all for the posh bastads like V."

"Posh bastards like the Prime Minister and his wife?"

I shrugged. "Don't know what you're on about, mate." Truth was Kira and Barclay *had* been there. Barclay was an alright lad for a politician but that woman of his was a proper liability, and the two bloody mini Lucas hooligans combined with Mia's niece had terrorized the Pig and Whistle, driving Fergus straight up the wall.

"I heard Mia's speech at the Action Against Domestic Violence conference," Dermot said. "It was impressive. She looks well."

I nodded. Mia was well. She carried her past with her and sometimes something would trigger that look in her eyes again – she still couldn't sit in the back seat of a car – but she was tapping less and less. Sometimes, if I was with her and she got that look back in her eyes, I'd found that if I held her hand in mine she didn't even need to tap. Having the confidence to speak out at conferences was recent. She'd turned down many offers to be an advocate for women in her position over the first year. But in the end she felt like she had to do it – like it was a betrayal if she didn't. It was the only time she dressed up.

"You're a lucky man," Dermot said, his face now serious.

"That I am, Dermot. That I am."

MIA

I took a deep breath through my mouth and let it out slowly through my nose. Crowds still weren't my favourite thing, not by a long way, but tonight was important. Max paused mid stride and turned to look at me. We were behind the others so they didn't see us stop.

"Max, what do you–?"

"We can go home, love," he said, reaching for my other hand so that both of mine were engulfed in his warm ones. I felt that warmth travel up my arms and into my chest. A feeling of calm settled over me and I smiled up at him.

"You just don't want to be trussed up in that monkey suit for a whole evening."

He searched my face and then leaned down to rest his forehead on mine.

"I know you don't like these chuffing things," he whispered. "We can go home, get a brew on and watch it on't telly." I squeezed his hands before removing mine so that I could wrap my arms around his middle. His arms came up to pull me into his chest, which I felt expand with a deep breath under my cheek.

"We are not going home to watch it on the telly, you daft article," I said, my words a little muffled in his shirt so I pulled back a little to look up at his face. "This is a big deal, Max. You're Young Architect of the Year. You've *got* to accept the award. I'm not going to let my neuroses get in the way of your success." His arms gave me a squeeze as his brow furrowed.

"Without you and your Number Five stuff I wouldn't even be here. I don't need a bunch of twats telling me I'm a *visionary* and all that bloody nonsense for designing something any Tom, Dick or Harry could have thought up."

"But nobody else *did* design it, Max. That's the point. You did. You deserve this award and I'm going to see that you get in there and accept it."

He rolled his eyes then focused back on my face.

"You'll tell me if you want to do one though, okay?"

"I'll be reight, lad," I said, lowering my voice to a poor imitation of his and causing his chest to shake with a low chuckle.

"We'll make a northern lass out of you yet," he muttered, his gaze falling to my mouth as I smiled up at him and his pupils dilating. "Love you, Number Five," he whispered as our lips brushed.

"Love you too, you grumpy bastad," I said against his mouth before deepening the kiss. The world fell away and it was just Max and his smell and the feel of his muscles through his suit. He may not have been comfortable in this get up but that didn't mean that he wasn't objectively gorgeous wearing it.

"*What* are you two horny cockwombles doing out here?" Kira's sharp voice cut through my Max daze and we broke apart to turn to her. Max kept one of his arms around my waist and pulled me into his side. "There'll be time for the funky mamba later, people. You're the star of the show, Maxy boy. Barclay will be presenting the award to thin air if you don't get a move on."

"Right," I said, determination lacing my tone. "Kira's right." I wriggled out from under his arm, grabbed his hand and gave him a sharp tug to get moving.

"Okay, okay," he grumbled as he let me pull him along with Kira on our heels as if she was worried we'd try to bolt again.

As soon as we got into the vast hall I stiffened. Crowds were still not my ideal environment. But I reminded myself that I knew how to do this, I'd had years of this. A group of people descended on us, some of whom I recognised as other architects Max had bid against in the past, some developers I didn't know, and the chair of the architecture commission. I pasted on the low-key interested smile I had perfected when I was with Nate. I could small talk the hell out of this party. I might not like it, but I would do anything for Max, and tonight was important to him. These were people he needed to network with. Nate was always saying how important connections were in business – Max would be crazy not to take advantage of opportunities like this.

He muttered a few greetings, shook a few hands and we both took an offered glass of champagne, which looked ridiculous in Max's huge paw. I almost laughed at the filthy look he gave it – Max hated champagne. He squeezed my hand as the chatter around us increased and I felt him turn and look at my profile. I was still using my polite smile as one of the other architects was asking me about my role in Max's company. When my eyes flicked to Max's face I was surprised to see him frowning and I felt an arrow of worry that I might be disappointing him. Old insecurities surfaced – was I saying the right thing? Did I have the right dress on? Was I embarrassing Max? He squeezed my hand and turned back to the crowd around us.

"Scuse us," he muttered. "I'm bleeding starving. Come on, Mia. Let's see if this gaffe has any decent sausage rolls." I barely had time to blink before he'd pulled me through the ring of people and across to other side of the room.

"There you are," said Yaz, linking her arm with mine and claiming me from Max as we approached. "I've already taken those bloody shoes off – and I don't care what V has to say about it. They are the devil's work." Yaz never seemed to really want any other footwear than flip flops.

"As long as your breasts remain contained in that dress I'm happy," Verity said, eyeing Yaz's dress which was split from her neck down to her waist.

"Exactly," Heath put in after he'd leaned forward to kiss my cheek. "Let's pray the dress from hell holds up. You've garnered enough attention already, Midge." Hostilities between Heath and Yaz had been ramping up in recent weeks for some reason. It was completely beyond me why the otherwise kind, reasonable Heath would be so carelessly cruel to Yaz but I was losing patience with him.

"Now hold on just a minute," Kira said, joining our group with her husband. I noticed her security lurking in the background. "That's *my* dress she's borrowing."

"Well yes," Verity said after everyone had greeted Barclay and Kira. "You could hardly wear it, could you? Nobody can risk the Prime Minster's wife flashing a bit of nip in public. I'm sorry if it makes me a frightful prude but I'd prefer Yaz didn't either. And there *is* a slight difference in dimensions between the two of you."

"She means I've got massive wazzers," said Yaz and I snorted out a laugh, relaxing into Max and feeling the tension drain from my body. Heath choked on the champagne he was drinking in an uncharacteristic loss of his usual cool.

"I think your wazzers are fabulous," I told Yaz and she gave me a big grin before launching herself at me and hugging me until I couldn't breathe.

"Thanks gorgeous," she said, rocking me from side to side, her "wazzers" restricting my oxygen supply. "You okay," she then whispered in my ear.

Max pulled me back into his side and pushed Yaz away. "She will be if you don't crush her to death, you nutter."

"She needs the positive tactile reinforcement, Max," Yaz huffed out, her hands going to her hips. "Hugs centre people in stressful situations."

Heath snorted and Yaz whipped around to narrow her gaze at him. "What's the problem Heathy baby? Do *you* need some centering?"

Heath took a step back and two flags of colour bloomed

across his cheekbones. "My oxytocin levels are more than fine thanks, Midge." He was trying to fake a bored expression now, but the choked element to his voice gave him away. What on earth was going on with them?

"Well, I think *Mia's* had a fair bit of *tactile reinforcement* already, Yaz, if what I caught her doing with your brother in the corridor is anything to go by," Kira put in. Heat rose to my cheeks.

"That's wonderful, Max," Yaz gushed, reaching up to pat his face. "I love how sexually open you are now. Oh! Oh ... you guys should go and bang in the bathroom. It'll centre you both and make the night less stressful – release tension."

Verity made a gagging sound. "Yaz! Please. Some of us don't require that level of information."

"Wow," Barclay was grinning as he stared at Yaz. "I don't think I've ever met anyone as bizarrely inappropriate as my wife before. That's quite an achievement." As I started giggling I noticed Max watching me again.

"You okay now?" he leaned down to whisper in my ear.

"Yes, of course," I said, turning to frown up at him. "Listen, Max, why didn't we stay and talk to those people before? I know that some of them are a big deal in the industry. Don't you think you should be using an opportunity like this to your advantage? Make some connections?"

He shrugged. "Either the stuff I design is good or it's bollocks. No amount of schmoozing changes that. Waste of bloody time."

"You know that's not true," I whispered, tugging on his hand so that he looked down at me again. "You know that –"

"Look," he cut me off, drawing me a little away from our small circle. "You got that weird smile on your face over there. And you had that thousand-yard-stare going on. But now, with our mates, you're back in the room again."

I rolled my eyes. "I can survive a bit of small talk, Max."

His mouth set into a grim line and his eyes flashed with annoyance. "I know you can *survive* small talk. You've proved you can survive just about anything. But with me you're not going to just survive. You're going to live and that does not include making small talk with a bunch of bastads that make you uncomfortable."

"But – "

"Listen, no amount of chat counts if you build crap buildings. I've never been good with the arse-licking stuff and I'm *still* getting this award tonight – because I can design the shit out of building."

I smiled up at him. "You're so modest."

He grinned back and his hands came up to cup my face again, both his thumbs sweeping the corners of my mouth. "That's the smile I want to see," he muttered. "I do love you, mind."

"I love you too."

"Ugh! Will you lot stop canoodling every two minutes," Verity snapped, giving Max a sharp punch on the arm.

"I think it's beautiful," Yaz said on a sigh. "And it's so good for their oxytocin levels to be –"

"I think their oxytocin is topped up for the moment, Yaz," Heath said in a dry tone. "They've been all over each other for months."

"Yeah, it's pretty gross," added Teddy as he joined the group. He'd taken some time off from his course in Cambridge to come down for the award ceremony.

"Why don't you canoodle *me* like that anymore?" Kira snapped at Barclay, whose eyebrows went up into his hairline. "My oxytocin needs a boost as well."

"Kira, I canoodled you pretty thoroughly this morning," he said.

"Oh yeah," Kira replied, a dreamy expression coming over her face as she leaned into him and wrapped an arm around his waist.

"I think we canoodle fairly regularly for a married couple with two out-of-control kids."

She huffed. "Well ... maybe I want more *public* canoodling."

"I publically canoodled you two weeks ago, Kira, and a picture of us snogging appeared on the front of pretty much all of the national newspapers just before the UN summit."

Kira bit her lip. "Right, I forgot about that." She patted his stomach and looked up at him with a smile. "Maybe I'll let you off whilst you're the Prime Minster."

He rolled his eyes and then pulled her around to face him, giving her a brief kiss on the lips. A click and a flash went off just as their lips touched but the pap was gone by the time they'd separated. "Bloody brilliant," Barclay muttered. "The British public will think I'm some sort of sex maniac at this rate."

Max's acceptance speech was brief. He thanked Verity, his family and me before saying, "Cheers then," and strolling off the stage. Not long after that he declared he'd had enough of "this poncy nonsense" and we all went off to the chippy round the corner. No small talk, no superficial conversations, no expectations of me to perform, no fear – just love and laughter and home and family.

And Max's mum was right. This was how I won. Living this unperfect life surrounded by love was my victory.

About Domestic Abuse

As a GP I work with victims of domestic abuse and those in a women's refuge. Unfortunately, the pandemic seems to have exacerbated this problem. For many people home is not a safe place and being trapped there during lockdown was a disaster.

I'm so sorry if anyone who is reading this does not feel safe in their own home. **You are not alone**. There is help available. This should **not** be happening to you. For those in the UK the Gov.uk website lists all the information and helpline numbers.
    https://www.gov.uk/guidance/domestic-abuse-how-to-get-help

Acknowledgments

I'll start by saying a massive thank you to my readers. I never dreamt that people would take the time to read the stories I have thought up in my freaky brain, and I am honoured beyond words. I am also eternally grateful to the reviewers and bloggers that have taken a chance on me – your feedback has made all the difference to the books and is the reason I've been able to make writing not just a passion, but a career. Special mention for Susie's Book Badgers - you are wonderful humans, and your support means the world.

Thanks so much to Jerry for your help and advice with all things eco-architecture. Your buildings and designs are inspirational. I am so proud of my big brother!

Thank you to my agent, Lorella Belli, for your support and encouragement. To Jo Edwards my fantastic editor and dear friend – thank you, thank you and I'm so sorry about all the semicolons! Thanks also to Steve Molloy for such a wonderful cover design.

Last but not least thanks to my very own romantic hero. I love you and the boys to the moon and back.

About the Author

Susie Tate is a contemporary romance author and doctor living in beautiful Dorset with her lovely husband, equally lovely (most of the time) three boys and properly lovely dog.

Please use any of the links below to connect with Susie. She really appreciates any feedback on her writing and would love to hear from anyone who has taken the time to read her books.

Official website:
http://www.susietate.com/

Join Facebook reader group:
Susie's Book Badgers

Find Susie on TikTok:
Susie Tate Author

Facebook Page:
https://www.facebook.com/susietateauthor

Email Susie at:
hello@susietate.com